SKIPPING STONES

A SILVER LAKE STORY

KATHERINE WARD

ISBN:

Hardcover 978-1-7382565-0-1

Paperback 978-1-7382565-2-5

Ebook 978-1-7382565-1-8

FICTION, ROMANCE, CONTEMPORARY

Cover design by Mary Ann Smith.

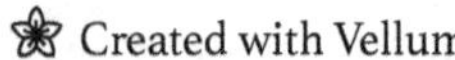 Created with Vellum

For Stephen,
who may be far from home,
but who is living his own adventure.

1

Linney McDonnell picked up a small stone, flat and smooth, in the chilly September dawn. She'd been at it for ten minutes or so, as the horizon turned a bright pink and now slowly morphed to orange. A loon called out across the misty lake and Linney turned the stone over in her hand, concentrating hard. Angling it just so, she sent it flying toward the lake and then tucked a stray strand of hair behind her ear as she held her breath.

One ... two ... three ... four ... five. Would there be a sixth? Yes! She jumped with pleasure as whoops of appreciation from her childhood friends carried across the water.

"Good one, Linney! I don't think I can do better than that." Derek's deep voice rumbled beside her and he high-fived her on the Silver Lake shore before they scrambled up onto the dock and under the blankets to join the warmth of the others.

Kirsten handed Linney an insulated mug while Anna pulled a striped Hudson Bay blanket more tightly around her shoulders. The fall mornings had turned chilly, but the four friends had been determined to get together for one last sunrise before Linney left them again.

"I wish this didn't have to end," she said with a sigh. "It's been so good to be home." It was the end of a month-long vacation, full of kayaking on the lake, spending time with Gran, and visiting with friends. She'd spent hours devouring book after book curled up on the porch of the house she grew up in. But real life awaited her on the other side of the Atlantic Ocean.

"One last hug," said Anna, as she regretfully shrugged off the blanket and stood up, her posture perfect as always. "I do need to get home. It's a school day." Anna had married right out of high school after falling head over heels with a local contractor. She now owned the town's dance studio and had two adorable daughters, just a few years older than the friends had been when Linney first moved to Silver Lake. She threw her arms around Linney. "We'll miss you. But we'll get our fix watching you on the news. The girls love it when they see their Auntie Linney on TV." Linney sniffed softly. "No tears, okay? And no goodbyes. We'll see you soon."

Linney nodded, and after another hug, Anna jogged off the dock, her long ponytail swinging behind her, heading past the house and back to her family.

Kirsten looked at Linney sadly. "I should go too if I'm not going to be late." Kirsten's nursing shift at Silver Lake General Hospital's emergency room started at seven o'clock. She'd come this morning in her usual boxy scrubs that hid her curvy figure. "But I'm glad we saw the sunrise with you. Safe travels, and don't be a stranger, okay? If you wait too long to come home again, I might have to come see you in London."

Linney wiped a tear away from behind her glasses with her forefinger as she pulled her petite, shapely friend to her. "You know I'd love that."

Turning her attention to Derek, Kirsten grinned. "Glad you could come up for a couple of days. See you soon." The dock bounced slightly as she jumped off and walked up to her car.

It seemed impossible to Linney that five years had passed

since she had been recruited to the TeleCan News bureau in England right out of university. Back then, while Derek finished his law degree in Toronto, Anna was already an exhausted and busy Silver Lake mother of two preschoolers and Kirsten had landed a job at the local hospital. But Linney and Derek always had big plans, and staying in Silver Lake had never been part of them.

Full of excitement for her overseas job, Linney quickly found a tiny, bright flat at the top of four flights of stairs in the London neighbourhood of Notting Hill and started at the bottom of the ladder as a fact checker for more experienced reporters. She raised her hand for every extra assignment and soon gained a reputation for her quick and thorough work. Linney hadn't slept much in those days, but it had paid off with a string of promotions. She still remembered how excited she'd been when she'd called Derek to proudly inform her best friend that he was talking to the latest TCN on-air reporter.

In the years that followed, she'd covered all manner of news stories, from business to politics, and from royalty to sports. Lately, though, she was feeling restless and was hoping for the challenge of an assignment further afield. Iran, Somalia, Ethiopia—she didn't care where. She just wanted to be where the action was, and she wanted to be there soon. Whether she made it or not, the whole population of Silver Lake, all 2,566—2,567 when she was home—was already proud of "their" Linney McDonnell.

The last colours of the sunrise faded as Derek and Linney sat on the dock in comfortable silence and the rising sun started to burn off the fog that had been hovering over the lake. The friends had been watching new days start together on this dock since they were young. A cool breeze made Linney shiver. Derek put a brotherly arm around her, and she leaned into his familiar broad frame as the loon called again. They sipped the last of their coffee as the sun slowly started to warm them.

It was Derek who broke the silence. "I'm sorry Olivia couldn't make it up to the lake this weekend," he said. "This deal she's working on has her chained to her desk. I've hardly seen her for weeks." Derek's long-time girlfriend was a successful mergers and acquisitions lawyer who was just as smart and driven as he was. They had sparred often during mock trials at law school. He'd won two more cases than she did—not that anyone was counting—but he had a softer heart.

As a teenager, Derek had developed a reputation around town for his volunteer work at the local food bank and by rescuing more than one stray animal. He'd been known to shovel sidewalks for some of the town's elderly population in the winter, and in the fall, colourful blankets of coloured leaves would mysteriously be raked from front lawns into piles by the roadway for pickup when Derek was around. As a lawyer, he had more tools to help people and these days, Derek could be found with his shirtsleeves rolled up as he fought the system for immigrants, refugees, and the poor at a bustling Legal Aid office in downtown Toronto. The cases Olivia and Derek worked on couldn't be more different, and neither could they. But opposites attract, and they had been together since they'd met in the law school library.

"She loves her job." Linney shrugged, always amused that Derek was smitten with a driven Bay Street lawyer.

"So do you." Derek turned to look at Linney and teased, "You can't fool me. As much as you're sad to leave, you're looking forward to being back in London with Mac as well." He stood up and jumped down to the shore, looking for another stone.

Linney rolled her eyes, but she knew he was right. She did love her job. And she couldn't deny that the heady, tempestuous romance she had with storied reporter Finlay MacGregor was an amazing bonus. The roller coaster ride was exhilarating.

A bone of contention between them was Mac's inability to

understand why Linney kept returning to her hometown, despite having been so eager to leave. Compared to the hustle and bustle of London and the adrenaline-filled news business, he often teased her that the Silver Lake community she described sounded sleepy and insular.

He had a point, she had to admit. Not a lot had changed since Linney had left for London. Silver Lake was a small town, and while it did have the benefits of being the county seat, that only went so far. The county offices were on the edge of town, in a nondescript brick building designed for efficiency, not looks, and Silver Lake was home to the county hospital, library, and schools. The not-so-cleverly-named Main Street curved around the crystal-clear lake and hummed with activity during the busy summer cottage season. It was home to a number of businesses in old Ontario heritage buildings, including Page Turners, the popular bookstore that Kirsten's family owned, and which drew people from many towns over.

Across the road beside the lake was grassy Centennial Park and the beach, where all Silver Lake holiday gatherings were held. On Victoria Day, the cottage season kicked off properly, and high school students served strawberry shortcake every year to raise money for activities. On Canada Day, a band played to summer crowds in the 1800s pavilion before the fireworks began. All through the summer, the ice cream stand where Anna had worked as a teenager was still the place where folks, old and young alike, held hands, flirted, and watched the sun set.

The annual Fall Festival in October was Silver Lake's last big celebration. It brought summer people back for one last week after Thanksgiving, to hike in the autumn leaves and visit festival booths that featured handicrafts, preserves and other local food, pumpkins, and hayrides.

But behind the spit and polish that brought the town of Silver Lake to life for summer people lay a far less prosperous one. When cottages were closed after the Fall Festival, many businesses also closed their doors for the season. On the other side of the summer facade, there were Silver Lake families who struggled, living paycheque to paycheque as the town limped through winter. At Christmas, when the park was just for locals, the huge spruce tree beside the pavilion, laden with snow, was lit with a few strings of lights. In January, volunteers groomed a section of the frozen lake for skating.

Away from the lakeshore and beyond the town limits, some families relied on a combination of social assistance and the food bank, reluctantly accepting the kindness of strangers to make it through the winter. What Silver Lake lacked in monetary wealth however, it made up for in caring and the town always looked after its own. Linney's grandmother taught her to pretend not to notice if a classmate's sister went to school in her hand-me-downs. Several women banded together in a group called KnitWorks, to ensure that nobody was ever without mittens and scarves.

The downside to all this caring—everyone poking around in everyone else's business—had driven Derek and Linney crazy as teenagers. He said you couldn't sneeze without the whole town knowing about it. They couldn't wait to escape for relative anonymity in big cities where not everyone knew everything about them. Others chafed less at the intrusion and these days, both Anna and Kirsten were avid KnitWorkers.

"Can I trust you with a secret?" There was a note of conspiracy in Derek's voice. They'd always been each other's confidants and there was no one Linney trusted more. Back on the dock, Derek picked up a blanket, folding it carefully, busying his hands and buying time.

"Go on."

"I bought a ring. I'm going to propose to Olivia." The gold flecks in his brown eyes glittered with excitement.

Linney squealed and leaped up to hug him, making the

dock sway beneath them. "I'm so happy for you. I know how much you love her."

"I sure hope she says yes."

Linney put her hands on her hips in a show of false exasperation. "Of course, she will. You're a great catch, and she's lucky to have you." She hugged him again and whispered in his ear, "You'll be a great husband."

"I hope so."

"I know so."

Derek pulled away and grabbed another blanket to fold. He threw a longing glance at the kayaks that sat on the shore. "And now, my friend, I really need to go. As much as I'd like to be out on the lake, I couldn't cancel my afternoon meetings. I need to get back to the city and my clients."

"Thank you so much for staying for the sunrise today. It wouldn't have been the same without you."

"Here." He pressed the stone he'd found on the shore into her hand. "Another one for your collection. Be safe, okay? Don't do anything dangerous, and come back home soon."

"Call me when she says yes. Love you!" He nodded, and then took long strides through the garden and up to the small single-story clapboard house painted a buttery yellow next door.

She waved as he turned back before pulling the door closed. Then Linney opened her hand to see the stone he'd given her. She kept a jar of them in London. Special stones with meaning—either gifts or souvenirs of places she'd been. Derek had been giving her perfect stones as gifts forever, it seemed. Tucking it into her pocket, Linney folded the rest of the blankets and, with one last longing look out to the lake, carried them up to the porch.

∼

"OH, LINNEY, THIS IS TOO MUCH!" Linnea McDonnell, after whom Linney was named, looked at the pitcher of black-eyed Susans and Michaelmas daisies that her granddaughter had cut from the garden and set on the old pine farmhouse table. Like the house and the china, the table had once belonged to her late husband's family. Four generations of McDonnells—five now, if you counted her great-grandchildren—had sat around the table and it bore the scars of many happy meals.

"I just wanted our last breakfast to be special."

Gran was the only parent Linney could really remember. She had landed abruptly at the century-old house at Silver Lake after her parents had been killed in a car crash. Her brother Jake was much older than her—she'd been her parents' surprise baby, born seventeen years after him—and had begun working at an architecture firm. Six-year-old Linney was a sad, skinny, and scared little girl with buck teeth, limp dirty-blonde braids and coke-bottle glasses. Time had healed Linney's pain, years of braces had fixed her smile, and she'd eventually learned what to do with her hair, which had darkened to a rich, warm brown, but the glasses had always been a constant, thinner now, thanks to new technologies, but still thick enough to correct her extreme nearsightedness.

It was a far more put-together Linney who pulled out a chair for her grandmother this morning, at least on the outside. On air, and in the newsroom, Linney exuded confidence and looked the part of the successful journalist. On the inside though, some of that insecure little girl remained, seeking affirmation that she was doing the "right" thing and looked the "right" way. It left her second-guessing herself, and she put a lot of faith in Mac's advice.

Her cooking was something she didn't question. She'd learned from the best. Linney filled Gran's plate and poured orange juice. Gran was eighty-four now, and time was beginning to catch up with her. Linney had listened to the same stories many times and walked more slowly than usual with Gran on this trip home. She knew she'd have to talk to Jake about it soon so that they could support their grandmother in these later years.

The sun streamed in the window as the two women enjoyed thick slices of French toast drizzled with maple syrup and preserves. Linney poured cups of coffee, adding milk and sugar for Gran and leaving her own black. They chatted while they did the dishes, putting them away in the old milk-painted cupboards that hadn't changed since Linney was young. So little had changed in the dove grey board-and-batten house with its wraparound porch and darker grey metal roof that during Linney's vacation, she had made a list of some updates that she wanted to make Gran more comfortable. The carpet in the bedrooms could use replacing, the living room needed new paint, and she'd noticed the porch was starting to peel. It would need to be dealt with before next summer.

"They'd have been proud of you, you know." Linney almost dropped a plate as she looked at Gran in surprise. "And Jake too, of course, but you're the one that followed in their footsteps. They'd have been so proud," she repeated, smoothing her blue dress.

Before the accident, Linney's mother had been a radio producer and her father a print reporter in Toronto. Jake had settled in the city too, but architecture was his passion. Linnea had encouraged her granddaughter's love of storytelling and supported her dreams. Linney was one of the few people allowed through the blue door and up the tight winding stairs to Gran's office above the sunroom—her personal creative space, built lovingly for her by her late husband. Linney knew the townspeople had whispered that the McDonnell family was putting on airs when they'd put on the addition back in the 1950s, but it made the house unique and she loved it. Gran had let her write her first stories there, curled up on a soft and well-loved leather chair.

"Gran, you're making me cry!" It was an emotional morning, and tears welled up again in Linney's eyes. She took off her glasses to wipe them away.

It was all the excuse Linnea needed, and she hugged her granddaughter tightly. Finally, Linney disentangled herself from her grandmother's arms. She squinted. It didn't help. The world didn't come clear again until her glasses were perched back on her nose where they belonged.

Slowly, she hung up the tea towel she'd been using to dry the dishes. "I guess it's time then," she said with a pang of regret. "I love you, Gran."

"Have a safe journey back, my dear."

Gran followed Linney out onto the porch and they shared one more hug before Linney climbed into her rental car and slowly drove away.

SEVERAL HOURS LATER, when Linney had dropped off the car, given her bag to the handling agents with crossed fingers, and passed through security, she sipped a cup of steaming coffee, nibbled on a cheese scone at an airport coffee shop and began the mental transition from small-town lake girl to sophisticated big-city journalist. She texted Mac.

> Boarding in half an hour. Can't wait to see you.
> Dinner at my place tomorrow? I'll cook.

> Sounds great. Grabbing a pint with the guys.
> Can't wait to see you too. Safe flight.

Her next text was to MJ, her best friend in London, and fellow Canadian. MJ—short for Marie-Josée—also worked at

TCN and provided radio and television reports for both the English and French sides of the network. When they weren't working, she and Linney could often be found thrifting around the city—looking for great TV-appropriate outfits and cost-effective second-hand furniture finds for their walk-up flats. The spunky francophone from the Ottawa Valley tolerated Linney's abysmal attempts to use her high school French and was helping her up her style game.

> Wheels up soon. See you in the office in two days.

> Bon. We need to set a shopping date. My clothes are all terrible.

Linney laughed out loud. MJ was built for clothes. She looked good in everything and always looked chic, even in jeans and tennis shoes. Linney, on the other hand, perpetually felt a bit of a mess. She pushed away a stray bit of hair—no matter what she did with it, it was forever falling into her face—and fretted about her weight. She'd been trying to lose the same few pounds ever since she arrived in London. Mac said it gave him something to grab onto, which made her blush, but she did need to do something about it. She shoved aside the last of her scone. That'd be a good start. She turned her attention back to MJ.

> Not true! But any excuse to shop, right? A bientôt!

THE FLIGHT WAS SOON in the air, and Linney reclined her seat. As usual, she told the flight attendant not to wake her for dinner, and she tucked her glasses away in her purse, replacing them with a silk sleep mask. But slumber didn't come easily as she thought about home.

Earnest, curly-haired Derek Blake was the first person she'd met when she arrived at Silver Lake. The serious little boy, with pants just a bit too short, had knocked on Gran's door with a plate covered in plastic wrap. Nibbling his mother's cookies together, their legs dangling from the same wooden kitchen chairs she'd sat on this morning, Linney learned that her next-door neighbour knew many of the children who would be in her class. They waited for the yellow bus together at the end of his driveway a week later as she picked at her cuticles nervously —a habit she'd picked up in the weeks since her parents died— and when they arrived at the small elementary school, he helped her find her teacher. A year older, Derek quickly became Linney's best friend and, encouraged by his mother, he looked out for her.

Derek introduced her to Anna and Kirsten at recess, and as she settled in, Linney smiled more and looked less forlorn. Her cuticles recovered, and in time, Silver Lake became her home, and she blossomed. She giggled with her friends, spent hours at Page Turners and scribbled stories in notebooks Gran bought. But for real-life adventures, it was Derek who Linney sought out. He'd rescued her too many times to count, from the first winter when she fell through the ice on the creek that fed the lake to the night of her junior prom when her date ditched her. In the winters, they skated and tobogganed, gleefully throwing snowballs at each other as they hiked up the trails to frozen waterfalls when they weren't studying. And as they approached the end of their high school years, when she wasn't poring over the latest teen magazines and practising makeup with the girls, Linney spent hours with Derek, exploring the marshes and little rocky islands in their kayaks, or on the end of her dock with their feet dangling in the water, while they sipped lemonade.

Early mornings and still evenings were for skipping stones along the shore and sharing their hopes and dreams for the future, far beyond the frustrating constraints of Silver Lake. Unlike most of their classmates, who stayed in town after high school, or attended the local college in Bridgegrove just up the road, they had big plans and chose highly respected universities in Toronto, several hours away from Silver Lake.

Even now, years later, hardly a week went by without several texts and the occasional video chat. They shared everything that was going on in their lives—celebrated the victories, shared the losses, and supported each other when things didn't go as planned. Linney was the first to know that Derek was losing his heart to Olivia, and he had been her sounding board as she struggled with the intensity of her feelings for Mac. Linney knew that Derek would always be there for her, just as she would for him.

Shifting uncomfortably in her narrow airplane seat, Linney yawned, and as sleep continued to elude her, her thoughts turned to London. Mac was a legend in the news business, reporting over the years from war zones and bearing witness to important international events. So of course Linney had known exactly who Mac was when she saw him in the newsroom on her first day at TCN. But that hadn't prepared her for the moment their eyes met.

Linney had read her fair share of romance novels and cynically perused descriptions of the heroine's breath being taken away. But that was exactly what had happened when their eyes locked across the newsroom. Time stood still and every hair on the back of her arms stood up as her heart began to race. The flutter in her stomach was something she hadn't experienced before.

Mac winked. Flushing scarlet with embarrassment at having been caught staring at the handsome star reporter, Linney tore her eyes away from his and scurried away. She was new—a nobody—and she had work to do and a reputation to build. Being caught making eyes at the senior correspondent wouldn't help that one little bit.

Still, she knew Mac had noticed her and something had happened between them. Over the next months, it happened again and again, with the same dizzying effect. Linney stole glances at him, and he met her eyes, but just as often, it was her meeting his gaze.

It was MJ who first told her Mac was making a point of checking out her work, and one evening at the pub after work with colleagues, he asked her opinion about the latest government change. Linney, newly promoted, stammered out an answer, blushing to the tips of her ears. Mac nodded, and she inferred that she'd passed some kind of test. The next day, he approached her desk, and they chatted for a few minutes. Mac was known for spotting raw talent, and he took Linney under his wing, mentoring and guiding her.

Linney soaked it all in, celebrating little successes but equally beating herself up when Mac's critique was less positive. Applying the lessons, she landed an on-air reporting position after just a year at TCN. As she progressed, and became more confident in her abilities and decisions, they often had professional disagreements, and their colleagues learned to ignore the raised voices from the editing suites and the heated arguments during story meetings as their opinions clashed. Because the end result was worth it. Linney's news stories made great television and viewers responded to her.

But the more they worked together, the harder it became for Linney to keep her feelings under wraps. She often turned to Derek to work them out.

OMG, what am I going to do? Yesterday, in the editing suite, Mac reached over my shoulder to show me something in the film we shot and I could feel his breath on my neck. My knees almost buckled. Whyyyyyyyyyy does he make me feel this way?

Get it together, Linney. He's almost 20 years older than you—and your mentor.

I know, but …

NO!!!!

Do NOT go there! Repeat. Do NOT go there!

But they did.

~

"WE WON!" Linney bounced out of her seat and grabbed Mac's hand, dragging him to the stage at the annual TV awards gala to collect a pair of statuettes for a story they'd collaborated on. She adjusted her glasses nervously as she thanked everyone at TeleCan News. She gestured to her co-winner. "And especially to Mac for all he's taught me since I joined TCN two years ago." Mac offered up his own thanks and followed Linney back to their table, his eyes trained on her shapely backside.

As their colleagues drifted out at the end of the evening, Mac suggested they have a nightcap. Linney was still riding high on the excitement of her first big win and agreed. Eyes dancing in the lights of the streetlamps, she suddenly stopped on the sidewalk. Mac almost bumped into her.

"Something wrong?"

Fuelled by the confidence brought on by a third glass of champagne, Linney reached up and kissed him. She pulled back quickly, realizing she'd probably just made the biggest mistake of her professional life. She started to offer an apology, but Mac's hand was suddenly on the small of her back and he pulled her in roughly. Fireworks went off in Linney's head as he kissed her back with the same passion as she felt. They never made it to the bar.

From then on, sometimes against their better judgement, they were inseparable, and whether in the newsroom or the bedroom, their relationship was a roller coaster of intense highs and lows. It was unpredictable and explosive, leaving Linney careening between exhilaration and hurt.

Mac never apologized when his words sliced into her self-confidence, but in the light of each new day, the passionate making-up more than compensated for anything he'd said. Linney found she was unable to describe it, despite her profession. Their relationship left her breathless and burning for more. Every single time.

Mac. Derek. London, Silver Lake. Linney finally slept, but her restless dreams were filled with a jumble of them all.

2

———————

Bump. The airplane shuddered. Bump. It shook again. It was a less-than-smooth landing, and after a fitful sleep coupled with the turbulence that had begun even before the descent, Linney felt unsettled and dishevelled. The customs line seemed endless, but eventually she was waiting with hundreds of other people for the luggage carousel to spit out their bags. The conveyor jerked to a halt and she could feel the frustration in the baggage hall rise. Digging around in her purse, she fished out an elastic band and raked her fingers through her hair until she had some semblance of a ponytail. Next was a cloth to clean her glasses. She rubbed it along the lenses, squinting, trying to make the blurry arrivals hall come into focus. No luck. At least the carousel was starting to rumble again.

Bag in hand at last, and clean glasses back where they belonged, Linney joined the crowd to reach the Heathrow Express. When the train arrived at Paddington Station, she splurged on a cab for the last leg. She couldn't wait to get back to her tiny sun-filled flat, where she shared more nights than not with Mac since that first time after at the awards three years ago. He was at work, so she'd have time to wash off the travel grime, unpack, and rest for a bit before making the promised dinner for two.

"Notting Hill," she told the cabbie as she slipped into the back seat.

"You here for business or pleasure, ma'am?" asked the driver as he pulled away from the curb.

"Oh, I live here," Linney said, explaining about her job.

"Well, welcome home then," he said and Linney realized, with surprise, that while London felt like home, she rarely called it that.

As the cab idled in London gridlock, she pulled out her phone and messaged her Silver Lake friends.

> Hey, everyone. Safely back in London. Thanks for a great vacation. That sunrise yesterday was amazing. Love you all and see you soon.

Looking at her watch, she realized it would be a few hours before anyone would be awake to respond. It was time to return her focus to London, and to Mac.

> Morning! Headed to my flat to shower and nap. Can't wait to see you tonight!

> Welcome back.

She hoped for more, but Mac was a man of few words, so she closed her eyes until it was time to pay the cab driver.

A LONG HOT shower had been just the ticket, Linney thought to herself as she wiped steam from the mirror. Leaving her long thick hair to air dry into gentle waves, she threw on some comfortable leggings and an oversized sweater. Yawning, she unscrewed the lid of the mason jar on a slim console table tucked inside the front door next to the umbrella stand and dropped in her newest stone. Among the collection were stones from Vancouver, Toronto, and Halifax in Canada, one from a Florida trip with Kirsten's family, and a slice of agate from a Lake Superior camping trip. There were English stones from Robin Hood's Bay and Brighton, and two from Ibiza and the Amalfi coast where Mac had rolled his eyes at her for looking for them when they vacationed together.

Linney padded over to the window and sank into an oversized chintz-covered chair—a re-covered thrift shop find and her favourite reading spot—pulling her feet up under her. She started turning pages of a magazine, not really reading, but glancing at the pictures. Yawning again, she pulled the quilt Gran had made over her lap and her eyes fluttered closed.

It was two hours later when Linney woke with a start. Her stomach grumbled. She hadn't eaten since pushing away the scone in the airport the day before, and she was suddenly starving. Time to go to the market. She bought a few essentials from Sainsbury's and then stopped at the Portobello Road vendors for fresh fruit and vegetables before lugging her bags up the steep stairs. That was the other downside of her shoebox-sized period flat. But the tall baseboards, wooden floors, crown moulding, and huge windows more than made up for it. And besides, it was good exercise. A good reason to splurge on a nice meal.

Linney didn't cook often. Tonight, however, for their first dinner together in weeks, she wanted to make something special for Mac. By that evening, there was salad on the table and apple crumble cooling on a rack on the counter. A glass of chilled white wine was by her side, and Linney took a small sip before she chopped the mushrooms. The broth was heating, and soon she'd start stirring it spoonful by spoonful into a pan of arborio rice and caramelized onions. She looked at her watch. Timing was everything with risotto, so she picked up her phone.

When Mac stumbled through the door with a kiss two hours later, the risotto was a congealed starchy clump, the limp salad was an unappetizing room temperature and Linney was steaming. She'd wanted tonight to be special.

"You're late," she said flatly.

At least he had the presence of mind to look sheepish. "The boys convinced me to stop at the pub for a pint. I guess we had more than one."

"Dinner's ruined."

He pulled her close and kissed her again, hungry after a month away from her. "You know it's not dinner I'm after. I've missed you." He kissed her neck and was rewarded with an involuntary sigh. Linney was losing her resolve to stay mad. She'd missed him too and her body was responding. His hands slid under her sweater and deftly unhooked her bra. Achieving the goal, they continued to roam and the last of Linney's anger melted. Dinner was soon forgotten in a tangle of bodies and bedsheets as they made up for lost time.

The next morning, Linney scraped wilted salad and cemented risotto into the trash while Mac was in the shower. It was a waste of food, but the welcome he had given her had been something else. She touched her bruised lips with her fingertips and then moved on to her collarbone, slightly irritated from the day's growth of Mac's beard. Oh, yes, it had been so worth it.

They left her flat together but headed in different directions

—Mac to a meeting with a source, and Linney to the newsroom. The city was already alive, and she revelled in the bustling activity as she entered the studio.

"*Bonjour*, Marie-Josée. Hi, guys." Greeting her colleagues as she entered the newsroom, Linney put down her purse and turned on her computer.

"*Bonjour*, Linney," MJ replied. "Welcome back. Are we on for shopping soon?" Nodding her head, Linney sat down at her desk. Her laptop had booted up and now several hundred unread e-mails stared back at her. Linney winced. It was going to be a long first day back.

DEREK SAT at his desk in Toronto, turning a small blue box over and over in his hands. There was a beautiful diamond ring inside that he could imagine on Olivia's slender finger. He hoped she would like it. He'd risen far beyond his beginnings, where winter coats came from the charity box at Silver Lake, but good as it was, his salary didn't compete with hers. He'd saved up for several months for the square-shaped diamond.

Linney's excited reaction had boosted his confidence. They had shared everything for as long as he could remember, and her opinion mattered to him. She'd listened to him lament his father's absence, and she was the only person he'd confided his fears of alcoholism being hereditary. He hated that she'd been so far away for the past five years. Texting and phone calls were one thing, but it wasn't like having her in the same city.

He put the box on his desk. Tonight was the night. Derek was meeting Olivia at her office, and the plan was to walk down memory lane through their law school campus. He was going to drop to one knee in front of the law library where they'd met and ask Olivia to make him the happiest man alive before taking her out to one of the hottest new restaurants she had been dying to try. Derek had only been able to get the reservation because it was a weeknight. It didn't matter. He was more than ready for them to begin the next stage of their lives.

She'd be shocked at first, then she'd say yes. He was pretty sure she'd say yes. He hoped she'd say yes. He ran over the details in his head one more time and reached out for the box again.

"Counsellor!" There was a loud rap on the open door to his office. "Pickup basketball this week. You in?"

Derek jumped at the clipped, but joking tone of his friend and colleague, Aiden. The ring box skidded away from his fingertips and his heart pounded in his chest. "Geez, you scared me!"

Aiden laughed. "You were so far away. Thought I'd put your feet back on the ground. You gonna do something with that ring soon?"

"Go back to work, Aiden!" Derek grabbed the ring box and jammed it into his jacket pocket.

"Just saying! And get back to me on the basketball." The two men sometimes joined a league of lawyers and other professionals at a gym around the corner from their office. Aiden closed the door behind him, leaving Derek to his thoughts.

Aiden was right. Derek had been holding on to the ring for a while now. And while he said it was so he could tell Linney first, he knew there were other reasons for the delay. He pulled the box out of his pocket again, opened it, and looked at the ring. Derek hadn't grown up with a male role model at home. Yes, there had been his uncle, his mother's bachelor brother, who ran Silver Lake's small hardware store, but he didn't have a healthy marriage to emulate.

Derek had only a few fuzzy memories of his father. He remembered his dad roughhousing with him in the living room and kicking a ball around in the yard. But he also remembered a lot of empty bottles on the kitchen counter and raised voices when he was in bed. He remembered his father napping during the day, sometimes on the couch, and once or twice on the floor —he'd been a teenager before he'd realized what those "naps" were. And he remembered his mother crying. By the time Derek started kindergarten, it was just the two of them in their little house. Santa didn't bring much that year. When Linney arrived a couple of years later, his mother was just scraping by, keeping the books for her brother's store. They often had dinner with Linney and her grandmother, and in his memory, those meals were feasts. A teenaged Derek understood better, and he showed his gratitude through his own acts of giving back to the community.

By then, his mother had explained about his father's relationship with alcohol and that one day he'd just left. Disappeared. They'd never heard from him again and she said it was for the best. She had never given Derek many details, but he understood that there had been some difficult years for her. He'd been careful around alcohol since his first bush party. It didn't do much for his popularity, but he didn't want to give his mother anything new to worry about.

Derek didn't talk about his dad to many people. Only Linney knew the whole story. She knew him, and back in Silver Lake on the dock, she'd understood what he was hesitant about. Her encouragement had helped. The ring twinkled under the harsh office lighting as Derek turned the box in his hands. He snapped it closed and gently put it in his pocket until later that day. It was time.

~

"THAT, *mon amie*, is stunning on you." MJ made a motion for Linney to twirl and she complied. The floor-length black dress she was modelling hugged her in all the right places. It had a high slit and showed more cleavage than she was used to.

Linney bit her lip with indecision. "Are you sure?" The dress was far outside her comfort zone, but she trusted MJ's fashion style.

"*Mais oui.* We will need to find shoes, of course, and a bag, but you must buy this."

Linney twirled again as MJ disappeared into the dressing room. She did look good, and it would be a perfect dress for the gala awards event, even if it was still a month away. She was nominated on her own this time, which was a huge honour. Mac was nominated too, as he was most years, and she was sure he'd win again. Linney twisted her hair and held it up on her head, imagining the updo she would have her hairstylist create for the event. She looked in the mirror, turning back and forth to see every angle. Almost, but not quite right. She took off her glasses with her free hand. Would that be better? Squinting suddenly at her fuzzy reflection in the mirror, Linney blinked several times, but couldn't make anything come into focus. Her shoulders slumped. Contacts had never been an option for her given her particular condition, so she was stuck with the glasses, even if she thought they marred the sophisticated image MJ was helping her create.

The door squeaked and a blurry figure approached. Linney jammed the offending eyewear back on and her jaw dropped. MJ was wearing a cobalt-blue dress with jewels embellishing her slim waist. Linney's eyes opened wide. "Wow," she said, as MJ turned around. "Just wow." The high-collared dress was conservative in front, but the back was where the drama was.

MJ swayed back and forth, looking at the way the fabric draped low showing off the small of her back.

"I think this will do," she said finally. "We'll be the two best-dressed reporters there. Let's go find shoes." They laughed and put their street clothes on before heading down to the shoe department.

"You're good for me, MJ," Linney admitted, as she stood in black patent stilettos with heels far higher than she would ever have considered on her own. "You push me to try new things."

"Ah, but this is my job as your friend, Linney. To stretch you a little bit. You should know how beautiful you are. You know, you can do far better than Mac."

Linney sighed inwardly. MJ rarely let her thoughts about Mac slip out. "Drop it, MJ. I love him and he loves me. We're very happy." Linney knew her voice was louder than it needed to be. She slipped out of her heels and led the way to the cashier.

3

Linney turned the page of her novel. She stifled a yawn and then turned the page back again. Her toes grazed Mac's under the covers at the end of the bed. The newly-released bestseller was excellent, but it was late and getting harder and harder to concentrate. They'd shared a romantic dinner and at least one bottle of wine at their favourite Thai restaurant earlier in the evening and now, close to midnight, her eyelids were growing heavier with every passing moment. Mac sat in bed beside her, scribbling research notes as sleep finally won and Linney's book slipped from her hands. Mac gently lifted her glasses from her nose, closed her book, and put both on the nightstand beside her cell phone. He kissed her forehead and picked up his pen again.

Silver Lake soon filled Linney's dreams. She was a teenager, back at Page Turners where she'd spent hours and hours with Kirsten in the back room—originally the old home's kitchen—doing homework and devouring as many books as Kirsten's mother would allow. Anna and Derek joined them, dropping backpacks and grabbing cookies. Soon they were all giggling over silly jokes when the bells on the front door jangled, announcing the arrival of another customer. Derek bumped her shoulder playfully as the bells kept jangling.

No, Linney realized, not bells. What was that sound? Waking with a start to Mac jostling her shoulder, she pulled her ringing phone close to her face, squinting to make sense of the blurry letters on the display.

"It's Derek," she yawned, as she slipped out of their bed and put her glasses back on. "I really should take this."

"Really? He's calling now? Doesn't he know what time it is here?" Mac, who'd just finished his work, but was not yet asleep, was clearly not impressed.

Their eyes met briefly and Linney felt a spike of annoyance but bit her tongue. She shrugged a dressing gown over her cotton nightgown to ward off the cool air of the late October night. Mac would have to deal with the fact that the bed would be cold for a while.

"She said yes, Linney! She said yes!" Halfway around the world, Derek was giddy with excitement, not even giving her a chance to say hello.

Fully awake now, Linney closed the bedroom door and padded into the front room. She curled up in her reading chair and wrapped herself in the worn quilt that had lain over its arm. "I'm so happy for you. Tell me all about it. How did you propose?"

"It was outside the law library where we first met back in school. We stopped to sit under the trees in the courtyard after work and I just got down on one knee, the old-fashioned way. We're going out to dinner to celebrate now, but I had to call you first."

There was scuffling and laughter and suddenly Linney could hear Olivia in the distance. "Linney, we're getting married! At the lake. You'll come, right?" The two usually ultra-composed lawyers were anything but, tonight, and they talked over each other, bubbling with excitement, to Linney's amusement.

"You can count on it!" Yawning, she reminded them of the time. "Send me pictures of the ring. And don't forget to tell me as soon as you set the wedding date. I wouldn't miss it for the world. Congratulations again!" She hung up the phone and turned back to the bedroom, but Mac was on his way out to meet her.

"What was that all about?" He slipped his hands around her waist.

"Derek proposed."

"Well, that deserves a toast!" Mac pulled Linney by the hand into the kitchen and poured them both a tumbler of whiskey. He knocked his back and as Linney slowly sipped hers, he poured himself another. He held up the bottle with a question in his eyes. Linney shook her head. One was more than enough for her, especially after the two glasses of wine she'd had earlier. She was about halfway through her drink when she covered a yawn with her hand.

"Go back to bed. I'll be right behind you."

Linney nodded, yawning again, and stood on her tiptoes to kiss his cheek. Mac finished her glass and poured himself another.

RAINDROPS on the bedroom window the next morning woke Linney even before the alarm. She showered, put on the coffee in her tiny kitchen and got ready for work adding a black blazer over a knit maroon dress because she knew she'd be in front of the camera that day. She was blotting her lipstick when she heard Mac groan and hit the snooze button. Hard. Linney went to the bedroom to kiss him.

"Good morning, sleepy head."

Mac grabbed her hips playfully. "Come back to bed." He had the gravelly voice of someone who might have had one too many drinks the night before.

"I can't. I have to—*we* have to—get to work." Mac kissed her hungrily but Linney stood her ground. "I can't."

"Fine, you go ahead then. I'll be about half an hour behind you." He let her go and gave her a playful smack on the behind as she got up.

"Mac!" With an exaggerated sigh of frustration, Linney smoothed her dress. Being involved with a colleague had complications and while everyone at work knew about their relationship, she still worried about people thinking she was a girl who slept her way to success. So she worked twice as hard to make sure everyone knew what she could do. Leaving her lover in bed, she pulled on some black boots. At the bottom of the stairs, she buttoned her trench coat, opened her umbrella, and headed out into the drizzly day.

Linney walked up one of Notting Hill's iconic streets of coloured houses toward the tube station thinking about Derek's call. It had only been six weeks since she'd seen him, Gran, and the girls at Silver Lake, but she missed them already. Somehow, with time and distance, the same nosy, annoying townspeople that she couldn't wait to get away from didn't seem quite so bad any more. They were starting to morph into warm, caring neighbours who she cared about and who cared about her. She shook her head. No. London was where it was at. She was lucky that her flat was tucked away from the tourist mayhem, on a quiet little close—a cul-de-sac she supposed she would have called it at home.

Linney turned the corner and smiled, watching the market vendors open their stalls and set up for the day. Jovial banter filled the streets as the city started to wake up. London was teeming with excitement and full of good restaurants, markets, museums, and galleries. She loved it here.

It was nearly two hours later when Mac finally arrived at work, his hair still damp from a shower. He had a folded newspaper in one hand and an insulated mug of coffee in the other. One could almost believe he was late because he was checking out the competition. Only his bloodshot eyes gave him away to those who looked closely. He strolled across the newsroom and slid into the day's story meeting just in time. Gemma, their bureau director, raised her eyebrows and tapped her watch. He ignored her but flashed a huge charismatic smile at Linney when he saw her across the table.

That look always made Linney's stomach do fluttery flip flops, and this time was no different. Despite herself, she smiled back. The things he made her feel. There was no way to stay angry at Mac.

WHILE OLIVIA proudly showed off the huge diamond on her left hand to her fashionable high-heeled colleagues in the tall glass Toronto tower where she toiled for long hours for TSX-listed clients, Derek shared the news with his own colleagues, including Aidan. There were congratulatory slaps on the back and good-natured jokes about his single days being over from his motley crew of Legal Aid lawyers while they drank the terrible coffee from the lunch room. Their offices were decidedly rundown and the coffee maker had seen better days, but they practised great law and helped people every day.

Derek and Olivia were as different as the kinds of law they practised, but they'd been in sync instantly from day one. He didn't mind at all that he'd had to scrimp and save to pay for that ring.

Derek always told the story with a slightly embarrassed grin on his face. He met Olivia in law school when he was sound asleep over his books in the law library one evening. Even with the scholarships he'd won, Derek worked two part-time jobs to help cover the cost of school and the grind had caught up with him. He woke with a start to this gorgeous woman telling him the library was about to close. She was so far out of his league that in any other setting, he never would have had the courage, but in his not-quite-awake haze, he'd asked her out for coffee to thank her.

As they left the library, and as his brain started working properly, Derek realized that from the cut of her dress, the scent she wore and the designer logo on her bag, Olivia Hastings came from money. He sighed inwardly—what bad luck. Once she knew he was just a small-town kid with no money, intent on righting the wrongs of the world, she'd disappear quickly enough and he'd have wasted money on coffee. Still, he'd invited her, and she'd said yes, so Derek guided her up the street to Common Grounds, his favourite café. He studied there often—one of the few places where he could hang onto a table for hours for the price of a single cup of coffee.

They chose a table in the front window and Derek dumped his frayed backpack on a chair as she settled herself. He took her order and returned shortly with a caramel macchiato and slice of biscotti for her and a cup of plain black coffee for himself.

"How do you–"

"Are you–"

They laughed as their voices overlapped and started again. Two hours later, they realized the café had emptied, and the last remaining barista looked like she wanted to go home. The world had disappeared until it was just them. Their hands brushed against each other as they reached for the last bit of biscotti and they looked up at each other in surprise. Derek had felt a spark and he was sure she had too.

Derek didn't want the evening to end, so when they reluctantly stood up and left the café, he walked Olivia home, insisting on carrying her heavy bag in addition to his backpack. When he kissed her tentatively at the door, it was like magic. Derek dropped the bags to the floor and gathered her into his arms. Olivia let out a soft sigh as their lips met again.

They spent every spare second together that year, snatching hours between his jobs and their studies. They picnicked on her living room floor, held hands while they drank coffee and walked arm in arm along the waterfront. They studied together, and on rare days off, visited art galleries and museums. The city seemed made for lovers.

"You don't drink much," Olivia remarked one evening when they were out in the Distillery District with friends, celebrating the end of mid-term exams. Derek was nursing the same beer he'd ordered when they'd arrived.

"No, I guess not. Does that bother you?" Derek hedged, not ready to share this part of his story with Olivia yet.

"Just an observation." She cocked her head at him. "Do you mind if I have another?" He shook his head, and it was never mentioned again. Some family history was best left in the past.

On paper, they shouldn't have worked. Olivia was from money. Derek wasn't. They were both driven, but where he wanted to save the world, she wanted to orchestrate big business deals. He loved to kayak. She was used to cruise ships. She liked to curl up in a cashmere sweater with a good book in front of stone fireplaces at ski resorts. He thought a plaid flannel shirt, a campfire, and long hikes to waterfalls were perfect ways to relax. A complete mismatch. But somehow they clicked, and with every day that passed, they grew closer and closer. When friends saw them together, they could see a special chemistry that was undeniable. Derek and Olivia were both driven, and there were early whispers that they could be destined to grow to be one of the city's important power couples.

Since graduation, they had been busy building their

careers, working the crazy hours new lawyers do, with little time for anything other than that—and each other.

Despite–or maybe it was because of–Derek's upbringing, he felt compelled to help people who were struggling. He didn't care that the Legal Aid office was worn at the corners, or that the perks were few. When he sat down with a young single mother struggling to get support from an ex-husband, a new immigrant who was threatened with being evicted by an unscrupulous landlord, or an injured worker who needed guidance to get government support, Derek knew he was making a difference. Olivia was on the partner track at a shiny, upscale law firm and she was laser-focused. She was being mentored by a friend of her father's, who made sure she was not only working on the right cases but also seen to be doing the right things.

From time to time Olivia and Derek attended charity events or went to the theatre or symphony, but most evenings, one or the other of them would come home late, with takeout from the local Indian place, or lately a new Ethiopian restaurant they'd found, to find the other sound asleep on the couch, covered in legal briefs. Once, Derek took a photo of Olivia and texted it to Linney. "My sleeping tiger" he'd typed. Linney had sent a laughing emoji back when she woke in the morning, but of course, Derek hadn't seen it immediately. He'd already scooped Olivia up and taken her to bed. She had woken as he pulled the covers over her and they'd found a way to use natural endorphins to relieve her tension.

He knew his new fiancée was more stressed than usual these days, working on a case that required her to have all her wits about her as she helped a client execute a hostile takeover. Truth be told though, he was no better. Derek had a habit of becoming emotionally invested in his clients' plights and it fuelled him to work hard to get them justice. His own humble beginnings meant he could relate to his clients in a very real way. He put in at least as many hours as Olivia did.

Although Derek was head over heels in love with Olivia, he had been nervous when he'd first introduced her to Linney. He'd heard stories that old friends and new girlfriends didn't always mix and that sometimes choices had to be made. It worried him. He couldn't imagine life without either one of them.

"She's different than I expected," Olivia had told Derek, as they got ready for bed.

"What do you mean?" Derek thought he'd given Olivia a pretty good description of his friend.

"Well, she's clearly as smart as a whip, but I expected her to be—I don't know—a little more worldly." She rubbed moisturizer along her long legs. "I mean, did you see her clothes? And those glasses—I've never known anyone with glasses that thick!"

Derek laid a hand on her arm and his voice had an edge to it. "She's my best friend, Olivia. No matter what she wears."

Olivia put up her hands in a gesture of apology. "I know. I'll stop."

"So when's the big day?" Derek was shaken out of his daydreams by Aiden's question.

"Soon," he answered. "Next summer, actually. We don't want to wait, so I've talked Olivia into getting married at the lake, where there are no long waits for venues. And that means you'll finally get to see where I grew up! You will be my best man, won't you?

"I thought you'd never ask." The guys laughed and another round of back slaps followed before the lawyers re-filled their mugs with coffee and got down to the gratifying business of getting justice for those who needed it most.

IN THE TCN editing suite after a day of shooting, Linney shrugged off her blazer, and reviewed the film, watching her standup critically.

"For TCN, this is Linney McDonnell, in Piccadilly Circus." The area had been buzzing, and you could feel it on the film, thanks to her cameraman's skill. It never got old. Never. She took great pride in the stories she told for viewers of the network, whether they were back in Canada watching on TV, or these days, international viewers watching on the internet.

Pleased with the work they'd done, Linney headed to the office kitchen, put on the kettle, and poured boiling water over the tea bag. Letting it steep for a while, she texted Anna and Kirsten.

Did you hear? Derek asked Olivia—they're getting married!!

Kirsten: Super news!! But more importantly— when are you coming home? We miiiiiisss you!

Anna: Yeah—soon I hope?

Linney smiled, as she tossed the tea bag into the compost bin. She was lucky to have friends who loved her as much as she loved them.

Miss you guys too. Home in the spring, I think.

Kirsten: Not for Christmas ˙ᴖ˙ ?

They'd made an unlikely trio back in grade school. Pretty, but shy and bookish Kirsten, gregarious dance-obsessed Anna, and little orphan Linney, bespectacled, bucktoothed and always getting into scrapes. But they were a tight group and stayed that way, even though as teens, their physical differences became obvious.

The summer before high school, Anna suddenly shot up. She was tall, slim, and graceful—the ideal dancer's body. That same year, Kirsten started wearing oversized sweaters and shapeless dresses trying desperately to hide a rapidly developing figure that she didn't understand and didn't welcome. She was mortified by her new voluptuous hourglass shape with full hips, ample chest and an impossibly tiny waist. Most grown women would be envious, but it made the boys—and a few grown men, much to her horror—lose their minds. Through gritted teeth, she endured stares, bra snaps, lewd comments, and more than the occasional hand where it shouldn't be.

Linney was jealous of both of them as they transitioned into beautiful young women, while she still had a little girl's body. She had waited another frustratingly flat-chested year, but finally, the day came when Gran took her to buy a bra. Her braces came off, revealing a lovely smile and some gentle curves emerged. They came with a few extra pounds, but not too many. When she looked at herself critically in the mirror, she saw no great beauty and decided she would have to be satisfied with being just the average girl next door type.

4

Derek shook his head, frustrated by the never-ending lists of wedding decisions to make, and the acute hunger that was making his stomach growl. He'd skipped breakfast to meet a client who couldn't be late to his minimum wage dayshift, and was now with Olivia at an upscale stationery store in Yorkville instead of eating lunch. Derek glanced at his watch. He only had a few minutes before he had to be back at the office. This wedding was beginning to be more trouble than it was worth.. He just wanted to be married.

"Olivia, my love," he said, irritably, looking at the identical sheets of expensive paper in front of them. "I honestly can't tell the difference. They all look white to me. You choose." He glanced impatiently at his watch again.

"The cream one," she said decisively, her manicured finger pointing to the sample in the middle. "Go on, I know you have a deposition this afternoon. I'll finish up here. But I'll be home late tonight."

With a quick kiss, Derek was on his way, relieved to have another decision made. The sooner this wedding was over, the sooner they could get back to their regular lives. He rushed back to the office apologizing profusely to his nervous client, a quiet woman who was trying to escape an abusive relationship, and who had been waiting for five minutes. His stomach growled again, but he pushed it to the back of his mind, as he sat down in the tired beige conference room and gently explained what was going to happen that afternoon.

It was a far cry from what Olivia would return to. He knew that when she left the stationer there would be lunch waiting for her at the office—sushi maybe—and her usual bottle of sparkling water. He could imagine her crunching numbers and scribbling notes on her legal pad as she ate.

It was another two hours before Derek finally had time to grab something from the vending machine. He pounded on the glass three times and the temperamental machine finally dispensed the bag of chips he'd selected. It wasn't lunch exactly, but with a cup of stale coffee, it would have to do. It was just another one of those days. Derek headed back to his office, loosened his tie, rolled up his shirt sleeves and lost himself in his work.

"Earth to Derek."

Derek looked up with a start. It was dark outside and Aiden was standing at his office door, coat on and briefcase in hand. He looked at his watch.

"Want to grab something to eat? It's getting late."

Derek shook his head. "Lots to do still."

"There'll always be lots to do. You need a break. Let's go get a burger."

Derek ran scenarios in his head. He could take work home. He could come in early in the morning. He could...he could just take a break.

"Good idea." He closed his laptop. "Olivia's going to be late tonight and work will always be here." He stood and as he stretched, his stomach growled. "A burger sounds good."

The two lawyers walked down the street to a diner they'd

been to many times before. They slid into a booth with red vinyl benches that didn't look like it had changed since the place opened decades before. They'd been coming here since their law school days. The food was cheap, plentiful, and Aiden swore they served the best milkshakes in the city. The owners had never bothered with a liquor licence, which suited Derek just fine.

"You wouldn't believe it," he said to Aiden after they ordered their usual meal. "The entire dining room table is covered in bridal magazines, fabric, wedding favour ideas, and lists upon lists. There are so many decisions to make." He slumped in his seat. "Olivia's obsessed with perfection and she's going to drive me insane."

"Well, you were the one who wanted to get married!" Aiden teased, always the joker. Seeing the pained expression on his friend's face, he changed the subject. "How's your abuse case going?"

"We'll win. She'll be good on the witness stand," Derek said confidently. Their milkshakes arrived, and he thanked the waitress before continuing. "We just need to get to court quickly, before the ex-husband does something stupid."

Aiden nodded. He'd had a case last year where his client ended up in hospital with a concussion and a broken jaw because the system moved too slowly. "There's a kid involved, right?"

Sipping the milkshake through a straw, Derek's face darkened. "Two. I don't want anything happening to them."

The two men lapsed into silence until their food arrived. With bacon cheeseburgers, fries, and coleslaw in front of them, the conversation turned to sports and stayed lighthearted until they were done.

"Thanks, Aiden," Derek said, as they stood in front of the diner preparing to part ways. "I needed this break."

Aiden clapped him on the back. "Glad to help. Now go back

to your fiancée and make some decisions!" He turned to go the opposite way from Derek and threw a final goodbye over his shoulder. "See you tomorrow!"

Derek walked home and opened the door to a dark condo. As he expected, Olivia wasn't home. He dropped his briefcase inside the door and flipped on the lights. He thought about texting Linney, but glanced at his watch and added five hours. It was too late.

The thought briefly flitted through his head that Linney would never make a wedding such a big production and that Mac was a lucky guy to have such an accommodating girl-friend. Derek thought Linney could do better, but this was the choice she had made and so he was there for her, even though he didn't always like what Linney had to say about Mac. And he heard a lot. Derek was always there when Mac's sharp comments stung. He gave Linney space to vent and tried to give her good advice.

Kicking off his shoes and dropping onto their comfortable couch, he picked up the latest issue of *Maclean's* from the coffee table and had almost read through it when the door flew open and Olivia rushed in, cheeks red from her brief walk from the streetcar. She looked stunning. Derek met her at the door as she hoisted up a takeout bag.

"I stopped for food at—"

"Shhh." He silenced her with a kiss that left them both breathless. Hunger instantly forgotten, Derek put his hand on the small of Olivia's back, pulling her close before leaning down to kiss her again. Before he knew it, they were leaving a trail behind them as they shed their clothing on the way into the bedroom.

Long afterward, Olivia threw on a negligee, retrieved the Ethiopian takeout and let her fiancé feed her in the comfort of their big bed before the stress of another day of law—and dreaded wedding planning—caught up with them.

~

"I JUST DON'T UNDERSTAND why you want to go back there all the time." Mac sounded more than a little whiny in his orange Christmas cracker crown as the candles burned low. "I am so tired of you always talking about a tiny little town in the middle of nowhere. You outgrew that place years ago—you've told me as much. Many times. There's nothing there for you now. Close the chapter." The ice clinked as he gulped his drink.

"It's Christmas Day, Mac, can you not just let it go?" Linney threw her napkin down on the table she'd so carefully set with flowers and candles several hours earlier. He was well on his way to ruining what had been a lovely day. They'd lounged in bed that morning with the sun spilling across the room, a rare treat with neither of them working. When they opened the gifts under the tree, Mac found a new briefcase and Linney was spoiled with a beautiful necklace with matching earrings. And then there was the silky red lingerie that had taken them back in the bedroom until lunch. While Mac poured over the latest issue of *The Times* in the afternoon, the flat filled with the scents of the holiday feast Linney cooked while talking to her friends and family back home. Mac called nobody.

The weather had turned just before dinner, and Linney closed the heavy curtains against the cold rain. They'd dined on turkey, roasted root vegetables and creamy mashed potatoes, accompanied by a magnificent bottle—which had mysteriously become two—of crisp Sancerre. Linney had even warmed up a Christmas pudding, which she'd lit on fire before bringing it to the festively decorated table with accompanying hard sauce, to Mac's amusement. It had been a glorious day.

But now, over post-dinner brandy, everything was falling apart. All Linney had said was that she was planning to spend a couple of weeks in Silver Lake over Easter and then again in the summer for Derek's wedding. She could feel Mac's instant annoyance with her. And it frustrated her. He just didn't get it. Despite having all of London at her doorstep and Europe just beyond, Linney simply missed home.

"Your career is here. I'm getting tired of you being gone all the time." Mac's words were beginning to slur together.

"My grandmother is there," she said quietly. Linney was acutely aware from their weekly calls that Gran's hearing was deteriorating. She was forgetting more as well, and Linney knew she'd need to start going home more frequently. Mac had to understand that. But then again, he didn't spend time with his own family. "And I have other friends there." Talking with everyone on the phone wasn't enough for her. She missed seeing the holiday excitement on the faces of Anna and Danny's girls.

Mac sloppily poured more of the topaz-coloured liquid into his snifter, spilling a bit as he missed the glass. Linney winced as the stain spread on the vintage tablecloth she'd thrifted recently. "I'm here. That should be enough." Linney was starting to wonder how much Mac had been drinking that afternoon while she'd been cooking.

"You could come with me," she suggested quietly, although she knew the answer before she opened her mouth.

"The city's the place for me. And for you." Mac leaned over to kiss her. She tasted the brandy on his lips, but the kiss made her quiver just like it did every time, and she leaned into it. She was rewarded with a low growl from Mac and he led her to the bedroom. She laughed as he playfully tossed her on the bed and then they celebrated Christmas once more.

Derek and Olivia's Christmas morning was spent on the couch wrapped up in cozy cashmere blankets, watching the snow gently fall. They had promised each other no gifts that year, as they saved for the wedding, but neither of them had been able to resist the temptation of at least one gift.

Derek had found a pair of unique hand-thrown ceramic mugs for Olivia. They were not quite identical, their colourful asymmetrical walls ideal for warming hands. They would be perfect for coffee on the quiet Saturday mornings he hoped they'd have one day once they were established and had children. He wanted at least two—growing up without siblings had been lonely sometimes, even with good friends.

"They're lovely," Olivia said, looking somewhat confused as she unwrapped them and held one up. When she got up to get them another cup of coffee, she poured it into the decorator china they used every day, but Derek shook it off. For him, there was an elegant set of cufflinks. Olivia said they'd be perfect for charity events, and they were growing in number, to his dismay. They were getting invited to more and more dinners, mostly through her work, and they were seen as the perfect upwardly mobile couple. Derek knew this was important for their careers—more hers than his, to be fair—but he sometimes bristled at the cost of the events, when that money would mean so much to his clients. Still, it was important to support his fiancée, and he would always put on the uncomfortable penguin suit for her.

They had lunch with Olivia's parents and then drove up to the lake to have dinner with his mother. As the three of them did the dishes, Derek reflected on how lucky he was. He'd grown up in this wonderful place under the loving eye of his mother, with great people he still considered friends. He'd achieved career success in the city now with the woman who was about to be his wife. He had it all. His eyes flickered to the darkened house next door.

"It's strange seeing it dark at Christmas, isn't it?" his mother said.

"Mrs. McDonnell went down to the city for the holidays, then?" he asked.

"Jake came up to collect her a few days ago. I'm sure she'll have a good time, but it's never the same as when the family comes to Silver Lake. I know she loves watching her great-grandchildren playing in the snow and skating on the lake." She looked at her son and soon-to-be daughter-in-law, her expectation obvious.

"It's very pretty here," Olivia said agreeably, skipping over the clear hint about children. "But the city is beautiful when it's all dressed up for the holidays. And there's so much to do."

"Bored already?" Derek joked. Although he loved city life, in recent years, he'd rediscovered, much to his surprise, how much he liked Silver Lake. He had a fleeting thought of building snowmen in the yard with their future children.

Olivia leaned over and kissed him. "Not as long as I'm with you."

On Boxing Day, Derek took Olivia around to Anna and Danny's house. Their daughters, Emma and Gabby, came bounding out to meet them. Derek, who saw them often when he visited Silver Lake, pulled them both into a big bear hug and swung them around, listening to their gleeful shrieks. Olivia stood back, taking in the chaos with wide eyes.

"Girls!" Anna said sharply, trying to regain control. "Come and say hello to Olivia. Uncle Derek's going to marry her this summer." She used the familiar title they preferred their children call close family friends.

"Hello, Olivia," they chorused politely and Olivia smiled tentatively. At eight, Gabby was still excited to share what Santa had brought her, and Emma, one year older, was curious about the wedding. They planted themselves beside Derek and Olivia on the couch and by the time Kirsten let herself into the cozy house half an hour later, the girls had hardly allowed the grownups a second to themselves.

"Hey, I've got an idea," she said to them, hearing the chatter about the wedding and winking at Anna. "Why don't you two go out and make a snow bride and a snow groom and let the grown-ups visit?"

"Thank you," Danny mouthed, and got the girls bundled up for their task.

Suddenly there were several more children in the yard, as Anna's sisters arrived with their families and Olivia tensed. Derek watched as she relaxed again, realizing it would just be adults for a while. She was introduced to the new arrivals, and Derek squeezed her hand. She'd get there, he told himself. She was an only child like him, but she hadn't had exposure to young kids. They'd fix that in time. He couldn't wait until they had a family.

5

———

"**S**mile!" The photographer at the awards gala snapped a photo of the TCN table. They were a handsome group. The men looked dashing in their tuxedos and the women were dressed to the nines. Linney was wearing the elegant black evening gown she'd bought with MJ and she'd been getting compliments on it all night.

Mac's eyes never left Linney. She could feel him staring as she laughed with colleagues, and she saw a cloud pass over his face as she deftly brushed off overly friendly compliments from other men. She couldn't decide if he was dying to get her out of her dress, or angry and possessive about the way other men were looking at her. That dress. Linney loved that dress and the way it made her feel. She looked sexy, sassy, and smart, and her eyes sparkled behind her glasses. Mac reached for the wine and filled his glass again. He offered her more, but Linney shook her head.

TCN was up for several awards, including Linney's first nomination. Linney caught Mac fiddling with his bow tie as their dessert was taken away, an unusual show of nerves. When his category was called, she held his hand and squeezed it tight. "You've got this," she whispered to him.

The table clapped politely when the nominees were announced and held their collective breath until Mac's name was announced as the winner. As their colleagues applauded wildly, Mac made his way to the stage. In his acceptance speech, he thanked Gemma and the network for their support. Linney felt a small pang of disappointment when he didn't mention her, but said nothing. MJ noticed too and rolled her eyes. All of the winners that evening had mentioned their spouses or partners. But not Mac. It was always all about him.

In total, TCN picked up seven awards that night, up two from the year before. Champagne flowed, and spirits were high. Linney hadn't won, but she hadn't expected to. It sounded trite, but she was honoured just to be mentioned in the same breath as the other journalists in her category. MJ grabbed Linney's hand when the band started playing and the two were soon dancing with abandon. Their exuberance attracted others to join them and soon the dance floor was full.

When they got home in the wee small hours of the morning, Mac put his statuette on the dresser and turned his attention to Linney's zipper. "I have been dreaming about getting you out of that dress all night," he whispered, as he kissed the back of her neck. The black satin puddled to the floor. She looked just as good out of it as she had in it, and Mac pulled her towards him possessively. It was a glorious night.

FEBRUARY WAS GLOOMY IN LONDON, but Linney hardly had time to notice. Gemma was giving her more and more interesting stories to cover. Linney had natural instincts, and she turned in consistently great work with unique and interesting angles. The whole newsroom knew it and nobody—except maybe Linney herself—was surprised the first time Gemma assigned her a top-tier story that any one of them would have wanted.

"Thank you, Gemma," she stammered.

"Go get 'em," Mac whispered in her ear when the story meeting was over and everyone had their assignments. Linney's star was rising, and he was proud of her. When the story aired, he took her out to a favourite neighbourhood restaurant to celebrate.

"You'll be outgrowing me soon," Mac joked with her over cocktails.

Linney blushed. "I've learned so much from you. And I value your opinion. I'm not sure I could ever outgrow you." She couldn't quite believe her own success yet.

They ordered a bottle of wine with their oysters and Mac toasted her again.

While they waited for their entrees, Linney went to the ladies' room to powder her nose and when she returned, she saw Mac beckoning the waiter over for a second bottle. Linney was surprised. Mac had only just poured her a second glass. How could they need a new bottle already? But as she bit into the best fish she'd ever tasted, she forgot to ask about the wine. Mac was spoiling her with this amazing meal.

"This is so good," she told him between forkfuls and Mac smiled at her enthusiasm.

He raised his glass. "A toast. To London's newest star journalist."

Linney blushed but raised hers as well. "And to the man who's helping me along the way." They drank, and Mac topped up his nearly empty glass before they turned their attention back to their meals.

As she finished a slice of decadent chocolate cake for dessert, Linney groaned. "I've eaten too much." She was fully sated and pleasantly relaxed from her two glasses of wine. "I don't think I even have room for coffee. This has been amazing, Mac."

Mac popped the last bite of his key lime tart into his mouth and gestured to the waiter for a whiskey. When his drink came —a double neat—he took a gulp. "Now," he started, leaning back in his chair and indicating a shift in the conversation. "We've celebrated enough. Let's talk about what you could have done better."

Linney looked at Mac in shock at this sudden change, but he continued, his words slightly slurred. "Your intro wasn't executed well, and you could have asked tougher questions." He waited for her to reply. "Have you nothing to say for yourself?" He waited another moment. "I thought you were a serious reporter," he taunted her, taking another drink from the brandy snifter.

Linney gritted her teeth. "I am a serious reporter. And I was pleased with that story. So was Gemma."

"It was fine. But fine isn't enough. You need to do better if you want to be great." His voice was loud.

"Mac, not now. Not here."

"Yes, right here and now." He banged the table and people were starting to stare. "How are you ever going to be more than average if you don't learn from your mistakes? I'm just trying to help you."

"Mac." Linney looked down at her lap, tears threatening.

"Fine. Be a crap reporter then. What do I care?" He drained the whiskey, slammed the glass down on the table and pointed at her. "Oh, and you should probably try and drop a few pounds. The camera will love you more." He waved down the waiter and gestured to his empty glass.

Linney had heard enough and embarrassment made way for anger. "I'm sorry you feel that way." The legs of her chair scraped on the floor as she stood abruptly and threw the linen napkin on her plate. "I think I'd better go. Do *not* follow me back to my flat." She turned on her heel and left the restaurant, bumping shoulders with the waiter who was rushing to refresh Mac's drink.

Her heels clicked on the sidewalk as she walked the few blocks home, blinking her eyes rapidly to avoid the tears. It took a long bath to calm her and Linney was getting ready for bed when her phone vibrated. She almost ignored it. She could *not* deal with Mac again tonight. But her hand hovered over the phone and when it buzzed again, she picked it up.

Wow!

Seriously, wow!

Linney climbed into her bed and under the covers before dialling Derek's number. She didn't waste any time with greetings.

"You saw it? What'd you think? I'm not sure it was that good." She chewed on her lip nervously.

"It was amazing! I'm so proud of you. You're as good as Mansbridge or LaFlamme! When will they send you somewhere dangerous?"

Linney chuckled. "Soon, I hope. As long as I didn't screw this up too badly. I still have things to learn."

"Good luck. You deserve it. Really, you were great on the news tonight."

She blushed at the praise. "You're the best cheering section." There was silence for a moment and she changed the subject. "How's wedding planning coming?

Derek groaned. "I can't wait for it to be over. The wedding that is. But I can't wait for marriage to begin."

"Not much longer. The next few months will go by in a flash." She stifled a yawn, but Derek heard it.

"It's late for you. Get some sleep. I'll talk to you soon. Congratulations again."

They put down their phones, Linney unwilling to spoil their chat by sharing Mac's outrageous behaviour and Derek equally averse to bringing up Olivia's wedding obsession.

Over coffee and pastries with MJ on a Kensington Park bench that weekend, Linney brought up her recent piece. "Honestly, MJ, how was it? I think—could it have been better, maybe?"

MJ put down her croissant and looked at Linney like she was crazy. "What are you talking about? It was great. Everyone said so, even Gemma. And you saw the viewer response."

"Well, not everyone thought it was great." Linney twisted the sleeve around her coffee cup, remembering Mac's criticism.

"Do you really think Gemma is in the habit of handing out compliments where they are not deserved? *Je pense que non.*"

"Well, no, I guess you're right. I thought it was good, but now I'm not so sure." Linney sounded deflated.

"Why are you doubting yourself?" The penny dropped and MJ's temper flared. "Did Mac say something?"

Linney's head shot up. "How did you know?"

MJ gathered up the paper bag and napkins, balling them up. She strode over to the rubbish bin and dropped them in. "You cannot let him get to you like this," she said as she walked back. "Gemma would not have given you that story if you were not ready for it, and you delivered. It will get nominated during award season, you know that, *oui*? Do not let Mac take away your confidence. You are going places. I think you will leave me behind here in London soon. But it will only happen if you believe in yourself." Lecture delivered, she held out her hand to Linney and pulled her in the direction of the park's pond.

"Thanks, MJ," Linney said, a little embarrassed. "You're a good friend."

Linney continued to mull it over in her head for several days, while she ignored Mac. To her surprise, he ignored her too and didn't apologize. Eventually, she decided that Mac had meant well and had been trying to share his experience. She was the one who had overreacted and had left him sitting alone at the restaurant.

"A peace offering," she said one morning, bringing two cups of strong coffee into his office. "I'm sorry. I shouldn't have walked out like that the other night. I know you were just trying to help."

Mac took one of the cups and nodded. "Glad you understand that now."

"Dinner at my place tonight?"

"Thought you'd never ask." Mac put down the coffee and walked around his desk. Kicking his office door closed with his foot, he backed Linney against it. With one arm around her shoulder, he pulled her so close that she could feel his heartbeat. His hand slid down further and his next kiss made her toes curl.

When Linney left his office, smoothing down her skirt and breathing deeply to regain her composure, she didn't see Mac open his desk drawer with shaky hands and unscrew the cap on a bottle of vodka. The coffee she'd brought, which had started to cool, needed a little something extra to get him through the day.

6

———

When Linney landed in Toronto a week before Easter there was still snow on the ground. Her brother Jake picked her up at the airport with his children in tow. "You've gotten so tall!" she exclaimed, hugging all three of them tightly.

"Welcome home, Auntie Linney," they chorused fighting to take one of her bags.

They found Jake's SUV in the parking garage and the kids hopped in the back seat. "Rachael didn't come." It was more of a statement than a question, but Linney was surprised not to see her. She'd been looking forward to chatting with Jake's wife.

"Things are a little tense at home," he said tersely. She looked at him with concern but he didn't explain and his tweens soon filled the space with chatter.

On her second night there, she was surprised to find Rachael had taken the kids out to the movies to give the siblings some time alone. Linney looked at her brother over the kitchen island. "Okay, Jake, this is weird. What's going on?"

"I just want to make sure you know what to expect when you get up to Silver Lake." Linney's brow furrowed. "Gran's getting older is all. You must have noticed when you were home last year."

"Yes, but she was fine."

"Things are different now," Jake continued. "I brought Gran's computer down to the dining room a few months ago, and there's been a big change since Christmas. You should know, she can't handle the stairs any longer. We're lucky she hasn't fallen."

Linney looked shocked. That office space upstairs was special. She still remembered the day Gran had taken a large ornate brass key off the shelf—a key she'd had been told never to touch—and unlocked a door Linney had never seen open. The door was unlike all the others in the house. It was narrow, and arched, with a circle of glass in the top. And it was painted bright blue like a clear summer sky. Gran beckoned her granddaughter to come.

Eyes wide, a young Linney tentatively climbed up a circular staircase that led to a room at the top. "This is my special room," Gran said in a secretive voice. "I don't share it with other people. But today, I want to share it with you. It's where I come when I need to be alone, or when I want to paint, or make up stories. I thought maybe you'd like to do the same. All that I ask is that you let me open the door when you want to come up here."

"I've arranged for someone to come in to clean for her now, and to cook twice a week," Jake continued, jolting Linney back to the present. "I don't know how much longer she'll be able to stay in the house.

"I ... I didn't know," she said sadly.

Jake reached out his hands to squeeze Linney's before continuing gently, "You're just too far away to know the day-to-day things. I'm telling you now, so you're not surprised."

Linney had been sure her brother was exaggerating, but she saw the changes immediately. Gran moved slowly and more cautiously now than she had the previous autumn. She seemed frail and was unsteady on her feet. Her slippers shuffled across the floor between the kitchen and the living room. She gripped the railing tightly when she took the steps one at a time from the porch to the driveway. But while repeating herself more than she used to, she could still be relied upon to recount family stories.

"Tell me about them, Gran," Linney asked one evening after dinner as they settled in front of the fireplace. She had just returned from the kitchen with mugs of piping hot chocolate. "Tell me a story about my parents."

"I remember when they found out they were pregnant with you." Linney smiled and settled back into her chair to hear the familiar story. "Your mother was in shock. Jake was a teenager already—almost ready to go to university—and she thought she was far too old to have another baby. But your dad? He was over the moon. He was so excited that another McDonnell was coming into the world. He calmed your mother right down and convinced her that everything was going to be alright. He always had that way about him. Your mother had terrible cravings with you and I remember him telling me he had to drive across Toronto to a specific bakery to get almond croissants for her. And when they named you after me? It was such an honour.

"He was a good father to you both. Your dad was the one who first noticed you squinting and sitting so close to the television. And he made sure nobody bullied you at preschool when you first got your glasses. He treasured you." Linnea's voice caught. "I miss him, Linney, even now, all these years later. I wish you'd had a chance to really know him."

Linney got up and put her arm around her grandmother. She hadn't meant to upset her. "It's okay, Gran. I know him—both of them—through you, and through the stories you tell me." They sat in silence, watching the fire flicker until they finished their hot chocolate.

After Gran had gone to bed that night, Linney unlocked the blue door and climbed the stairs. Jake had moved Gran's computer, but the well-worn leather chair was still there, and she could see the moon reflecting off the lake through the windows. She ran her fingers across the spines of so many favourite books from her childhood. She pulled one from the shelf and curled up on the chair, remembering all the times she'd done that with Gran, and realized for the first time, with a lump in her throat, that she wouldn't always have Gran to come home to.

THE NEXT MORNING, Linney walked across the yard and knocked on the familiar door at the little yellow house next to hers

"Linney!" Mrs. Blake looked happy to see her. "Derek told me you were coming home. He'll be up tomorrow with Olivia. You know, I always thought it would be you. But she's lovely, and he seems so happy."

Linney laughed. "Yes, they're both in love and ecstatically happy. And I'm happy for them."

"You sure?" Mrs. Blake looked carefully into Linney's eyes.

"I'm sure. And I have Mac."

Mrs. Blake knew when she was beaten. "Come in, my dear. Tell me all about your latest adventures. I love watching you on TV."

Linney soon found herself in the Blake kitchen, with a mug of coffee in her hand and a plate of ginger cookies in front of her.

"How is Gran doing?" Linney broached the reason for her visit carefully after several minutes of chit-chat. "Jake's worried.

And I'm seeing changes too." She paused to break off another piece of warm cookie and pop it in her mouth. "Mmm. So good. You've always been such a good neighbour and friend to her. I don't want to put you in an awkward position, but I'm wondering if you think there's anything we should be doing to help Gran stay in the house."

Mrs. Blake thought carefully before answering. "Your grandmother is fine for now, dear. I know your brother worries. The time will come when you may have to consider something different for her, but right now, she's fine. And after all she did for Derek and me, I'll keep a close eye on her."

"You'd let me know, wouldn't you, if anything changed?"

"Of course, Linney dear. You can count on me."

LINNEY AND GRAN cooked up a storm for Easter. Well, mostly Linney cooked, with the help of Gran's supervision and her old, stained *Canadian Living* cookbook. The house got louder when Jake arrived with his family. Jake and Rachel seemed to have patched things up, Linney noticed happily. Whatever it was couldn't have been too serious.

Later in the day, with the Easter lamb in the oven, Linney closed the door on the noise for a few minutes, and with one of Gran's knitted shawls loosely around her shoulders, walked through the last of the melting snow down to the lake. Lifting her face to the warmth of the bright afternoon sun, she suddenly realized she wasn't alone. Turning, she saw Derek walking across the dock.

"Hey!" She greeted him with a smile.

"Hey, yourself. Escaping the chaos?"

Linney laughed. "It's not as bad as it was when Jake's kids were little, but yes, you caught me! What are you escaping?"

"Wedding plans! Olivia and Mum have been at it for hours. I needed a break."

The two friends stood there, enjoying the quiet simplicity of the lake until the call of a migrating loon broke through their thoughts.

"I do miss hearing that sound. I don't get home enough."

"You do pretty well for someone who lives in London."

"It's still not enough. Gran's getting older and I'm not sure how much longer—" She broke off, not wanting to finish the thought.

"Mum says she's doing okay," Derek said softly.

Linney shrugged. "I'm not sure for how much longer though."

Derek put his arm around her shoulder and squeezed. They stood there for a few more minutes before she pushed her glasses up her nose. "Okay, back to the chaos. I'll see you in the city before I leave. Happy Easter." Linney left Derek on the dock. He stared out at the lake for another few minutes before squaring his shoulders and heading back into wedding madness.

On her final night at the lake, Linney had dinner with Anna and Kirsten. Glasses of wine in hand, the three women gathered in Kirsten's cozy apartment above Page Turners. The store had recently changed hands when Kirsten's parents retired.

"It doesn't seem as busy," Linney mused. "I popped in earlier today, but there weren't many customers. It was strange not seeing your mother at the till."

"I'm afraid you're right," Kirsten agreed. "I'm not sure the new owners knew what they were getting into. But they have a couple more months to get it together before summer." They all knew that the seasonal cottage crowd was a big source of income for Page Turners. "I am a bit worried though. They haven't even rented out the other apartment yet."

There were two identical well-proportioned apartments above the store, which had taken up most of the first floor of the heritage home for decades. Over the years, businesses had come and gone in the small section of the main floor that Pages didn't take up and it was currently a paper shop in the summers. Kirsten had grown up in one of the apartments with her parents, and her grandmother had lived across the hall until her death almost seven years ago. When Kirsten finished nursing school, her parents redecorated it for her as a graduation gift. She'd lived there happily since then, spending a couple of evenings a week with her mum and dad. But since they sold the store—the deal included the provision that Kirsten could stay in her apartment as long as she wanted—and moved to Florida to enjoy the warm weather year-round, the other apartment had remained empty.

Linney changed the subject. "Do you ever see my Gran in town? How does she seem to you?"

"I don't think she's driving much anymore, but Mrs. Blake brings her to KnitWorks most weeks," Anna offered, "and we're watching out for her." Envisioning the gossipy knitting group usually made Linney cringe, but today, the thought of community made her feel better.

Kirsten interrupted her thoughts. "I can stop by from time to time if you like and keep an eye on things for you.

"Me too," Anna added.

"That'd be great. Thank you both. I'm not sure if I've appreciated how much everyone takes care of each other here. Now, Kirsten," she said, changing the subject and looking pointedly at her friend, "tell me about who you're seeing."

Kirsten shook her head. "Sadly, nobody right now. It's hard to find someone who will look beyond this." She gestured to her chest, hidden behind a boxy sweater, "and see me for who I am. Besides, the hospital keeps me busy."

"Don't sell yourself short," Anna chastised her. "Don't give up. The right guy is out there for you."

"Easy for you to say. You found the love of your life the summer after high school!"

Anna blushed. She and Danny were still madly in love. "You know, Danny's just hired a new electrician. He's cute. Maybe we should set you up."

Kirsten shook her head. "Not interested in another blind date." She stood up. "Cupcakes?" She brought a plate from the kitchen.

"Not for me," Linney said. "They look delicious, but I need to watch my weight." Anna rolled her eyes as she took a chocolate cupcake. Even her fingers were long and delicate.

Linney put her hands on her stomach. "I wish I had your metabolism. I need to lose some weight for the camera." She'd been careful, watching everything she ate since she'd been home. "Mac says ten pounds—or even better, twenty—would help me look better."

"He's crazy." Kirsten sounded offended for Linney. "You're gorgeous just the way you are." She pulled the wrapper off a red velvet cupcake and licked the icing off her fingers.

"You don't know what you're missing," Anna taunted her.

Linney sighed. She wanted one, but she knew she shouldn't.

"How is it with Mac anyway?" Kirsten asked. She gave her friend an impish look. "Still hot and heavy?"

"When it's good, it's really, really good," she admitted sheepishly. "I miss him."

"And when it's not good?" Anna asked perceptively.

Linney thought for a moment. "Mac just wants what's best for me. So sometimes he's a little harsh. It's all part of the business. I don't mind." She drained the last of her wine and changed the subject. "Did I tell you? Gemma's promised to let me spread my wings when I get back. A European story. It's the first step towards a foreign assignment!" Linney was excited about this new development, but she was nervous. "I hope I'm ready."

"Of course you are!" Anna exclaimed. "It's what you've always wanted!"

"Not somewhere dangerous, right?" Kirsten asked.

"I can't promise that," Linney said, giving into temptation and reaching out for a lemon cupcake. "But wherever it is, I'll be careful." The icing was delicious. To heck with Mac's suggestions.

7

———

"Linney, dear, it's so good to hear your voice. When are you coming home?"

Linney's brow furrowed. She seemed to have this same conversation with Gran every week now since she'd been home for Easter.

"Hi, Gran. Remember, I'm coming in a few weeks when Derek and Olivia get married."

"Yes, that's right." Linney could hear the disappointment in her voice. She knew that just like Mrs. Blake, Gran had always hoped that the boy next door would propose to her granddaughter, but that was just wishful thinking. Derek and Linney were friends. Good friends, but just friends. Sure, there had been that one spin-the-bottle game and an awkward kiss at a party when she was thirteen, but there'd been no spark, and they had never thought of each other that way.

"But first, Kirsten's coming to London, remember? And Jake will be up to see you this weekend. Maybe he can help you get out the summer cushions for the porch furniture."

"That would be lovely. Do you think he would help me plant the flower boxes?"

"I'm sure he will. I'll call you in a few days."

Linney had always been a bit disappointed none of her friends had visited her in London. Of course, they had good reasons. Anna and Danny were busy with their businesses and their family and Derek didn't take much vacation to begin with. When Kirsten made good on her threat and finally booked a trip, Linney had planned a great holiday for them together.

But a few days before Kirsten arrived, Gemma popped by Linney's desk with a file. Linney opened it and looked up at her boss with surprise. This was a big opportunity to show how much she'd grown as a reporter. Suddenly her face fell. Was she ready for this? Mac had plenty of criticism for her work these days.

"Are you sure, Gemma?" she asked.

Gemma's forehead wrinkled. "Why would you even question it? You're the best young reporter we have. You were ready for this months ago." Linney bit her lip hesitantly and Gemma spoke sharply. "Linney, this is a tough business. Especially for women. I don't know what's going on, but you need to get your confidence back. You are a great reporter. Don't second guess yourself."

The smile returned to Linney's face. "I'll do my best. Promise." As Gemma left, Linney started reading through the research, getting excited. It would eat into her time with Kirsten, but it would be so worth it.

LINNEY BOUNCED on her toes as she waited for Kirsten to come through the doors at Heathrow. It was her friend's first international flight, other than family trips to Florida. Finally, she caught a glimpse of a tired and nervous Kirsten and shrieked. Kirsten's head spun around and soon Linney caught her up in a hug.

"You're here! How do you feel? That flight can be something."

"I feel tired and grimy, but excited all at the same time!"

"Well, first things first then. Let's get you back to Notting Hill. A hot shower and a nap will cure almost anything.

Linney had only been able to secure a few days off work and fortunately, Kirsten was happy to fill her days with sight-seeing on her own. She gawked at the royal palaces, took in the parks and museums, and visited both St. Paul's and Westminster cathedrals. She splurged on a matinee ticket to Les Misérables and rode the London Eye. On the weekend, Linney showed her the Portobello Road Market, sharing the secrets she'd learned to furnish her flat with vintage finds so close at hand.

Kirsten's introduction to MJ took place at a favourite fish and chips shop. The petite Quebecer hugged her and then looked her up and down. "Wow, you have a great figure under there. But why do you hide it?" The stylish woman was genuinely confused.

Kirsten turned beet red and tugged at her oversized T-shirt. "I don't—I mean, I've always—well, you know, guys-" She shrugged. "I just don't like the attention," she admitted.

"I can help you with that," MJ said gently. "If you would like me to."

The three women sat at their table and quickly ordered battered cod and thick-cut chips.

MJ's a magician," Linney added when the waitress disappeared. "You know how I look on air? And how I look better off air too than I used to?" She grinned, knowing that Kirsten had noticed the change in her wardrobe since she'd been in London. "That's because MJ's taught me how to dress properly." Then she laughed. "Gran wasn't a lot of help, and even though Anna and her sisters tried, I just don't look like them."

Kirsten smiled weakly, and Linney understood. Kirsten's

mother dressed like a stereotypical librarian, and what worked on willowy Anna wouldn't suit Kirsten any better than it would suit Linney. She looked between the Londoners with a combination of fear and horror in her eyes. "You're kind to offer," she stammered. "But I don't think so." She lowered her eyes to her lap, willing the nervous flush in her cheeks to dissipate.

MJ looked quizzically at Linney, who shook her head almost imperceptibly. Kirsten wasn't ready yet.

Their meal arrived and MJ acquiesced. "Okay, no problem. But if you change your mind, just ask." She reached for the malt vinegar.

Kirsten shook her head emphatically and popped a hot chip in her mouth as if to put an end to the conversation. Linney worked hard to put the awkwardness behind them, and somehow, by the end of the meal, MJ had convinced Kirsten to at least get her hair cut.

Linney spent the next day toiling in the newsroom and when the women met up outside a Covent Garden pub for a before-dinner drink, she couldn't believe her eyes. Kirsten had always been beautiful, but under MJ's expert guidance, she'd been transformed.

Linney whistled. "You look amazing!" Her friend's curly hair had been styled in a way that suited her round face and looked shinier and bouncier than usual. She was wearing makeup that accentuated her hazel eyes and made her look sophisticated. And while her clothes still hid her figure, Linney thought MJ was responsible for the colours that made Kirsten glow. Maybe there had been some shopping after all.

"You like it?" Kirsten's voice was unsure, but the way she touched her hair showed Linney she was pleased.

"You look great! But how do you feel?"

"I love it," Kirsten whispered, her eyes sparkling with delight. "I feel pretty.

"Now, let's show London the new Kirsten."

The three women found seats at the bar and were soon enjoying the attention of three handsome men. They sipped cocktails, flirting harmlessly. Taking their leave after an appropriate amount of time, the women headed to dinner, arm in arm.

"I'm embarrassed to admit how much I enjoyed that," Linney said, helping herself to some calamari from the centre of the table.

MJ looked at her sharply. "I keep telling you, you can do better."

"MJ," Linney warned.

"What do you mean?" Kirsten asked. She hadn't met Mac yet, despite being in London for close to a week.

"Let's just say Mac is not always the kindest," said MJ. "And he—"

"Enough, MJ." Linney snapped.

"Okay, okay." MJ knew when to change the subject, and turned the conversation deftly to elicit stories of Silver Lake.

The next night, Mac joined Linney and Kirsten for dinner. To try and avoid criticism, Linney wore his favourite silky shirt with sleeves that fluttered in the breeze and black capri pants with heeled sandals that made her legs seem to go on for miles.

"Mac! Over here." Linney waved when she saw him and he joined the women, kissing her almost proprietarily, which didn't sit well with Kirsten. She immediately knew what MJ had meant.

She didn't warm up to Mac over their main course. Despite his sexy Scottish brogue, he was dismissive and condescending. He drank a lot, and she bristled when he spoke to her. After his initial greeting, he treated her like he thought her intelligence was diminished by her small-town address and less than fashionable clothes.

"You never left," he stated suddenly as they finished their main course, his words starting to slur. "Why?"

"I never wanted to," she replied. "Silver Lake is my home."

"But you could have. You didn't want to work at a cutting-edge practice?"

"I love my work. And people in small towns deserve health care just as good as those in big cities."

"But what is there to do after work is done? There are no museums, no art galleries, no lectures to go to. And you don't have restaurants and pubs like we do. It must be so boring."

"Leave her alone, Mac." Linney jumped in to rescue her friend. "Small-town life isn't so bad—and of course, Silver Lake has a restaurant! More than one in fact. And the landscape is our art."

Mac caught a waiter's arm and asked for another drink. "You ran away from it. You told me you hated it."

"Yes, I did." Linney had to give him that. "But that's because I wanted to do something that I couldn't do there. And I appreciate that Kirsten and Anna stayed. They're part of a community that's helping me take care of my grandmother. You know that."

Mac knocked back his drink as the waiter came by with dessert menus. "I think we'll have to agree to disagree." He stood up. "Now ladies, I'm going to let you enjoy the rest of your evening." Linney looked up at him with surprise. He wasn't staying. "I have to go join my mates. Kirsten, good to meet you. MJ, Linney, I'll see you at work tomorrow." He leaned down and put his hand behind Linney's head, kissing her roughly. It wasn't a kiss she was used to getting in public and Kirsten was so embarrassed she had to look away.

Kirsten didn't see Mac again until her last night when she and Linney met Mac and MJ for a late dessert. "This has been such a great trip," Kirsten said, as she took another bite of the sticky toffee pudding that the table was sharing. She looked at Linney with gratitude. "Thank you for everything. I know you've been busy, but I've had such a good time. And it's been

great to meet the storied Marie-Josée, who is now a friend!"
Kirsten then glanced at the man with them. "And you too, Mac.
I had to meet the man who keeps Linney in London." She
smiled weakly.

"Don't be fooled," he replied a little too loudly. "She stays
for the work. I'm just a bonus." The table erupted into laughter.

"I don't mind saying, though," he began when they quieted,
"I am looking forward to having her back to myself."

Linney kicked him sharply under the table and did her best
to repair the damage. "You are always welcome, Kirsten.
Always."

MJ jumped in. "Now that I know two people from Silver
Lake, I might just have to stop in the next time I'm home."

Mac rolled his eyes. "Silver Lake. Always Silver Lake." He
caught the waiter's attention. "I'll leave you to one last
evening together." He paid the bill, and they all stood up for
parting hugs. Mac whispered in Linney's ear. "Tomorrow
night you're all mine. I've missed you." Linney's knees almost
gave way.

EVEN KIRSTEN COULDN'T HELP but notice the attention her new
hair and makeup were getting. It was ridiculous, she thought.
She was still the same person underneath, but she'd noticed
some admiring glances, which felt very different from the
leering she was sadly used to. She mentioned it to Anna when
she visited shortly after getting home.

"You look amazing," Anna told her. "You should be getting
looks."

Kirsten took a sip of her coffee. "It's a bit unnerving," she
admitted. "I'm used to stares, but this time people are looking at
me, not my—" She gestured to her chest, always feeling
awkward.

Anna rolled her eyes. "You're a beautiful woman, with a figure most would die for. I'd love to have a few more curves."

"You already have your guy. And he loves you just the way you are."

"Yeah," Anna said, a faint blush coming over her cheeks as she smiled. "I got lucky."

Danny's truck rolled into the driveway. When he came to a stop, their daughters tumbled out of the back seat.

"Go put your wet things in the dryer," Danny called out to them as they ran into the house. He'd picked them up from a pool party.

"Wow!" he said admiringly, as Kirsten stood up to give him a friendly hug. "What happened to you over there?"

Kirsten blushed at the compliment and explained about MJ's magic. "It's just a haircut and some new makeup," she said.

"Well, whatever it is, you look great." Danny sheepishly looked over at his wife. "And so do you, dear."

Anna shooed him away and asked Kirsten more about her trip.

"You'd like MJ, but I have to admit, I don't know what Linney sees in Mac—I mean, he's handsome, and there's the accent and all—but he's a bit of a bully, and he drinks an awful lot. She seems happy with him, but I just wonder ..." Kirsten trailed off, not sure how to explain what she was thinking.

"Do we need to be worried about her?" Anna's brow was furrowed, and she stirred her coffee aggressively.

"No, I don't think so. He's just not the kind of guy I would have pictured her with. I always thought she'd be with someone more like Derek.

Anna laughed and Kirsten playfully tossed a throw pillow at her friend. "Not *our* Derek of course," she explained. "They've been friends for too long for that. But with someone like him."

"Well, she'll have to take care of herself over there," Anna said. "Maybe MJ can help her. But back here, this new look of yours will surely help your dating life. I think I know a few good options!"

Another throw pillow came her way, and the women giggled like schoolgirls.

DEREK RUSHED to the tailor before they closed. His wedding suit was ready, and he had to ensure it didn't need last-minute alterations. It was a pain in the neck, but at least it wasn't like Olivia's gown. His fiancée seemed to have had endless fittings, probably because her schedule was keeping her from eating properly. Olivia had lost several pounds she couldn't afford to lose in the run-up to the nuptials.

As the tailor tugged on the jacket and smoothed its lapels, Derek thought once again about how much he wanted this wedding to be over. It was just two weeks away but had become a huge source of stress for both of them. They simply had too much going on and he was frightened something was going to break. They'd bickered about it, Derek trying to get Olivia to slow down just a little bit. He hadn't been successful.

The old tailor nodded his approval. The groom would look perfect. As he headed back into the dressing room to change, Derek admitted he wasn't taking his own advice. He was deep in a domestic violence case and was bound and determined to get it tied up before the honeymoon. His client, impoverished since birth, had chosen the wrong man. She'd been routinely beaten by her husband and Derek was going to get results for her and her children.

Heading home, Derek stopped at the local market. It had been ages since either of them had cooked. Maybe, if he planned a nice meal tonight, they could have a quiet evening with no talk about their cases or the wedding. He had a basket full of food when his phone rang.

"Hi, Derek. I'm going to be late for the charity event tonight," Olivia said in a rush.

Derek felt deflated. He'd forgotten about this one. He turned and started putting things back on the shelf. "Why don't I come and get you from the office when you're ready and we'll go together?" he suggested.

"No, this event is important," she said. "You should be there for the whole thing. I'll come as soon as I can. Promise."

"We need a vacation."

"Honeymoon's coming. Just two more weeks."

Derek smiled. "I love you, Olivia."

"Love you too! Now I have to run so I can finish. See you soon!"

Derek walked home slowly. Yes, this wedding couldn't be over soon enough.

8

———————

Derek stood on the top stops of the Silver Lake church. The sun was shining, but he hardly noticed. By his side was his beautiful bride, the diamonds in her ears almost as bright as her eyes. Aiden had kept him calm that morning—the best best man ever, he joked—and all his friends and family were there to be part of it. A perfect day. The fact that the hassle of wedding invitations and the million other decisions was behind them was just a bonus. Now he was married to the most beautiful, most talented, most driven woman he knew. They were a family and their whole life was ahead of them.

"Can you believe it?" he whispered to Olivia as they started down the steps hand in hand. "I'm your husband."

"And I'm your wife," she whispered back, glowing with the excitement of the day. "I love you." She stopped at the bottom of the steps and kissed him. A light breeze carried the sensual jasmine scent of the perfume Olivia always wore, and which she matched in the bouquet she was carrying. "For now and for always." Olivia's lace overlay gown was deceptively simple, hugging every curve and flaring out at the bottom slightly, mermaid style. She wore a satin bolero for church, but it would be coming off soon. The dress had a plunging neckline, with netting to hold everything together, but it was the deep cut of the back that was the star of the show. Derek's hand crept up under the cropped jacket now, touching her bare back. He was anxious to get her alone tonight.

~

LINNEY HAD WATCHED the service with her grandmother on one side of her and Kirsten on the other. Anna and Danny, who were sitting in front of them had just turned around to chat.

"It was a beautiful wedding," Linney said. Anna was dabbing at her eyes and Danny stroked her arm tenderly. Kirsten sniffed and Linney reacted. "Don't you start crying too! It'll be your turn soon enough," she teased.

"Or yours, maybe," Anna jested, as she folded her handkerchief and put it back in her purse.

"That would be nice," Linney's Gran said. "I'd like to see you settled, dear. Maybe you'll bring Mac home to meet me."

"I'm working on him," Linney said, but her voice was flat.

The group made their way to the back of the church, following other guests. Danny took her grandmother's arm as she shakily descended the steps. "Thank you," Linney mouthed to him at the bottom, and he nodded. Gran seemed even more frail than she had at Easter, and Linney realized she needed to put on her research hat and start looking at retirement homes. For when they needed to, she told herself. Gran didn't need one just yet. She put that thought away as they reached an impromptu receiving line in the church gardens.

The wedding party had been small—just Aiden, who Linney had met several times in Toronto—and Olivia's best friend from law school. Linney gave Aiden a friendly hug, and a perfunctory kiss on the cheek to the maid of honour who she didn't know well. Moving down the line ahead of her, Gran congratulated Derek's mother.

"Well, you did it!" Linney said to Derek and Olivia when she reached them. "Congratulations, you two. May you have all the happiness you deserve."

"Thank you, Linney." Olivia reached out politely to hug her.

Derek's hug was warmer, almost crushing her. "I'm so glad this part is done!" he whispered in her ear.

They both looked much more relaxed listening to Aiden's best man's speech as dinner came to a close. Aiden had everyone in stitches, telling stories of when he'd first met Derek in school. "I predated Olivia," he joked, "but as soon as Derek met her, it was like he completely forgot who I was." There was laughter, and he moved smoothly into his closing. "I'm hardly one to give marriage advice, so let me draw from literature. Antoine de Saint-Exupery wrote that love does not consist of gazing at each other, but in looking outward together in the same direction. Derek and Olivia, may you always look outwards together." He raised his glass. "Please join me in a toast to the bride and groom."

Linney lifted a slim champagne glass along with the other guests, and there was much applause. She looked over at Olivia and Derek as they kissed. The happy couple was savouring every second of their reception under a big white tent at Derek's home on the lake.

There were many more toasts and laughter as friends told stories until the sun set, the twinkle lights came on, and music filled the air. Derek and Olivia wound their way among the tables, thanking their guests for coming. Olivia charmed the Silver Lake locals while Derek impressed guests from the city with his earnest devotion to Olivia and his job.

When the dancing began, Olivia took her father's arm and Derek offered his to his mother. Olivia's father, after dancing with Derek's mother, approached Linney.

"Thank you, but I'm sure my gran would like to dance first."

With a wink, Linney set off to find Anna and Kirsten, leaving her grandmother to enjoy a slow spin around the dance floor.

"He should have been here, Linney," Anna admonished when Linney slid into a slip-covered chair between her friends. "If Mac loves you the way you say he does, he should want to meet your friends and be part of our celebrations." Linney had no answer for that, so she deftly changed the subject.

"Can you believe it's been ten years since Kirsten and I were your bridesmaids? Where has the time gone?"

"It just gets better every year," said Danny, smiling down at Anna and it was clear they were still as much in love as they had been at their own wedding. "You two should try it!"

Suddenly the music sped up and Linney grabbed Kirsten's hand. "Let's dance!" she said, pulling her friend from her chair.

Derek and Olivia spent their wedding night at Silver Lake's tiny inn. It had seen better days, but the rooms were large and you could tell they'd been luxurious in the past. It was either that or leave their reception early to drive back to their city apartment before their flight to Mauritius the next day, so Olivia had reluctantly agreed to stay at The Manor House.

Derek battled back a yawn as they climbed the stairs to their room just after one in the morning, his tie already loosened. He'd been careful not to drink too much, but the energy he'd felt on the church steps had been sapped from the excitement of the day. Was this how every groom felt, he wondered, as he thought about giving Olivia a proper wedding night.

They stopped at the door to their room and Derek put the key in the lock. He pushed it open.

"The traditional way?" he asked.

Olivia nodded, and he picked her up and carried his wife over the threshold. "I love you," he said, setting her down gently.

"I love you too." Olivia stifled a yawn. She stepped out of her rhinestone-encrusted high-heeled sandals and Derek kissed her shoulder, undoing the few buttons on the back of her dress. The gown slipped to the floor, and she tried to hide another yawn behind her hand. The relief of planning the perfect day, coupled with perhaps one too many champagne toasts, had caught up with her and she was drained.

"Tired?" Derek asked as he unbuttoned his shirt.

"Honestly? Exhausted." She sat on the corner of the bed, and Derek was unable to fight back a huge yawn of his own, making her laugh. "You too?" Derek nodded. "How weird would it be if we just slept tonight?" she asked.

Derek looked at her, surprised by the suggestion, but honestly relieved. "Sure," he replied, drawing out the word. "As long as you're okay with that, and we make up for it when we get to Mauritius tomorrow."

"Deal," Olivia said, taking her earrings off and sliding under the covers. Derek joined her and spooned her tightly. They were asleep instantly.

The beaches of Mauritius were exactly as advertised, and although Derek and Olivia had planned to spend a few days relaxing and then do some hiking and other watersports, they found they spent far more time in their honeymoon suite than out of it—making up time and time again for the wedding night.

~

LINNEY FULFILLED a promise to Derek to have breakfast with Aiden the morning after the wedding. She'd spoken with him about it at the reception and he'd agreed to join her for a quick spin in the kayaks.

"Great speech last night," Linney said, as they pushed off from the dock. Linney had a small picnic basket in the stern hatch.

"Thanks," Aiden said as he concentrated to avoid tipping over his kayak. "When do you go back?"

"Tonight, actually," she said. "It's a short visit. Too short in fact." She looked over at him and laughed.

"What?"

Linney pointed to his paddle. "Make sure the long edge is up."

"This is harder than it looks!"

"We're not going far." Linney pointed to a small island off to the right. "We'll have breakfast over there." The pair paddled silently, except for the splashes when Aiden dipped his paddle into the water less than gracefully.

They arrived at the island and Linney hopped out of her kayak to helped Aiden get his to shore. She pulled out the hamper, and they sat on the stone outcrop as she poured coffee from an insulated carafe and began arranging plates of pastries, eggs, and fruit. Linney raised her coffee cup.

"To the married couple."

"To Derek and Olivia. They've beaten us both to the alter!"

Linney tore off the end of a croissant. "You didn't bring a date to the wedding. I'd say the alter is a ways off for you."

Aiden laughed. "A very long way! But what about you? You've got a pretty serious guy in London, right?. Why didn't he come?" He grabbed a hard-boiled egg.

"Mac had things to do. He couldn't spare the time." Even to her, the excuse sounded thin, so she was thankful Aiden didn't pursue it. Instead, he stood up and stretched.

"I think I understand why Derek loves it here," he mused. "I read somewhere that the human eye can see far more shades of green than any other colour. And that being in nature can lower your heart rate, reduce stress, and even speed up healing times."

"I've read those studies too. And I believe it. I love London, but my trips home are what keep me grounded. I think Derek feels the same way. I know I always feel so much calmer after I've spent time back home at the lake."

They finished their breakfast, and as they put away the empty containers into the hamper, Aiden spoke. "Thanks for bringing me out here. Way better than breakfast at a restaurant."

"Anything for Derek's best man. But we have some good breakfast spots. Make sure you come up sometime when Derek and Olivia are here and have them take you out to Vi's Café or the Doughnut Hut. Two different experiences, but both great."

"I'll take your word for it. I don't have a lot of spare weekends."

"You work as hard as Derek, then."

"Guilty as charged. But it sounds like you work just as hard."

Linney reddened. "You caught me!"

The pair kayaked back to the dock, and Aiden thanked her again as he got ready to go. "Maybe I'll see you in Toronto sometime when you're here to see the newlyweds."

"You never know. Safe drive back to the city." Linney waved as he backed his car out of the driveway and took off.

Her phone buzzed, and Linney sat on the porch stairs with the hamper to read MJ's text.

Your boyfriend is grumpy.

??

He looks like crap. Comes in late every day,
barks at the interns. Gemma's pissed.

Sigh.

Gotta be honest with you. He's been out late at the pub every night since you left. And I wouldn't be surprised to find out he has a bottle in his desk. You need to know. He's acting strange and people are noticing.

It was like a kick in the stomach and Linney put her phone down and closed her eyes. MJ wasn't one to sugarcoat the truth, but the fact she'd said it so plainly was a surprise. Linney knew Mac had always been a heavy drinker. But he'd always been professional in the newsroom and his work had never suffered. She felt a tension headache forming and realized she hadn't had one since she'd been home.

Linney got up and moved to the porch swing, clutching a throw pillow tightly. If she were honest with herself, she knew that Mac had been drinking more in the last year. A lot more. She'd had suspicions about what was in his coffee in the morning for several months but had never asked. She didn't want to know. Linney gulped. Maybe it was worse than she thought. She was afraid she was going to have to face some unpleasant truths soon. Squirming uncomfortably, she picked up her phone again.

Oh no.

Miss you.

Miss you too. Hurry back.

Later that day, after Linney put dinner in the oven for her and Gran, she leaned against the kitchen cupboards. Six o'clock. So eleven in the UK. She pulled her phone from the back pocket of her jeans and her fingers hovered over the keyboard. She started typing and then deleted it. She started over but deleted it again. Finally, the words came to her.

> Hey. Hope all is well. Miss you and can't wait to see you.

Linney held her breath, waiting for a reply. Nothing. She looked at her watch. Had she got the time difference wrong? If MJ was right, Mac should still be at the pub. Suddenly her phone buzzed.

> Ha ing a pint witg the boys. Miss you. Miss you i bed with me. come jome soon. Thr things I want to do witj ypu …

Linney's heart sank. She did not want to deal with this. A tear rolled down her cheek as she typed.

> Be safe, ok? See you in tomorrow.

"I'm back!" Linney called as she opened the door to her flat, breathing heavily after dragging her luggage up the stairs. Mac had promised to be there, but he wasn't. Charitably, Linney guessed that Gemma had him out on an assignment. Still, she wished he had left a note. She unpacked and took a long hot shower, rinsing the travel day away. Starting the laundry, she sat down to sort through the mail. It was probably for the best he wasn't there, she justified to herself. Gave her a chance to acclimatize.

Her phone dinged later that afternoon.

> Going to the pub with the gang. Come!

Linney was still tired, but if she wanted to see Mac, she

supposed she'd have to go to him. She sent a heart emoji back and pulled on her coat. When she arrived at the familiar watering hole, she waved to colleagues and gave Mac a quick kiss. "Just one drink, okay?" she murmured. He nodded, and she pulled out her phone to show the wedding pictures to the group.

Conversation soon turned to the latest stories of the day, and who was working on what. MJ was working late, Linney learned, which explained why she wasn't there. Linney nursed her beer, stifling several yawns behind her hand, while Mac had a second, a third, and ordered a fourth, his stories getting wilder and louder with each one. He loved being the centre of attention.

When it was clear he wasn't ready to leave, Linney finally gave up. She needed some sleep, and so she tugged at his jacket. "I'm going home, okay? Don't be too long."

"Spoilsport," he sneered. "You just got here. Can't you stay and wait?"

"Seriously, Mac. I'm tired and jetlagged."

"Fine," he huffed, snapping at her. "Go home. You left me for a week already for some stupid wedding. What's another day? I'll see you tomorrow."

Linney wiped a tear away as she walked the short distance to the tube station. What she would have given to be able to text Derek for advice. But her best friend was on his honeymoon.

9

———————

Linney hoisted the gold statue over her head, as the crowd clapped enthusiastically at the annual TV awards gala banquet. She'd worn her hair up, to show off the keyhole detail of the back of her dress and now, with the spotlight on her, she was glad she had. Linney had been cautiously optimistic this year, but nothing was ever certain. She was so overwhelmed when her name was called that her knees knocked together as she stood up, and her voice wavered when she accepted her first solo award. She thanked Mac for his support and Gemma and the rest of the crew at TCN for their ongoing confidence in her. Nobody clapped louder for her than MJ did.

She held up the hem of her garnet floor-length gown—another purchase MJ had helped her make—muttering, "Don't trip, don't trip," to herself under her breath as she carefully made her way down the stairs from the stage and back to their table, where MJ stood up and gave her a huge hug.

"Congratulations," Mac said, kissing her sloppily when she slid into her seat beside him. Linney tensed. Mac was drunk. She knew conversations stopped in the newsroom when she walked by these days and she'd heard the whispers that his work was suffering. Gemma was giving him less air time too. Linney had meant to confront him in the fall, after she came back from Silver Lake, but the time never seemed right. Even though the evidence was right in front of her, she was frightened to have confirmation. So it was easier to stay silent and soldier on.

Mac was up for a production award, despite his issues, and Linney expected now that they'd go home to celebrate a pair of trophies. She laced her fingers with his and they both tensed in expectation when his category was called and he fidgeted nervously with his bow tie. To Linney's surprise, the award went to a competitor.

"You were robbed," she said quietly. "He didn't deserve that." Others at the table murmured agreement as the winner made his way to the stage, but Linney felt it was forced, as if they were just being polite.

Mac took the bottle of wine from the centre of the table morosely and filled his glass again. His hands were unsteady, and the wine spilled on the tablecloth. Linney leaped to mop it up.

"Next year, Mac," Gemma told him tersely over the applause. "Stay the course." She and Mac had worked together for decades, and Linney wondered if Gemma's words held deeper meaning than they seemed to on the surface.

Mac sulked for the rest of the ceremony, draining the last of the wine from the bottle. As soon as the formalities were over, he headed to the bar, weaving his way among the tables to get there. Heady from her win, Linney was oblivious and joined MJ and others on the dance floor to celebrate. Mac watched, with a sneer on his face and a whiskey in his hand.

"She's good, Mac," said Gemma, as she joined him at the bar. She wasn't ready to let this go. "She's good. Don't hold her back."

"Whatd'ya mean?" he slurred.

"She's ready to fly. Do not make it hard for her to go."

"Gemma."

"And I think it's time you switched to water tonight." A dark cloud passed over Mac's face, but Gemma put a hand on his arm and then slipped away, as Linney joined him at the bar and asked the bartender for a soft drink. A few strands of hair had slipped from her updo and her cheeks were pink with exertion. Her eyes danced, but all Mac could see was her with an award and his hands empty. Gemma's words rang in his ears. But Gemma wasn't there. Linney was.

"You know," he began, poking her in the shoulder with his finger as his frustration overtook any sense of decorum. "The only reason you got that award was because of me." His voice rose as he tapped his own chest. "I made you. I gave you your first chance and taught you everything you know." He turned to the bartender. "Another one."

Linney flushed with embarrassment. "Mac, not here."

"Why not here? It's no secret. Everyone knows it." He was shouting now, and his new drink spilled with his oversized gestures. "You wouldn't have had half the opportunities if you weren't sleeping with me. That award should be mine. You'd be nothing without me." He threw back the whiskey and raised his glass, once again empty, signalling to the bartender to fill it again.

Silence fell over the bar and Linney's eyes darted around, noticing that people dropped their gaze as she did so. They had all heard. She took a deep breath and clenched her hands into fists. "Mac, let's go home." At least there, she would be the only audience for his biting and condescending words. She was used to that.

But he wouldn't be quieted. "You think you're a big shot now, don't you, now that you have an award?" he sneered. "It doesn't mean a thing. The whole thing's rigged." Linney put a hand on his arm, trying to make a connection, but he shrugged it off. "Don't fool yourself." He finished his drink in one swallow and slammed the glass on the bar. "And another thing. It had to go to a woman this year. That's why you got it. Don't fool yourself into thinking it had anything to do with talent." Mac turned his attention to the bartender. "Gimme another." He stumbled and only just caught himself on the bar.

People were openly staring now. MJ made her way over to Linney for support.

"I'm sorry you feel that way, Mac," Linney began, squaring her shoulders against the hot tears prickling in her eyes that prevented her from continuing.

MJ picked up Linney's statue and put her arm around her friend's shoulders. "Let's get out of here," she whispered. They could both hear the murmuring as they left the room.

"I'M OKAY, MJ." Linney took a few deep breaths as they stood in the lobby. All she wanted was to go home. "I love him. I really do. It's just hard when he's like this."

"Let me call Gemma." As they left, MJ had seen Gemma take Mac's arm firmly and lead him away from the crowd with a grim look. Gritting her teeth, she spoke to their boss and as she put Linney in a cab, she confirmed. "Gemma says not to worry, okay? She's got it. You're sure you don't want me to come with you?"

Linney shook her head. "Thanks, MJ. You're the best. But I need to be alone tonight."

"Okay, but call me if you need anything. Anything at all."

Somehow, Linney held her emotions in check during the cab ride. When she closed the door to her flat behind her, she unclenched her fists and saw the fingernail marks in her palms. In her bedroom, she placed the award on her bureau and hung up her beautiful dress, and she finally let herself cry. Salty tears rolled down her face, and she sobbed as she pulled hairpins out of her updo, letting her hair tumble down her back. She put on her pajamas and splashed water on her face, but the tears kept coming. Her phone buzzed.

> Hey, how'd it go? Am I now the friend of a twice-awarded journalist?

> Yes, you are! I'm home now but I keep pinching myself.

Linney's phone rang, and she climbed into bed and took a deep breath before answering quietly. "Hey."

"Hey to you—and well done!

"Thanks. It was a magical evening. I can still hardly believe I won." Linney paused. "Mac didn't take it well though."

"What do you mean?" Derek was on alert. Linney didn't sound as excited as she should be.

"He had too much to drink and said some things he'll regret tomorrow. I'm home now. It'll be fine tomorrow." She swiped her finger on her cheek where new tear had fallen." She sniffled. There was silence on the other end of the line. "Seriously, it'll be alright.

More silence. Linney's training had taught her not to fill silences. People usually said what they really felt if you waited them out and if Derek had something to say, she could be patient. While she waited, Linney picked at her cuticles. The stress was getting to her.

"Why do you do that? Apologize for him. It's not right."

"Derek—"

"You're upset. What did he say?"

"That I didn't deserve it. That he made me." Her voice hitched and eventually she continued in a quieter voice, "Maybe he's right."

"That bast— Linney, don't listen to him. You are a great journalist. Is ... is everything okay over there? I'm worried about you."

She pulled her knees up to her chest. "Don't be."

"It's just ... Look, I don't want to pry, but you keep talking about Mac's drinking and it reminds me a bit of my mum. I'm worried. Are you sure you're alright? You should be out celebrating, not at home and upset."

Linney's temper flared. She was tired, aggravated, and hurt, and now Derek was piling on too. "Thank you for your concern, but it's nothing like that. And I can take care of myself." How dare he, she fumed. He was comparing her and Mac to his mother and father. She was educated, she had a career, and she wasn't beholden to any man. He didn't know what he was talking about.

"Linney—"

"I'm tired. I'll talk to you tomorrow." Linney hung up the phone and silenced it wondering how today had gone so wrong.

THE NEXT MORNING, Linney pulled herself together and headed to TCN ready to take on new challenges. Her self-confidence had taken a hit, but she was an award-winning journalist now, so she needed to act like one. She'd texted Mac before she left the house and she was concerned he hadn't replied as she sat down at her desk.

"Good morning. Gemma wants to see you," MJ told her as she turned on her laptop.

Linney grabbed her notebook and headed upstairs. The senior offices were in a ring around the open newsroom, the mezzanine convenient for announcements to the reporters and editors working on the floor.

"You asked to see me?" Linney stood in the door of Gemma's office.

Gemma ushered her in and closed the door. "I wanted to talk to you."

Linney's brow furled. Closed door? Was something wrong with her performance? Had there been a mistake? Did they want to take her award back? Had something happened to Mac? Her heart lurched.

"This is off the record," Gemma continued, confusing Linney even more. "Human Resources would tell me I'm not allowed to talk to you about this, but I think it's important. I think you know that I consider Mac not just a colleague, but a friend."

Linney knew that, but didn't quite understand where this was going. She nodded and adjusted her glasses nervously.

Gemma smiled sadly. "Linney, I've worked with him a long time."

Linney listened as Gemma told her more. "It's no secret that journalists drink. Many of them drink a lot. It's a taxing industry, with impossible deadlines and not always the nicest people. We drink to relieve the stress. We drink to celebrate great interviews and we drink to commiserate ones that fall through. We drink to dampen the ugliness that we see in the world. We drink to quell the fears that we're not good enough."

Gemma stopped for a moment while Linney absorbed her words.

"There are studies about the propensity for alcoholism in our profession. It's real, Linney." Gemma took a sip of coffee from the TCN mug on her desk. She looked Linney directly in the eye. "Some people can manage the drinking. Some can't. You may not know this, but Mac is probably what people sometimes call a 'high-functioning' alcoholic. He's come close to the edge a couple of times before. This isn't his first flirtation with full-blown alcoholism, but he's always been able to pull himself back. This time? I'm not so sure." Linney's head started to swim and her heart pounded in her chest. She sat down suddenly. What had happened after she left the gala?

Gemma noticed her anxiety and put a hand on Linney's shoulder. "It's alright. I got him home last night, and I spoke with him this morning. He's okay."

"Thank goodness." Linney took a few deep breaths and her heart rate slowed a bit.

Gemma leaned on her desk. "Now for some advice. You're a rising star here at TCN. To be blunt, even if he gets healthy, Mac's glory days are behind him. He could be a great editor. But right now he's not even a good reporter. As your boss, I'm not going to get involved in your love life. But you need to know—I haven't seen him this bad before." She sighed and rubbed her temples. "I'll stand by him. We've walked this road before. But you're good, Linney, and I don't want you derailing your career over him. I think you may have a tough decision to make. And you may need to make it soon."

Linney breathed, taking in what she'd learned. "Thank you, Gemma," she said, standing up. "I appreciate your candour."

"And Linney? This conversation never happened."

Linney headed back to her desk, her head swimming as she tried to understand exactly what Gemma had been telling her. She didn't get a lot of work done, as she wrestled with the two sides of Mac that she knew. There was the Mac who she was passionately in love with and who took her to heights she'd never experienced with anyone else. And then there was the Mac who cut her down and belittled her when he drank to the point that she didn't believe in herself. Like Gemma said, she had a career to think about. But surely she also owed it to him to stand by him in his time of crisis. To support him. To be by his side. Didn't she?

By mid-afternoon, Linney had convinced herself that Gemma had been exaggerating. She'd been too exuberant at her success at the gala. No wonder he had been upset. She shouldn't have been so unfeeling about his loss. It had been her fault that he'd drunk so much. And now she had to make it right.

> Hey. I'm sorry if I lorded my award over you. I didn't mean to. Love you. ♥ ♥

> Dinner at my place Saturday? We should talk.

It was hours before he replied.

> Deal.

~

NERVOUSLY, Linney chopped up vegetables for the stir-fry she was cooking. Hopefully, the only tears tonight would be from the onions she'd just added to the wok. She wondered which Mac she'd get tonight. After thinking about her conversation with Gemma she was more confused than ever. She loved Mac, and she knew he loved her. They could be so good together when he wasn't drinking. Gemma seemed to be suggesting she distance herself from Mac. But how could she do that? Linney was twisting herself into knots when she heard Mac's keys in the lock. She smiled. Mac was here.

Mac stumbled slightly over the threshold and then dropped his keys on the kitchen passthrough before joining Linney in the kitchen and putting his hands around her waist. He reached beyond her to turn off the burner and spun her around. "I missed you. I don't like spending nights without you."

Linney instantly melted when he whispered in her ear, but then she smelled booze on his breath. A flag went up, but the thought flew away when he nibbled on her neck and with a hand on the small of her back, pulled her close.

"Do you suppose," he murmured, "that dinner can wait?" His lips crushed hers hungrily and Linney felt the room spin. No matter what, Mac always had that effect on her. She reached up around his neck and before she knew it, he'd scooped her up and taken her to the bedroom.

THEY LAY side by side under the covers staring at the ceiling, not touching. Linney twisted the hem of the bedsheet in her fingers. What had gone wrong?

"I gotta go." Mac sat up suddenly and shoved his legs into his boxer shorts. He pulled on his pants and buttoned his shirt in a rush. "You just don't do it for me anymore," he slurred. "You think you're so hot. You're just another wannabe journalist. I'm outta here." He weaved his way out of her room and slammed the door to her flat. She heard him stumble down the stairs.

Sitting up in bed with her arms around her knees, Linney wept.

Later that evening, she put her glasses back on, got out of bed and cleaned up her kitchen. When she dumped the stir-fry into the garbage, she remembered the risotto that she'd scraped into the bin. Had this been going on that long? Just the thought of it made her feel ill. Tonight was a disaster. Linney picked at a torn cuticle while she waited for the kettle to boil. She made herself a cup of chamomile tea and curled up in her reading chair with her laptop. It was time for some research. With shaky fingers, she started to type the word "alcoholism" into the search bar when her phone buzzed. Linney slammed the computer lid shut.

> There's a great exhibit at the Tate. Want to go tomorrow?

Linney sighed. All she really wanted to do was hole up in her flat and try to figure out what to do next. But an afternoon out with MJ would be a good distraction.

> Sounds great. Thanks for the invite!

The women texted back and forth for a few more minutes, deciding where and when to meet. When they finished, Linney muted her phone, left it in the living room, and drew a bath. She needed to think.

Because her phone was on silent, she missed several texts from Derek. Reading through them the next morning, Linney realized she'd been pulling away from her best friend. She just didn't know how to talk about this problem with him.

Olivia and Derek enjoyed a rare Sunday when neither of them had work to do. They took a sunny stroll, gloved hand in gloved hand along Queen's Quay and then stopped to warm their frozen fingers and fill their stomachs at the trendy bistro up the street from their condo. They sated themselves on the world-class brunch menu and drank mimosas. They'd been married for almost eight months and with the stress of the wedding behind them, they were deliriously happy.

The waiter brought another mimosa for Olivia, and coffee for Derek along with the bill. Derek put his credit card in the folio and then reached across the table and laced his fingers through Olivia's. He looked deeply into her eyes and brought up what was on his mind. "I think it's time we started trying for a baby."

"Derek, it's way too early!" Olivia pulled her hand from his. "I can't afford to take time away now. I'll look like I'm not serious about making partner. Maybe in a few more years."

Derek was crushed. "I thought maybe we could slow down a bit. I can take fewer cases, and you could–"

"No." Olivia cut him off. "Not now. It's not the right time."

Knowing he wasn't going to win, Derek raised his hands in defeat. "Fine, not now. But I want to start talking about when is the right time. I want a family."

Olivia nodded. "I know you do. Just not yet."

IT WAS the dreariest April Linney had experienced in London. She couldn't remember the last time she had seen the sun, and the damp cold had seeped into her bones rendering her permanently cold. London was miserable, and Linney's mood reflected it.

She was on edge all the time now with Mac, and the state of her fingernails betrayed how stressed she was. Sure, they'd made up, and there hadn't been any more problems in bed but Linney agonized about Mac's drinking and felt powerless to do anything about it, watching helplessly as he changed from Jekyll to Hyde at the flip of a switch without warning. Some days she internalized what he said about her. Her research was poor. Her stories were shallow. Her scripts were trite. She looked fat on camera. She was lucky to have him. It went on and on. His words were at odds with how Gemma treated her, but somehow she believed him more. She dressed badly, she wasn't attractive, she couldn't cook well. He had put on weight, but he blamed her for taking his clothes to a dry cleaner that shrank them. How could she be so stupid?

Linney's hands weren't the only ones showing the state of

things. Mac's own hands often shook during morning story meetings, but stopped after he emerged from his office with a fresh cup of coffee. The little bit of research she'd done told Linney that the tremors meant alcohol was starting to leave his system and that when they stopped shaking, he was probably doctoring his coffee with something so there was booze in his system all the times. There was always a drink at lunch, and he was at the pub almost every night now. Linney finally started acknowledging how many empty bottles were in the recycling bin. She knew from the nights he stumbled home to her, that he wasn't sleeping well. Nothing made him happy and how he was keeping up with work was beyond her. She couldn't bring herself to share any of this with anyone. Not Gemma, not MJ. Not even Derek.

Linney sat at her desk, head in her hands, trying to battle through the dull throbbing behind her eyes. Dealing with Mac, on top of the stresses of the job, was hard and her head ached frequently these days. She'd had a tough week at work, putting in long hours on a story that would air tonight. She was looking forward to a quieter day tomorrow, when Gemma called her into her office and handed her a Eurostar ticket. "Go home and pack a bag. I need you in Rotterdam," her boss said. "The port is in trouble. I want both TV and web copy from this." Gemma was nothing, if not direct.

Adrenaline surged as Linney recognized the opportunity in front of her—her first story from Europe. "Thank you, Gemma. I'm on it." She took the tickets and popped her head into Mac's office before heading back to her desk to collect her purse. She waved the tickets. "I'm heading to the Netherlands," she told him.

Mac looked up at her, unshaven and rumpled. "Grant's your cameraman?" He grunted as she nodded and leaned back in his chair to take a sip of tea. "When do you go?"

"Now. I'm heading home to pack." Linney pushed his door

closed and walked around to the other side of his desk. "I just wanted to say goodbye."

Reaching his hand out as he stood up unsteadily, Mac pulled her close. Still holding the tickets, Linney put her arms around his neck and they shared a passionate moment. "I hate that you have to go," he whispered in her ear. "I had plans for us tonight."

"I'll miss you too," she whispered back. "I won't be gone long. Two nights at most. Probably just one."

Linney smelled the alcohol on his breath—it was a constant now—but she gave Mac a quick peck on the cheek. She put that aside and headed out, excited by the assignment, but also aware that Mac might brood for a time. A few years ago, that story might have been his. She just hoped he wouldn't pour another shot into his mug of tea.

Linney and Grant strategized on the three-and-a-half-hour train trip. Rotterdam was the biggest port city in Europe, so troubles were concerning. They worked out where Linney could do her stand-up pieces—they thought the Delft Gate would be a good backdrop—and where Grant could shoot B-roll. Linney called the contact Gemma had set her up with to confirm the interview time.

Confident they'd done everything they could, the conversation turned personal. "You know, I think he fell in love with you the first time he saw you," Grant said, seemingly out of nowhere. Linney stared at him, wondering what the long-time TCN employee was getting at. "I hope you know what you've gotten yourself into, Linney," he continued. "We all love Mac. But we also know—" he broke off, not sure how to approach this with her.

"Don't worry, Grant. I'm not naïve. I'm taking care of myself." As she said the words, she willed herself to believe them.

"Gemma and I have seen this with him before. It could get

ugly." He swallowed hard and his cheeks coloured as he stared intently at his shoes. "Linney, he's starting to talk about you when you're out of the newsroom. It's not flattering, personally or professionally. I agree with Gemma. You're a great reporter. Don't let your career get blown up because of Mac."

"Thank you for telling me," she said after a moment and then they lapsed into awkward silence, her stomach churning with the new information.

The interview went well the next day at the Port Authority. Linney made everyone feel comfortable on camera and asked probing questions, based on all the research she'd read on the train and late into the night.

After the interview, they headed straight to the wharf where Linney would do her standup. Grant nodded his head approvingly as she finished. This was shaping up to be a good story. Unfortunately, they wouldn't make the last train home that evening but booked the first one in the morning. They had an early dinner together and then went to their rooms. As Linney pushed the door open, her phone buzzed. When she saw the text from Derek, she smiled.

How's my favourite reporter? I haven't heard from you in ages.

So sorry. I've been busy.

Coming home soon?

Linney felt a sudden pang of homesickness. Maybe if she was at home, she could talk to Derek. Or maybe she could do it now. Bravely she typed:

Not soon enough. Can I ask you something?

Go for it.

Derek waited while the three dots danced.

I don't know how to start.

Just say it.

I'm scared. You know Mac drinks a lot.

Too much. I'm not sure he's in control anymore.

Derek took his time answering and she wondered what he was thinking.

Is he hurting you?

Not physically, anyway.

But he's horrible to me when he drinks. Sometimes I just feel so small. And I just learned he's talking about me in the newsroom too.

You have to leave him.

I can't. I love him.

Nobody's worth losing yourself over. Can I call you?

Linney panicked and typed quickly.

No. I'm fine. It's not that bad. I'm just tired.

I don't believe you.

No really. I'm in Rotterdam for a story and it's been a long day. Forget I said anything.

Don't shut me out. I'm here for you.

> I'm not. I'm just exaggerating. Things will be fine when I get back.

> If he's not ready to get help, you HAVE to leave him.

> Now you're the one exaggerating.

> Please listen to me. I'm calling you now.

> Derek, let it go. I'm fine.

Linney's phone rang, and she dropped it on the bed, ignoring the sound. Another call. A third. Linney silenced her phone, and pulled the covers over her head. She couldn't deal with this. Not now. Not even with Derek.

AFTER A RESTLESS NIGHT, Linney appeared for breakfast with Grant quiet and pale, and he asked if she'd slept alright.

She shook her head. "Lots on my mind."

"I hope I didn't contribute to that with what I said yesterday."

Linney lay her hand on Grant's arm. "It's fine. I'm fine."

When the train pulled out of the station, Linney remembered her phone and took it off silent. Five missed calls from Derek. She slumped in her seat. He needed to let it go.

Almost immediately, her phone buzzed. MJ had news.

> Heads up. Loverboy didn't make it in this morning.

> On our way home now.

> You might want to go over to his place when you get back. Even Gemma couldn't reach him and she looks like she's ready to strangle him. She had to give his story to Ron.

> Ron'll do a good job.

> Not the point. Mac's out of control.

> I know. I'm scared.

> I'm here for you when you need me.

> ♥ Thanks.

Linney felt the dull ache in her head return. She propped her glasses on the top of her head and rubbed her eyes. It didn't help. And she spent the rest of the journey fretting. She wasn't going to be able to ignore this anymore. She flagged down a taxi at Kings Cross station and picked at a hangnail until it bled. Soon she arrived at Mac's place. The hinges creaked as she used her keys to open the door and crept into his dark flat. "Mac? Are you here? It's Linney."

She heard a thud from the bedroom and then some scuffling. Mac appeared in the doorway with a tumbler in his hand. He had a black eye and a scraped cheekbone. "Hey, Linney," he slurred as he weaved his way toward her, stumbling into the coffee table on his way. "Ouch!"

"Mac, you're drunk. It's not even lunchtime." The sight of him confirmed all the things she'd been worried about. "What happened?" Mac threw back the amber liquid in his glass and set it down roughly. He put his arms around Linney, who stiffened at his touch.

"I'm glad you're back. I missed you." Mac kissed her sloppily and she tensed and wrinkled her nose at the taste of his boozy breath and the smell of stale sweat.

"What happened?" she repeated.

"This?" Mac asked, touching the bruise under his left eye. "Disagreement at the pub. You should see the other guy."

"Oh, Mac. You can't keep doing this," she said sadly.

"I'm fine," Mac insisted. "Just fine."

"Okay, I can't keep doing this."

Mac didn't respond, and she followed him into the bedroom, where he picked up a bottle and took a swig. He certainly wasn't trying to hide it anymore. When Linney looked around the room, she saw another empty bottle by the side of his bed, and judging by the state of the covers, if he'd slept at all last night, it hadn't been soundly. She hadn't missed the bloodshot eyes and his grey pallor.

Mac lay down on the bed and pulled up the rumpled sheets. "You gonna join me?" he asked, but she shook her head. "Your loss," he grumbled, but it wasn't long before his eyes closed, and he began snoring loudly.

There were no tears left to cry as she cleaned up the liquor bottles in the bedroom, and then the beer bottles she found in Mac's reception room. She put on a pot of coffee, drinking a cup to steady herself, and planning to pour the rest down Mac's throat when he woke up. Time to let MJ know.

I found him. It's bad.

What are you going to do?

I don't know. But I have to do something. For real this time.

Will he get help?

IDK. He's sleeping now.

Sleeping? Or passed out.

Either way …

Let me know if you need anything.

Just let Gemma know I'm here?

Consider it done.

Late in the afternoon, after she'd thrown away the first pot of coffee, Linney heard retching in the bathroom. She found Mac sitting on the floor in his boxers and T-shirt, leaning against the wall, holding his pounding head in his hands. "Mac?" He looked up and groaned. She'd never seen him look so bad. "Take a shower. And then we'll talk." Linney made fresh coffee and waited for him.

Mac joined her in the kitchen half an hour later. His hair was damp, and he'd shaved, but his black eye seemed to have darkened. "Linney, why are you ... How did you—?" he rasped and lapsed into a fit of coughing. She handed him a cup of strong coffee.

"MJ told me. I'm worried about you—you missed work today."

Mac had the presence of mind to be embarrassed. "Gemma." He winced. "The Downing Street story."

"She sent Ron. It won't be the same, but he was the only one available." Linney's voice was flat as she gathered her things to go. "I meant what I said, Mac. I can't keep going on like this. You need to get some help. "

"I'll be fine. I've stopped—well cut back—before. I can do it again. You believe me, don't you?"

Linney shrugged her shoulders. She slipped out of his flat and left him to think about it.

~

DEREK WAS elbow deep in legal briefs, the remains of his lunch pushed off to the side of his desk. His latest battle with an unscrupulous employer was proving to be more difficult than he'd hoped. The guy had a lawyer who was burying him in legal papers. Derek would win, and his client would have his rights restored, with restitution, but it was taking longer than he liked. When his phone buzzed on his desk, he glanced over.

Do you have time to talk?

His brow furrowed. It wasn't like Linney to reach out this early in the day and he did want to push this case a little further.

Just finishing something up. Can it wait an hour?

Absolutely. It's not important. I just need to pick your brain.

Derek had a funny feeling, and he shoved his chair away from his desk. Taking a drink of the cold coffee on his desk, he dialled Linney's number.

"You called. It could have waited."

"What's up, Linney?"

"I just…I just wanted to hear your voice. It's been a while since we talked."

"Too long."

"How's Olivia?" She was stalling, and Derek knew it.

"She's fine. Working too hard, but that's not new. What did you want to talk about?"

"It's not important. I'm sorry for bothering you."

"Linney, it's me. You can tell me anything. Is it Mac?"

There was silence. "Things aren't good," she said finally. "No, things are awful."

It was like a dam broke and suddenly Linney told Derek all about how bad it had gotten.

He was aghast. "Linney, you have to get yourself out of this relationship. Now, before he hurts you." Derek had too many clients—admittedly in very different circumstances—who had been in abusive relationships, and often alcohol was at the root of them. "I'm serious about this. Do you know how many women—"

"I know." He heard a vulnerability in her voice that he had never heard before. "I just don't know if I can."

"Linney, you know I love you, right? You're my best friend in the world. And I am frightened for you." He heard her crying on the other end of the phone. "You can do this. You are strong enough to do this. You must do this."

"Thank you, Derek," she whispered and hung up the phone. He hoped she believed it.

10

The following night Linney was in bed early and sound asleep when she suddenly jolted awake. There was a noise at her door. Was someone trying to get into her apartment? Then she heard a key in the lock and the door open. It was Mac.

"Anyone home? Linney? Where are you?" This did not sound good. She jammed on her glasses and saw the time. Two o'clock. Linney slid out of bed and tiptoed into the hall to see what state he was in just in time to watch him stumble into the console table. He put out his hand to steady himself and knocked over her mason jar of stones. It crashed to the floor with a loud noise and the glass shattered. The stones scattered and the largest, from the lake, bounced and landed on Mac's foot. He swore and hopped around in pain. "Linney, why do you keep that stupid jar there?" he yelped.

"Stay still, I'll get the broom," she said, making her way quickly to the kitchen. "Seriously, don't move. You'll get hurt."

Linney swept the entire mess into a dustpan and decided to deal with separating the glass from the stones in the morning.

Mac went into the kitchen and poured himself a drink. Waving his glass around wildly he asked Linney if she wanted one too. Shaking her head, Linney quietly went back to bed.

When Mac joined her in the bedroom a few minutes later, she was curled away from him. "You asleep already?" Linney squeezed her eyes shut and stayed quiet. "Fine," he muttered. "I can get better sex somewhere else." Linney held her hand over her mouth to keep from sobbing. He left the bedroom and headed to the bathroom. When the shower was still running fifteen minutes later, Linney found him passed out on the floor. She turned off the water and roused him enough to put him into her bed. Then she spent what was left of the night on the couch.

As Linney painstakingly pulled her stones from the shards of glass the next morning from her stones, she sliced her hand open. Cursing under her breath, she ran water over the cut and wrapped it in a clean tea towel. When she couldn't rouse Mac, she took herself to urgent care. Six stitches and a tetanus booster later, she returned to her flat. Mac was gone.

"Where did you go this morning?" Mac asked when she finally made it to the newsroom. He noticed her bandage. "What happened to you?"

Linney stared at him, open-jawed, seeing him critically with new eyes. Gone was the devastatingly handsome man she'd fallen for when she arrived in London. This man was dishevelled and both his face and midsection carried the weight gained from years of drinking. In a sudden moment of clarity, she knew, without a shadow of a doubt. It was time. Still, she answered him.

"You broke a jar last night. Don't you remember? I cut myself cleaning it up. I had to take myself to hospital." It was clear Mac had no recollection of the night before.

It was the final straw. With a quiet resolve she didn't know she had, Linney called a locksmith and met him at her flat at lunchtime. He drilled out the old lock, put in a new one and handed her the keys. He left and she leaned against the door and then slid down to the floor. This was not going to be easy.

Pulling herself together, Linney splashed water on her face and headed back to work.

"*Bonjour*," she greeted MJ, who instantly knew something was amiss.

"What's wrong?" she asked.

Linney shook her head. "Later. First, I have to talk to Gemma."

Linney climbed the stairs and knocked on Gemma's door. "Could I have a minute?" she asked seriously. Gemma waved her in with a premonition. Linney hadn't looked well since she'd returned from Canada, but today, she looked awful.

Linney sat in one of the guest chairs. "I'm done," she said flatly. "I've had the locks changed. Tonight I'm going to tell him."

Gemma started to speak, but Linney put up her hand. "I know this isn't great timing, but I have to do this now, while I still have the courage. I still haven't even told MJ. But I thought you should know. Because I don't know what will happen. How he'll react. Or for that matter, what it means in the newsroom." She looked Gemma straight in the eye. "You said you're his friend. Maybe he'll listen to you."

Gemma chose her words carefully. "This is very brave of you. Don't worry. I'll figure out the newsroom. Thank you for telling me, so I can be ready."

Linney nodded, not trusting her voice and stood up slowly. "Thank you for listening."

She outlined the plan to MJ over a cup of tea. "Will you be there?" she asked, looking for support.

"Of course. You do not have to do this alone."

Mac was busy in the editing suite all day. Linney texted him after she got home and asked if he could come by so they could talk. She and MJ ordered takeaway and sat quietly on the couch, eating it, yet tasking nothing. MJ finally turned on the television to break the silence—and the tension.

Seven. Eight. Nine o'clock. "Do you think he'll come?" MJ finally asked.

Linney nodded and put her finger in her mouth to stop the bleeding. She'd been picking at her cuticles constantly. They finally heard him fumble with his key just before ten o'clock and Linney took a deep breath. Getting up from the couch, she walked slowly to the door and opened it.

"Yer lock's broken," Mac said, walking past her. He took a bottle of whiskey out of a paper bag and a glass from the cupboard. Then he saw the look on her face. He was confused for a moment and then he remembered. "Oh, yeah. You wanned to talk. Whazzo 'mportant?" He leaned over to kiss her. She turned away. "Aw, c'mon, gimmie a kiss." He saw MJ in the living room. "Whazz she doing here?"

"Mac, it's over."

"Whad'ya mean it's over?"

"We're done, Mac. I can't do this anymore. You need help. Serious help. You're a brilliant journalist and a wonderful man. The world should see all of that."

"Wha'rya talkin' about? I don't have a problem. I got it all unner control." Mac swayed and tried to take Linney's hands. She pulled them away with tears in her eyes.

"No, you don't," she said quietly. "Maybe you did once, Mac, but you don't anymore. I don't want you to lose everything. Please get some help."

Mac grabbed her by the shoulders and pushed her hard against the wall. Alarm bells went off in Linney's head as she shrank from him. It was one thing to put up with verbal abuse. It was another thing entirely for him to manhandle her. Time seemed to stand still and even when MJ jumped up to help it seemed to happen in slow motion.

But Mac wasn't done yet. "You don' mean that. I don't have a problem." His words were slurred, and he was getting worked up now. "An' I don't need you either." He let go of her shoulders with one last shove. "I was gonna break up with you anyway. I don't love you. Yer nothin' special. The whole world will find out just how much you're nothing without me," he finished with a sneer.

Linney opened her mouth to speak, but Mac kept on talking as he turned away. "Stupid bitch. I'm outta here." He took the bottle with him as he stumbled into the hallway.

MJ closed the door. "Good riddance," she muttered under her breath while Linney rubbed her upper arms where he had gripped her. She started to shake, all her nervous energy collapsing and when she sank to the couch, she put her arms around her knees and rocked back and forth. MJ sat quietly with her—there were no words to say.

Eventually, the rocking stopped and Linney put her head on MJ's shoulder. "Thank you for being here," she said. MJ stood and held out her hands to help Linney up. Linney followed her robotically into the bedroom and climbed into bed fully clothed. MJ lay on top of the covers stroking Linney's hair until they both fell asleep.

LINNEY CALLED in sick the next morning and left a message for Gemma that she'd followed through. MJ reluctantly left her for the newsroom. As soon as the door closed, Linney went back to bed until midafternoon, trying to process the past few days. Finally, she turned on the shower and stepped in, allowing the hot water to wash everything away. She pulled out her favourite leggings and sweatshirt and made a mug of tea and some toast.

She was emotionally bruised and battered, but okay. Linney took a second sick day, still not ready to face her colleagues staring and whispering.

On the third day, she dragged herself into the newsroom, having used enough makeup to cover the dark circles under her eyes. Gemma called for her immediately.

"He's gone to rehab." Gemma didn't waste time with pleasantries.

"What? How did you convince him?"

"Mac showed up yesterday afternoon, totally out of control and reeking of booze. He was dishevelled and ranting. I don't think he'd slept. I gave him a choice. He could either take my offer of help, or I would fire him on the spot."

"He must have hated that." Linney looked at her recovering cuticles and resisted the urge to pick at them.

"Very much. But I knew there was room in a great program and told him he was leaving TCN one way or the other. He did not take kindly to that and tried to call my bluff. It did the trick, Linney. Somehow those words got through to him. I took him up to the rehab centre myself and got him checked in. He's there for six months."

Linney's eyes flickered up to Gemma's. Six months. This was a serious commitment.

"He knows how badly he screwed up this time. And not just here. With you too." Gemma's voice softened. "Leaving him was brave of you. But now you need to hold your head high out there and do your best work ever. Show the world what strong stuff Linney McDonnell is made of."

Linney went back to her desk. It was hard to pull herself together, but she knew she had to.

That evening she texted her friends back home.

I did it. I left him. It's too raw to talk about yet, so please understand if I don't. MJ was with me. It was hard but I know I did the right thing. Gemma found him a rehab place. Thank you all for your support. ♥

Linney put her phone on "do not disturb" and closed her eyes trying to gather her strength. A new chapter was about to begin.

11

———

Derek breathed a huge sigh of relief when his phone buzzed with Linney's text. He'd been worried about her and the choices she'd been making to stay with Mac. Now he was worried about how she was coping. She clearly didn't want to talk about it, and he knew MJ would be there for her. Still, it took everything he had not to text her back. Instead, he reached out to Kirsten and got MJ's number. The women had stayed in touch since Kirsten's mini makeover. It was only after MJ repeatedly assured him that the whole newsroom had Linney's back and that she had booked them a trip to Greece to get away that he was able to turn his attention back to the case on his desk.

The case needed his attention. It had been haunting him for a few months. Derek was representing a young mother and her son who had no social safety network. The husband had isolated his wife and then disappeared. She was being taken advantage of by a landlord whose apartment building was a whisker away from being condemned. Derek couldn't help but compare it to his own upbringing. He and his mother had benefitted from the close-knit community he'd grown up in and this woman had none.

His client was reliant on the food bank and a local charity for clothes as her toddler grew. Derek could relate. He'd had at least one winter coat from the local church, and mittens from the KnitWorks ladies. And then there were many dinners he and his mother had eaten with Linney and her grandmother. Years later, he came to understand that Linney's gran had allowed his mother to keep her dignity by letting her "babysit" to pay Mrs. McDonnell back for the generosity when the two children played together.

Derek was determined to get his client justice. So it was quite late that evening when he joined Olivia at her law firm's box at the Rogers Centre. It was mostly used to entertain clients, but from time to time, it was a nice perk for employees and their families to watch a Blue Jays game.

"So, Derek," her boss began after drinks had been handed out, "when are you going to give up on Legal Aid and come and join us on Bay Street, where the real money is made? Word on the street is that you're good. But they're paying you peanuts."

Derek pasted a smile on his face. He'd heard this more than once from Olivia's colleagues and it irked him every time. He did not understand why people couldn't accept that he wanted to make a difference in people's lives. At Legal Aid, he was able to help people. One at a time, he made families better than they were before they'd met him.

"Thanks, but I'm happy where I am. You're right, I could make more at a big law firm, but that's not what practising law is for me."

"You're a bright guy. Why not leave Legal Aid to the new grads?" The organ started up, whipping the Blue Jays fans into a frenzy.

"I could have had my pick of the Bay Street firms," Derek

said through gritted teeth. "I chose to work where I do, and I'm proud of my work."

Olivia came to his rescue, sliding in beside him. "Leave my husband alone. He's an idealist. And I love him for it. Someone's got to help the less fortunate."

"Fine," her boss said, turning as the crowd cheered for a home run by the home team. "But if you ever change your mind, Derek, you know where to come. We'd have you in a heartbeat."

"Thanks for getting me out of that," Derek said to Olivia, giving her a quick kiss.

She sipped her wine and looked at him seriously. "Would you ever consider it though? A comfortable office, a great view, a paycheque that matches mine? We could buy a house up in Lawrence Park."

Derek stiffened, thinking of the excess of the tony neighbourhood. "Our condo is pretty great, don't you think? I'm happy with how things are. Now, if you'd tell me you're ready to start thinking about a baby, I'd be even happier!"

"Derek!" She playfully swatted his shoulder, and he understood the message. Not yet.

THE GREEK SUN was high in the sky and it felt warm on Linney's legs. She'd initially resisted MJ's urging to leave everything behind for a few days in the Mediterranean, but the getaway was turning out to be just what she needed. She dug her painted toenails—regal rebel, the colour was called—in the sand. Beside her, MJ's periwinkle-coloured toenails were drying from a recent dip in the sea. Linney lowered the brim of her straw sunhat, thinking about how nice these first two days in Greece had been. They had spent much of their time swimming and lazily lounging on the beach or by the pool drinking up the sun. No thoughts of home. No news. No worries. Just two friends on holiday. To MJ's unending amusement, Linney kept picking up stones as they walked along the beach. She tried to skip some in the sea, mostly losing to the waves, and had tucked several perfect pebbles into her pockets.

"Ready for a swim?" MJ interrupted her train of thought. Linney nodded and got up out of her lounger tossing her hat behind her.

It was a glorious escape from reality. While her colleagues had mostly been great, Linney still felt awkward when people glanced her way, and when conversations stopped as she approached. They swore off newspapers and pledged not to watch the news. But truth be told, by the third morning, they were both going crazy with boredom.

"I wonder what's going on back at home?" Linney mused, as she dipped a spoon into the pot of honey on the breakfast table and drizzled it into her yogurt.

"I wonder what stories we're missing out on?" MJ added. She was as eager as Linney to know what was going on in the real world. "What do you think? Should I go and get a paper?"

"Well—"

MJ laughed. "We're like news junkies desperate for a fix!" Then her hand flew to her mouth as she realized the comparison she'd made. "Linney, I'm sorry. I did not mean to be insensitive."

Linney shook her head. "It's fine, MJ. You shouldn't have to walk on eggshells around me. Go get that paper!" MJ pushed her chair back and then hurried across the dining room to the front desk where the news they'd been ignoring was free for the taking.

As she went, Linney thought about it. Yes, there had been a brief moment where she felt pain, shock, and shame all at once, but it wasn't as bad as it had been a few weeks ago. She was going to be okay.

They gorged themselves on the news that day—print, TV, online, catching up on what had happened around the world. The break had been good, but they both lived for news. They bantered over dinner about a falling dictator in Eastern Europe, the American economy, and the rumblings of Brexit in the UK. Familiar territory for both of them.

"What's the next move for you?" Linney asked as they hiked up a steep scrubby trail on their last afternoon in Greece. Despite the hour, it was scorching, and Linney was melting. She was starting to wonder if the promised spectacular sunset views of the islands off the shore were going to be worth it. She stopped to take a sip of water and wipe her brow, where tendrils of hair were stuck with sweat. Behind her, MJ seemed as cool as a cucumber.

"I am thinking of moving to editing on the digital side," she said, cryptically.

"Really?" Linney screwed the top back on her water bottle and started to walk again, waiting for MJ to elaborate.

"I've already talked with Gemma about it. I think editing is where my future lies, not in reporting. I don't have the same desire to travel that you do. I want to settle down and have a family one day."

"With an Englishman?"

"Why not? They are not all so bad!" MJ caught up with her as they crested the hill before continuing jokingly, "And besides, I like the city fashions."

The two women let their daypacks fall to the ground and took in the view.

"Thanks, MJ, for making me come," Linney said. "This is spectacular."

"It is. Maybe it signifies a new beginning for both of us. But first, you are going home soon, *oui*?"

Linney nodded her head. "In a couple of months. I need to spend some time with my grandmother. She's getting on, you know, and it's not fair on my brother. It's not like your big family, where there's lots of people to share the load." MJ was one of seven siblings, and she was the only one who'd moved away. "And of course, I want to catch up with Jake, and my friends back home."

MJ smiled knowingly. No matter where she travelled, or the beauty in front of them, Linney was always drawn back to Silver Lake.

12

———————

Linnea found the porch stairs difficult for her creaky knees these days, and she took her time descending them, needing to put both feet on each step for balance. Her arthritic hands ached and she had reluctantly stopped going to her beloved KnitWorks. She'd given up her car a year ago, and these days felt every one of her ninety years. Derek's mother stopped in every other day now and they had tea together, and Linney's friends often came by. Linnea knew they were all checking in to make sure she was alright; she appreciated that they didn't say so.

In addition to the lovely lady who cleaned her house every Tuesday and cooked her a meal with enough leftovers to last several days, Jake had arranged for someone to shovel snow in the winter and take care of the gardening and the grass in the summer. She just had to water the flowerboxes on the porch, although even that had left her tired and short of breath this summer. Six months ago, Jake had also organized a service to deliver a meal on Fridays. Linnea could split each one into two, the portions were so big.

Her computer beeped with an incoming email from Linney

in London and she shuffled slowly to the dining room table to read it. Jake had amended the settings so the type was big and easy for her to read.

> *Dear Gran,*
> *Ten more days until I'm back with you at the lake.*
> *Work has been crazy, and I can't wait to come*
> *home. I'll stay with Jake for two nights and then*
> *rent a car and drive up. I miss you. Please let me*
> *know if there's anything I can bring you from*
> *London. Maybe that nice hand lotion from*
> *Marks & Spencer that you like? Or anything*
> *at all.*
> *Love you!*

A cough rattled in Linnea's chest and she took a moment to catch her breath. She needed to see Linney, to talk to her and share her family stories one more time. It was time for her granddaughter to come home.

LINNEY LOOKED for Jake and Rachael. Scanning the crowd at the airport, she found them, and waved, a huge smile on her face. Jake waved back, and it wasn't long before he was giving his sister a welcome home hug.

"You doing okay?" he asked, and she nodded. It had been a difficult few months, but she was much better now.

"Let's get you to the house," Rachael said. "The kids are dying to see you. They're so excited to see their Auntie Linney in real life rather than just on TV."

"I know they're really too old for them, but I've brought them some Buttons," Linney said, referring to the British chocolates, "and some of that tea you two like."

"Lovely. We'll have some when we get home." Rachael unlocked the car and Jake put Linney's bag into the trunk.

"So tell us your plans," Jake said, after he paid the parking fee and the arm raised, allowing him to drive out of the parking garage and onto the busy highway.

"I'm having a quick lunch with Olivia tomorrow. Derek's out of town. He's in Calgary for a couple of weeks helping out their Legal Aid office," she explained. "I'm not sure I'll even get to see him before I fly back. Dinner tomorrow with you two and the kids. And then up to the lake. Nothing exciting." She yawned and leaned her head against the car window. Jake and Rachael glanced at each other and let her rest. There was silence the rest of the way home.

Linney was up early the next morning, her internal clock not yet set to the right time zone. She padded out to the kitchen, put on the coffee maker and then went to the front door to pick up the newspaper from the porch. She stood at the window and watched the sun begin to rise. She'd sensed tension in the house last night and hoped her brother and his wife weren't having troubles again. Soon the kitchen was bustling with activity as Jake came down for coffee and the kids followed, dressed in their school uniforms. Rachael was right behind them and pulled premade lunches out of the fridge.

"Everyone into the car!" she shouted above the din. It was her turn to drop them off.

"Have a good day," Linney said, and she noticed that Jake kissed the kids, but not Rachael.

"Something going on with you two?" she asked, as she poured another cup of coffee.

Jake rolled his eyes. "Same old, same old," he said. "We go through these rough patches from time to time. We'll get over it. We always do. I'm just sorry it's happening while you're here." He grabbed an apple from the bowl. Over his shoulder, as he left for the day he said, "Enjoy your lunch today, but save your appetite. The kids are making a cake for dinner!"

Just before noon, Linney pushed on the big heavy door of the Bay Street building that housed Olivia's firm. She'd never been there before and she was plenty intimidated. Feeling self-conscious about her casual dress and simple rubber-soled ballet flats, she pushed the button to call the elevator. When she reached the sixty-eighth floor, she stepped out into a sleek, modern lobby. Even the receptionist looked sophisticated and polished with her hair pulled back into a bun, and flame-red fingernails. Linney took a deep breath, pushed her glasses up her nose and walked to the desk.

"Hello. Linney McDonnell for Olivia Blake—I mean Hastings." Olivia had kept her maiden name.

The receptionist's head snapped up. "McDonnell? Linney McDonnell? From TCN News?"

Linney blushed and nodded. "That's me."

"I watch you all the time. I'll let Ms. Hasting know you're here." The receptionist called Olivia's number. "Of course. I'll let her know." She turned back to Linney. "Unfortunately, Ms. Hastings has asked if you can wait about ten minutes. I love your news reports."

Linney made polite banter with the receptionist, surprised and amused to have a starstruck fan, until Olivia arrived.

"Linney!" she called out as her heels clicked on the marble floors. Linney took in Derek's wife in a designer suit that hugged her lean body perfectly, and the four-inch heels that went with it. "Thank you for waiting. I'm so glad you could make the time." The two women hugged politely and were soon sitting down at a chic boutique restaurant where Olivia had made reservations.

"Derek is so disappointed that he's missing you," Olivia said after they ordered. "Tell me all about the Rotterdam Port story. I feel like there was more than made it into your report."

Linney smiled and launched into a story about the near calamity of shooting the final standup for that story, which had Olivia in stitches. They'd shot in front of Delft Gate as planned and then headed to the nearby botanical gardens for a contrasting backdrop. The lawn irrigation system had gone off just behind her while the camera was rolling, drenching the back of her jacket and pants. "Fortunately, when Grant reshot it, you couldn't tell that water was dripping down the small of my back. But the worst? By the time we got back to the newsroom, the whole news crew had seen the raw footage and there was a sprinkler sitting on my desk!" she finished and they both laughed. "What about you? Can you share what you're working on?"

"I'm afraid not," Olivia said as their lunch arrived. "It's an international acquisition but I'm under a nondisclosure agreement so I can't say much. The whole thing is very hush hush."

Linney was impressed. "When is Derek back?" she asked, changing the subject. "I'd hate to miss him altogether."

"Not for two more weeks," Olivia sighed, and Linney deflated. This would be the first trip home she wouldn't see her old friend. "I miss him so much when he's away. But being asked to help out in Calgary? They don't ask for help for just anything. This is huge, and it could change his career. He wins this and he can have his choice of Bay Street firms."

"Are you sure that's what he wants?" Linney couldn't picture Derek in Olivia's over-the-top, yet somehow still cold office.

"Of course it's what he wants. And he can still do pro bono cases from time to time."

Linney nodded absentmindedly. It didn't sound like the Derek she knew.

Dinner that night was a decidedly more relaxed and raucous affair. The kids ganged up on their dad, who gave as good as he got. Linney missed this camaraderie more and more the longer she was away from home. Over the kids' cake, they laughed until they cried and caught her up on all the news from promotions to dance competitions and sports trophies. Despite their busy lives, Jake made it a point to visit Silver Lake often, although it was too disruptive with the kids now to spend the night with their gran.

"I get up at least once a month," he told her as they cleared the table. His voice dropped. "She's been ill more than once this winter and she has a cough that won't go away. You probably know that from talking with her." Linnie nodded. "Her doctor's worried about her heart and she's not always as clear as she used to be. The last couple of times we were up, she thought Abby was you. I think it's time to consider a nursing home."

"It was weird, Auntie Linney," Abby said as she stacked the plates. "She sent me upstairs—you know, through that blue door. I wasn't sure I should go, but it's kind of neat up there."

Linney paled and Jake quickly moved the conversation along. "That's enough now," he said to his oldest child. "I'm sure your Auntie Linney would like a good night's sleep to get rid of the last of her jetlag before she drives up to Silver Lake tomorrow."

As LINNEY DROVE out of the city, she replayed the sound of the low voices arguing that she'd heard last night when she'd gone to bed. She hoped Jake was right about this just being a rough patch. With her overseas, he bore all of the responsibility of taking care of Gran. He deserved a happy home life.

Linney drummed her fingers on the steering wheel of the cute little blue hybrid she'd rented but brightened up when she saw a familiar sign ahead on the road. Soon, she pulled over at the Tim Hortons and into the drive-thru. Getting back on the highway with a double double, she put her concerns aside and started looking forward. As she rounded a long curve, she smiled, knowing she was getting closer to Silver Lake. The tension left her shoulders. Life slowed when she was home and she felt like she breathed more freely. She couldn't wait to get out in her kayak and skim across the lake.

Linney drove past the hospital and the hardware store before turning onto Main Street. She saw the town law office, the grocery store, and the park across from Page Turners. Taking a hard left, she turned the corner and parked behind the bookstore. She took a deep breath and pasted a smile on her face. It was Wednesday, so there was one more stop to make before seeing Gran.

"Room for one more?" she called out as she entered the back room of the bookstore.

"Linney!" There was a huge noise as the KnitWorks ladies dropped their knitting and rushed to greet their local superstar. She got the biggest hug from Anna, who set her up with a mug of tea and a cookie and told her Kirsten was working a shift at the hospital that day. The new owner gushed over the celebrity in her store, much to Linney's embarrassment.

She spent the next hour chatting with old schoolmates, neighbours, and a few newcomers to town. Jennifer's baby was due in another month and Mr. Jones was recovering well from a bypass operation. Carrie was engaged, and Mrs. Masterton had a new grandchild she was going to visit in Halifax soon, where her son and daughter-in-law lived. The Carvers were having trouble paying their bills. And the Soulier boy was in trouble again. The warmth that Linney had felt enveloping her when she arrived had turned to the gossip that irked her, so with hugs all around, she left the knitters and drove the final couple of kilometres home. She'd catch up with Kirsten tomorrow.

The gravel crunched as Linney eased the rental car into the driveway. She called out to her grandmother, who was napping on the porch. Linnea woke with a start, and soon the two women were in each other's arms. "I'm so glad you're home, Linney dear," Gran said. "I've missed you so much."

Linney squeezed her grandmother again. "Me too, Gran. Me too."

THE FIRST DAYS SPED BY. The fall weather was glorious and Linney took the kayak out every morning. Her muscles hurt more than she wanted to admit, but every day got easier, and she loved the meditative time on the water. She took photos in the marshes she traversed and of the wildlife she came across. She hadn't seen a moose this visit, but she was still hopeful.

In the afternoons, Linney often read or scribbled notes about stories she'd like to cover while Gran napped in her comfortable armchair. Some days she headed into town and caught up with Kirsten or Anna. She cooked whenever Gran would let her, and in the evenings they sat together with mugs of tea. Despite bouts of coughing and shortness of breath that put a knot in Linney's stomach, Gran insisted on recounting family stories of years spent at the lake. They were stories Linney knew so well from so many retellings over the years, that she could recite them alongside her grandmother, but she was happy to hear them again and they laughed often, remembering all the scrapes she got into as a child. Some nights, Gran told stories of her mother and father, and even of her own early years in Silver Lake. To Linney, each story felt like a warm hug as she listened to Gran reminisce.

One evening, she left Gran at home for a proper girls' night out at a Bridgegrove bar with her friends. Dressed in her best dark denim jeans and a silk blouse, she first picked up Anna, finding her similarly attired in black jeans and a pink ballet sweater showcasing her long lean limbs. Anna climbed into Linney's car and squeezed her hand.

"I'm so glad we're doing this," she said. "It's been far too long."

"I agree," said Linney, putting the car into reverse and backing out of the driveway. "We'll have fun tonight!"

After pulling into the parking lot behind Page Turners, Linney slipped out of the car and ran upstairs to get Kirsten. "You look great!" she said, pleased her friend had continued with the hair and makeup tricks MJ had taught her. Sure, the loose tunic Kirsten wore wasn't very figure-flattering, but it was a pretty colour at least and played up her eyes. "Ready to go?"

"Absolutely. It's been a while since I've been out." Kirsten locked the door, and they joined Anna.

"Here's to girls' night," said Linney, putting her key in the ignition.

"Girls' night!" chimed in the others in stereo and soon all three were singing along with the radio as Linney drove out of Silver Lake.

All eyes turned to the pretty trio as they entered the bar in Bridgegrove. They grabbed a table and a handsome waiter brought them three beers and a plate of nachos to share. They told their latest work stories, but soon the conversation turned to men.

"Is there anyone new, Kirsten?" Linney asked, always hopeful.

"Well, maybe. It's just been three dates, but there's an administrator at the college who I like a lot." She popped a tortilla chip in her mouth.

"Details!" demanded Anna. "You've been holding out on me."

"Well, you know that I've almost part way through my master's degree. I might try teaching," she explained to Linney in an aside. "When I signed up for a course last summer, Alan asked if I'd be interested in coffee. I agreed, and we've had dinner a couple of times now. He's handsome, and he's such a gentleman."

"I'm so happy for you," Linney said, squeezing Kirsten's hand.

"Now what's new with you? Are you dating anyone new?"

Linney took a swig of her beer. "Honestly? I'm not ready for anything new. I need a break. I really thought I loved Mac. But even as he was falling apart, he hurt me so much." Her eyes teared up, and she swiped at them, frustrated that she could still be emotional about it. She needed to change the subject.

"How are the cottages, Anna?"

Anna and Danny's cottage business had taken off, and they now owned seven that they rented out for good money in the summers and somewhat less in the off-season. Nevertheless, they were almost always full and supplemented their income from the dance studio and contracting business nicely.

"Danny has his eyes on another couple of properties," Anna said proudly, if with a bit of worry. "We'll need to hire someone to help turn them over—the ones we have already are difficult for us."

"It's amazing the businesses that you guys have built," Linney said. "Who'd have thought we'd all have turned out the way we did? Me in London, Kirsten working on her master's and you a savvy businesswoman. We've done well for ourselves."

The three women brought their beer glasses together. "To us!" Kirsten toasted their success.

~

"Hold on, Olivia." Halfway across the country and two time zones earlier, Derek covered the phone with his hand and gave instructions to a colleague. "Sorry, sweetheart, I'm back. I think we're just about halfway done out here." He stood up to stretch and scratch his five o'clock shadow. "I can't wait to get home."

"Me too. This bed is awfully empty without you. Especially when I'm wearing the lingerie you bought me for my birthday," Olivia said in a sexy voice, having some fun with her husband. "Should I send you a picture?"

Derek was standing in the middle of a conference room filled with banker's boxes full of paper, with other lawyers and paralegals. It was going to be another late night. "Um, maybe not just now," he said quietly into the phone. "Too many people around. Give me a minute" He flushed beet red, and fled the conference room.

"Okay, I'm alone now," he said, and a photo of Olivia in a wispy black chemise quickly came his way. "I miss you so much. Tell you what. How about we start trying for a baby when I get home and you get back from your Singapore trip?" Olivia was about to head out of town to close a deal. "For real this time."

"I still think—" Olivia lapsed into silence before continuing. "Well, maybe." She left the door open for the first time.

Derek's smile couldn't have been bigger. "Oh, we'll have so much fun trying."

LINNEY FRETTED over Gran's obvious decline. Together they walked down to the dock after lunch every day, but Linney was distressed at how heavily Gran breathed after these short excursions. She insisted on seeing her grandmother's doctor and was given a realistic report on her health. It turned out that Gran had not been entirely honest with her grandchildren.

"Ms. McDonnell, let me be frank," said the doctor, putting down his file. "I know neither you nor your brother live close. And your grandmother is a fiercely proud woman. But her blood pressure has been high since I first started treating her several years ago, and since her first bout of angina—" Linney's head snapped up. Jake had mentioned heart concerns, but angina sounded serious.

The doctor sought to reassure her as best he could. "We're treating it, so there's no imminent threat as long as she takes her medication regularly. But it will only get worse." He folded his hands on his desk and looked at Linney seriously. "Your grandmother is over ninety. She doesn't like to complain, but her health is in decline."

"What do we do?" Linney asked, ashen-faced.

"I've been suggesting it for a couple of years now, but it's time that you and your brother convince your grandmother she needs to accept more support. Maybe she could move in with him?" Linney shook her head. Gran would never leave Silver Lake. "Or perhaps she'd consider Graceful Care? In any event, she needs more care than she can get living on her own."

Linney stood. "You've given me a lot to think about, and I know Jake agrees with you. I'm home for a while longer. I'll see what I can do." She left the hospital, not even looking for Kirsten, mulling over all she'd learned.

Linney suggested Graceful Care to Gran, but she wanted no part of it.

"I do not need to see that place," she insisted, referring to the long-term care home. I am not leaving my house. I'm just fine here." And no matter how gently Linney brought it up, or how many suggestions she made that Gran would have more company, would have better meals, would have all her friends visit, nothing would change the old woman's mind.

"I don't know what to do," she complained to Anna and Kirsten. Gran slept most afternoons, and Linney had met them at the renovated tea house that seemed to be the new meeting place. "She needs more help, but she's stubborn." She threw her hands up. "It's so hard being so far away."

"Danny's grandparents were at Graceful Care in their last years and we visited a lot. They took care of them really well," Anna said, sipping her tea.

Kirsten nodded. "Their reputation is well-deserved," she said. "Everyone at the hospital says Silver Lake is lucky to have such a good facility."

"That's all very well and good," Linney said. "But she won't even consider it."

"You could consider hiring someone to live with her," suggested Anna. "There's room at your house. It's expensive, but it's another option."

Linney licked her finger to pick up the cookie crumbs on her plate as she contemplated that idea. "I'll look into that." A live-in caretaker. It was a good idea.

After saying goodbye to Anna and Kirsten, Linney stopped at Page Turners and was surprised to find herself the only customer. She bought a novel to support the store and read the first few chapters in the autumn sun in the park across the road. She hoped things would turn around for Page Turners. It was an institution in Silver Lake and she couldn't imagine the town without it.

13

Two weeks of kayaking every afternoon of the glorious Indian summer that had settled in had given Linney's arm muscles better definition, and they no longer screamed at her when she pulled the double-edged paddle through the still water. Today, she'd been out a little longer than usual, paddling over to the island she and Derek would take a picnic to back in high school, and she'd found a pretty pink granite rock to add to her collection.

Gran always said the lake healed people, and while Linney had laughed at her as a teenager, now she was sure she was right. The distance from the UK and time with her friends was closing the wound and giving her the strength to advocate for the next step for her career.

As Linney pulled her beloved boat up to the dock, she could see Gran on the porch, as usual, waiting for her to come back. Giving a quick wave as pulled the kayak up onto the shore, Linney opened the boathouse and hung up her paddle before shrugging out of her life jacket. Closing the door, she was surprised to see Gran still sitting in her chair. Usually, her grandmother made the effort—and Linney knew it was an effort—to come down the stairs and shuffle partway down the path to greet her and give her a kiss.

But today, something was different. As Linney approached the house, she somehow knew Gran had slipped away quietly, at her beloved lake house, watching the water and waiting for her granddaughter to come home. She stood there for a moment, trying to process the scene. Suddenly it all made sense. Gran had desperately wanted her home for this visit. She'd told all of the old stories. She refused to consider leaving. She'd known.

She'd known this would be her last visit with her Linney. It was her time.

Putting emotions to one side, and taking a deep breath, Linney called an ambulance. It seemed like an eternity before it arrived, so while she waited, Linney put an afghan over her grandmother's lap. It was pointless, she knew, but she felt she had to do something. She sat down beside her and numbly, held Gran's hand, rubbing it gently.

She stood aside silently, watching the paramedics work when they arrived. She understood they had to do it, but she knew in her heart that Gran was long gone. She followed the ambulance, and when the news was official, she called Jake from the hospital. Gran had been lucky. She hadn't been seriously ill, and she'd been able to stay in the house right to the end. She'd passed peacefully, and they were all grateful for it. Jake kept clearing his throat gruffly as he offered to get in the car right now if she needed him to, but she told him she'd be fine until he and the family came the next day.

When she got back to the house, she walked across to the yellow house next door. Mrs. Blake had seen the ambulance and the look on Linney's face told her all she needed to know. "She was a wonderful lady, Linney, and a good friend. More than you probably know. Your grandmother was very good to us when Derek's father left." Linney nodded. For the first time, she realized that maybe Mrs. Blake and she had more in common than she'd thought. "Let me know how I can help." Linney nodded again, not quite trusting her voice.

In a moment, she pushed her glasses up her nose and said quietly, "I think I'm okay for now, but thank you. You were a good friend to Gran too, and I know you've helped a lot since I left. I can't thank you enough." After another hug, she headed back home. There was a lot to do. Her Gran, her rock, was gone.

"Hi, Mum. What's up?" Derek picked up the phone quickly when he saw his mother's ID pop up. She didn't often call, and she knew he was away. "What?! How is she?" Derek raked his hands through his curly hair. Linney's world must be shattered. "Why didn't she call me?" This was the second big blow for her in a few months. His colleagues looked at him, surprised at the strident tone of voice.

"Everything alright at home?" a grey-haired paralegal asked. "Your wife?"

"What? No, no. It's not Olivia. It's my best friend." He strode out of the conference room and leaned on the glass wall outside before turning his attention back to his mother. "I can't believe she thought I'd be too busy for this. I'll text her right away. Thanks for calling."

Mrs. Blake hung up, knowing she'd done the right thing. She looked out the window, and when she didn't see cars in the driveway except for Linney's rental, she texted her son. She didn't think Linney had called Anna or Kirsten either.

Back in Calgary, Derek messaged Linney right away.

> I just heard about your Gran. I am SO sorry for your loss. Tell me what I can do to help. What do you need?

When she didn't answer, he tried again.

> I'm worried about you. I know we haven't talked a lot recently. Please let me know you're OK.

Ten more minutes went by.

> Linney? Please answer me.

> I don't think I'll ever be OK again. Jake's coming up tomorrow.

> You're alone?! I will ALWAYS be there for you, no matter what. Do you need to talk? Call me if you do.

> Thanks, but there are no words. Funeral on Wednesday, I think.

> I'll be there. Love you, Linney.

Derek called his boss and spoke with the head of Calgary Legal Aid. He knew he would be leaving them in a pinch, but this was important.

ANNA AND KIRSTEN leaped into action when they received Derek's text Within half an hour, they were at Linney's door and they gathered her up into their arms when she let them in with a tired, sad smile.

"Thank you for coming," she said quietly.

"Where else would we be?" asked Anna. "We're so sorry for your loss."

Kirsten held up a container of ice cream and a bag of chips. Comfort food. Linney pushed her glasses up and pointed to the ice cream. Anna got spoons, and they spent the night telling stories about Gran, their spoons dipping into the container until the softening ice cream was all gone. They fell asleep on the couch, and Linney's friends woke early in the morning only when Jake's car pulled into the driveway. Linney was still sound asleep.

"Thank you," he said to both of them gruffly, when they expressed their condolences. Jake looked pale and distraught, no better than his sister. "And thank you for being with Linney last night. I couldn't get up here any earlier."

Kirsten spoke for them both. "She'd have done it for us. And Jake? Let us know if there's anything at all we can do. Your grandmother was so loved in this town. There will be a lot of people who want to do something, anything. Even if you just want to use us to spread information, we're up for the task."

Jake smiled for the first time since Linney had called the day before. "Thanks, Kirsten. I think we'll be alright. But I appreciate the offer. Rachael and the kids will be up tomorrow. Now you two had better get home."

They left, and he smoothed Linney's hair and gave her a kiss on the temple. Best to let her sleep a little longer, he thought. Yesterday had been tough for her, and the coming days wouldn't be any easier.

It was windy and grey when Derek arrived in Silver Lake. He slipped into an aisle seat at the church beside his mother just as the funeral was beginning. In the front pew was Rachael and with her children—Mrs. McDonnell's great grandchildren—looking sombre. Jake and Linney walked down the aisle together. Jake was stoic, but his red-rimmed eyes betrayed the depth of his feelings for his grandmother. Linney's eyes were blank behind her glasses. She stood pale and ramrod straight in her black dress, looking like she might shatter into a million pieces at any moment. Derek managed to grab her hand and squeeze it for just a second as she passed by. He saw just a flicker of recognition, and he was glad she knew he was there.

Despite the weather, it was a lovely funeral, and the church was full. Anna and Danny were there with their girls, and Kirsten sat with them. Jake did the eulogy and only choked up twice. Derek watched Linney closely. She sat with a straight back and never moved. He was worried about her. Several other people from Silver Lake got up and said nice things about her, including one woman representing KnitWorks. Derek's mother spoke eloquently of her kindness and how she knew her neighbour was in a better place, with her beloved husband and son, which even left him with a lump in his throat.

Derek knew that after the funeral the house would be full of townspeople paying their respects. There would be so many people for Jake and Linney to speak with that he decided not to add to the chaos. When everyone was gone, and the empty hours stretched out endlessly, he would be there for Linney. For now, he went next door to visit with his mother and wait until things got quieter. After all, he had to tell her that her wait for a grandchild might be coming to an end.

FINALLY, thought Linney. Finally, it was quiet. She'd made it through the day. There had been so many people to talk to, and after they had gone, the family had spent some time reminiscing together. But now that Rachael had taken the children home and Jake was getting into his car, she was alone.

She stood on the wraparound porch of her grandmother's house as the storm that had threatened all day made its way across Silver Lake and the white caps on the waves grew bigger. Shivering, she pulled the finely knit grey shawl more tightly around her. It was the exact shade of the angry sky. Gran had made it years ago and Linney could almost hear the clicking of her steel knitting needles. It seemed appropriate, she thought, that the sky was angry. She was too. The lake, usually a source of peace and calm, was anything but that today.

She waved as Jake backed his car out of the driveway and Linney felt the first raindrops whip into her face as she walked around the porch and opened the door. She stepped inside the house, surveying the canapes and empty glasses littered around. She kicked off her high-heeled black shoes and walked silently through the front room in stocking feet, drying the rain from her glasses with the edge of the shawl as she went. The mess could wait.

Linney took the ornate key off the shelf and looked at the arched interior door it belonged to. Taking a deep breath, she unlocked the blue door. Slowly, as if each step was more painful than the last, Linney made her way up the circular staircase to the study. As the old family story went, her grandfather had added it onto the cozy little house when their son—Linney's father—was small. The front half of the rounded room facing the lake was all windows, with a built-in desk and cabinets in front of them. The back was lined with her grandfather's handmade bookshelves and filled with favourite books. Linney ran her fingers along the spines and pulled one out at random.

Curling up in the familiar battered burnished leather chair that gave her an almost 180-degree view of the lake in front and the woods to one side, Linney opened the book and tried to read. The wind was getting stronger and she could hear tree branches creak and moan as they moved against each other. It was as if they were crying. She shut the book and looked up as the rain came thrashing against the window. It seemed all the elements had come together to mourn as they buried her grandmother today.

Linney wished she could cry. She felt like she had an

elephant on her chest. She'd screamed. She'd stomped. She'd railed. But she hadn't been able to cry.

DEREK HEARD the last car drive away, and he looked across the lawn just in time to see the rain start, and Linney close the door behind her. He checked his watch and decided to give her half an hour.

Thirty minutes later, he kissed his mother goodbye. The storm was in full force by then, the rain coming almost sideways off the lake. Derek knew his umbrella would be no match for the weather so he put on a baseball cap, pulled the collar of his trench coat high on his neck and ran quickly the short distance between the houses.

He pulled open the screen door and rapped on the solid wood door behind it. There was no response. He turned the handle. It was open, as always. "Linney?" he called. "It's Derek."

Nothing.

Derek took off his wet hat and shoes and peeled off his dripping coat, hanging it over a dining room chair. He saw Linney's discarded heels. He took a few steps and called again. Getting worried, he went further into the house. And that's when he noticed the blue door. In all the time he'd spent in this house, he had never seen it open. Linney had always spoken of her Gran's private space in reverent tones. He started up the steps. "Linney?" he called again. "Are you up there?"

Derek climbed the tight circular stairs and when he reached the top, he found her standing in front of the window, clutching a book to her chest and rocking silently back and forth. She'd discarded her glasses, so he knew she was staring at nothing, and her face was as pale as it had been in the church. He put his hand on her shoulder and she jumped. "Linney, I've been calling you. Are you alright?"

"I can't cry, Derek," she whispered, still staring out to the lake. "I keep trying, but I can't cry. I should be able to cry for my grandmother. Jake did. But I can't cry, Derek. Why can't I cry for my gran?"

Derek put his arm around her shoulder and gently pulled her close. "It's OK, Linney. I'm here. You're safe."

Linney jerked with a start as if realizing he was there for the first time. "Oh," she said exhaling. She took one ragged breath in and another out. And another. Her eyes filled and her shoulders started to shake. Finally, release. She buried her head into Derek's chest and clung to him as he guided them both to sit, sobbing in the comforting arms of her best friend.

"I ALWAYS WONDERED what was up here," Derek said when Linney was finally spent and had wiped her tears.

"Remember when I got sick after falling through the ice on the creek? She showed this room to me way back then. And she let me write here. Then and whenever I wanted to. I wrote my first story right here on this chair. I knew right there and then that I wanted to write and tell stories for a living."

"I remember that," he said, smiling at the memory. "You were what—seven? You were so proud of that story when you came back to school. And you let me read it!" Derek stood up and held out his hands to her. "Have you eaten today?"

Linney's stomach chose that moment to growl.

"I guess that answers the question," she said, putting her cold hands in his warm ones. "Honestly, I can't remember the last time I ate. I haven't been hungry."

"Well, clearly your body is trying to remind you," said Derek gently. "Mum says people have been dropping off casseroles all week. Come downstairs and let's find one."

He turned on the oven and pulled a glass dish out of the

fridge. It was wrapped in foil with a strip of masking tape across the middle marked "roasted vegetable ziti" in black marker. While they were waiting for it to heat, he made some cocoa. "This always cheered you up when we were kids," he said. He lay a fire in the living room fireplace and lit it, cheering up the room a bit as the storm continued to rail outside. Derek busied himself, clearing the remains of the reception. Linney sat at the kitchen breakfast bar sipping her cocoa, staring into space.

The oven beeped. Derek pulled the casserole out and let it sit for a minute while he chopped up some lettuce and tomatoes for a salad. Linney picked at the meal robotically, not tasting it. Once he was satisfied that she had eaten enough, Derek poured some whiskey—just a bit—into her remaining cocoa. "This should help," he said, rubbing her shoulders.

He washed up the dishes and joined Linney in front of the fire. Her phone started to buzz. Jake was home now and checking in to make sure she was alright. She closed her eyes. Answering him seemed like a huge effort.

"Tell him I'm here with you," Derek said.

Linney nodded. She sent the message and turned the ringer off. They sat for a while, saying nothing.

"Now what?" she asked. "What do I do now?"

"Tonight you sleep, my friend," said Derek. "We'll figure out the rest tomorrow."

"Will you stay? I don't want to be alone tonight."

14

———

Derek made coffee the next morning, stretching his back from an uncomfortable night on the couch, while Linney called Gemma and told her it would probably be a week before she'd be back. There were things to take care of, and she needed some time to grieve. "And Gemma," she concluded, "I've made some decisions while I've been here." She mouthed her thanks to Derek for the mug he pressed into her hands.

"Take the time you need. Our thoughts are with you." The two women hung up and Linney texted MJ.

Hey—just checking in.

How'd it go yesterday?

Hard.

But a good send-off. Derek made it in time. It was good to have him here.

♥ When will you be back?

Next week. Will text details when I have them.

Reste forte, mon amie. See you soon.

Linney and Jake had met with the lawyer on the morning of the funeral. It was no surprise that Gran had left the bulk of her estate, including the house, to Linney. After all, it was the house that she had grown up in. There was some money Gran had divided between them, and Jake was to inherit many of her husband's tools, untouched for decades now, if he wanted them. If not, they were to be donated.

Linney was surprised to hear from Mr. Graham again that afternoon. There was one more thing in her grandmother's will that he wanted to discuss with her. "I can't imagine what he wants," she said to Derek, as they walked into town.

"You can tell me all about it when you're done. Meet me at the park." Derek was planning to say a quick hello to Danny, and then get them both a cup of coffee while he waited for Linney.

Linney sat down in the small law office—she loved the red brick farmhouse-style building with its steep dormer above the door—while she waited for Mr. Graham to finish with another client. She was intrigued. Surely they'd discussed everything when Jake was there.

"What do you want me to do about the royalty cheques, Linney?" The lawyer wasted little time with pleasantries.

Linney looked at him with confusion. "Royalty cheques?"

"The royalty cheques. There haven't been any new books since you were young, but the older ones are still in print and bring in some money."

"Books? I'm sorry, I don't understand. What books?"

"Linney," Mr. Graham started again kindly, "you know your grandmother wrote and illustrated children's books under a pen name, don't you? Ingrid Larsson."

"I ... I had no idea." Linney looked as shocked as she felt. Gran had read Ingrid Larsson books to her when she was little, and she'd poured over the watercolour illustrations. How had she not known that those were Gran's books?

She texted Jake right from the office. He hadn't known either, but it did help explain how she'd managed a few extravagances. Gran's royalties had topped up her husband's pension and the life insurance policies on her son and daughter-in-law. The royalties weren't large after all this time but they continued to come each quarter. And it turned out Gran had wanted them to go specifically to her. Linney left Mr. Graham's office with an entirely new appreciation for her grandmother, and what she had given up to raise her.

"So?" Derek asked as he handed Linney a white cardboard cup as she approached him on the park bench.

"You're not going to believe this. I still can't!"

The look on Derek's face as she explained told Linney he was as astonished as she was.

"And there are still royalty cheques. I have to figure out what to do with them."

"Don't make any decisions in a hurry," Derek advised. They sat quietly, sipping their coffee, until Derek turned to her,

"I hate to do this, but I do have to fly back to Calgary tomorrow. "I need to wrap things up there. But if you ever need anything—even just to talk—I'm there for you. All you have to do is call. You know that, right?"

Linney nodded. "You have no idea how much I appreciate that you came. But it's time I stood on my own."

After Derek left, Linney went upstairs to Gran's office. She started going through her grandmother's papers and sure enough, right at the back of one of the drawers, she found a folder of correspondence between Gran and a literary agent dating back several decades. She leafed through the yellowing pages slowly. The agent had begged Gran to write more books but reluctantly accepted that the writer was too busy. Linney noted the date and winced. It was the year she came to live at

Silver Lake. She shoved the folder back into the drawer feeling guilty that her arrival had been the cause of the end of Gran's writing career.

A few minutes later, she came across another folder marked "drafts." Linney's eyes widened. There, in her grandmother's handwriting was what appeared to be at least one full manuscript—maybe more, plus notes about other books she might have written. A treasure trove of ideas.

As Linney's time in Silver Lake came to a close, Anna left her girls at home with Danny and the three friends cracked open a bottle of wine at Kirsten's apartment. Linney asked their opinion about the house. She didn't want to sell it, but she was hardly ever in Canada. It seemed silly to keep it just for sentimental reasons and to visit a few weeks each year.

"You could rent it out," Anna suggested. "I'm sure Danny wouldn't mind if we managed your place in addition to our cottages," she said. "I bet we could even find a winter renter for you, so you could come home in the summer.

"How would that work?" Linney asked, intrigued by the possibility.

"Well, you could put a lock on one of the bedrooms and put everything in there that you didn't want someone using. And your gran's study, of course. And then the renter has access to everything else. You pay the utilities and internet, but make the rent high enough to cover it. At least that's how we're doing it."

Three wine glasses were raised together to solidify the deal.

15

———————

It didn't take long for Anna to find a tenant for Linney's house. "He's been renting in the area for years, just from October to June. In the summers, he flies rich tourists up to fly-in fishing and hunting camps. He's looking for something new immediately."

"So quickly? Isn't that a bit strange?"

"I forgot to tell you. The place he's been renting was just sold—a quick sale—so he has to vacate. But Danny knows the guy he was renting from and he has a solid reference. If you want, we can do up a one-season lease agreement and if it doesn't work, you don't have to renew it. I think this is the perfect solution for you." She covered the phone. "Girls, settle down!"

Linney smiled. "You have to bring those girls to London sometime." She returned to the business at hand. "If you think this is the right move, Anna, then I trust you. I don't want the house to be empty. Just send over anything I need to sign and tell him he can move in whenever he's ready.

~

DEREK HAD exciting news that fall. It was really too early to tell anyone, but he couldn't wait any longer. The fun that he had promised Olivia after she'd returned from Singapore paid off quickly.

At first, they thought she had food poisoning when she was sick the morning after Thanksgiving. Maybe the stuffing had sat out too long. But when it happened three mornings in a row, she took a test. They hadn't been using protection, and he knew it could take a year or more, so when she showed him the stick with a hesitant smile on her face, Derek was surprised but ecstatic.

"You'll be a great father," Linney congratulated him. "When is Olivia due?"

"Late June."

"Your mother must be so thrilled."

"We haven't told her yet," Derek said sheepishly. "We haven't told anyone because it's so new. Olivia wants to wait until three months. But I had to tell someone!"

Linney smiled—the first real smile in a long while. "I'll keep your secret, counsellor."

Linney was still smiling when she was told the boss wanted to see her. Gemma suggested they get out of the newsroom and grab a cup of coffee.

"I don't know how much, if anything, you want to know about Mac's progress," she began as they sat down at a local café. It had been almost five months since he'd gone into rehab.

"Just the highlights, I guess." Linney's smile disappeared, and she sat on her hands to keep from picking at them as the urge came over her anew. She didn't think about Mac often, but from time to time, she still beat herself up about all the signs she missed—or ignored—and how long she had stayed with him. She wasn't sure how close to his recovery she wanted to be. These days, she was also starting to wonder whether she could stay at TCN after he was out.

Gemma stirred sugar and milk into her coffee, and Linney felt her boss taking her time. "I'm told the detox was particularly difficult. I won't go into the details, but it wasn't pleasant. But since then he's been doing group therapy and individual therapy and all signs are good. He's doing the work. It won't be easy and it won't be fast, but I've been to see him and I'm optimistic we'll get our Mac back at the end of this."

Linney let out a breath she hadn't known she was holding. "That's good news."

"What about you, Linney? How are you doing?"

"Me? I'm—" Linney didn't know what to say. "My best friend called me today to tell me his wife is pregnant. And my house in Canada is rented. So good things are happening. But—"

"But?"

Linney let out a deep sigh and decided to be honest with Gemma. "I'm not sure I can work with Mac again. I'm not sure I want to. I thought a lot about it when I was home last. I don't know if I can look at him across the newsroom when he gets back." She sat up a little straighter and took her best shot. "I'm ready for a foreign post. You know I'm ready. Is there any way we can make that happen?"

"I wondered when you'd ask me that. Because I will have him back in the newsroom if he stays sober. He's too good to lose."

Linney took that in. Was Gemma going to choose Mac over her? Her boss' next words surprised her.

"Would you consider a different network? I've got connections, and lots of other networks would be thrilled to poach you."

"I ... I guess so. I'd never thought about it." Linney's mind calculated the situation quickly. Maybe Gemma was doing her a favour. It was an unusual suggestion, but she was ambitious and this might work for all of them.

"No promises, but let me make some calls."

Linney felt a huge weight off her chest. Maybe she hadn't blown up her career after all.

Just days later, she was scribbling notes after a press conference all of the networks in London had attended, when a voice broke her concentration.

"I wonder if you have a few minutes." Linney looked up and saw Rob Smith, Gemma's equivalent at BTN, a British network.

"Sure, Rob. What's up?"

"Not here. Let's grab a cup of tea." He led her around the corner to an out-of-the-way spot.

"You're wasted at TCN, you know." Linney looked at him with interest. Was this the result of Gemma's promise to make some calls? "You know Rory's retiring in a few months." Rory Finnegan was BTN's correspondent in Jerusalem. "I'm looking for someone to replace him. Join us in London and I'll guarantee you the spot. Think about it." And with that, Rob left her slightly stunned, to finish her tea. Without thinking she pulled out her phone. Derek, who was thrilled she'd reached out, was full of questions.

> Sounds amazing but are you sure? You love TCN.

> Not enough to wait forever. And maybe not enough to work there when Mac comes back. It's time for a new start.

> He's coming back?!

> It's been almost six months. Gemma says yes, if he gets his act together.

> At BTN I'd have to shadow Rory for a while.

> What will Mac say?

He doesn't get a say anymore. This is my career. My life.

I'll be worried for you if you go to Jerusalem.

It's always been WHEN, not IF, I get an assignment like this.

New subject. How's Olivia?

OMG. Nobody told me morning sickness could be this bad.

Oh no!

It's hard on her for sure. And I love her even more for it.

Give her healing wishes and love—and keep some for yourself.

You too! Let me know when you decide.

It didn't take her long. Linney called Rob back the next day, and they negotiated a great compensation package.

"I won't let you down," she promised.

"I'm counting on it."

Linney met MJ for dinner. She owed her friend the courtesy before she told everyone in the morning.

"BTN? Wow. I'm so pleased for you." MJ reached across the table to squeeze her friend's hand. "This is a giant step for you. I'm sad we won't be on the same team, but let's toast to the next chapter of your career. And mine."

"What do you mean?"

"I've been talking with Gemma. My move to the digital side of the business is official in a month. I'll be editing full time, with regular hours. I'm really excited."

"To a fresh start for both of us." Linney raised her glass and

MJ brought hers up to meet it. A satisfying clink shared their toast to new beginnings.

"*Santé!*"

The next morning, Linney handed in her official resignation and on her last day, she knocked on Gemma's door.

Gemma gestured for Linney to come in.

"I would have preferred to stay at TCN, you know, all other things being equal."

Gemma nodded. "I know. But it will be good for you to spread your wings a bit. And to do it without Mac in your face. Besides, BTN is thrilled to have you. They didn't even know you were interested." Gemma smiled. "You need to learn to network better. Rob can offer you things I can't here right now. You know it and I know it. And like any good reporter, you're impatient. I'm sad to see you go, but I understand. I hope one day you'll be back."

Linney took a deep breath. "I haven't talked to Mac since he went to rehab. And I still don't want to. Will you tell him?"

"Of course. Now get out of here and knock 'em dead. Just don't scoop us all the time."

Linney left TCN with a laugh.

16

BTN was different from her old network, but Linney had interesting assignments to help prepare her for reporting from overseas. One of the first she worked on was the Eurozone economies, when it appeared they were heading to a third recession in five years. When Greece called a snap election and the stock market crashed, Linney went to Italy, France, and Greece to do a series on the future of the EU. She returned to Greece when the Syrian refugee crisis began, to cover stories of families escaping the horrors of the war, and economic migrants looking for a better life. And when Britain voted to leave the European Union, Linney knew she could be busy for months, if not years, reporting on everything the vote meant and how it would affect the country.

Mac was back at TCN. It was an editorial position, MJ said, and he looked better than he had for a long time. He was still in counselling, he'd told them, and he laughed that he shouldn't be expected in the pub any time soon. Linney appreciated MJ's update but didn't need to know more or to talk to him. She'd moved on and the passion she'd felt for Mac had been permanently extinguished.

The industry was small, however, and Linney and Mac eventually ran into each other at a lunch sponsored by the Associated Press. He saw her first, and Linney noticed him walking across the room with purpose. She steeled herself and decided to be the first to speak.

"Mac. How are you?" He'd lost some weight and looked healthier, but the years of alcohol abuse had permanently changed him. The lines on his face were deeper now, and spider veins around his nose told the world a story. A story she'd been blind to for a long time.

"I'm good. Really good. How are you?"

Linney nodded.

"I have a lot to apologize for. I don't know if we can ever be friends again, but I want you to know how incredibly sorry I am for what I put you through."

"Thank you, Mac. I appreciate that." Linney was polite but did nothing to suggest she wanted to prolong the conversation. She waved to some of her new colleagues who wanted her to join their table. "I have to go now. I'll see you around," She turned on her heel and left Mac in the middle of the room. He might be ready to apologize, but she wasn't ready to hear it yet. And besides, she'd just been given great news. Rob had told her that she could expect to be in Jerusalem by November, a month earlier than she expected.

"Can you believe it?" she asked MJ when they caught up on a Saturday picnic in Hyde Park. "It's finally happening!"

"I told you you'd be leaving me behind. I'm so happy for you!" MJ would miss Linney fiercely, but she was proud of her friend's success.

Linney spent the next weeks getting paperwork together and deciding what she needed to take with her. The network had promised her six months there, and then they'd evaluate. So, for now, she was keeping her London flat and would be back a few times during her foreign assignment.

DEREK WAITED on Olivia hand and foot through her pregnancy. He suspected he was more excited than she was, especially through first trimester morning sickness that seemed to last all day long. She spent a lot of time on the cold marble floor of their ensuite and Derek knew she was horrified when her stomach revolted at work. Unfortunately, it didn't go away entirely, and Olivia lived on saltines and ginger ale for months as nausea continued to plague her. Her exhaustion irked her, and she was disheartened at her enormous belly. By her final month, she was miserable. Pregnancy did not agree with her.

When Leo joined them after a long labour Derek was instantly besotted and he was sure Olivia would be too. Everything she'd been through would be worth it.

Leo was a good baby, but Derek hadn't accounted for how hard motherhood would be for Olivia. When he came home from work, exhausted and emotionally worn out from the stories he heard from his clients, his wife thrust their son at him often before he'd even had a chance to change out of his work clothes. "I just need some time alone," she would say to him, and retreat into their bedroom, where order reigned, and the room wasn't filled with baby things.

Most evenings, Derek would give his son a bath and sing the songs to him that he remembered from his childhood while he rocked him and fed him a bottle. Derek loved this time—he would have liked it better if he'd been in jeans and a T-shirt, but he loved it just the same. He did as much as he could to lessen the burden on Olivia, while he drank in the wonder of being a father. When Leo cried in the night, Derek got up with him at least as often as Olivia, despite his early alarm. He found himself needing more coffee to stay alert, and on more than one occasion, he missed his subway stop, having fallen asleep to the rhythm of the train.

Still, he loved every second he spent with his son and snapped endless pictures to send to his mother and Linney. He beamed with pride when he took Leo out to the St. Lawrence Market in the stroller. It quickly became a Saturday morning routine for them, letting Olivia sleep late. After a morning alone, Olivia was more herself, and the new family slowly settled into a rhythm. Sure, there was less time to catch up on reading legal briefs than there used to be, but the more Leo gurgled and smiled, the more Derek fell in love with his son. He wouldn't let anything or anyone hurt his precious little boy.

Perhaps he shouldn't have been surprised when Olivia announced matter-of-factly over dinner one night—they'd gotten a babysitter for the evening, and she'd dressed up for the first time in ages—that she was cutting her maternity leave short to get back to business deals for her clients. When Derek asked if she'd reconsider, she made it clear the decision was already made. She explained how she'd been interviewing nannies and had found the right one. While Derek listened with disbelief, she told him that Zuzanna would be coming by his office the next day to meet him.

"This will make me happy, Derek," she insisted. Doing his best to be supportive, he agreed to meet the nanny she'd selected, but turned to Linney to vent.

I just don't get it. I want to spend every second with Leo. Why doesn't she?

It'll come. Not every woman is a natural mother right off the bat. And look at me. I don't even want kids. I guess you're right. But she seems to want to run away from it.

Give her time.

I'm trying.

Hang in there.

> You really don't want kids? You're so good
> with Leo.

> I'm happy to be an auntie. I can't have kids
> and the job I want.

> I'm sad for you. I can't imagine anything more
> amazing than being a parent.

> I made my peace a long time ago. I'm sure
> Olivia will come around, especially when she
> gets back to work. Like I said—give her time.

The next day, a slight blonde woman knocked on Derek's office door. "Mr. Blake?" Her voice was gentle. "I am Zuzanna. Your wife sent me?"

"Please come in," he said. "Would you like some coffee?" She nodded and Derek went to find some. He met Aiden in the hallway. "What do I ask a nanny?" he hissed.

Aiden was little help. He wasn't married yet and nannies were far outside his area of expertise. "Maybe ask her—I don't know—what she thinks of Dr. Spock." Derek rolled his eyes at the reference to the baby specialist.

When he returned with the coffee, Zuzanna asked what he'd like to know about her.

"I'll be honest with you. I didn't know anything about you— or my wife going back to work—until last night."

"Let me start then," she said in accented, but clear English. "First, I am older than I look. I am twenty-nine years old." That was a surprise. Derek had her pegged for twenty at best. "I was an au pair in Poland for English families at the embassy. Now I am working in Toronto, but the family I work for does not need a nanny anymore. Mrs. Hastings has told me all about your baby. I will take good care of Leo."

Derek sat back, taking in all of this information.

"Has she sorted out schedules with you?"

"I will live in during the week and go to my boyfriend's apartment on weekends." It seemed Olivia had thought of everything. Derek wasn't sure if he was surprised or annoyed.

"And you'll look after him while we're at work?"

"Yes, and in the evenings if you need."

"Wow. Well, Zuzanna, it is good to meet you. This is all new to me, but I will look forward to your help. He shook her hand and after she left, he sat back in his squeaky chair wondering how he'd ended up here.

The week that Zuzanna moved in was the same week Linney moved to Jerusalem. Derek would need to remember he seven hour time difference between them now—two more than before. Texting her on the subway home from work was probably off the table. He'd have to think about it at lunchtime now, or very late at night when he was up with Leo. Or perhaps Zuzanna would be up with the baby, he realized. It would be strange to have another person in their condo.

He quickly got used to it. His reliance on caffeine diminished, and the change in Olivia was amazing. She spent her days in silk blouses and pencil skirts, buried in law books, and gaining energy from her work. She smiled again, and there was a bounce in her high-heeled steps. She was finally able to give a little bit of herself to Leo. And to Derek.

Linney settled quickly in Jerusalem with the help of the fixer and cameraman who had worked with Rory before her. In some ways, it was what she'd expected—a city unified on paper, but meaningfully less integrated between East and West in reality. What did surprise her was how international the city was, with expats from many countries. Among those expats were fellow foreign correspondents in the city, and Linney was pleased to discover that the community shared information freely.

While Jerusalem was where the government was headed, it was Tel Aviv that was the heart of the country's economy, so Linney frequently travelled the short distance. Other times, she went to Beirut, Tunis, or Cairo. Her stories were sent back to London to wide acclaim. Still, something felt not quite right about it. Linney couldn't put her finger on it, but the job wasn't as fulfilling as she'd expected.

BACK IN TORONTO, Olivia and Derek celebrated Leo's tenth month in April in the middle of an unseasonably late blizzard by simply sitting with him on the beautiful warm Persian rug they'd recently purchased as he got close to taking his first steps. It would be any day now, and Derek had his phone ready to capture the moment.

Olivia had been working extra hard to make up for her six months away, so the quiet Saturday was welcome, and she took a nap while Leo slept in the afternoon. Even Derek dozed on the couch, pretending to read. He was working just as hard right now on a difficult refugee case, and he missed putting Leo to bed most nights. They couldn't have managed without Zuzanna. When Leo woke, Derek put his son into his highchair for a snack. Half an hour later, when Leo was knocking over stacks of blocks Derek built for him, Olivia stirred. A few minutes later, she came out of their bedroom, looking pale, and holding up a stick with two pink lines.

Derek's eyes widened. "Another baby?"

She nodded, and Derek missed the look of panic in her eyes. "You're pregnant." It wasn't a question, simply a statement. This would explain Olivia's recent exhaustion.

"It's too soon."

"It's wonderful news! Leo will have a little brother or sister."

Another stack of blocks was knocked over, and even Olivia laughed at that. But she turned serious quickly. "Are we ready for this?"

Derek couldn't remember the last time she sounded so vulnerable. He kissed her tenderly. "We will be. I'm sure this time will be easier for you."

But he was wrong. Very wrong. Being pregnant was everything Olivia remembered, and then some. Her morning sickness was worse and even landed her in hospital in her ninth week. Derek was frantic with worry for her over the four days they kept her. But intravenous fluids helped her dehydration, and she seemed to listen to the stern lecture from her doctor about taking it easy. She had no choice.

When Linney saw them in July, she was shocked. Derek had been texting her, of course, but she didn't expect to see Olivia still throwing up every day. She had none of that pregnancy glow and her face was gaunt and grey, despite being very pregnant. She looked like a stick figure that had eaten a melon.

"Derek, you have to get her to take it easy," Linney admonished him when she joined him and Leo for their Saturday St. Lawrence Market visit. "She works too hard at the best of times, but she's pregnant and you have Leo. She's driving herself into the ground."

Leo reached for a rice cake, and Derek handed one to him. "I know, and I can't get her to stop. She'll be in the office this afternoon, trying to catch up."

"Does her firm not understand this is serious?" Leo reached his arms up and Linney gently pulled him from the stroller and sat him on her lap. She sighed as he snuggled into her. She was in baby heaven.

"I'm beginning to think I may have to talk to her boss myself. But she'd kill me." Derek picked up the hat Leo had thrown on the ground and popped it back on his son's head.

"Sometimes you have to do hard things to protect the people you love." She kissed Leo's chubby baby cheek. "Do you want some juice?" she asked him when he reached out for his sippy cup.

"Are you sure you don't want kids," Derek said.

Linney shook her head. "My job is too unpredictable. And besides, soon you'll have another little one for me to spoil when I come home." Linney was completely satisfied with her decision.

At least about kids. The move to BTN was another thing. She liked her job, and Jerusalem was an amazing city. But it wasn't TCN, and she missed working with the team there. She was stopping in London for a week on her way home, but she'd heard that Gemma was retiring. A return option might not even be open to her any more. Still, she hoped to have a few quiet meetings while she was there. Linney had some soul-searching to do as her first six months with the British network drew to a close.

17

───────

It was MJ who told her. "I waited until you were here in person," she said. "I didn't want to tell you on the phone or in a text." Linney had been out of touch with the changes in London and didn't know that when Gemma retired, the TCN executives had promoted Mac. "There was a lot of chatter and raised eyebrows in the newsroom and around the city, but he's settled back in. I'm almost ready to forgive him for what he put you through," she admitted. "But not quite!"

"You don't have to hold a grudge for me. I'm past that," she assured MJ.

It was true. Linney was pleased for Mac, and she texted him a quick congratulations. She was surprised when he returned it the next morning.

Can I interest you in a cup of coffee? I have an interesting proposal for you.

I'm only in town for the week.

Better make it quick then. Day after tomorrow?
At that little café near you. You know the one,
right?

I do. See you then.

She was intrigued, but also realistic. The chances of returning to TCN were slim. It was probably time to double down on making her current job work.

Linney caught the tube to the studio the next morning to meet with Rob for a quasi-performance review.

"Splendid work you're sending back," he began. "I'd like to see you commit to two years. What do you say?"

Linney hesitated. "I'm flattered. It's a great team out there, and I've loved the travel. But I have a few concerns."

Rob listened and scribbled some notes. "Let me take this up with the suits. Can I come back to you this afternoon?"

Linney nodded. She was more than pleased. She spent the rest of the morning catching up on training and meeting with younger reporters who wanted to know about her journey. True to his word, Rob came back just before the end of the day with a proposal.

"Give us three months with these changes," he countered. "And if we can't make it work for you by then, we'll bring you back and look for another bureau. BTN wants you out there, Linney. But we also want you happy."

"That's very generous. Let me think about it and I'll give you an answer soon." They shook hands, and in Rob's mind, the deal was done.

～

MAC WAS WAITING for her the next morning with two cups of coffee in front of him, at a table in the familiar café. "Still like a flat white?" he asked.

"Especially in the morning," she said, sitting across from him as he slid a cup over to her. He hadn't tried to welcome her with a hug or a kiss, and for that she was grateful. Mac looked older, and his greying hair had started to recede. "Well, this is awkward, isn't it?" Linney took a sip of coffee to cover her nervousness.

"That would be my fault."

Linney almost spat out the coffee, she was so surprised by Mac's forthrightness. During their relationship, he hadn't taken the blame for anything.

"I have a lot to apologize for," he continued, looking her directly in the eyes. "And I will, but that's not what this meeting is about. I want you back."

Linney stood up abruptly, upset that she'd been taken in. She did not need to entertain this line of thought.

Mac cracked a sad grin. "For the network, Linney. TCN wants you back. Please sit down."

After Linney composed herself, Mac spent the next half hour outlining his proposal. It was incredibly tempting. She kept thinking of the great people she'd worked with, not the least of whom was MJ. Mac was offering her a return to the network, with two months in London to get reacclimatized, followed by her choice of several bureaus. Even setting up a new bureau in Syria was on the table. "I know BTN and I know you," he said. "You can't be entirely happy there."

"It's an amazing offer," she admitted, and the salary beat what Rob had offered by quite a bit. "I have some options to consider. Can I let you know soon?"

"That's all I can ask. But there's just one thing. I can't make this happen right now. I need three months." Linney's eyebrows shot up and he continued quickly. "Don't worry. We can paper it over while you're here so it's firm. Think about it and call me if you have any questions. And no matter your answer, I do owe you an apology. I'd like to take you out to dinner tomorrow." Linney reluctantly agreed to dinner, and after Mac left, she mulled over what he'd told her while finishing her coffee. She needed to bounce this off Derek. When it was late enough, she picked up her phone.

I'm shaking. So many great options presented to me today.

Do tell. The case I'm working on is depressing and I don't want to open the file.

Am I just entertainment to you?!

Pfffffttttt!!!

OK, here goes. Rob agreed to 3 months and then we re-evaluate. If it's still not right, they'll find me a new bureau.

That's great!

And here's the interesting bit. Remember I told you the other day that Mac had Gemma's old job? I met with him this morning.

Wait—WHAT???????

No, it's fine. I met with him as a TCN rep, not as my old boyfriend.

Aaaaaaannnnnddddd?

They're offering me a choice of posts, after two months in London.

OK, that sounds good too. What do you want to do?

Here's where the stars align. TCN needs 3 months to make it happen.

Perfect - that's amazing!

Mac wants to apologize.

I should certainly hope so.

Linney waited while the dots blinked indicating Derek had more to say.

Do NOT get sucked back in.

Don't worry. He's the past. I've grown a lot since then.

You have.

Crap. Client's here. Thanks for sharing. Gotta run. Love you!

Love you too!

Linney arrived early and waited for Mac in a restaurant they'd never been to together. That was a smart move, she thought to herself. No chance of bad memories. Still, she bit her lip and twisted her napkin in her lap as she counted the minutes until he arrived.

"Linney, thank you for coming." Mac slipped into the seat across from her. "You look nervous. Don't be. Please."

"Okay," she said cautiously.

"Would you like something to drink?" Linney's eyes flew up to his. "It's alright. Just because I don't drink anymore doesn't mean you can't have a glass of wine if you like."

Linney's cheeks coloured, and she dropped her eyes to her lap. "I'm sorry. I just don't..."

Mac waved away the waiter. This wasn't his first apology, but it would be his hardest. They weren't ready to order yet. "Linney, we're going to have to get past this if you're going to come back to TCN." His words were kind, but she was flustered. "Look at me. Please." Her eyes flickered up tentatively. "Part of my recovery journey is to make amends. Or at least try. I've apologized to a lot of people. You're the only one left. I was horrible to you. I let alcohol kill a wonderful relationship. There is no excuse for my behaviour."

His words sounded sincere, and from what MJ had said, Mac was stable. Linney did her best to be open as he continued.

"I let you down time and time again and I said horrendous things to you just to build myself up. And I can only imagine the effect that had on you." Mac continued shakily. "I have nightmares about the things I can't remember that I need to ask forgiveness for." Linney blanched and put her hand to her mouth, remembering him pushing her against the wall. "And then there's that scar." Linney pulled her hand from her face and rubbed the thin white line that remained from where she had cut herself on a shard of the mason jar he'd broken. "I hurt you in too many ways. I am so deeply sorry."

Mac took a deep breath. "You may not realize it, but you and Gemma—the shock of you leaving me and then her ultimatum—that's what made me finally realize I needed help. Before then I actually thought I was handling things. Rehab was the best thing that ever happened to me. Six months of intense therapy while I was there and then another three months afterward. I learned a lot about myself, and why I react the way I do. And I learned some coping mechanisms."

"And you're confident that will keep you from drinking again?" She had to ask it.

He nodded. "Yes. I'm still seeing a therapist—I probably will for years—and I go to AA meetings at least twice a week. I have a sponsor—he's a journalist too, so he gets it—and we get together for coffee every Friday." He laughed. "No more Friday pub nights for me."

"And the other nights?" Linney's eyes were steady on his now. "Because it wasn't just Fridays."

"And the other nights I go to the gym or go home. And if I have the urge to drink, I go to another meeting. It's working, Linney. And I'm doing everything to make sure it does."

Linney let out a breath. "I'm glad for you, Mac. But can we redefine our relationship? Put it back in a professional box?" Her hands mimed the shape.

He nodded. "We can. I already have. I might pine for you forever, Linney McDonnell, but I am under no illusion that you would ever take me back." Her smile was tentative. "My sponsor would probably kill me if you did. That's not why I'm doing this. I asked you to come back to TCN because you are a fine journalist, and the network would be foolish not to pursue you." Mac beckoned the waiter. "Now let's get you a glass of wine, and sparkling water for me and you can ask me all the questions you need to."

Ever the journalist, she grilled him, and he was forthright, not sugar coating anything. Linney deserved the truth. He told her about the horrors of detox—how badly his hands had shaken, how every inch of his body itched one moment and was drenched in sweat the next. Linney winced when he told her about the vomiting and hallucinations of that first week. He'd needed diazepam to keep him calm and get him through it. Detox was not for the faint of heart.

"Just as it started to get easier, it got even harder," he explained, spearing asparagus with his fork. "I still craved a drink with every fibre of my being. I just had no access. So they taught me how to build new habits. Gemma came to see me a few weeks in."

"I remember. You asked for me too."

Mac nodded. "That was unfair. I was still a little bit crazy, and I thought I had a chance with you. I still had work to do. I meditate now, did I tell you? Imagine, me, meditating!" He chuckled, and Linney did too. They were finding their way.

"Was it hard when you got out?" she asked.

Mac put down his fork. This was where it got real and he wanted to be honest with her. "Linney, not a day goes by when I don't want a drink." He saw the cloud cross her face, but he continued. "Suddenly temptation was everywhere. I went to AA meetings every day for a while. Sometimes twice a day. Paddy —that's my sponsor—got calls and texts from me constantly."

Linney nodded. "But you've never faltered?" It was a tough question, but she needed to know.

"Not once. It was a miracle that Gemma was willing to offer me a second chance professionally, and I will *not* blow that. And if it means I never socialize with the news team, then that's the price. I'm happier and healthier than I've been my entire adult life. My fifties are going to be the best decade ever!"

They ordered dessert, and the conversation turned to how they would work together at TCN. The more they talked, the more comfortable Linney became with the proposed arrangement. Crazy as it sounded, this could work. Maybe she really could come home to TCN.

In the end, Linney promised Rob his three more months but told him he'd need to look for someone else at the end of it. After several meetings with Mac and with HR, they hammered out a deal that everyone was comfortable with. She'd return to London in December. The TCN team would always be family to her.

OLIVIA WENT into labour at home a few weeks before her due date. Derek had been with her when her water broke and they left Leo with Zuzanna. He was frightened both his wife and child, but the doctor assured him the baby would be fine. Olivia just wanted it over. She was never doing this again.

It was a quick delivery, and just a few hours later, tiny but perfect, Ivy joined their family. Fortunately, her lungs were well-developed and Ivy was big enough that she didn't need to be in the NICU. For that, Olivia was relieved, but she was exhausted and all she wanted to do was sleep. So that left an ecstatic Derek to make late-night phone calls to family and friends. Checking his watch, he realized it was the middle of the workday for Linney.

Derek sent a few and Linney sent him back several heart emojis. She was in a rush. Moving day—back to London was just a few days away.

Zuzanna brought Leo to the hospital the next morning and Derek introduced him to his sister.

"Baby!" said the toddler, seeing Ivy in Derek's arms. He kissed his little sister, as his nanny taught him to do. He reached out to put his arms around Olivia's neck, but she pushed him away. Nurses had been in and out of the room all night and she hadn't slept. Leo and a newborn were just too much for her to cope with.

"Take him home, please," she asked Zuzanna, and Derek's heart broke.

Even the new baby seemed too much for her. Ivy and Olivia stayed in the hospital for three nights and Derek split his days between home and the hospital. Olivia didn't seem to want to hold Ivy at all, choosing to let her husband or the nurse soothe their daughter. She just turned her back and claimed she was too tired. Derek talked to the doctor, who explained it was just a touch of the baby blues and not to worry. She would be tired, after a very difficult pregnancy and with a toddler at home.

Derek accepted this, but once they got home, it didn't get better. Christmas was coming, but Olivia showed little interest, preferring to read law books than read to her children. Zuzanna was there, after all, to take care of them.

LINNEY SPENT the dull grey workweek days of December getting reacquainted with TCN staff in London and hanging out on weekends with MJ. It took the better part of the month, but she finally decided where she wanted to be posted after several conversations with Mac—always with his office door open, lest anyone think something was happening.

On Christmas Eve, she shook the rain from her umbrella outside MJ's door and rang the bell. Good smells were wafting from under her door. MJ's traditional Québécois *tourtière* was divine, and Linney couldn't wait to taste it. "Merry Christmas! *Joyeux Noël!*" she shouted and held up a bowl of trifle she'd made. They'd have a multi-cultural celebration this year, just the two of them.

"So tell me," MJ asked as they got settled on her couch. "Have you decided yet?"

Linney smiled. "I have. And Mac's on board."

"Well, where?" MJ bounced with excitement for her friend.

"Damascus."

"Syria. Wow." It was a big bold move for both TCN and Linney. This would be a start-up location at a time when the situation in the area wasn't stable.

"The bad news, or good news depending on how you look at it, is that I'll probably be in London for longer than we'd originally thought. It looks like it will take a few extra months to get the paperwork in place to get the new bureau set up there."

MJ looked delighted. "I don't mind that at all!

They had a lovely dinner and as she poured cups of tea, MJ announced some news of her own. "They're going to announce it after the holidays, but I'm going to manage the whole digital team in London." This was a big promotion, but MJ deserved it.

"That's amazing—congratulations! Maybe your team will be able to use some of what I send back."

"I'm counting on it!"

THE CHRISTMAS SEASON in Silver Lake was always beautiful with the tree in Centennial Park lit up for the holidays. It was a peaceful time of year when the town could focus on its own. The schools held concerts, the church rehearsed for the Christmas Eve pageant, and Anna's dance studio held recitals. Emma and Gabby were older now, and at thirteen and twelve, didn't have the same enormous "Santa high" as Anna called it. Instead, their Christmas mornings were quieter affairs—the real excitement started when friends and extended family stopped by on Boxing Day for apple cider and cookies.

This year, Derek arrived first, with brand new baby Ivy and big brother Leo in tow. "I left Olivia at Mum's to rest," he explained. Zuzanna was with her boyfriend for the holidays and with Ivy keeping them both up most of the night, her parents were perpetually exhausted. Emma and Gabby descended upon Ivy and declared her beautiful, but the baby began to cry.

Kirsten stomped the snow off her boots in the entry. "What's all this noise?" she asked, as Danny took his turn trying to settle Ivy. He was happy to turn the baby over to Kirsten, but she had no better luck. Leo toddled up to her holding a book, and with an apologetic look, she handed Ivy to Anna and took Leo to a quiet corner. She was more than happy to read to Leo and he seemed comfortable sitting in her lap.

Anna seemed to have the magic touch and as she bounced Ivy gently, in the swaying dance most mothers seemed to know how to do intuitively, the baby's eyes fluttered closed. With relief, Derek ran a hand through his hair and yawned.

"Is it the company?" Danny jested.

Derek shook his head, failing magnificently at stifling another yawn before holding his hands up in defeat, making everyone laugh.

"Is everything alright at home?" Anna asked, still swaying back and forth. She'd never taken to Olivia, but she did know how hard babies were.

"Ivy's fussy so we're not sleeping, and Olivia's just having a bit of trouble adjusting. Two babies close together, and she's not—" He hesitated, wondering if he should say it. "She's not the most natural of mothers."

"Give her some time," Anna counselled. "The baby blues are a real thing."

Derek nodded his head. "I've talked to her doctor. She had another tough pregnancy, and I think she's just finding it hard to get her energy back. We're a lot older than you and Danny were when you had Gabby and Emma."

"You're right there. I don't think I could do it now." Anna looked lovingly at her husband, and then back at Derek. "At least you have Zuzanna."

The bells at the door jingled as Anna's sisters and their families arrived. The teenagers took Leo with them to play in the snow, and Derek kept an eye out for him while everyone cooed over his slumbering daughter. A few neighbours came by and when Leo and the teens came in for hot chocolate, the house was full to bursting. It was a bit much for Leo, who was ready for a nap. When he started rubbing his eyes, Derek decided to cut the visit short. "It's been so good to see you guys again," he said as he gave hugs all around. "I'm sorry we can't stay longer. I'm hoping by summer that things are a little more stable and we can spend some time at the lake as a family."

"Merry Christmas, Derek," Danny said, clapping him on the back. "We'll look forward to it."

18

———

Derek came up out of the subway into the cold winter air one stop before his own. Tonight he wanted the walk to shake off the day. He'd done everything he could, but he'd been unable to keep his client in the country. Now a single father and his two young children were going to be deported, where they would be plunged back into a dangerous and violent situation. It infuriated him that he couldn't help and all he wanted was a hug from his wife and to hug his children.

The walk helped, but he was still under a cloud of melancholy when he greeted the doorman, collected the mail and headed up in the elevator. When he reached his front door, he hesitated before putting his key in the lock. It was Zuzanna's day off and he could hear both of his children crying.

He took a deep breath and headed in, plastering a smile on his face. Olivia was standing in the middle of the living room, trying to soothe Ivy by bouncing her perhaps a little too hard and ignoring her teary son, who was pulling at her leg, trying to get her attention with a toy car. Her face was expressionless.

"Hi, sweetheart." Derek dropped the mail on the counter

and took long strides to join his wife. "Tough evening?" He took Ivy from her arms and started humming. The baby reacted to the change and quieted almost immediately. Derek sat on the couch with her and turned his attention to Leo. "What have you got there, sport?" Leo climbed up onto the couch and started "driving" the car over his father's shoulders.

"How do you do that?" Olivia asked. "I've been trying to get them to stop for ages."

"Sometimes all they need is a change," he said, but he wondered how long the crying had been going on. "Why don't you go have a bath and I'll put these two to bed."

"Thank you." Olivia walked silently down the hall and closed the door behind her.

Derek tousled Leo's hair. "Let's say good night to Ivy, and then I'll read you a story." The baby stirred when Derek lay her down in her crib, but he kept humming and she soon settled again, thumb in her mouth.

Derek sent Leo to his room while he changed out of his suit and pulled on a pair of sweatpants and a T-shirt before heading back to see what his book his son had chosen. Leo wasn't satisfied with just one so Derek began a second. He was three pages in when he yawned and rubbed his eyes. Leo's eyes were fluttering closed, so Derek planned to read three more pages. He didn't make it that far before his own eyes closed as well.

Ivy's crying woke him a few hours later. He was disoriented but quickly realized he'd dozed off in Leo's bed. He rolled his stiff neck as he closed Leo's door and went to see if Olivia was fixing a bottle. But his wife was sound asleep, so Derek scooped up his daughter, changed her diaper, and humming a soft jazz favourite, took her to the kitchen where he warmed a bottle for her.

A few minutes later, Ivy's tummy was full, and she was dropping back to sleep. Derek put her back in her crib and climbed into bed beside Olivia, spooning into her and breathing in the scent of the lotion—rose and jasmine like her perfume. It would get easier soon. It had to.

LINNEY FELT like she was just passing time. The paperwork for Damascus still hadn't been sorted out, and she was stuck in London. MJ's new job took all her time, and back home Derek had two children and no time to text with her.

For now, she was considering a trip home, and it was Anna she reached out to.

> How much snow do you have?

> Lots! Why? Homesick?

> Maybe a little. I'm thinking of visiting.

> Kirsten's down south visiting her folks.

> Danny & I are going down too, to enjoy some warmth.

> So maybe in a month or so?

Linney felt dejected. She wasn't fitting in anywhere right now. Working with Mac was still strange. It was getting easier every day, but she couldn't wait to get out in the field.

> I'll think about it.

She needed the battle of bureaucracy to be won. And soon.

IT WAS DARK, and the office was just about deserted when Derek leaned against the kitchen counter in the law office while the kettle boiled. His head was down, and his hair was standing on end from the number of times he'd raked his hands through his curls in frustration. The wheels of justice moved too slowly for his liking sometimes.

"You look like you need a break." Aiden's voice broke through Derek's thoughts and he turned around to see the taller man with a gym bag over his shoulder.

"Just gotta break the back of this new case," Derek muttered.

"You need to get out of here for a bit. Come join me tonight at the gym. Work-life balance and all that." Derek hadn't been to a pickup basketball game in months. A busy career and two kids under two were clearly taking a toll.

The kettle whistled and Derek poured himself a big mug of tea. "Sorry, can't. I have to get home too. Olivia's having a tough time still." His stomach growled loudly.

"At least join me for dinner," Aiden said. "Burgers and fries. On me. Olivia can manage without you for an extra hour. And the case can wait until tomorrow."

Sensing he wouldn't win this one, Derek poured his hot tea down the drain. "Fine." He scratched the stubble on his chin. "But just a quick dinner."

At the aging diner, they ordered and talked sports. Derek yawned.

"Am I boring you?"

Derek yawned again. "Sorry. There's just so much on my plate right now. And Ivy's not sleeping through the night yet. It's a lot." Their meal arrived, and they dug in. "When did we do this last?" Derek mused as he sprinkled malt vinegar on his fries.

"Too long," said Aiden. "I know you're overwhelmed, but you need to carve out some time for yourself. You've got Zuzanna. You should be able to do that.

Derek nodded. "Yeah, you're right. It's hard to see the forest for the trees sometimes." He took a bite of his burger. "I'd forgotten how good these are. I might need basketball if I eat them more often."

Aiden laughed heartily. "I like the way you think. Can I tell the guys you'll be back soon?"

"Give me a few more weeks until the baby's sleeping, but yes. I've missed the game too."

IVY WAS THREE MONTHS OLD, and Leo closing in on his second birthday when Derek came home late one Friday night to find Olivia sitting quietly in the darkened living room with a suitcase beside her. Zuzanna's weekend had begun and she wouldn't be back until Sunday evening.

"Kids in bed?" he asked as he kicked off his shoes and loosened his tie.

Olivia nodded silently, and he noticed the tracks of dried tears on his wife's face. He leaned down to kiss her gently, and she stiffened.

"What's wrong?"

"I can't do this anymore," she said flatly.

Derek was confused. "Can't do what?

"I can't be a mother. Don't you see? I'm trapped here. This is not who I'm supposed to be. I have to leave."

"What?"

"I've taken a job in the New York office. I was never cut out to be a mother." She looked up at him. "You're an amazing father. You light up whenever Leo or Ivy are around. When I look at them, all I see is years and years of drudgery, my partnership slipping further and further away, and years before I get back to being me. You'll all be better off when I'm gone."

Derek stood frozen in front of her as she continued. "This isn't who I am. I should never have let you talk me into having children. I'm not mother material." Her voice was void of emotion as she stood up.

"But—" Derek trailed off, finding it difficult to find words, but his eyes were wild with panic as her words sank in. "You ... you can't go. Let's see a counsellor. Let's get some more help. I love you. You love them. You're their *mother!* You're my *wife!* You can't just *leave*." His voice cracked.

"I've seen a therapist. I've been seeing someone for months. Since before Ivy was born. And yes, I have to leave. To get myself back. For my own sanity." Her voice broke. "It's best for all of us." She picked up her suitcase and walked to the door before turning around and clearing her throat. "Don't try to find me. I have to start again. I love you, Derek, but I just can't do this. I'm so sorry." And with that, she strode out of their condo and shut the door firmly behind her.

"Olivia!" Derek's voice echoed through the living room. He opened the door, but she was already in the elevator. "Olivia! Don't go!" He could hear his voice, strident and tormented, echo through the hallway. The elevator door closed. His wife— the love of his life—had left him and their children. Just like that. Just like his father had left him and his mother behind. He stumbled back into the condo and collapsed on the couch. This could not be happening.

It was the sound of the baby crying hours later that startled him out of his shock. Robotically, Derek prepared the formula, sat down in the rocking chair in the nursery, and fed his daughter. His motherless daughter.

"She'll be back," he promised Ivy as he rocked her to sleep. "I'm sure she'll be back."

So confident of this was Derek, that he didn't even text Linney. He took the kids out on Saturday morning as usual and then brought them home for an afternoon nap. He kept checking his phone, expecting a message of apology from an embarrassed Olivia. She'd be so sorry she'd frightened him.

She'd say she hadn't been thinking clearly, and that she was on her way home. Of course, she loved her children. And him. She'd never actually leave them all. Surely, she'd never do to him what his own father had done.

But the call never came.

Derek dialled her number on Sunday morning. The phone rang and then the robotic voice of the cell phone provider said, "The number you're trying to reach is not in service. *Le numéro que vous—*" Derek's face went as white as his knuckles. What had Olivia done?

As he fed the children on Sunday evening, Derek finally faced the reality that Olivia might actually have left them. He called his boss and explained there was a family emergency, and that he'd need at least a few days off work. Then he called Zuzanna and told their nanny—his nanny, he realized—to take a week off. Derek needed time alone to figure out what was next. He put the kids to bed, promising them their mummy loved them, and then sat in the dark in the living room staring out over the waterfront. How on earth was he going to find the words to explain to people what had happened to his family?

A week passed, and nothing had changed. Derek hadn't heard from Olivia, hadn't told anyone, and was no closer to having answers. He'd ignored a few concerned texts from Aiden. The house was a mess, the laundry pile was the size of a mountain and the kitchen floor was sticky. Leo could tell something was wrong and was throwing tantrums—and food. Derek barely had time to shave most days, and he had almost run out of diapers. He'd never realized just how much Zuzanna did and he was grateful that she was coming back. He'd asked his boss for a few more days.

If Zuzanna was surprised by the state of her employer's condo or, in fact, of her employer, after her week away, she didn't say. But Derek felt he needed to explain. To tell her something that made sense.

"Olivia's been called out of town for a few days. She'll be back soon." He desperately needed to believe it. But when he called her office anonymously, he'd been told that Ms. Hastings had transferred to New York. Did he want another attorney? He wanted to scream. He just wanted his wife back. He left messages at the New York office every day but she didn't reply.

Derek couldn't eat. He couldn't sleep, and when Zuzanna took the children out to the park each morning, he broke down, the pain of abandonment by his wife and his father co-mingling into one. the kids were going to grow up without a mother, just like he'd grown up with no father. How could she do this to all of them? Each day, he pulled himself together just in time for them to return. But Zuzanna saw his swollen blood-shot eyes, and he could tell that even if she said nothing, she knew.

Nights were even worse. His bed was cold and empty and the condo was silent, except when Ivy woke up for her bottle. At least, Derek thought morosely, this was one positive of Olivia having not breastfed either of the children. This was one less loss for their daughter.

Finally, he had to go back to work.

"Is everything—what happened to you?" Aiden stood at Derek's office door with takeout coffee cups in his hand.

"Close the door."

Aiden kicked it closed with his foot and handed over the coffee. "Derek, what's wrong? Is it one of the kids? Olivia?" Derek knew just how bad he looked when Aiden added quietly, "Or is it you?"

Derek took a sip of the coffee. "It's Olivia." Aiden's eyebrows rose. "She left. She left the kids. She left me and the kids. She said—" Derek swallowed hard and Aiden saw his Adam's apple move above his knotted tie. "She said she wasn't cut out to be a mother. It was hard enough before. I...I don't know how to do this, Aiden." He put his head in his hands.

"What does Linney say?" Aiden knew how close the old friends were.

"I haven't told her yet. I ... I just don't know how." Derek took a ragged breath. "How do I tell her everything's so screwed up?"

"Call her." Derek shook his head. Aiden put his hand on Derek's shoulder. "If you don't, I will." He pointed to Derek's phone.

Linney still hadn't left London for Damascus, but there were positive signs that the tedious bureaucracy would soon be conquered. It had been nice, though, to be back in London, and the spring weather had put a bounce in her step. She had her coat on and was just about to sneak out of work early to join MJ when she felt the phone vibrate in her back pocket.

"Hey, Derek, what's new? I haven't heard from you in ages!" They hadn't gone this long without talking or texting since Linney was dealing with Mac's alcoholism. When it took Derek a moment to answer, her senses were suddenly on high alert.

"She's gone."

Linney was confused. "Who's gone? And what's wrong with your voice?" Derek sounded grim. She listened as he explained, sounding detached and cold. It was unbelievable.

"I don't know what to do. I'm drowning." A strangled sound escaped.

Linney was shocked at the news, and worried about Derek, who sounded desperate. The comparison to his father was unavoidable.

"I'll be on the next flight."

"You don't have to—"

"Yes, I do. Don't argue with me on this. Now, where are the kids?"

"Zuzanna's with them. I'm at work. Linney, she left almost two weeks ago."

"Two weeks? And you're only calling now? Is Aiden with you?" Hearing a sound she took to be confirmation, she continued. "Stay there with him. I'll call you back in half an hour."

Linney quickly texted MJ to cancel and managed to find a late flight. She'd have just enough time to throw a few things in a bag. She texted Mac on the way to the airport. He'd just have to understand this was an emergency.

She called Derek back. "I'm on my way. I'll be there in the morning. I'll come straight to the condo. Hang tight, okay? Everything will be fine. I promise." Olivia couldn't just disappear. Linney would track her down and bring her home.

It felt like the longest flight of her life, but when the plane touched down in Toronto, Linney strode quickly through the airport to the taxi stand. The sun was not up yet. She directed the driver to his waterfront condo and spoke with the doorman, who recognized her from previous visits. He sent her straight up. She knocked on the door, not sure what to expect. When Derek didn't come to let her in, she tried the doorknob. It was unlocked.

Linney cautiously stepped into Derek and Olivia's living room. It had always reminded her more of Olivia than of Derek. He was standing at the window, barefoot and in jeans and a rumpled T-shirt, but she didn't think he was seeing the day come to life. He certainly hadn't heard her come in. She glanced at her watch. The babies would be awake for the day soon. She stood beside Derek and put her hand lightly on his arm. He turned his head toward her and she almost gasped at how pale he was. He hadn't shaved and his hair was standing up. The golden flecks in his eyes had been extinguished, and she saw nothing but pain. "I'm here, Derek. Tell me what you need." He opened his mouth, but no words came out. "It's okay," Linney assured him. "We can just stand here if you like."

Even if it had been two weeks, it was soon clear to Linney that Derek hadn't processed what was going on yet. She would need to take care of him so he could take care of his kids. Thank goodness they'd kept Zuzanna. Linney led him to the kitchen and sat him down in a chair while she dug through his cupboards for coffee beans. She ground them and started the coffee in silence.

"Who have you told?" she asked eventually, trying to get a handle on the situation.

"Nobody. Just Aiden. And now you."

"Are you sleeping?" she asked gently, pushing a mug across the breakfast bar.

Derek shook his head. "How can I?" He looked anguished and Linney's heart broke for him again. Derek's world had been shattered.

"You need to."

"Mama mama." Linney could hear Leo calling for Olivia. Derek took a long sip of coffee and wordlessly went to get his son. He came back with two sleepy bundles and handed Ivy to Olivia. Leo buried his face in his father's neck.

"Now, Leo, do you remember Auntie Linney? She's Daddy's friend. She brought you the fire truck." Leo turned his eyes shyly toward her and then grinned.

"Fiah tuck." He squirmed to be let down and ran off to get his toy, bringing it back to show her. Derek took advantage of the moment to prepare Ivy's bottle. Robotically, he put Cheerios in a bowl for his son and poured some juice into a sippy cup.

Derek's nanny appeared, somewhat taken aback by Linney's arrival. She recovered quickly. "Nice to see you again. Miss Linney."

"Nice to see you again too, Zuzanna. I'll be here for a while, helping Mr. Blake." It had always amused her that Olivia kept them on formal terms. Zuzanna nodded, and as she took Ivy from Linney's arms, the women shared a meaningful look that Linney took to be a bit of relief that Derek had finally told someone who could help support him.

Derek had turned back to the window, staring blankly. Linney took things into her own hands. "Zuzanna, would you be able to take the children out for most of the day? To the Science Centre? Or a museum? Or—well wherever kids go." Linney realized she had no idea. "I'd like some time with Derek.

"Of course, Miss Linney. I'll pack their things. We will come back about two or three o'clock."

It took Zuzanna twenty minutes to get the children dressed and a diaper bag ready. She packed extra clothes, diapers, toys, a couple of bottles and snacks. To Linney, it looked like they planned to be gone for a week.

And then suddenly it was just Derek and Linney. Linney held out her arms and Derek buried his face in her shoulder as he gave in to two weeks of hurt and confusion.

"You need to sleep," she said and he shook his head. "Lie down here right here, on the couch. Let me carry the burden for a while."

Derek was too exhausted to argue. He put his head on a pillow in Linney's lap and her fingers carded his hair. "Thank you for coming," he whispered, as his eyes slowly closed.

LINNEY SLIPPED OUT from under Derek when he'd been asleep for an hour. She made soup and had biscuits in the oven when she heard movement from the living room. Derek stretched out his huge frame on the extra-long couch. Sitting up, he rubbed his eyes, gritty with sleep and worry.

"Thank you for coming," he said again, clearing his throat and joining her in the kitchen.

"Where else would I be at a time like this?"

"That smells good." He tilted his head. "Like your grand-mother's." Linney nodded. He'd noticed. "But I should go take a shower before the kids get home."

"Go take your shower. Soup can wait."

Linney puttered in the kitchen while she listened to the sounds of Derek in the bathroom. The pipes shuddered when he turned the water off, and a few minutes later, he returned in fresh clothes, clean-shaven and with damp curls.

They talked, and as Linney convinced Derek to tell his mother and their Silver Lake friends, she gave him a bowl of soup and a plate with biscuits and butter. Derek ate it all, and an apple.

"You know, it doesn't matter if there were signs or not," Linney interrupted when Derek berated himself for missing them. "What matters now is that we figure out how you go on from here." They talked quietly and Linney squeezed his hand when he needed support.

"I'm just so glad you're here," he said to her, feeling clearer than he had in a long time.

By the time Zuzanna arrived back with the children, and he offered to put them down for their naps, Linney thought she saw the stirrings of life in his eyes again.

Zuzanna pulled her aside after she folded up the stroller. "Miss Linney, you can help Mr. Blake? He is so sad. And the children can tell."

"I hope so, Zuzanna. Do you happen to have Aiden's cell phone number?" Zuzanna nodded and Linney smiled.

The next day, as soon as Derek left for work Linney made use of the number.

Hi, it's Derek's friend Linney. I'm in Toronto.

How's he doing?

> Not great, but at least he slept yesterday. He's on his way in to work.

> Glad you came. How can I help?

> Don't know yet. I can't stay for long, but I can get him back on his feet. You might have to help him stay there.

> Do you think she'll come back?

> I'm going to try and find her today and see if I can convince her.

> Good luck.

It didn't take too long, with Linney's investigative skills, to track Olivia down. She had used her credit cards to book her flight to New York City and for the hotel she was staying at. She'd got a new cell phone number and Linney knew she'd put down a deposit on a condo there. Linney told Derek all she'd found that evening.

"Derek, do you want me to go? Try and convince her to come home? Maybe she'll talk to me."

His eyes gave her the answer. "Would you? I'm desperate. She won't answer my calls. I've tried. She just disappeared."

LINNEY SAT in the hotel lobby, waiting. Eventually, Olivia would have to sleep. It was dark when she walked through the lobby door, beautifully dressed. She wore a chic coat over a form-fitting suit and carried an expensive-looking briefcase. Judging by how it was bulging Linney thought it looked like Olivia was planning to do more work that evening. There was a smile on her face and no hint of the exhaustion of a working mother of a baby and a toddler.

"Olivia." Linney met her in front of the elevators, prepared to plead with Derek's wife.

The taller woman stopped but didn't lose her composure.

"Linney." She shook her head firmly. "You shouldn't have come. There's nothing to say. They're better off without me."

"How can you say that? Derek loves you. Leo and Ivy need you."

Olivia shook her head again. "I just can't do it. I was drowning, and I didn't recognize myself anymore. I wasn't meant to be a mother. Now if you'll excuse me, I have work to do." Olivia pushed the elevator button, and the door opened. She got in and turned back to Linney. "Linney," she said definitively, in a cold detached voice. "Tell him to forget me. I'm not coming back. The children are so much better off with him than they ever would be with me."

The door closed, leaving Linney staring, open-mouthed. Something told her this was the last time she would see Olivia.

In the end, Linney stayed with Derek for a week, helping him build a new routine and working with Zuzanna to see where she could help a little more. She was by his side when he called his mother and together, they told Kirsten, Anna, and Danny. Aiden came for dinner and Derek began to understand he had people he could lean on. He made an appointment to see a therapist at Linney's encouragement. It wasn't going to be easy, but by the time she left for London, he knew he was going to be okay.

19

———————

Linney arrived back in London to the exciting news that they'd finally cracked the bureaucracy and she'd have all her papers for Syria within two weeks. Suddenly the threat of danger became real, and she was alternately terrified and exhilarated. She, Linney McDonnell, was going to open TCN's first bureau in Damascus.

Grant, her cameraman, would join her in a few weeks, once she got the in-county bureaucracy out of the way, with the help of Hassan, the amazing fixer they'd found. Hassan, who was fluent in English and French along with his native Arabic, would use his local knowledge to help her arrange interviews, to translate, and smooth the waters for anything TCN wanted to do in Syria. But before that, he would be indispensable in getting the bureau set up and introducing her to the city so she could get around on her own. From Damascus, Linney planned to travel to other countries to report on elections, uprisings, and other world events. It was a great place to be situated.

When she met Hassan, greeting him in the little bit of Arabic she'd learned so far, she was so pleased with the choice. He was a well-educated, honest, liberal-leaning man who sometimes wrote for a Syrian media outlet that was critical of the government. He knew what she needed, and he made sure she got it. Nobody would be ripping Linney off with Hassan by her side. And Hassan was equally pleased to be working with Linney, and TCN in particular.

Grant was equally impressed when he landed. "*Salam Alaykum*," he greeted Hassan.

"*Alaykumu salam*," the young man answered back with a warm smile and they knew they'd both passed some kind of test.

Time roared by as Linney and Grant climbed a steep learning curve. They spent time with the expat journalism community getting the lay of the land. One evening, they were sitting in a local tea garden when a slim unassuming man who Linney guessed was in his late fifties approached them. "You are from TCN, *ja*?" he asked. "I am Ernst Zimmerman. I work sometimes with ATV in Germany as a photographer and they have space in the same building as you. Please let me know if I can help. I'm only here for a few days now, but I know Damascus well."

Linney's eyes lit up, and she stuck out her hand. "Linney McDonnell. We'd love to pick your brain. Will you join us for a cup of tea?" One tea turned into three and soon Grant called it a night while Linney and Ernst continued to trade stories, tossing out names to figure out who they had in common. It turned out that they'd covered many of the same international events recently, but somehow had never run into each other. Ernst was lovely—and modest it turned out. Over the next weeks, Linney met with him for tea or a drink at least once a week and managed to tease out of him the number of awards he'd won for his photography. She was beginning to feel settled in Damascus in a way she never had in Jerusalem. Her apartment was spartan but functional, and it was close to the office. Hassan spoke with the caretaker regularly and he had helped her find the best souks and a good grocery store. Linney was more interested in work than making a home.

Hassan invited Linney and Grant to his house for the Eid al-Fitr celebration, which marked the end of Ramadan. They met his wife, a beautiful hijabi with a university degree in chemistry and good, but tentative English. This was a dichotomy Linney was learning to understand and accept. Their son was keen to show off his language skills in English and French. Linney and Grant enjoyed their visit in Hassan's fig-tree-shaded garden. At the end of the afternoon, they were stuffed with Syrian delicacies and sweets, along with gallons of strong black tea and dates. It was a lovely peaceful afternoon amid the chaos of reporting the news and Linney made plans to see Hasan's wife outside of work, trading English conversation or Syrian cooking lessons.

DAMASCUS WAS GETTING MORE DANGEROUS, Linney could tell, but that just made the job more thrilling. As time went on, the wait times at checkpoints grew longer and mortars became more frequent. She'd stopped jumping at the sound of shelling in the distance. It was still safe in the so-called green zone, where she lived, with cafés and restaurants doing good business. But Syrians were fleeing the country and she could see the signs of tension on their faces of those who remained every day.

From time to time, Linney travelled to other cities in the Middle East to cover other stories. She and Ernst were both in Beirut when demonstrators and police became violent in Lebanon's capital city. Water cannons were pointed at citizens who were peacefully protesting the government's actions. Reaching a line of police, Linney waved her press credentials. Grant and Ernst did the same, and they were allowed into the area where citizens held placards and shouted slogans. She plunged in further. It was going to make great TV.

Suddenly a canister was thrown into the crowd right in front of her and Linney's eyes and lungs burned from the white fog of tear gas. Further behind her, Ernst had been quick to put on goggles, pull a scarf over his nose and mouth, and run into the crowd. Grant had done the same. Coughing and wheezing, Linney stumbled away, and when she reached safety with several others in the doorway of an apartment building, she tore off her glasses as tears streamed down her cheeks from the gas. Residents brought down bottles of water to rinse their eyes and Linney gratefully accepted.

After some time, she was able to put her glasses back on, and despite continued irritation, Linney plunged back out into the street to talk to as many people as she could. Grant arrived back first and rushed back to their hotel to upload footage. Linney waited for Ernst for as long as she could before she had to join Grant to record a standup so their story could be filed. When she didn't see him by dinner time, she was concerned, but he turned up in the hotel bar later that evening, his shirt ripped and a bruise forming on his cheekbone.

"Ernst!"

"Hey, it's okay. I'm fine. Next time you wear goggles, *ja*?"

Linney laughed, and then coughed from her irritated throat. Her eyes were still red, and she'd learned a valuable lesson that day.

Ernst asked the bartender for schnapps and tossed it back. "It was a long day. I will go to bed now."

"I'll walk up with you," Linney said. Their rooms were on the same floor. As they got off the elevator, she looked up at his face, wiping away the dirt still on his cheekbone with her thumb. "I was so worried about you." Before she knew what was happening, they were hungrily kissing each other. They made it back to her room, where the adrenaline-fuelled kissing continued at a feverish pace. Two consenting adults, who had experienced something terrifying, came together to create something pure and primal.

"This should not have happened, *Liebling*," Ernst said as he sat up in bed later that evening.

"I'm on the pill."

"No, not that. But that is good too." Ernst pulled his shirt over his head. "This—what happened—is just a reaction to danger. We are not ... Linney please don't let yourself think this means anything."

Linney nodded. "Don't worry, I understand. I know what this was. And what it wasn't."

DEREK WAS DOING HIS BEST, but six months after Olivia had left them, he was still struggling. Leo hit his terrible twos right on time and was a holy terror throwing tantrums and toys constantly. Ivy was teething, and the pain in her gums had her drooling and fussing. Derek loved his work, but his days were long and whenever he was in the office, he felt he should be home. If he left early, he knew he was letting his clients down. Between the demands of two young children and his job, he was bone tired. He never made it back to basketball.

The final straw was when Zuzanna reluctantly handed in her notice. Her family needed her back in Poland after her mother had suffered a stroke, she told him. It was another shock for Derek, and it made him worry for his own mother's health, just one more thing adding to the growing list of concerns that kept him up at night.

A nanny agency helped to fill the gap, but Derek couldn't find someone who was the right fit for him and his children and that he could afford. He was far too proud to pursue child support from Olivia—she'd made her feelings about mother-hood more than clear. So with only one income , he knew he had to make a change—a big one, if he wasn't going to lose his sanity. Some days, the only thing that kept him going was the early morning and late night texting with Linney. She was far enough away to give him perspective, but close enough to him to tell him what he needed to hear. He pulled out his phone. He needed to work something through with her. An idea that just might work.

> Where are you today? What time is it? Can you talk?

Cairo, for their elections. 7 hrs difference. Can text though.

> I need advice.

Lay it on me.

> Mum called me today. Mr. Graham is retiring and selling his law practice back home. She thinks it would be a good idea for me to move up there. Slower pace, money at least as good as I'm making now, and she could help with the kids until they're ready for preschool. What do you think?

There's a lot to like about being at Silver Lake, my friend. But what do YOU think?

> I love the city. I've spent my whole adult life here. There's so much to offer Leo and Ivy. But...

But?

> But if I'm honest, I'm dying here. I still see Olivia around every corner. I can't find a nanny to replace Zuzanna.

I used to love my job, but these days it's hard to get up the enthusiasm to go to the office. There's not enough time for the kids. Life would be simpler at the lake…

Maybe that's telling you something.

But give up my work? A small-town law office was never my dream.

No, but maybe it's what you *need* now. You could always go back to the city later when the kids are older. I'm sure your mum would be thrilled to have you home.

She's even talked about us moving in with her, but that's impossible. The house only has two bedrooms. And it's way too small for all of us. We could renovate when I sell the apartment, but that would take time. So there's that.

I bet Danny would fit you in. And maybe Jake could be your architect. But what about my place while you wait?

???

Seriously. My tenant has already told me he's retiring and moving south. It could work for you for a few months—or longer if you need it to. And then your mum is right next door. Close but not on top of you.

Are you serious?

Yes, of course!

That's incredibly generous. I don't know what to say.

Derek's brain was spinning. He drove up to Silver Lake to meet Mr. Graham in person and they talked at length about the business. Derek's mother was excited about the chance of having her son and grandchildren closer. Linney had given him the perfect solution. Her house would give him his own space while they expanded his mother's house next door.

Derek took the kayak out and spent an hour skimming across the lake and thinking, his broad shoulders powering even strokes that created a meditative rhythm. He could teach the children to enjoy the lake. He would be home for dinner every night. They could skip stones together and hike up to the waterfalls. By the time he pulled the kayak up onto the shore, he'd decided. For the first time in a very long time, something felt right.

"There's something different about you," Aiden said when they had lunch at the diner the next week. "And I can't figure out what."

Aiden ordered his usual burger and fries, but Derek surprised him, asking for a clubhouse sandwich.

"See, that's what I mean," said Aiden. "Something's off."

"I have news," Derek said, leaning back in the booth.

Aiden sat up straight, with interest. "Don't tell me you've found a woman." Aiden had been bugging Derek about dating for a couple of months now.

"Afraid not. Something bigger. I'm leaving Legal Aid."

"What? Did one of the big firms make you an offer? You know you'll see even less of your kids if you get on that ladder."

The waitress brought their plates, and the conversation stopped until she brought the ketchup and vinegar around.

"Seriously, Derek. There has to be a better way." Aiden shoved some fries in his mouth.

"There is. I'm leaving the city. The lawyer in Silver Lake is retiring. It's a great opportunity to be my own boss, set my own hours, and my mum is there to help with the kids."

"Whoa. That's a big change." Aidan sat there with a fry halfway to his mouth, thinking. "I guess that probably makes sense for you right now. I'll miss you though. When do you leave?"

"Soon. Within a couple of months. I'll have a house—you can come up and visit if you like."

"Maybe. It's always hard to get away. You know."

Derek nodded. He did know, and it was part of why he had to make the move. "Well, if you can."

Derek handed in his resignation and put the temporary nanny on notice. As if to punctuate the end of this chapter, divorce papers showed up the week before he left Toronto. Derek signed the papers with sadness and sent them back along with a note about the move. Olivia should know where her children were, but he knew now that she was never coming back. And after what she'd put him through, Derek wouldn't have taken her back anyway. He would build a whole new life for his family in Silver Lake.

They threw him a great going away party at the office, and Aiden took him out for one last drink.

"To new beginnings." The two friends lifted their frosted beer mugs.

"It's not going to be the same without you down the hall," Derek admitted. "I'm starting to feel a bit nervous about all of this."

"You're doing the right thing for your family." Aiden's gruff voice betrayed his emotions. "But, yeah, I'm going to miss you too." He munched on some bar nuts to compose himself.

"I hope you will come up to the lake from time to time," Derek said. "Check out the slow life, make sure I haven't become a hermit!" He laughed. "Seriously though. There's room at Linney's place. Consider it an open invitation."

"I'll do my best," Aiden assured him, and the men turned their attention to the game on the TV behind the bar. For once, Toronto was winning.

"Another beer to celebrate?" Aiden held up his empty mug when the game ended.

"No thanks. One's my limit." Derek always stuck to his rule, and a time when things were unsettled was no time to break it. "I'd better get going. Lots to do before the truck arrives in a couple of days."

Aiden slid off his barstool and clapped him on the back. "It's been a good run, man. Good luck and safe travels. I'll come and visit as soon as I can."

Derek pulled his coat around him and nodded. "Thanks, Aiden. For everything." With that, he plunged into the dark night. This chapter of his life was over.

20

____

Derek dressed nervously on his first day alone in his new office. He used the crossbody strap of his briefcase and pulled the diaper bag over his shoulder before scooping Ivy up and holding Leo's hand as they crossed the lawn to his mother's house. "You be good for Grandma, okay," he told the little boy. "I'll be home in time to make dinner." Leo nodded. Derek kissed his mother on the cheek and then turned to his children. "Have fun, okay?" There were hugs and kisses all around and then the kids waved goodbye to their father. The butterflies in Derek's stomach were receding. He could do this.

The front door of the old red brick Ontario farmhouse was finicky, Derek remembered when it didn't open on his first try. Mr. Graham had warned him he'd have to jiggle the key. Mission accomplished, Derek opened the door to his new life. He walked into a reception room full of legal books, that had seen better days. The floors could use refinishing he thought, but the bones of the place were great. Maybe he'd bring in some of the furniture he'd put in storage to freshen it up. Off to the left was his paralegal's desk. Janet was in her mid-fifties, and he was glad she'd agreed to stay on for continuity. Behind her desk were two doors. One served as the firm's current file room, and the other as a small kitchen. To the left, stairs led to upstairs rooms where they stored historical files. To the right, another door led to his office. Derek put his lunch in the fridge and then put his briefcase down on the old desk in his office. He'd spent the last week going over files with Janet and Mr. Graham but today was his first day solo. Maybe it wasn't the kind of law he'd planned to practice, but it would be good for his family. And that made it the right law for him. At least for now.

The outside door opened, startling Derek out of his thoughts. "Mr. Blake? You're here already! I'm so sorry I wasn't here when you arrived. I wanted to have coffee ready. Such that it is."

Janet's nerves were showing, he thought, and he wanted her to feel at ease. "Thanks, but I can assure you that coffee at Legal Aid is dreadful. Yours is a step up." When the gurgling from the machine stopped, Janet brought him a cup, and he flashed her a sincere smile. He took a sip. "This is great. Now what do we have today?" The pair got down to business.

Derek's phone buzzed just before noon and he put down the file he'd been reading.

Hey! Hope your first day is going well.

So far so good. Good coffee, great assistant, I had breakfast with my kids and I'll be home for dinner. Nothing to complain about! What about you? How was your day?

Sad one. We were at an orphanage in Idlib. So many kids whose parents have been killed in the war. It's heartbreaking. Give your two a hug and a kiss for me when you get home.

Will do. Be safe.

∾

IT TOOK Derek some time get used to the slower pace of small-town lawyering. Janet encouraged him to take his lunch hour every day and once he realized that meant he could pop in and check on the children, he was ecstatic. And when five o'clock rolled around, the day was done. He and Janet turned off the lights, locked the door, and Derek was home within ten minutes, ready to give Ivy and Leo hugs, and make dinner.

Today, though, was Thursday, and somewhere along the way, Thursday had started to mean dinner at Anna and Danny's. Kirsten was often there too, and between the two women, and two newly teenaged girls, Ivy and Leo were well occupied. This left the guys with lots of time to get to know each other better and they could often be found after dinner in the basement, shooting pool.

"Curling season's starting soon," Danny mentioned, as he lined up his cue and then successfully knocked the ball into the side pocket.

"Nice shot. Curling?"

"We've got a good rec league in town," Danny said. "Wondered if you'd like to join us. I can put in a good word."

"Thanks, but I'm sure I won't have time, with the kids and the business."

Danny put down his pool cue and said authoritatively. "You're back at Silver Lake now. You'll have the time. And if your mother can't watch the kids, Emma or Gabby will babysit. It's time you started getting out a bit."

"Okay, okay!" Derek knew when he was beat, and meeting some new people did sound good. As it turned out, the same group of guys played basketball in the warmer months, which reminded him of the pickup games he and Aiden had played.

Derek and Danny met often for coffee in the early months, finalizing the renovations Derek wanted to make to his mother's house. They were significant and would turn the tiny old two-bedroom cottage into a four-bedroom lake home with modern efficiencies. Derek wanted his mum to have some of the luxuries she deserved after raising him alone. She'd have to move into Linney's house for some of the renovations, but it would be worth it in the end.

Derek and Linney texted constantly and called each other often as he got used to his new life in Silver Lake. After they adjusted to the change, the children settled in and the community rallied around Derek the way he had known it would. Aiden called from time to time, and he kept making the noises about coming to visit, but it hadn't happened yet.

Small-town law turned out not to be so bad. It was certainly varied. Wills, real estate, and the occasional prenup for sure, but Derek also saw some clients in conflicts with neighbours, fighting police charges, or sad cases where proud people facing bankruptcy needed help staying in their homes—not so different from his work in Toronto. Derek realized he could find satisfaction in making a difference in Silver Lake lives.

It afforded him some luxuries too. When Ivy got an ear infection, Derek could leave the office in Janet's hands and take her to the doctor. When Leo cut his head falling down the stairs and his mother called in a panic, Derek rushed home, scooped up his bleeding son and took him to the emergency room. Kirsten was working that day, and when she saw a crying Leo in Derek's arms with bloody cloth pressed his forehead, she rushed over.

"We'll get you triaged quickly," she said, "but let me take a quick look now." Fortunately, it wasn't deep, and she said she thought a few stitches would take care of it. Derek was incredibly relieved to know she was there. He would never have gotten that kind of personalized service in the city.

~

DEREK KNEW his mother loved having him and the kids close. And she was just as happy when she moved next door while the renovations were going on. They'd just celebrated Leo's fourth birthday and Ivy was close to two.

"You take the little ones out before it gets dark," she told him after dinner. "I'll clean up the dishes."

"Are you sure, Mum?" he asked. "I could help and then we could all go together."

"No, you go. Take them down to the lake."

"As long as you're sure." He grabbed a light windbreaker. Together, they went down to the shoreline to look at the rocks. Leo loved throwing them into the lake and Ivy laughed and clapped her little hands when they made a splash. It wasn't exactly skipping stones, but it was a start.

After their walk, Derek read bedtime stories and doled out kisses before coming down into the kitchen to make some tea for his mother and himself. He had an hour or two of work to do and his mother would likely watch television.

"Just another few weeks, Danny tells me," he said to his mum, who was looking across the lawn to her house.

"I hardly recognize it," she said, somewhat sadly. "All those memories."

Derek put an arm around her shoulder. "We'll build more memories, Mum," he assured her. "There's room for all of us, and room to grow."

"You're a good boy," she said. "Thank you for bringing my children home."

"Your grandchildren!" he corrected.

His mother's hands flew to her face. "Oh my, I can't believe I said that."

They both laughed and then went on with their evenings.

～

Finally the day came when the house was finished. Derek's mother watched the children while Derek and Danny moved furniture across the yard and removed dust covers from things that had stayed during the renovations.

"I know I keep saying this, but this is amazing," Derek told Danny. "Your team did great work here. He ran his hand over the counter in a kitchen that his mother was going to love." "I can't thank you enough."

"Write me a good review," Danny said. "That, and your cheque are thanks enough." He pulled his phone out of his back pocket. "Anna's on her way with some lunch. We should be ready to give your mum the grand tour by midafternoon if we make it a quick one."

Derek felt a small twinge when Anna arrived and gave Danny a kiss. It had been a long time since he'd had that in his life and he envied their easy relationship.

"Is it okay if I set this up in Linney's kitchen?" she asked and Derek nodded. "Come on over in about ten minutes."

Anna pushed the door open. "Hello, Mrs. Blake." Seeing confusion on Derek's mother's face, she added, "It's Anna. Derek's friend. I brought lunch for everyone."

The confusion cleared. "Oh, that's so kind of you, dear."

Anna set up the crock pot of chili on the counter and looked into the cupboard for a bowl to put the rolls in. With her height, reaching the top shelf was easy. When that was done, she joined the kids on the floor.

"Hi, Leo. Hi, Ivy. Are you doing puzzles?" The children nodded earnestly. "Your daddy and Uncle Danny are coming in soon for lunch. Shall we get you cleaned up?"

They scrambled up and Anna took them to the powder room to wash their hands. Derek and Danny came in and Derek kissed his mother. "Where are the kids?"

"Linney took them to get washed up," she said. "She brought lunch."

Derek was taken aback. "You mean Anna."

"What? Oh yes, Anna. She told me her name. What a nice lady."

Derek and Danny exchanged a look, but the kids ran into the kitchen and the incident was forgotten.

THEY'D BEEN in the new house for a month and everyone had settled in when Aiden finally made it to Silver Lake. After introductions, Derek gave him the grand tour. The light and airy upstairs bedrooms for the kids, and the more masculine one for him. There was a big family bathroom and a space for the kids' toys. On the main floor, the great room had huge windows to the lake. It was open to a big kitchen and the whole space had wide hickory plank floors. Derek's mother had a main floor bedroom with its own sitting room and with an eye to the future, an accessible ensuite. A small office had a Murphy bed which Derek pulled down for his old friend's visit

"You've got a great place here," Aiden said. "The location was beautiful before, but with this house—wow!"

"Thanks. You'll meet the builder tonight. But first, Mum has made us dinner."

They sat down to a simple meal of chicken, scalloped potatoes, and glazed carrots.

"You spoil me, Mrs. Blake," said Aiden appreciatively. "I have to rely on my own cooking, and I can promise you I don't eat this well."

Derek's mother blushed. "Have another piece of pie," she suggested, to which Aiden was happy to agree.

Ivy was shy with their visitor, not willing to make eye contact with him, but Leo asked Aiden questions about his shiny red sports car—he was car obsessed these days—which Aiden answered patiently until it was time for them to leave.

They met Danny, who was waiting at the local bar. Danny put his hand out immediately.

"Aiden. I remember you from the wedding." Danny winced and glanced at Derek. "Maybe I shouldn't have said that.

"Good to see you again. I remember you too. Your wife, and another woman—shorter, brunette." He searched his memory. "They were always with Linney."

Danny nodded. Kirsten. She and Anna have been tight with Linney since grade school. I was a few years ahead of them. And Derek too. Beer?" He pointed to the bottles on the table. He'd ordered for all of them.

"Thanks." Aiden took a drink from the bottle. "Great job on the house, by the way. It's perfect for him." He nodded his head toward Derek.

Aiden and Danny had a second beer, as they traded stories about Derek, all in good fun.

"I'm sure he'll show you his office tomorrow," Danny said to Aiden, when Derek went to the bar to pay for their beers. "Being a former big shot Toronto lawyer and all that! But honestly, he's really well respected in Silver Lake and people have nothing but good things to say about him. It's a good fit— for him and his kids. I hope you're not here to convince him to go back."

Aiden took a last swig of beer. "I won't lie. I miss having him around. But I can tell this is way better for him. He wasn't coping in the city. But here? It seems to really suit him and he's got a whole community looking out for him."

Derek returned to the table. "All ready to go?" he asked his friends, and they headed out. The house was dark when they returned, and when Derek opened the door, he found his mother standing in the kitchen in her nightgown.

"Mum? Everything alright?" he asked with concern.

She looked at him blankly and then shook her head as if

returning from a dream. "Derek. This house is just so big now that sometimes I forget where I am."

"That was a little odd, don't you think?" Aiden said, after Derek walked his mother back to her suite.

"You're overreacting. Mum is over seventy now, and I completely changed her house around. She's bound to be a little confused from time to time."

"If you're sure. Now show me where I'm sleeping. I can't wait to see your laid-back office tomorrow!"

21

———

As Derek's life slowed down, Linney's took off. She'd been busy before, but it was a whirlwind now, and TCN had her travelling from city to city and country to country covering regional events and providing a window into everyday life for people in the UK and back home in Canada. Mac sent accolades, ratings soared, and the Silver Lake community was happy to see Linney on TV again.

She now had a wardrobe of loose-fitting linen skirts and blouses that covered tank tops and worked in almost every environment. Her khaki trousers replaced skirts when she was in the field. MJ would not approve of any of it as being fashionable but it suited its purpose. Linney kept a pashmina in her purse in case she needed it to go into a mosque or a conservative neighbourhood or village. Her Arabic was improving, but she relied on Hassan for anything complicated.

The pace of work made it impossible to find enough time to get back to Silver Lake. Suddenly she'd been in Damascus for almost two years and the only holidays she'd had were a few stolen days here and there to see the pyramids in Egypt, the lost city of Petra, and the modern marvels of Dubai.

A lot had happened since she'd been home last and Linney hadn't been there to see any of it. Things were changing at Silver Lake and not all of it was good. What started as Derek's mother's forgetfulness and confusion quickly became more than that. Linney heard how Derek had found her book in the freezer one day and her keys in the medicine cabinet another. When his mother had trouble finding the right words, he took her to the doctor, but didn't want to believe the diagnosis. When he couldn't trust her to look after the kids anymore, Ivy joined Leo in daycare. Eventually, he hired someone to come in to make lunch for his mother and stay for the afternoons.

One evening, when he was talking on the phone with Linney in his home office beside the kitchen, he smelled smoke. His mother had turned on the stove and started a fire when she wandered away leaving the pan unattended. Derek brought in more help. She was his mother, after all, and it was his job to look after her, early-onset Alzheimer's or not. But the aggressive disease progressed rapidly and when Kirsten appeared at the law office one cold winter day with his mother, who was wearing her nightgown under her winter coat and slippers on her feet, despite the snowy streets, he knew he had no choice. Kirsten had found Mrs. Blake in the supermarket, confused about where she was, and anxious about getting home. It was agonizing, but his mother needed full-time care, and for their family, the Silver Lake Graceful Care facility was the right choice.

Derek visited her at lunch every day and he took the children to see her twice a week after dinner. Linney cried with him when he told her that he could see his mother slipping further away with each visit. Still, even if she didn't remember who they were, she lit up whenever Ivy and Leo ran into her room. She knew they were important to her.

Anna and Danny had bought another cottage recently, adding to those they already managed. The cottages were full from spring to fall, and sometimes in the winter. Anna had hired a couple of local ladies to clean them between guests.

Master's degree in hand, Kirsten was now a nurse manager and blended caring for patients with managing a team of nurses. She still went to KnitWorks when she could, sang in the church choir and now she was volunteering for Silver Lake's Fall Festival organizing committee. Unfortunately, Page Turners was not doing well. It had been six years since the new owners had taken over and they had just never found their groove.

All of this Linney learned about at a distance, and as time went on, she felt further and further away from her friends. So she was firm with TCN back in the UK. She needed to take some time off and go home. They agreed, if reluctantly, to a full six weeks. But first, there was Kabul.

Linney and Ernst met up in the Afghan city after another bombing attack. She and Grant were there to do interviews and Ernst was on a freelance photography job. The fighting between the government and the Taliban was intensifying. Linney wasn't sure the TCN brass would agree to let her and Grant go to Afghanistan again, so they worked extra hard to get as much on tape as they could. After the work was complete, Linney and Ernst found themselves in bed again. It wasn't really a surprise and had happened often since Beirut. They lay together now, breathing heavily, their khakis strewn about the hotel room. She sighed as he began the same speech he always did about how their sleeping together was a bad idea. It was as if he needed to hear her confirm it every time.

Linney rolled over and looked at him. "I'm not asking anything from you," she assured him. "I'm not looking for anything serious. These moments we share are enough." That satisfied him, and he kissed her again. They were both hungry for a moment of sweetness amidst the horrors outside the door before they headed their separate ways.

A few days later, Linney wiped the sweat from her brow as

she finished things up in her office. As much as she loved Damascus, it was hard to deal with the heat. Even with air conditioning in her apartment, it was sticky and tendrils of hair curled on the nape of her neck as she forced a few last items into her suitcase. Linney was ready to go home.

DESPITE THE VIDEO tour of all the renovations, Linney was still surprised when she pulled into her driveway in the early evening. The little yellow house next door wasn't so little anymore, but it looked like it had always been there. Her place looked a little neglected in comparison, she thought, as she noticed peeling paint. When she opened the front door, scuff marks on the walls and her outdated kitchen made her wince. Her house needed a little TLC.

Someone had been in and left her a vase of wildflowers. Derek probably—he knew they were her favourites. She'd thank him later. But first, she wanted to get out on the water. Linney unpacked quickly, changed from her travelling clothes, threw on a bathing suit and some quick-dry shorts and headed down to the shore. She slid her kayak into the water and was soon on her way. It wasn't long before her shoulder muscles were burning, and she rested her paddle over the front of the kayak and drifted for a while, watching the willow trees on the shoreline wave in the gentle breeze and listening to the happy shrieks of children playing down on the beach. The sun was warm on her back and she heard a loon cry in the distance. Linney propelled slowly down the lake for a few more minutes and then rolled her sore shoulders and reluctantly turned around. Clearly, she was going to have to work up to a longer paddle.

Linney saw Derek and the children down at the shore when she pulled her kayak out of the water. Derek looked relaxed and tanned. Summer life in Silver Lake agreed with him. Ivy and Leo, with sunhats on their heads and life jackets over bathing suits, were gleefully throwing stones into the lake.

"Starting them young?" she called over to Derek, remembering their childhood stone skipping contests.

"Welcome home! I saw a car in the driveway. Come and join us." Linney walked over a few minutes later when her kayak was safely stowed.

Derek took off his sunglasses as he bent down to talk to his children. "Remember Auntie Linney? We talk to her on my iPad. Can you say hello?" Taking her cue from him, Linney came down to their level too.

"Hi, Auntie Linney," Leo said. A shy Ivy buried her face in Derek's chest and he put his arm around her.

"Hi, Leo." Linney put her hand on Ivy's shoulder. "Hello, Ivy." The three-year-old shrank deeper into Derek's arms.

Linney's eyes flitted to Derek's, questioning, but he just mouthed, "Give her time." She nodded, but it still hurt. She'd been gone for far too long.

"Your daddy is a skipping stones champion," she tried again. "Did you know?" Leo looked up at her with wide eyes and shook his head. Linney looked over at Derek. "Shall we show them how it's done?"

Derek picked up a smooth, round stone and stood up. "You're on!"

His first stone skipped four times and Linney matched him. They continued for several minutes, Ivy and Leo cheering their father on.

"Remember when we did this as kids?" Derek asked. "Your gran would have to bribe us with milk and cookies to entice us up from the shore." Linney nodded, the memory strong. "We only have store-bought cookies, but you're welcome to come up to the house. It's just about bedtime for these monkeys."

"I'd love that." Linney took Leo's hand and Derek scooped

Ivy up and they headed up to the house. "I still can't get over how much you've changed this place," Linney said to Derek as they sat in the kitchen after a tour. "It's perfect."

Derek poured glasses of milk and pulled out a box of assorted cookies. "Two each," he told the kids.

"What's your favourite kind?" Linney asked Leo and Ivy, trying to build some rapport.

"I like chocolate chip," Leo said. "And Ivy likes the ones with sprinkles."

"Rainbow," added the little girl, shyly holding one out to Linney, which she accepted with pleasure. By the time they finished, it was getting late.

"Okay, kids, time for bed," Derek said when they'd finished. "Say goodnight to Auntie Linney."

Linney yawned. "I think it's my bedtime too. Thanks for the snack, you guys. Sleep well." She turned to Derek. "Jetlag. I'll see you tomorrow."

DEREK'S CAR was gone when Linney emerged the next morning and looked across to his house. She'd been lulled to sleep the night before by the sounds of waves lapping against the shore and had slept until nine o'clock. Humming to herself, Linney put on the coffee maker and got dressed in a T-shirt and tan shorts after showering. She left her long hair to air dry and took her mug out to the porch. It was going to be a warm day, but not as hot and sticky as Syria, thank goodness. Linney noticed her glasses didn't fog up when she went outside. She didn't miss that!

Linney filled her mug again and brought her phone back out to the porch with her. She sent a photo of the lake to MJ and then Anna and Kirsten to see if either of them were free. There was no response, but Linney didn't mind. She took her kayak out and headed into town, across the lake. This was something they'd done as teenagers. Gran would give her money for ice cream and then she'd join Derek to get a cone from the summer stand at Centennial Park where Anna worked during the summers in high school.

Shoulders a little stiff from last evening's kayaking, Linney was determined to paddle steadily and ignore the pain. She found a rhythm, and as she settled in, started to think about Ivy's hesitance with her. She'd have to find a way around that. The town docks came into view and Linney doubled her determination. Her muscles were screaming when she pulled up and slipped out of her kayak to tie it up. But she'd made it, and for that, she was happy.

A single scoop of raspberry ripple was her reward, sold to her by a lovely girl who told Linney her family cottaged at Silver Lake every summer. Linney sat on the steps of the band shell with her bare legs stretched out in front of her, enjoying every last spoonful and then headed up to Main Street.

By the time she got halfway down the street, the local storekeepers already knew she was home and many came out to greet her. Small town life, thought Linney with hints of both amusement and irritation. It never changed. Linney turned the corner at Willow Street and soon found herself at Anna's dance studio. She watched Anna give some instructions to a trio of teenagers—summer staff, she supposed—and then knocked on her office door.

"Got time for an old friend?"

"Linney!" Anna was up on her feet and across the room to hug Linney. "I wasn't sure we'd see you today."

A frown crossed Linney's face. "Didn't you get my text?"

Anna rummaged through her purse and looked at her phone. "Sorry," she apologized. "It's a busy day and I haven't even had a chance to sit down." She used her hands to smooth back her dancer's bun.

"I won't keep you then." Linney was disappointed, but understanding. Her friends couldn't upend their lives just because she was home.

"But will you come to dinner tonight? Danny and the girls are anxious to see you."

"I'd love to. Now go back to work. I'm going to check out Page Turners and get myself a new book."

Linney entered the bookstore expecting to see a large summer crowd. There was an older couple browsing, but the cash register was certainly not ringing up sales quickly. She found a couple of books—a light romance and a meatier historical thriller and then decided to poke her head in at the local law office. But Derek was leaving as she arrived.

"How's the jet lag this morning?" He asked and then looked at his watch. "This afternoon, I mean." It was almost one o'clock.

"Not bad. Have you had lunch yet?"

Derek shook his head. "I was just heading out to get a sandwich. Want to join me?"

"I've just had ice cream. And books!" She held the bag up. "I shouldn't."

"No problem. I don't have time to linger anyway. See you around ... neighbour!"

Linney laughed. "Sounds good ... neighbour!"

The kayak ride home was more leisurely, and Linney allowed herself to stop a few times and just drift. Life was unhurried at the lake, and she was starting to slow down. When she had pulled the kayak up onto land, she made a sandwich and spent the afternoon getting lost in her book.

∼

"WE THINK it's time that Derek started dating," Anna told

Linney matter-of-factly, when she joined the family for dinner that evening.

Danny nodded his head. "He won't listen to me though. We're hoping you can help us with that."

"Do you have anyone in mind?" Linney asked, curiously. She hadn't thought about it, but Derek had been alone for more than two years. It was time.

"Well, Kirsten does," Anna said, as she passed the salad. "She knows a couple of people who'd be interested in a handsome man and wouldn't be put off by the fact that he's a father."

Linney put some potato salad on her plate. "Count me in."

"Good," Danny said. "Kirsten's coming for dessert, after her shift. The girls and I will let you three plot!"

Linney couldn't get over how Gabby and Emma had grown. The teenagers had inherited their mother's grace but their father's dark hair and eyes had fought with their mother's blonde genes. Gabby, who was driving already, had lighter hair but Emma was more like her father. They both wanted to know all about her adventures, and she kept everyone entertained through dinner.

When Kirsten arrived, looking fabulous despite a twelve-hour shift, Danny made them all some tea and then took dessert for himself and his daughters out into the garden to let the women plan.

"He won't agree to go on a date, from what Danny said," Linney summarized. "So we need to orchestrate a situation where he meets someone."

"Like what?" Kirsten asked. "It needs to feel natural."

"Let me think a bit. Where does Derek go out these days?" Linney realized she'd lost track of the details of her friends' lives.

"Basically it's just out with us, or basketball with Danny and the guys," Anna said. "And I'm not sure how that would work."

"Is there any reason either of you would need to throw a party?" Linney asked.

"What about a picnic for Danny's birthday?" Anna suggested. "I was just planning something small but the girls want to try and surprise him. That might be a good opportunity."

"If we can't figure out something sooner," Kirsten added.

By the time Linney went home that evening, they were in agreement. Danny's party would be a surprise for more than one man.

LINNEY HAD ARRANGED for the newspaper to be delivered, and it quickly became a morning habit to sit on her porch with coffee and the news to start her day. Despite her impatience with everyone in town wanting to know all about her, she thoroughly enjoyed her quiet, leisurely mornings. After breakfast, before it got too hot, she would take the kayak out and after a couple of weeks, her shoulders were strong and tanned. If it was raining, she did yoga on the porch instead. Most days she walked into town, and she'd bought herself some shorts and sundresses that were more appropriate for her vacation than her linen khakis. Because it was summer, Knitworks was on break, or it would have been the perfect place to get caught up on all the local news. Instead, regular lunches with Anna or Kirsten took care of that. The only disappointment was that MJ hadn't been able to get the time off to come and join her. They'd have to leave her initiation to Silver Lake for another time.

Linney mentioned dating to Derek briefly once or twice but backed off when he got bristly. It was going to take some time to warm him up to the idea. Good thing they still had Danny's birthday.

Afternoons were reserved for reading, a real luxury, but one Linney needed to decompress. She had a long "to be read" list on her phone that she was working her way through, but she'd also added a couple more paperbacks since her first Page Turners visit.

Linney was used to the familiar sounds of the children coming home from camp and daycare with their dad in tow now, and it signalled that it was time to put away her books. She spent a lot of evenings with her neighbours. Sometimes she'd cook for them and other times she'd eat at Derek's place. Tonight they were planning to take the youngsters out for an evening kayak ride after dinner. Ivy had warmed up to Linney finally and was like her shadow now, always wanting to sit with her or hold her hand.

"Do you want to go in Daddy's kayak or mine?" Linney asked Leo as she helped Derek buckle the kids into their life jackets.

"Daddy's," Leo said.

"Okay, then the girls will go together, right Ivy?" The preschooler nodded. "In you get!" Linney scooped her up and placed her in the front of her kayak's cockpit. Derek helped Leo climb into his, and after they adjusted the seats, they were off.

Derek was first to spot a heron in the reeds along the shore, but the big graceful bird flew off before they could get too close. "Shhhhhhh," they both said to their passengers. As the sun got lower in the sky, Derek guided them along the shoreline and Linney knew what he was hoping to see.

"Let's be quiet like mice," she whispered to Ivy as her paddle sliced through the water almost silently. Derek beckoned her to come closer. She raised her eyebrows in question and he nodded with a huge grin.

Linney pulled her kayak up to Derek's, and he grabbed hold of her cockpit rim to keep them together. She could see that Leo was almost vibrating with excitement. He pointed ahead of them. And there it was. A huge specimen of a moose, at least six feet tall with an enormous rack of antlers. "Wow," she whispered. No matter how often she came across one, seeing the majestic animal was always humbling.

Ivy twisted around in front of her. "Can we pet it, Auntie Linney?" Linney smiled and shook her head.

"We can only watch him, sweetheart." And they did, as he munched on lily pads and reeds. "We'd better turn back," Derek said, as the sun slipped toward the horizon. "Or else we won't get home before dark."

Linney nodded and turned her kayak. She and Derek pulled hard strokes, and they got back to the dock, just as the sun disappeared.

"Alright, up to the house and into pajamas," Derek told the kids. "I'll be up soon after we put the kayaks away."

"Auntie Linney too?" asked Leo. "She reads good stories."

Derek looked over at her. "You don't have to."

She shook her head. "I'd love to."

When the kids were finally in bed, Linney and Derek shared a glass of cider in his front room.

"Thanks for tonight," Derek said. "I've never been able to take them out before." There was silence while he gathered his thoughts. "Sometimes it's really hard being a single parent."

"You're a great dad," Linney reassured him. And it was true. From what she'd seen, he lived only for his children.

Derek looked at her with a touch of melancholy in his eyes. "Even here, where it's easier than the city, I sometimes feel I'm not measuring up. There's just not enough of me to go around and I can't always give them what they deserve."

"You're doing a great job. But Derek, you need to put yourself first sometimes." Linney shifted in her seat to look Derek directly in the eye. "I know you don't want to talk about it, but the only way you're going to find someone else to be in their lives is to start dating."

"Linney." His voice was tight, warning her not to continue.

"Derek, you at least need to think about it. You deserve someone in your life."

He shook his head. "I'm too busy. And they're too young."

Linney stood up. "I'll let it go for now, but not forever."

LINNEY INVITED her brother and his family for the long weekend in August. Bringing family now meant including girlfriends and boyfriends. The kids pitched tents on the lawn between the house and the lake and the waterfront was busy with kayaks, canoes, and even a jet ski that they rented from the marina in town. The noise level was high as they played games of horseshoes and lawn darts, the young people mixing with the adults.

When they ran out of ice on the second day, Linney popped into town for more and added extra marshmallows, graham crackers and chocolate.

"You've got everyone home this weekend, I hear," said the woman who cashed her out.

"I do. It's nice to have them at the lake." Linney was surprised the news had spread so fast. This town was quite something. She hurried back with the ice and makings of s'mores.

Linney found herself telling her brother about the renovation plans she was drawing up with Danny to update the kitchen and refresh the hardwood floors.

"Are you doing anything big enough to need my help?" he asked.

Linney shook her head. "Nothing structural that would need an architect, but thanks. This is just some simple upgrades—but you're welcome to have a look."

"Are you thinking of selling?" Rachael asked with interest.

"Both those projects would help your resale value." Rachael had taken her realtor courses when she'd been downsized from her company a few years ago.

Linney shook her head. "I could never sell this place. No matter where I am, it's home."

"Well if you ever change your mind..." Rachael said, trailing off.

"She won't," Jake said firmly. "If I know my sister, no matter how infrequently she comes back to Canada, she'll always want to come to the lake. She grew up here. I just visited." He had a sad, faraway look in his eyes and Linney knew he was remembering times before their parents' death, something she had only fleeting memories of.

"I want you guys to be able to visit whenever you want. Even when I'm not here. You know that, right? The renovations will make it more comfortable for you too."

Jake nodded and gave her a hug. He cleared his throat. "I think it's a great plan." He helped Linney put away the last of the lawn chairs.

She waved as all the cars pulled out of the driveway and then collapsed onto the porch swing. It had been a lot of work having the whole family, and she was exhausted.

THE NEXT WEEK, Derek and Linney sat out by the dock one evening watching the fireflies. The night had turned chilly and Linney was thankful for the warmth from the mugs of tea in their hands.

"It's strange," he said pensively, one ear tuned into the baby monitor he'd brought down so he could hear if the kids woke up. "All the things I hated as a kid here are the things I appreciate now."

"What do you mean?" Linney asked with a furrowed brow.

"This town really cares about people. It's so reassuring to know that if, say Leo ran off at the park, someone would make sure he found me again. Or like when Ivy got sick, and I had to go to court, the KnitWorks ladies took turns rocking her while they knitted until I could get back."

"And you don't find that stifling?" While she appreciated it more these days, Linney still chafed at the town's embrace.

Derek laughed. "Not like I used to. You wouldn't understand. You're loving your life abroad and you don't have kids. Things change."

"They do." Linney saw an opening. "Olivia's been gone a long time now. You really should start dating. I can babysit while I'm home. You deserve a night out."

"Linney." Derek clenched his jaw. The tone of his voice in that one word gave her pause. "I do not want to talk about this."

"It's not working," Linney reported back to Kirsten and Anna over coffee and treats at the Doughnut Hut. "I can't get through to him!" She huffed in frustration and sat back in her chair. "He just won't talk about it."

Kirsten licked her fingers. "I think we're just going to have to spring it on him." She didn't love the idea, but Derek was being obstinate. "I can bring Will too, so there won't just be one new person there." Kirsten was dating an insurance adjuster from Bridgegrove.

Anna snapped to attention. "Wait, is it getting serious with Will?"

"We're having fun for now, but I don't think it's going anywhere." Kirsten sighed dramatically. "I'm beginning to think your girls will have partners before I do."

"Don't even say it!" Anna looked aghast and the women burst into fits of laughter.

"Seriously," Linney said after a minute, wiping the tears from under her glasses. "I'll try again, but he gets really annoyed at me when I bring it up."

"You don't have much time left," Anna said. "I'm going to send email invitations about the picnic in a few days."

Kirsten and Anna lingered after Linney left.

"You know," Anna began, "if Linney would ever come home, she'd be perfect for Derek. They've known each other forever. I bet they could finish each other's sentences."

Kirsten looked over at her, her mouth hanging open. "I thought I was the only one who thought that! You're right, they'd make a great couple. The kids already love her, and imagine what beautiful babies they'd have." She sighed, to Anna's amusement. "Of course, that will never happen. Do you suppose they've ever thought of each other that way?"

Anna shook her head. "Linney's never said anything and Danny would have told me if Derek had. I guess it'll only ever be in our imaginations."

"WHAT'S THIS ABOUT A PICNIC?" Derek asked Linney a week later as he scrolled through his email after putting Leo and Ivy to bed. He'd dodged the raindrops on the way to her place tonight with his laptop and the baby monitor, and they sat in her sunroom, listening to the rain and enjoying each other's company while they worked.

"A surprise party for Danny. So don't say anything." Linney didn't want him spilling the beans on one of their basketball evenings. "It's small. Just a few people. You, me, the kids, Kirsten. I think she's bringing a date."

"You can be mine," Derek jested.

"I'd make a pretty bad date. I'm going back soon, remember?"

"No chance I can convince you to stay in Silver Lake?" His eyes danced, teasing her, and knowing that was out of the question.

Linney stood up and looked out into the darkness. "I'll admit it's been good to have all this time at the lake. And I've loved spending time with you and your kids. But my job is waiting for me. I'll be back—but never to stay."

They lapsed into silence, Derek continuing to clean out his inbox and Linney sketching out kitchen ideas. She had a meeting with Danny soon to finalize what she wanted him to do. She'd assured him already that he could do it over the winter when things were slower. She wouldn't be back until next summer at the earliest.

22

On the day of the picnic, Derek saw Linney head out for her daily paddle. The weather was glorious—perfect for the surprise birthday celebrations—without a cloud in the sky. Ivy had pestered him all morning, so after lunch, he finally gave in and picked up his phone.

> Would you like a helper? Ivy wants to cook with you and I have some errands to run.

> Send her over—door is open!

Derek had gotten awfully used to having his best friend next door. He watched his daughter skip across the lawn and up onto the porch, and a lump formed in his throat. He wasn't the only one who would miss Linney when she went back to Damascus in a week. Shaking it off, he called out to Leo, who climbed into the car with him and they headed into town. They picked up ice for the cooler, juice for the kids, and some pop for the adults. Then they headed to the beer store.

"Daddy, what's Auntie Linney making?" Leo tugged on Derek's hand as he paid for the beer and coolers.

"Salad, I think. And maybe something from Syria. Why?"

"She makes yummy things."

Derek nodded, amused at the innocent, but honest, assessment of his culinary skills.

"Do you think she'll make apple crumble?"

"You can ask her when we get home, okay?"

That satisfied Leo and they packed up the car and headed back. Derek put the drinks in the fridge and the ice in the freezer before he and his son went to Linney's.

"Knock, knock," he called out, rapping on her screen door and then opening it.

"In the kitchen," he heard Linney reply.

She'd made falafel, and Ivy was scooping watermelon with a melon baller, to make salad with feta and mint. Linney had sliced apples and now was making crumble topping.

"Your daughter's going to need a dip in the lake before we go."

Derek had to press his lips together to keep from laughing. The kitchen was a mess. Ivy was sticky and pink from the watermelon juice dripping down her shirt—and her face. Beside her, Linney stood in front of her stand mixer . Several strands of hair had escaped from her ponytail and were now hanging down on each side of her face. She looked like she'd had quite an afternoon.

"She's not the only one," he joked, using his thumb to wipe flour from her cheek.

Linney flushed. "I'm ... I'm not used to having so much help in the kitchen." She made air quotes around the word help.

"Is that for crumble?" he asked, hopefully pointing at the mixing bowl.

She nodded and Leo cheered. She knew it was a favourite of both father and son, so of course it was on the menu.

Derek took charge. "Okay, kids, let's leave Auntie Linney to finish up, and we'll see her at the picnic. Ivy, don't touch anything!" he added as he picked his daughter up off the kitchen stool and set her on her feet. "You're going right into the bath."

WHEN THE KITCHEN was finally clean, Linney changed into a sundress and put on mascara and a little bit of lipstick, probably the first time she'd worn makeup in the last five weeks. She left early so she could help Anna set up. Danny had found out about the party, but Emma and Gabby were still keeping him away so he wouldn't see the decorations.

They were not quite finished when Kirsten pulled in with Will and Elise. Elise was a medical sales rep who Kirsten knew from the hospital. She had a large territory and travelled around it from her home base in Bridgegrove. She wore a sundress like Linney, but where Linney had hers paired with a pair of practical flat sandals, Elise wore three-inch espadrilles, and a face full of makeup. She brought an orchid for the host and was happy to sit in a lawn chair while the rest of them scurried around with last-minute preparations.

They heard a car in the driveway and quickly Emma and Gabby appeared. "Is everything ready?" Gabby asked. Receiving confirmation, she continued, "Okay, Dad, you can come back!"

Danny came through the house to rousing birthday greetings from family and guests. Anna delivered a beer and a kiss.

"Derek and the kids?" he asked his wife, knowing they were meant to be there.

"I'm sure they'll be here soon. You remember how we were always late when the girls were young," she reminded him. "And there were two of us!"

Soon enough, the last guests arrived. "Sorry, everyone," apologized Derek. "We had a temper tantrum to deal with."

Leo's sulking face made it clear who his father meant. "But we're here now. Happy Birthday, Danny!" He gave him a clap on the back and looked around, his eyes stopping on the man and woman sitting next to Kirsten. He let go of his children's hands, getting ready to meet the unfamiliar guests. Ivy made a beeline for Linney and Leo dropped to the ground melodramatically.

Linney jumped up to make introductions. "Derek, this is Kirsten's friend Will. And this is Elise."

"Good to meet you both," he said, shaking hands.

"Elise works in medicine, Linney continued. "I'll get you a drink and you two can get to know each other." For a fraction of a second, Linney saw the equivalent of a thunderstorm in Derek's eyes, but he recovered and started making forced small talk.

HE WAS TRYING to be friendly with Elise. He honestly was. It wasn't her fault she was here, but Derek was beyond furious that Linney was setting him up, at Danny's birthday party of all places. She was trying to foist a woman on him when he'd been abundantly clear to all of them he had no interest in dating.

"Thank you," he said through gritted teeth when Linney returned with the cold drinks. There was no way she couldn't know he was annoyed at her.

Before too long, Anna fired up the barbecue and soon hotdogs, hamburgers, and corn were on the grill. Leo joined Gabby on the swings, but Ivy wanted to stay where she was. It wasn't lost on Derek that it was in Linney's lap his shy daughter was opting to find comfort, with all the barbecue activity.

It turned out Elise liked her beer and was on her third before the food was ready. She was getting loud and had touched his arm one too many times for his liking. Ivy hadn't left Linney's lap. This was going to be a problem in a week when Linney left again. His head felt like a band was being tightened around it.

The day went from bad to worse when Leo tripped and skinned his knees, howling as blood dripped down his dusty shins.

"Excuse me," Derek said to Elise. "I'd better deal with this." He scooped up a wailing Leo and took him into the house.

Kirsten followed behind him. She wanted to make sure it was just a scrape and nothing more serious. She found the pair in the powder room, Leo sitting beside the sink with his Dad pressing damp washcloths on each knee. "Everything okay?" she asked. "Can I help?"

Derek didn't turn around. "Leo's fine. We don't need any more help today, thank you very much." His voice was tense. He wasn't going to let any of them off the hook.

"We just thought—"

"None of you thought. I said no. More than once."

"But—"

"But nothing. Go back out there and just let me take care of my son."

Kirsten rejoined the picnic where people were loading plates with food. Everything smelled delicious, and she was going to join the line when she realized Linney was sitting off to the side with Ivy.

"Everything alright?"

"She says she doesn't feel well, and I think she might be a bit warm."

Kirsten lay her hand on Ivy's forehead. "Hmmm. You might be right. But for now, if she's happy with you, let her stay there. I'll get you some food." She knelt beside Ivy. "Do you want something to eat?" Ivy shook her head.

Linney hummed to the little girl while stroking her hair. Suddenly, Derek appeared in front of her.

"Come on, Ivy, let's get some supper." Ivy shook her head again. "Ivy, I'm sure Auntie Linney wants to eat too."

"It's fine, Derek. Kirsten's getting me something."

"No, you go and eat. She's my daughter." He picked Ivy up and set her on her feet, taking her hand and leading both children to the food tables.

"Daddy, I feel icky." Derek turned his head just in time to see his daughter throw up on the grass.

People sprang into action. Anna took Leo off to get food and to distract him. Kirsten, who was closest to the kitchen got a wet cloth, while Linney tried to console Ivy, who was crying now. Danny brought her some water to drink.

"Well, folks, I guess my evening is over," Derek said, his voice tight and clipped. "Elise, I'm sorry for this. It was good to meet you." He picked Ivy up and went to get Leo. "Danny, happy birthday, and my apologies for all the drama."

"Do you want me to come with you?" Linney asked.

"I am perfectly capable of taking care of my family," he said in a forced, formal tone. "You should stay and get better acquainted with the new folks." And with that, he strode off.

Derek settled Leo in front of the television and put Ivy in the bath. He gave her some medicine and put her to bed. Heading downstairs, he apologized to Leo for having to leave. "I didn't get any of Auntie Linney's apple crumble," the little boy whined. Ivy threw up twice more before midnight, and after Derek changed the bedsheets, he sat on the landing, head in his hands, emotionally exhausted from the day.

What had his friends been thinking? No woman wanted to deal with two young kids—look at what a disaster the day had been. Derek was angry with all of them. He didn't want to open himself up to being hurt again. It was just too hard. And Linney, who they had all gotten used to being next door would be leaving soon.

"How's Ivy?" Linney asked the next morning when she stopped by. Derek stood in the doorway with a tea towel over his shoulder and circles under his eyes. He didn't move out of the way to let her in.

"Twenty-four-hour bug," he said with a yawn. She'll be fine."

"Can I help with anything?"

"We're good. I think today the three of us will just have a quiet day ."

"Oh." Linney was a little hurt to be shut out when they'd spent so much time together. "Well, if you change your mind, I'm right next door."

Derek nodded. "We'll be fine. Thanks for coming by." He closed the door.

To take her mind off the confusing frostiness she felt from Derek, Linney reluctantly started to think about work. She was well-rested now and full of ideas for stories she wanted to pitch when she got back. She went into town and picked up several little gifts for Hassan's son from the dollar store and some locally-made lavender soap for his wife.

Her vacation was hurtling to a close and she really felt it when she handed a cheque over to Danny for the renovations.

There was one last dinner for Derek and the kids, including all their favourites. "I'll give your dad the recipe for apple crumble," she promised Leo, and she read Ivy three stories before bed. "I'm going to miss you guys so much," she told them both and showed them where she was going on a map. "Promise me we'll do video chats so you don't forget who I am." She turned her attention to Derek. "I have to go and finish packing. You'll come over after they're asleep?" He nodded.

Derek knocked on her door an hour later. "I can't believe

you won't be here tomorrow," he said, taking a mug of hot chocolate as they settled themselves on the porch swing.

"I know. The time has gone by so fast. Too fast. I'm starting to understand why you're so happy here. And yet ..."

"And yet what?"

Linney shifted in her seat, tucked her hair behind her ear, and made one last attempt. "I know you were angry when we tried to set you up. But, Derek, I say this as your friend. You can't sit here every night by yourself. You—"

"Enough, Linney," he exploded at her. "I'll date when I'm good and ready. Whenever that is. But it's not now." Derek yanked at the neck of his T-shirt. It suddenly felt like too tight.

"Come on. You're stuck. It's time," she shot back, her voice rising. She needed to make the point to push Derek out of his comfort zone. "You're acting like a monk. You're hiding. You can't live like this, with just the kids for company! You need someone. They need someone." Linney held her breath. Had she gone too far?

Derek turned purple and Linney could see the veins in his neck.

"Do not bring my kids into this. I live for those kids. I have turned my life inside out for those kids. It isn't easy being a single father." He slammed his mug on the table and hot choco-late sloshed out, leaving a sticky mess as he continued, his temper getting the better of him. "And you're one to talk. You date guys old enough to be your father, and Ernst is no closer to being there for you than Mac was. So don't be lecturing me!"

The chair legs scraped on the floor of the porch as Derek stood up suddenly, grabbing the baby monitor and striding down the steps. At the bottom, he turned around. "And speaking of my kids, I need to get home to them. Have a good flight. I don't want to talk about this ever again!"

Linney just sat there. She knew she'd been pushing, but she never expected Derek would react like that. She was angry and hurt by his attack on her too. It hit closer to home than he knew. She tossed and turned that night, uncomfortable with what they'd both said. When she got up in the morning, the car was gone from Derek's driveway. She left goodbye notes for the kids on his porch and texted him before she left Silver Lake and again from the airport, but she got no reply.

DEREK FUMED for weeks about the way he and Linney parted, but he couldn't bring himself to apologize. But after one of his monthly sessions with Dr. Aslan—he'd continued therapy when he moved to Silver Lake— he finally conceded that maybe she had a point. When school started, Ivy joined Leo at the local primary school. She was in junior kindergarten, the smallest one in her class. Leo, a year ahead, looked after her in much the same way his father had looked after Linney.

"So maybe she was right," Derek told Danny sheepishly, at lunch a few days later. It had been a while since they'd talked and between the harshness of Linney's words, and Dr. Aslan's gentle probing, he was finally starting to admit he was lonely. There was a hole in his life that he was almost ready to think about filling. "If you have anyone in mind, you can introduce us. Just don't say anything to Linney."

"You really should end this silence between you." Danny was well aware from his wife that they weren't speaking.

"She pushed too hard, and at the wrong time."

"She just has your best interests at heart. We all do."

Kirsten set Derek up with a locum doctor who had come to Silver Lake to take over while one of the emergency room doctors spent a year with Doctors Without Borders. Misty wore suits with tight pencil skirts and high heels that made her a little exotic for Silver Lake. She and Olivia were cut from the same cloth, so Kirsten thought Derek would like her.

They met for dinner after her shift at the hospital. Emma was babysitting. Derek couldn't believe how loud his heart was thumping as he waited for his date to arrive. It was ridiculous to be so nervous. When she approached the table, he stood up and took her coat. Kirsten had good taste, he had to admit that. He could appreciate Misty's good figure and expensive salon hair. She'd worn high heels and a pair of expensive-looking black pants. An emerald green sweater with a deep v showed off her assets.

Derek ordered a glass of red wine and she did the same. He soon learned that Misty could carry on conversation enough for both of them. When she did stop long enough to let him speak, she laughed at his jokes and it was clear she was enjoying the date. He wasn't sure if he was, but he'd promised Kirsten he'd try.

"Oh, Derek," she breathed, placing one dainty hand on his chest as they said goodnight at the door. He was surprised by the touch.

He gave her a chaste kiss. "Thank you for a lovely evening."

"I had a good time, Derek. I hope we can do it again some-time soon."

He felt flustered and wasn't quite sure what to say. "Umm. Sure. I'll give you a call."

The next morning, Danny dropped by the law office with a pair of double doubles. Sitting opposite Derek, he took a swig of his sweet milky coffee.

When Derek didn't offer information, he came out and asked. "So, how was the date?" Derek raised one eyebrow but said no more. "Come on!" Danny cajoled.

"Let's just say it wasn't as easy as I remember."

"How hard could it be? Kirsten wouldn't set you up with someone bad. Pretty woman, good conversation." His eyes twinkled as he added, "A hot kiss at the end of the night, maybe?"

Derek rolled his eyes. "Okay, she was pretty. Great career. Laughed a lot."

"And?"

"And nothing. It just felt weird. The last woman I was with was my wife. And we all know how that turned out.".

"They're not all going to be like Olivia. Give this one— Misty, right? — another chance. What do you have to lose?"

"We'll see," Derek replied unenthusiastically.

"I'm going to hold you to that," Danny said, standing up. "Gotta run. The Henderson house won't build itself." He turned to go, throwing his parting words over his shoulder. "Derek? I'm glad you're getting out there."

Surprisingly, Derek and Misty did go out on another date— three more, in fact, and he did kiss her several times. But he felt nothing, and he didn't want to lead her on.

"It's been fun," she said when he told her. "But I'm not surprised. I could never live full time in a place as small as Silver Lake and I'm not sure you can live anywhere else. I hope you find someone here one day." She reached up and kissed him then turned and left him sitting in the bar. Derek ordered a beer. Misty hadn't been right for him, but at least he'd gotten his feet wet. He wouldn't be so quick to shut down the idea again.

Christmas came and went but the longer he and Linney didn't connect, the harder it was for Derek to pick up the phone. Even texting felt wrong now. Derek's mood was as grey as the weather. Silver Lake had several blizzards and everyone was suffering from cabin fever. The schools were closed for several days because of the storms.

Leo lost his first tooth that spring and another soon after-wards. Derek almost picked up his phone to send Linney a picture of his gap-toothed smile. But he couldn't. It had been too long. Surprisingly, Ivy lost her first one just a few months later and he tooth fairy began making regular visits to the Blake household.

One evening, after Derek tucked a loonie under Leo's pillow, he turned the TV on and started flipping through the channels. When he reached TCN, he stopped and leaned forward when he heard a familiar voice talking over pictures of a refugee camp.

Linney's face appeared on screen to wrap up the story. She looked tired, Derek thought, as he scrutinized her face. He knew she wore makeup to cover dark circles under her eyes, but he knew her so well, he could still tell. It was in her voice and her eyes too. It must be difficult over in Syria.

"For TCN News, I'm Linney MacDonnell, in Aleppo."

Derek's eyebrows raised. So not Damascus. He wondered how long she'd been there. He hoped she was safe.

The news anchor introduced the next story and Derek turned off the TV with the clicker—it hadn't left his hands. He looked at his watch. The sun hadn't come up yet over there. Too early to text. He wanted to wait until Linney would be able to reply. Tomorrow or the next day. They'd reconnect and he would apologize. And then everything would be right again.

23

The bombing in Aleppo had been going on at a distance most of the day. Linney and Ernst—he had arrived in the northern Syrian city just the day before her—had eaten dinner at the hotel restaurant after she filmed her standup, and then fallen into bed with each other.

While they lay together, they felt the rumblings getting more intense. Something had changed and their instincts kicked in. Ernst threw aside the covers and pulled on his pants and a khaki shirt. He grabbed one of his favourite cameras and slung it over his shoulder. Work was work, after all. Linney dressed quickly as well, knowing Hassan and Grant would be doing the same. She sat on the side of the bed, her heart pounding, as she tied her hair up on the top of her head—the heat and humidity in the city were oppressive—and then grabbed her laptop and phone. "I'll go down and work in the bar with the others," she told him. Whether you were drinking coffee, tea, soft drinks, or liquor, the hotel bar had become a central meeting point to trade information and to get away from some of the horrors they saw. "Please be careful out there."

Ernst leaned down and kissed her tenderly. "See you soon." He grabbed his camera bag and headed out to take more of his award-winning photographs.

Linney sat down at a small table alone, wanting to work rather than socialize. She texted a source who would probably speak on camera and then waved at friends from Agence France-Press and another reporter she knew from Associated Press, who were drinking coffee together. Linney furrowed her brow and concentrated hard to put words down on the page for this story. They'd shoot her standup, and maybe an interview, when the guys returned but the more she could write now, the faster they could get it on the air.

Suddenly the bottles in the bar began clinking against each other and the hanging pendent lights swayed back and forth. The explosions were closer now. Linney was scared for the first time in her career and she wasn't alone. Adrenaline wasn't enough to combat it, and her heart thumped loudly in her chest as the journalists around her made macabre jokes trying to relieve the tension.

Linney pushed her glasses up her nose and shivered. She jumped when the room shook again. She looked at her watch. Where were Grant and Hassan? And Ernst. It had been too long. They should have been back by now. She glanced around, wondering if they should take cover somewhere else, and pulled out her phone to text her colleagues again. But before she could, there was a deafening noise and Linney was thrown across the room by a force she didn't understand. Her head slammed into a wall and she slumped to the ground as debris fell heavily on top of her, pinning her down. The world went black.

～

MAC AND MJ saw the first reports of the devastating bombing in Aleppo, and they both had to sit down. Mac had sent Linney and Grant there and knowing them, they'd be right in the middle of things. MJ tried Linney's cell. Nothing. Mac couldn't reach Grant either. He tried every contact he had and finally got through to someone. It sounded like chaos. Nobody knew anything.

The newsroom was solemn, knowing two of their own were unaccounted for. Finally, there was a shout. "Video from Grant!" Somehow their cameraman had found a satellite link and had uploaded what he had. They watched in silence, and MJ's jaw trembled as she fought to stay composed. Mac grabbed the phone, dialling the number he knew by heart and this time, it went through.

"Grant, it's Mac. You're good?" Without waiting for an answer, he barrelled on. "I haven't heard from Hassan or Linney. Do you know where they are?"

"Hassan is fine. He was with me. We were out shooting. But Linney? I left her in the ... I have to go Mac. I'll call you when I know something." And the call dropped.

Mac ran his hands through his thinning hair. He jammed his arms into his jacket and barked at the staff. "I'll be back." MJ jumped at the tone of his voice, but she still couldn't tear her eyes away from the video feed.

LINNEY MOANED. She felt pain so excruciating she couldn't decipher where it was from. Her head was throbbing, her hair was matted with blood, and she couldn't move. She could taste concrete and dust and she could hear shouting. She blinked several times, but everything was a blur and the room was spinning. She felt a hand on her shoulder and thought she heard someone talking to her, but she couldn't make out the words through the whooshing in her ears. She tried to take a deep breath to clear her head. There was a stabbing pain, and she fainted again.

MAC HAD BEEN GONE TOO LONG. MJ pulled herself together and looked around the newsroom. She was terrified for Linney, and she could only imagine how the news had affected him. As much as she didn't want to get involved, she knew she needed to go and find him. And she had a pretty good idea where he'd be.

When MJ arrived at the pub, she saw Mac sitting at the bar beside another man. There was a glass of scotch in front of Mac and she wanted to scream. He was in charge now and she'd begrudgingly grown to respect him, despite his history with Linney, and he could *not* go down this rabbit hole. Then she realized his hands were in his lap.

"You gonna drink that, mate?" MJ heard the dishevelled man in a stained suit speak to Mac with a slurred voice. "You've been lookin' at it for a long time."

"I don't know," Mac muttered morosely, half to himself. It would be so easy. He took a deep breath and picked up the glass. The smell was like an old friend, enticing him, promising comfort. He put the glass down but kept staring at it.

MJ walked up beside him. "Mac!" she said sharply, trying to shock him back into the present.

"It's all yours, pal." Mac threw a ten-pound note on the bar and left the building with MJ. They didn't speak, but his phone rang just as they reached the studio. He grabbed MJ's arm to stop her and they stood outside as he answered curtly. "Just tell me."

MJ could see relief on Mac's face, but she still held her breath as he continued to listen to Grant, his phone to one ear and a finger in the other. The background noise must have been intense.

"So?" she asked quietly after he hung up. She needed to know before they went inside.

"She's alive, but Grant said four are dead." MJ blanched as he continued. "It sounds like chaos over there. They found Linney under some rubble inside the hotel. Broken bones for sure and he said there's a bad head wound. They're worried about internal injuries too. She's being airlifted with some others to Germany now."

"Did he talk to her?"

"He tried, but he wasn't sure she heard him. He said she whispered Derek's name."

"You need to call him." MJ knew that wouldn't be an easy call.

Mac's shoulders drooped. "Yeah, I know."

Together, they entered the busy newsroom. All professionals, the TCN team had temporarily put their personal feelings and fears aside and were busy reporting the news. MJ went to her desk and Mac climbed up the stairs, never happier for the design of the newsroom that would let him be able to speak from there. He felt eyes following him. "Can I get everyone's attention," he yelled over the din. Instant quiet. They had all been waiting for news.

"She's alive," he said sombrely, and the tension in the newsroom went down a few notches. He went on to tell them what he knew. And then, in a moment of humility, he added, "I know a lot of you saw me leave. I know what you thought, and yes, I went to the pub and ordered a scotch. But if there's any good news today, it's that I didn't drink it. Now back to work." Mac turned and walked into his office and closed the door. Now that the worst was over, he started to shake.

MJ gave him a few minutes and then slipped into his office. "You walked away from that drink," she said and he nodded.

"Mac, that's a big deal. You should take a moment to recognize that was a huge win today. I'm proud of you. She would be too. *Bravo*"

Mac gave MJ a tired smile and then she slipped out as quickly as she'd come in. Now was not the time for self-congratulation.

～

DEREK'S CELL phone was ringing as he pulled the keys out of the door to his Silver Lake law office. He glanced at the unfamiliar UK number.

"Derek Blake speaking," he answered formally, putting down his briefcase and starting to shrug out of his coat.

"Derek. It's Finlay MacGregor, calling from London. People call me Mac. We've never spoken before an you probably think the worst of me, but don't hang up. I have some news about Linney."

Derek felt the blood drain out of his head and he lowered himself shakily into an armchair. He'd been planning to call her in just a couple of hours.

"What's happened?" he said sombrely. "Is she okay?" All he could think of was the argument they'd had and how they hadn't talked to each other since then. What if ... no, he couldn't go there.

Mac interrupted his thoughts. "Derek, I don't know if you've seen the news yet, but there was an incident in Aleppo. Four journalists were killed. Linney was there but the good news is that she's alive. I just heard from her colleague on the ground. Grant." He figured Derek might know her cameraman by name. "But she's hurt. They're taking her and some others to Germany. I don't know a lot yet, but she's one lucky woman. I'll call you when I know more. Can you tell her family? I have to go. I'm sorry." And with that, Mac abruptly hung up.

Derek was still sitting in the waiting room holding his phone when Janet arrived several minutes later. A million things had been running through his head.

"Everything alright, boss?" she asked, jokingly. When he didn't reply she tried again. "Derek?"

"Linney's hurt. I need to call Jake." He got up and went into his office and made one of the hardest phone calls he'd ever had to make. He promised to connect him with Mac later. Derek didn't mind passing on information in the early stages, but he knew Jake would feel better getting it firsthand. And as busy as Mac was, he owed it to Linney's family. Derek briefly considered booking a flight, but he didn't know where in Germany she would be, or how long she'd be there. And he didn't have his mother to fall back on for overnight care, although Danny and Anna would probably step in. The clock moved infuriatingly slowly as Derek waited for Mac to call him back. Janet quietly cancelled his meetings, and he checked news site after news site on his computer. Not much work got done that morning.

Five long hours later, his phone rang again. "Please give me some good news," Derek said.

"Are you sitting down?" Mac was more composed this time and relayed what he knew. "She's probably got a concussion in addition to some fractured ribs and a shattered hip. Recovery will be tough and she'll need physio, but she's going to be fine. That's really all I know still."

When Derek couldn't find words to reply, Mac continued. "Listen, Linney's told me how close you two are. I know you're going to want to get on a plane, but it's better if you stay put for now. I'm at the airport now and I'll let you know how things are. Then you can decide."

Derek heard him sigh deeply, and an announcement over the PA system interrupted them momentarily. "I sent her there, so I owe her that. You should be able to call her by tomorrow morning your time. I don't know how long they'll keep her but we should know more by then. And Derek? She's going to need someone to talk to. On top of her physical injuries, she lost a good friend over there. Plane's boarding. I have to go."

Derek sank into his office chair as he hung up with Mac, trying to process it all. Linney had been his best friend since childhood. The argument they'd had was so stupid. He owed it to Linney to be there for her now, just like she had been there for him.

24

———————

Linney tried to open her eyes, but her eyelids wouldn't cooperate. Her body screamed in pain. She heard muffled voices and suddenly she was walking along the shoreline of Silver Lake. The call of the loons echoed clearly as the sun set. The pain disappeared as gentle waves covered her feet and ankles before rolling back out again. She was in her happy place and Gran was calling to her. "Linney, Linney!" The voice changed, getting louder and deeper, drawing her away from the lake.

With great difficulty, she blinked. It was bright. So bright. She managed to keep her eyes open and then instinctively reached for her glasses to bring the brightness into focus, but her hand hit a railing. Where was she?

"Linney? Linney?" She was confused. That brogue could only be Mac, but that wasn't possible. Was it?

"Wha ... what happened? Where am I?" Her voice sounded like sandpaper. The last thing she remembered was being in the hotel bar.

"You're awake." Mac rubbed his eyes. Linney lifted her hand and realized she was hooked up to an IV.

"Mac? What happened?" she asked again, groggily. "Where are my glasses? Why are you here?" She coughed and felt another wave of pain.

He held her hand. "Don't worry about any of that for now. How are you feeling?"

"Hurts. Everywhere. What happened?" she asked a third time, grimacing. "Tell me."

Mac gave her a high-level view of what he had learned from Grant and other news sources and assured her that he and Hassan were both safe and unhurt.

"Ernst?" she whispered.

Mac shook his head and told her that Ernst was one of the four journalists who had been killed, all of them photographers or camera people who had been closest to the action. "I know he was special to you," he said, and a tear slipped down her cheek. Linney turned her face away from him and let the waves of darkness come over her again.

When Linney woke again, the pain was still there, and so was Mac, slumped over in a vinyl hospital chair pulled close to her. He had fallen asleep with his head on his folded arms on her bed. How long had he been there, she wondered. How long had *she* been there?

Suddenly there was a knock at the door. The noise startled Mac awake, and he jumped to usher someone in. A fuzzy white shape got clearer as a doctor approached her bed.

"Ms. McDonnell, I'm pleased to see you are awake." The clipped German-accented English almost made her smile, it was such a stereotype. "I'm Dr. Fischer. I'd like to examine you now. How do you feel?"

She winced. "Everything hurts. And—" Linney put her hand to her throat. It was dry and scratchy. Dr. Fischer poured some water into a cup and let Linney take a sip with a straw. She struggled to sit up but gave up when another surge of pain made it clear that wasn't an option. "Mac told me what happened, but I don't remember anything."

"It will come back to you in time. When you arrived last night, the first thing we had to do was put pins and a plate in your hip." He pointed to her left side. "It was badly damaged. It was a difficult surgery, but I am confident you will recover fully, with no issues. You have a lot of bruises and some broken ribs, which will heal on their own, but no internal injuries. You are a lucky woman."

Linney touched her temples—her head was pounding—and found a significant bump and several painful spots. "Ah, and we sutured several deep lacerations," the doctor explained. Linney realized there were stitches near her hairline and on the left side of her head. She squeezed her eyes shut. "It's so bright in here."

The doctor frowned. "We have been watching for a concussion too. I can lower the lights, but first let me look. He shone a light in her eyes, which made her head hurt even more. Frowning, he scribbled something in her chart.

"Is something wrong?" Linney asked.

"Nothing to be worried about just yet," he said, not divulging any details.

Linney squinted, trying desperately to bring the room into focus. "I'm terribly nearsighted. I've worn glasses since I was little," she said, anxious to be able to see clearly and feel more in control.

"If you know your prescription, we can help with that."

"It's on my phone," Linney said, but then it occurred to her. "Oh."

"Don't worry. I've brought you a new one," Mac answered the unspoken question. "I had the tech guys download everything you had backed up on the cloud, so you're ready to go. I guess you'll want to call your family."

Dr. Fischer finished his examination. "Now, Ms. McDonnell, we're going to get you sitting up this evening and tomorrow you can take a slow walk around the hall. It seems fast and it will hurt. But moving is important for healing. We will take it slow, given your head injury and those broken ribs. For now, I prescribe more rest." He scribbled one last note and left the room.

The doctor may have wanted her to rest, but Linney was awake now and despite the pain, the journalist in her wanted answers.

"We don't know much more than I told you earlier," Mac said. "Grant and Hassan were out shooting—they're both still there—there are a lot of unknowns." He blinked several times and then continued huskily, making sure he was near enough for her to see him, "We were all terrified for you back in the London newsroom."

Her face clouded over and Mac understood what she was asking. "I'm good. I was scared for you—I sent you there after all—but I'm sober and I'm fine."

Linney closed her eyes again, letting darkness take her away.

25

When she woke next, Linney's head was clearer, and a nurse helped her sit up and have a proper drink of water. The effort exhausted her. Even without her glasses, Linney could tell from the darkness outside the windows that it was evening. She still had an IV in her arm, which they said was delivering medication to dull the pain. Linney wasn't sure how much good it was doing, but the nurse—her name was Freida—told her she wouldn't have it for much longer.

Alone again with Mac, who looked rumpled and exhausted, Linney knew she would have to summon the courage to deal with him.

"Mac, why are you here?" she asked wearily.

He shrugged. "I had to come. We've got too much history." He took a ragged breath and raked his hands through his dishevelled hair. "And I sent you there." It was an apology of sorts.

"Don't be silly. You send reporters everywhere." It wasn't his fault that she was there.

She reached for her phone and when she turned it on, it

started buzzing frantically with notifications. So many people were desperately trying to get hold of her. She held it to her chest and closed her eyes, tired just thinking about having to explain this to everyone. She opened them again. "I need to call home."

"Already taken care of. I've been keeping Derek updated regularly since you arrived yesterday and he's been passing information on to your brother." He gave her a sad smile. "You only beat me here by a couple of hours."

What he'd said sank in. "You called Derek?" She could only imagine how that went. She'd poured her heart out to Derek many times while she and Mac were together.

"He's worried about you."

"Thank you. Still, I should talk to Jake." She raised the phone again and squinted at the screen. "Can you help get me some new glasses?" He looked relieved to have something useful to do and jumped up quickly. "And then, Mac?" He turned back to look at her. "Go home. You look like hell."

WHEN THE TCN "BREAKING NEWS" theme music started playing —Linney had programmed Derek's phone with it years ago as a joke and he'd never changed it—he answered quickly. He'd never been so happy to hear the sound.

"Linney?"

"I'm okay, Derek. Tired and hurting, but okay."

"It's so good to hear your voice. I'm so sorry about what I … we've been so worried about you."

"I don't think I'm going back to Syria any time soon," she said, her mouth twisting up into a wry smile.

"What do you need? Do you want me to come to Germany? Whatever you want. We're all here for you."

"Don't come. At least not now. I need some time to figure out what's next."

"You're not alone, are you? Mac's still there?" It pained him to ask, but he didn't think she should be alone.

"He's here, but I'm trying to send him back. He's got work and I can't have him here feeling guilty about this. It's not good for either of us."

Derek waited as he heard Linney suck in a breath between her teeth and then whimper. She was clearly in a lot of pain.

"Did he tell you about Ernst?"

"He did. I'm so sorry for your loss, Linney. And I'm sorry for what I said."

"We all knew the dangers." She swallowed hard. "And we weren't in love. But I'm going to miss him." A wave of exhaustion came over her. "I'm so tired, Derek. Can I call you back later?"

"You can call me any time of day," he answered, and he heard her yawn. "You rest now and I'll give Jake a call to keep him up to speed."

"Don't let him come," she mumbled, as sleep overtook her and the phone fell from her hand to the bed.

Derek pulled up Jake's number and proceeded to pass on all the information he had.

"Have you spoken with her doctor? What does he say?" Jake was desperate for information.

"I haven't. I didn't think that was my place. But Mac gave me his name and I have the number of the hospital. I'll text you the details when we're done."

"Honestly, Derek, how did she sound to you?"

"She sounds weak and tired, but that's to be expected after what she's been through. She did at least attempt a joke, so that's a good sign."

"I need to get on a plane." Jake wanted to take action.

"I know what you mean. I feel the same way. But she doesn't want it. Not yet."

"I'm not sure my sister gets a vote in this. I need to get on a plane," he reiterated.

"Jake, listen to me for a minute. They don't keep people in the hospital long for hip surgery these days. This may be a little more complicated because of her other injuries, but I expect the hospital will want to release her sooner than we think."

"Release her?! They can't do that!"

"Exactly. I have a feeling they'll find a local rehabilitation centre where she can recover and get physiotherapy. And when she gets there, that might be a better time for visitors. I'm guessing after that, TCN will get her back to London." Linney had kept her Notting Hill flat.

"London? No, when she's released, she'll come home." Jake was adamant. "She'll stay with me."

Derek tried to be delicate. "We don't know if she considers Canada home anymore, do we? And even if she does, home would be Silver Lake, not Toronto. Remember, she's been away for a long time now. Almost her entire adult life." It saddened him, and could tell this wasn't something Jake hadn't thought of yet. "If I hear anything else, I'll text you. But I wouldn't be surprised if Linney calls you tomorrow."

Derek spent much of the evening pretending to catch up on work but thinking back to the adventures he and Linney had as young children. Linney had arrived in Silver Lake a grieving child not much older than his Leo was now.

She never had been one to shy away from adventure, and once she got over the loss of her parents, she dragged him along with her. She'd always been the more impulsive of them, and it had landed her in trouble more than once. Derek smiled, remembering she'd fallen out of a tree and broken her arm just in time for her tenth birthday. Derek had run for her grandmother. He dried her tears when her high school boyfriend dumped her. When they were in university, he took her to the hospital when she'd somehow put a skate blade through the skin of her calf at a city skating rink. And then there was that time, he remembered, when she stood up in a canoe quoting poetry during one of their evening paddles and toppled over the edge, coming up from the water sputtering. It hadn't surprised him at all when Linney had taken an overseas journalism position and then parlayed it into a job as a correspondent in a war zone. But this was something Derek didn't know how to rescue her from.

As Freida had promised, the IV came out the next day. Linney was still in a lot of pain, but it was time to wean her off the strong drugs. When she struggled to her feet with a great deal of assistance, she turned green and the room started to spin.

"I'm going to be sick." Linney's hand flew to her mouth.

Freida sat her down quickly. "Breathe," she ordered and Linney took a few shallow breaths and then some deeper ones. It took three attempts but finally, she was upright, clutching to a walker like an old lady. Mac watched her, like an anxious father.

She sent him away. "You're making me nervous," she snapped.

Reluctantly, he set off to give her some space. He could use the time to pick up her new glasses and get a much-needed cup of coffee from the cafeteria. Despite what she told him to do yesterday, not only had he not gone home, he hadn't left the hospital. Caffeine was the only thing keeping him going.

Freida helped Linney navigate through the wide hospital doorway. "He must love you a lot," she said. "He hasn't left your side since he got here."

Linney grimaced as she began to shuffle slowly down the

out-of-focus hospital hall. She hated being so entirely reliant on Freida, or on anyone, truth be told. Her head was feeling marginally better but her ribs hurt almost as much as her hip.

"We're not a couple. He's my boss." She saw Freida's eyebrows raise, and she continued more softly, "But we were together once." Linney stopped to catch her breath. This was harder than she thought it would be. Finally, she made it around the little loop and Freida helped her back into bed.

"The doctor will be pleased," she said. "We'll do it again later, and I can teach your boss how to help you stand up. For now, you rest."

Linney nodded and yawned. Another frustrating wave of fatigue was already threatening to overtake her and her eyelids fluttered closed.

～

DEREK WAS at the kitchen counter pouring cereal into bowls for Leo and Ivy's breakfast before summer camp when Linney's TCN theme played on his phone. "Shhhhh," he said to them, as he tried to listen to Linney.

"You sound better this morning," he said after she greeted him.

"Maybe it's because I was up walking," she said. Derek was surprised, but she explained it helped prevent blood clots and other complications. "It's a lot harder than I remember," she joked. "The walker makes me feel like I'm ancient. Even Gran never had one of those!"

"How long will they keep you there?" he asked.

"A few weeks at least, I think. It's complicated by the fact that to get back to London, I have to get on a train or a plane, and then I have four flights of stairs to deal with."

"I've been passing news on to Jake," Derek told her as he

poured a cup of coffee. "But I think he'd like a call if you're up to it."

Linney sighed. "It's so much easier to talk to you, but I know you're right. I'll call him later today. Kiss the kids for me. I have to go now. Someone's at my door." She heard the muffled sounds of Derek passing on the message and the little ones shouting their thanks before she hung up the call.

"You have children?" asked Doctor Fischer as he read her chart.

"They're my best friend's kids," she rushed to assure him. "But I love them like they're my own."

He checked her over again, had a look at the swelling on her head that was starting to go down, and checked her eyes again with a frown. Just then, Mac joined them, fuzzy in the distance, but becoming sharper as he got closer.

"Look what I have," he teased.

"Thank goodness." Linney couldn't wait to be able to see properly. She opened the case, perched the new glasses on her nose, and the world finally came into focus. "That's so much better." She frowned and blinked several times.

"What's wrong?"

"I don't know. Something's just different. Not quite right." She turned to the doctor. "You were looking at my eyes. Is there a problem?"

"There's something I'm a bit concerned about," he admitted. "We know you hit your head, so it may resolve itself as the swelling continues to go down, but right now, your right eye isn't responding normally to light. That's what I was checking yesterday and again today."

"What?"

"I expect that it's just some swelling around the optical nerve. We'll watch it over the next day or two and do some tests. I will probably resolve. The nurse said you felt dizzy and nauseated when you first stood up. That's probably why. You're seeing in two dimensions rather than three right now."

"But you think it will get better on its own?" Mac was the first to ask the question.

"Quite likely," confirmed the doctor, putting down the chart, where he'd been writing notes. "I'll be back to check on you tomorrow, Ms. McDonnell." Mac walked out with the doctor.

Linney tapped her finger nervously on the hospital tray table before finally pulling up Jake's name on her phone.

"Linney? Is that really you? How are you? Should I come? What do you need?" Questions tumbled out of Jake's mouth, betraying how worried he was.

Slowly the details of the bombing were coming back and Linney explained what she could remember and what had happened since she'd arrived in Germany. "I'm okay. I mean, I get tired easily, and it's going to be a rough road, but I'll be fine." She chose not to share her vision issues until they knew if they were real. She continued quietly, "I'll be here for a while though."

"I want to come," he said, gruffly, his voice full of emotion.

"You'd just be sitting around, Jake. There's no point in it. Maybe later, but not yet."

They talked for a while and Linney yawned. "Give Rachael and the kids my love, okay? I'll call again soon. But now, I need to rest for a bit."

"Take care, and remember we love you."

LINNEY WAS UP WALKING TWICE MORE that day, determined to do all she could to speed up her recovery. She spoke with Freida and with Dr. Fischer about the next steps after she was released from the hospital. She couldn't go back to her flat in London, but a long flight to Canada wasn't advisable yet either. They suggested a respected rehabilitation facility on the other side of the city, where the staff spoke English.

The physical exertion tired Linney out more than she wanted to admit, but she insisted Mac go to his hotel that evening and she slept peacefully. In her dreams, she slipped back to Silver Lake. Anna was sitting on the end of Linney's dock with her toes dipped in the lake, and a glass of iced tea in her hand, looking as if she'd swallowed a watermelon. Kirsten and Linney were sitting on either side of her, each with a hand on her stomach, grinning each time the baby inside kicked.

"It's amazing. Do you have a whole football team in there?" joked Kirsten.

Linney's dream skipped forward. Anna had two little girls in her arms now and looked tired but happy. Her dream skipped again to university, when she came home each summer and working at Page Turners. She would kayak home at the end of each day and walk up from the dock through her grandmother's perfumed cottage garden. It always smelled so lovely.

The floral scent pierced through her dream and opening her eyes slowly, Linney saw a huge bouquet beside her. She put on her glasses and the pretty wildflower blooms came into focus. Reading the card, she smiled. It was from the newsroom —with so many of her favourites that she knew MJ must have been involved.

> They're beautiful. Please thank everyone for me.

> Mac driving you crazy? Say the word and I'll invent an emergency to bring him back.

> You're the best. I miss you.

Thought I'd come this weekend if that's OK.

You don't need to.

But I'd really like that.

I'll be there.

Knowing she'd have a friend there soon gave Linney the strength to finally read and respond to the multitude of emails and text messages she'd received from family, friends, and colleagues. There were so many messages of concern that she had tears in her eyes just reviewing them.

She was relieved to find out that her friends were fine. Most had escaped with just a few scrapes, and sent their condolences about Ernst. Linney hadn't known the other three journalists who were killed, but she knew their families must be mourning. Hassan and Grant sent many messages and were keeping up the bureau with the help of a stringer until she could return.

She texted Jake suggesting a call a little later. She'd caught sight of her face in a mirror and didn't think a video chat was a good idea just yet. And she needed a shower.

26

"Good morning, Dr. Fischer," Linney said, seeing the familiar man come into her room.

"You're looking better," he said, matter-of-factly. She felt better. Freida had helped her wash her hair and until she could shower properly, it would do. She felt almost human. A broken human, but it was a significant improvement.

As usual, he examined her to see how things were coming along, but she noticed he had a serious look on his face the whole time. "How do things look?" she asked tentatively.

"I'm happy with how you're healing," he said. "Your bruises are starting to fade. The incisions look good and I like that you are walking so much." He flipped through her chart. "This is good."

"I hear a 'but' in your voice, Doctor." Linney was nervous. An ophthalmologist had been to see her yesterday and carried out several tests. "Is it my eye?"

"I'm sorry to say, Ms. McDonnell, but it seems you have suffered some permanent damage to your optical nerve." Dr. Fischer got straight to the point. "We will observe for another day or two, but it is possible you may not regain sight in that eye." Linney noticed Mac in the doorway. He'd heard, and she hated the pity in his eyes. The doctor went on to explain about therapies that would help her adjust, but she didn't hear much.

Mac talked about how enriching a career in the London newsroom would be. It was clear he didn't want her back in the field and she was sad as she felt this phase of her career slipping away, years before it should. When he left to take a phone call from the newsroom, Linney had a little cry and then wiped her tears. She didn't have time to feel sorry for herself. She was looking forward to MJ coming in a couple of days. Mac being there was one thing, but she needed a girlfriend.

"You okay?" Mac asked when he came back. Linney's nose looked a little pink, and he felt like something was off.

"Yep. Just thinking about all the things I have to do."

"Like what?" he demanded. "All you should be thinking about is resting."

"I will," she promised, "First I need a new laptop. And something to read!" Linney knew that as she spent more hours awake, she would need something to keep her occupied. Mac helped her order a new computer, which would be delivered straight to the hospital and she sent him to buy magazines from the gift shop in the hospital lobby.

Later that day, Linney steeled herself for a different conversation with Mac. It was time. When she signed the last of the rehab paperwork she shoved away the clipboard. "Well, that's it. So you know what that means, Mac."

He looked pained.

"Go home, Mac. Go back to the newsroom. You can't keep babysitting me here. It's not good for either of us."

"No. Not yet."

"Yes, now." Linney's voice was quiet but strong. She couldn't let him feel guilty about this. "You have a whole newsroom to run."

"Are you sure? Maybe I should stay longer. Until you're feeling a little better."

Linney sighed. Just like before, it was going to be her who had to be strong. "Mac, it hasn't been your job to take care of me for a long time, and anyway, MJ's coming. I appreciate you being here, but you are my boss. Let's remember that."

Mac took her hand and squeezed it tight. "It's because of you that I'm even here at all. Almost six years sober. I thank God for that every day but I don't know if I ever thanked you."

"You did all the hard work," Linney reminded him, and then she grinned wryly. "Gemma and I just gave you a swift kick in the rear. Now go. Pack up your stuff and get back to London. It's where you belong."

Mac opened his mouth to object, but Linney held her ground.

"If that's what you want."

"It is. And it's what we both need."

Mac nodded slowly and with a final squeeze of her hand, he admitted defeat. "I'll see you back in London."

And then he was gone.

Linney sat with the silence for a while. Initially, she wondered if she'd done the right thing. The room was empty without Mac's presence. To fill it, she called Derek.

"Do you have any more news about your eye?" he asked.

"It's not good," she said and Derek held his breath waiting for her to continue. "The damage is permanent. My hip and my ribs will heal, but my eye won't."

"I don't know what to say. Are you sure I can't come?"

"No," she sniffled. "Just tell me something good. Tell me what your kids are up to." Derek launched into the latest escapades of Leo and Ivy, keeping up cheery one-sided banter while she listened, trying not to cry.

❧

FREIDA CONTINUED to help Linney go on frequent short walks, but cabin fever was setting in. She was glad when her new laptop arrived. After unpacking it and doing all the setup, she wasted no time. She ordered some loose pull-on pants, T-shirts, sweaters, slip-on shoes, and a nightgown and slippers that could arrive quickly and would be easy to put on. She couldn't wait to get out of her hospital gown. The hospital was being quite accommodating in letting her have deliveries. She sent MJ a list of things to pick up from her flat including the quilt from her reading chair, with some face creams and makeup. She wanted to start covering the bruises on her face that were all now turning nasty shades of green and yellow.

Linney's eyes lit up when MJ arrived. She held out her arms as MJ dropped her bags on the floor. She hadn't even stopped at her hotel first.

"Can I hug you? I need to hug you." She did her best not to react to the state of Linney's injuries, but Linney saw it in her eyes.

Linney nodded. "But gently. My ribs!" She sucked in a breath as MJ squeezed her.

"Did I hurt you?" MJ sprang back. "I'm so sorry. I'm just glad to see you. What about here? Can I sit on the corner of your bed?"

"Sit down. Tell me everything new with you? I'm so tired of hospital talk," she said, closing her eyes wearily.

MJ perched on the end of the bed. "I am so glad to see you. I'll save my questions for tomorrow." And with that, she was off on a monologue about London and the newsroom that didn't stop until she saw Linney yawn.

She pulled the quilt from her bag and held it out. Linney reached for it gratefully. "A little bit of home. Thank you." She stifled another yawn and with a kiss, MJ took her leave.

"Sleep well. I'll be back tomorrow."

MJ was better prepared the next morning, both mentally

and with treats. She arrived with German pastries and steaming cups of coffee—far superior to the hospital food Linney had been eating. Linney had more energy, so they took a very slow stroll around the hospital floor. When they came back to her room, Linney's package had arrived. MJ helped her dress, jokingly admonishing her for the plainness of the pull-on pants and T-shirts, but she understood they were required for the time being.

"When will they let you come home?" MJ asked tentatively after lunch.

"It's complicated," Linney admitted. "I think I'll be sprung from the hospital in about a week. But I can't travel. So I'll go to a rehabilitation facility for a while. And then? Well, I guess I'll come back to London to the newsroom. Mac will find me an editing job. I think my foreign assignment days are over."

"I'm sorry."

"It's not your fault. It's not anybody's fault. I just hoped I'd have longer in the field." She was still frustrated by that, and felt like being back in London would be a demotion. "But before anything else, I have to get back on my feet." She blinked back tears.

"Another spin around the floor?" MJ asked, trying to change the subject. Linney swiped at her eyes, nodded her head, and slowly stood up. "Your forehead is looking better today," MJ said.

"Yeah, I think the bruise will be gone soon. And the stitches are getting itchy. I hope they come out soon too. I guess it's all signs of healing."

They turned the corner, Linney shuffling a little less than she had yesterday. MJ glanced at her. "And are they sure about your vision?" Linney had told her the diagnosis, but her friend's bright blue eyes looked exactly the same to her.

"It looks that way. I'll have another specialist look at it when I get back to London, but it doesn't seem likely. I'm still learning about what restrictions that will mean for me." They walked in silence, and when they got back to her room, Linney winced as she bumped her shoulder on the doorframe. "I'll be so glad to get rid of this walker."

Together, they watched a movie on Linney's laptop to pass the afternoon and MJ snuck out to get a takeout meal of bratwurst and sauerkraut. "And black forest cake for dessert!" she exclaimed. As they tucked in, MJ told Linney she had news. "Toronto called. They're courting me for a position back in Canada to head up digital globally."

"That's amazing—congratulations! I'll miss you, but we can catch up when I get home for the holidays."

"Don't get ahead of yourself. I'm considering it, but there are still things I want to do in London. I'm not sure this is the right time."

After dinner, MJ and Linney made one last lap around the floor before MJ reluctantly said she had to go. "My flight is early tomorrow. The news never stops."

"Even if I'm not the one reporting it," Linney joked. "Go on. I'll be fine. But you'd better let me know what you decide about Toronto!"

MJ leaned down to hug Linney—gently this time. "I will. Now you call if you need anything. I'm coming back when you're settled at rehab. And I'll freshen up your flat when they let you come home."

"You are one of my favourite people," Linney whispered in her ear. "Thank you so much for coming."

With just her laptop to keep her company, Linney willed herself to heal. Little by little, she was starting to feel more like herself, but she was impatient. The bruises continued to fade, and when her stitches were removed, she could cover the last of them with makeup, but her ribs continued to bother her and walking was ridiculously tiring, she complained to Derek. She still needed a walker, but she was determined.

Finally the day came when Dr. Fischer came into her room wearing a big smile to give her the news.

"Today is the day, Ms. McDonnell," he told her. "You are healing nicely. I can't think of any reason to keep you here any longer."

Linney thought that news would make her happy, and it did, but it also filled her with nervousness and she was on the edge of her seat all day. She called MJ who instantly started planning to visit again. She called Jake to tell him she was done with hospitals. And of course, she called Derek, excited to be one step closer to getting her life back.

Unfortunately, moving to rehab was not quite as quick and easy as Linney expected. It took all day for the papers to be ready for her release from the hospital and for arrangements to be made with the facility and the transfer service. She had hoped to be graduating to crutches or a cane so was disappointed to learn that the walker was coming with her, and worse, that the transfer required a wheelchair.

It was late in the evening before the service attendant picked her up from the hospital and wheeled her into the beautiful facility. Linney carried her few possessions—the duffle bag of pull-on pants, a couple of books, and her computer—on top of the quilt on her lap. The attendant left her in the hands of a young nurse, who took her place behind her chair and wheeled her into the reception area.

"I am Ilse," she introduced herself. "After you have filled in some forms, I will take you to your suite and we will get you settled in."

"More forms?" Linney couldn't imagine there could be any more.

"*Ja*, I am afraid so." Ilse laughed brightly. "Our German bureaucracy demands much paperwork."

Fortunately, it was only one last signature, and Ilse whisked Linney off to a suite with a bedroom, a sitting room, and a tiny kitchenette with a fridge, a kettle, and a microwave. "I think you will like your new home. We'll have you more independent in no time." Linney saw all the new bouquets. "You seem to have a few admirers," Ilse continued as she spun around to face Linney with friendly, laughing eyes. "Linney knew right then that she was going to like Ilse.

27

———————

Linney hated Ilse. The sweet nurse who chatted with her when she arrived turned into a vicious taskmaster in rehab. As hard as Linney worked, Ilse pushed harder. Walking more often each day. Taking longer walks out into the flat concrete path in the gardens.

Within a few days, Ilse insisted Linney start tackling stairs, which made her hip ache all over again. But Ilse knew what she was doing. She taught her patient how to move in ways that she wouldn't twist her healing hip and ribs and every day, and Linney could do more. Ilse gave her a grabber so she could pick things up from the ground without having to bend over. The tiny kitchen in her suite meant she could supplement her meals, and Ilse took Linney to a local grocery store to get some basics. It was a humbling beginning.

When MJ returned two weeks later, she brought Linney a small suitcase of comfortable—but stylish—clothes and shoes with her, which cheered her up instantly. She could dispense with the fleece pants and T-shirts! Linney's bruises were gone now, and her ribs were finally beginning to hurt less.

"Not much," she answered honestly when MJ asked if her

memory of the explosion was getting better. "It was a complete blank at first, but parts of it are coming back to me. One minute I was working away, then there was this huge noise and a force that slammed me against the wall. The ceiling collapsed, and that's all." Linney shrugged her shoulders. "Next thing I knew, I was in a bed, in incredible pain and as blind as a bat, trying to figure out what had happened." She pushed her glasses up her nose.

"How is the pain now?" MJ asked.

"There's still a fair amount. But it's getting better every day. And you should see how fast I can get around with my walker now." She saw MJ react to that. "It's okay, I need to be able to joke about it. And actually, you're just in time to see it for yourself." She eased herself up from the chair slowly, put her hands on the walker and started toward the door. She banged the walker into the doorframe, a common occurrence. Ilse and a counsellor were helping her understand that was less due to the cumbersome walker, and more to do with her compromised depth perception, and they were teaching her how to deal with it. The bump jostled Linney's ribs, and she sucked air in through her teeth. MJ ran to help her. Linney sighed. "I'm fine," she said. "I bang into lots of things now, because of my eye."

"You used to bang into lots of things before, too," said MJ with a grin, and suddenly they burst into laughter, breaking the tension.

"Oh," Linney gasped. "Don't make me laugh. Ribs!" But she grinned, holding her midsection tightly.

They slowly walked the paved path around the quadrangle twice and then Linney took them back to her room where she proved she was competent enough to prepare coffee and snacks. She was happy for the company, but she was equally happy when MJ went home a few days later.

Linney had a lot of time to think in rehab and the counsellor helped her talk about Ernst. They dove into what it was about her that led her to look to older men. Ernst had been almost old enough to be her father. They hadn't had a relationship per se, and neither of them expected anything more from each other than the comfort they found in each other's arms when world events saw them end up in the same city. But it was a pattern, Linney realized. She'd always fantasized about her male high school teachers and then her university professors. Mac was the most significant relationship she'd ever had, and he too was almost twenty years older than her. Maybe it was time she started looking for men closer to her own age. Once she could get around properly, that was.

"So are you dating anyone?" Linney demanded, talking to Derek one evening—lunchtime for him.

Derek almost spat out his water. "Where did that come from?"

"I'm tired of talking about me. And my counsellor got me thinking about my own terrible track record. But what about you?" Linney let that hang in the air remembering the last time she'd asked, and then added softly, "I know I've been pushy. And I am sorry about that. But it's been four years. You can't be alone forever."

She could almost hear Derek rolling his eyes on the other end of the phone and she braced for an emotional response, but then he continued quietly. "First, you shouldn't be sorry. I know it comes from a good place. But it's hard. I have a full-time job, two young kids, and a mother in long-term care. And the dating pool in Silver Lake is not exactly huge."

"Those sound like excuses."

"Maybe they are, but please don't push me too hard on this. I've been on a few dates, but nobody's been special. And honestly? I don't want to be hurt again."

Linney nodded. She understood that. It was hard to let

someone new in when you'd had a relationship that had left scars.

As her hip and ribs continued to improve, Linney had more time to think not just about the past, but also about what was next for her. She graduated to a cane, but it became abundantly clear she wouldn't be able to handle the four flights of stairs to her London flat for a long time. And despite what the doctors told her, she worried that she would always have pain, and maybe a limp. She thought about taking a leave of absence from work and going home to Silver Lake to recover fully. And the more she thought about that, the more appealing going home felt and the less she wanted to go back to the network at all. She didn't know what was next, but it no longer felt like London was where she should be. She mentioned it on a call with Jake.

"I always thought you'd come home," he replied. "You'll stay with Rachael and me until you know what your next move is."

Linney shook her head, tiredly. "No, I need to go up to Silver Lake."

Jake had heard something in her voice and knew there was no point in arguing. "Just promise us you won't do something silly like try to go up the stairs to the office any time soon." At least he'd have his sister closer than if she was in London. He could go up and check on her from time to time if necessary.

With that decision made, Linney worked harder than ever with Ilse to increase her mobility and with a visual therapist to help her develop strategies to deal with her monocular vision. When she told her medical team she was going back to Canada, not the UK, they decided to keep her a couple of extra weeks because of the long flight. Linney talked every couple of days with Jake and with her Silver Lake friends. Everyone was full of questions about how she was progressing, and they were delighted to learn she was coming home.

"We'll be neighbours again," Derek said, making her smile.

Linney called him during his lunch every day. It was just after dinner time for her, and she insisted they talk about normal things. She needed someone who wasn't always asking her how she was.

MJ packed up Linney's flat and organized a consignment shop to take most of the hard furnishings and gave the linens and cushions that she hadn't wanted for herself to a charity shop. MJ had turned down the job in Toronto in the end—for now, she said—and told them to think about her again in a few years.

Linney had one last phone call with Mac, when she'd handed in her notice. "You go knock 'em dead back home," said Mac gruffly. "Any news shop would be glad to have you." Linney knew he would write her a glowing recommendation, but she also knew she wasn't ready to go back to a newsroom. Not now. Maybe never.

28

As nice as the rehab facility was, Linney couldn't wait to be in her own bed at the lake. It was early September when days were still hot, but nighttime temperatures were perfect for sleeping with the windows wide open. She was ready. Ilse had worked her hard, and it showed. Linney was comfortable with just her cane, her ribs were healed, and she was mentally and physically strong. Finally, her team agreed she could go home. Jake travelled to Germany to get her, while Anna and Kirsten readied the house at the lake.

When Jake arrived, Linney was walking steadily—if slowly—down the corridor, using her cane. She saw him coming and waved. He put down his bag and walked toward her. She saw tears in his eyes and rolled her own. She was tired of this reaction from people.

"Hey you," he said tenderly, gathering her into a big brotherly hug. He pushed back his emotions and finally released her.

"Jake, I'm fine," she said. "Not one hundred percent yet, but I'm good. Honestly." The hug had hardly bothered her ribs at all. Jake only believed his sister after he'd had a long talk with her doctors, who'd insisted on her having a travel companion.

The trip home was uneventful. Jake rolled their carry-on bags through the airport and Linney remembered to tell the security people that she had a metal plate and screws in her hip and showed her documentation when she set off the security alarm. Jake walked slowly beside her as she leaned on her cane through the departure hall. Linney didn't remember the Frankfurt airport being quite so big. Obstinate, as usual, she refused a wheelchair or a ride on the in-terminal shuttle service. "I'm not an invalid," she insisted, as the driver pulled away, beeping the horn to get other passengers to move. But she had to admit that she was tired when they finally got to the gate.

They'd splurged on business class tickets so Linney could lie down properly, but she was restless, dozing fitfully through the flight. There was no luggage to collect in Toronto, so they walked straight from the airplane through the airport. Just like Frankfurt, it seemed to have doubled in length since Linney had last flown home and her steps were slow as she limped through customs. She was visibly relieved when they finally made it to the exit. Jake had phoned his wife when they landed, and she was waiting with their big SUV at the curb, watching for them.

"Welcome home," Rachael said when they reached her. She gave Linney a gentle hug and took her bag, putting it in the trunk beside Jake's. "Linney, do you need help getting into the car?"

"I can do it, Rachael. Honestly." But once she was in, and Jake closed the door, Linney closed her eyes. She was exhausted and frustrated by her limitations.

Jake jumped in the back of the car and Rachael pulled gently into traffic. She looked at her passenger. "Are you sure you won't stay for more than one night? Just until you're feeling stronger?"

Linney opened her eyes and shook her head. "Thank you, but I just want to go home."

THE NEXT MORNING, Linney was still tired, but there was some colour back in her face. Rachael quietly dished up eggs and sausages for the family. A hearty breakfast, Linney supposed, designed to build back her strength.

"Linney, can you pass the pepper, please?" Jake asked her.

"Sure," she said, reaching out for the pepper mill. She missed it by several inches. Seeing the shocked look on the kids' faces, she explained, as she concentrated hard to pick it up and passed it to her brother. "My brain isn't compensating yet for the fact that I only have one working eye. Depth perception is hard for me. So is peripheral vision." She continued for Rachael's sake. "Jake will tell you I keep bumping into things on my right side. It will get better. But it will take a bit more time."

Rachael smiled weakly.

Linney slept in the car as Jake drove up to the lake, stirring only when they got close to town. "Will you drive down Main Street?" she asked. I always love to see what's new and I'm not sure how long it will be before I can get into town myself."

"You know, I'm still not sure I love you being up here without a car," Jake said, protective as ever.

"You know they won't let me drive yet," Linney replied. "My hip should be good enough in a few more weeks, but I'll have to have my vision assessed too."

"That's why we all wanted you to stay in the city."

"I'll be back. But for now, I need to be here. I won't be alone, Anna and Kirsten are here and Derek is right next door. And besides," she teased, "they have this new-fangled thing called home delivery. I can get just about anything I need sent straight to the house." She yawned. "I think I need to sleep for a few days first! I can't believe how tired I am."

Jake slowed the car as they drove down through Silver Lake. First she saw the elementary school she'd gone to, and that Derek's kids attended now. She was pleased to see that the bakery and the wool shop were still there, along with the Doughnut Hut and a number of little restaurants and cafés that had made it through the winter. Anna's dance studio came into view and they passed Derek's office. A block away from that was the long-term care home where his mother had moved last year. Page Turners still looked grand, taking up most of a heritage building. Linney wondered for a moment whether the store had seen its last summer. Kirsten had told her that the owners had never quite gotten it off the ground and that there were rumours they were about to give up.

Finally on the end of the street closest to her house was the variety store that a refugee family that the local church had sponsored a few years ago had recently bought. As they turned onto the road that ran along the lake, Linney noticed that the trees were starting to turn. A little bit of yellow here, some orange there, and just a touch of red at the tree tops. October was right around the corner and soon the trees would be in full fall foliage, and the accompanying town festival would be in full swing.

A few minutes later, the house came into view and Linney felt a sense of calm come over her as the wheels of the car crunched on the gravel driveway. Jake put the car in park and turned to face her. "You have to promise to take things easy, and to call if you need anything. Anything at all. Even if it's just to talk." He helped Linney out of the car and she used her cane to gingerly climb the few stairs up to the porch one at a time, and then into the house.

Linney came to a halt as soon as she opened the door. It was the first time she had seen the renovations Danny and his team had done. Her sketches and ideas had come to life.

"They did a great job, didn't they?" Jake said, putting his hand on her shoulder. "The kids and I spent some time up here this summer, so thank you, but I'm glad you can enjoy it now." He put her bag down. "Kirsten and Anna unpacked the boxes that your friend MJ packed up and shipped."

Linney nodded. "You've all been so good to me." She was still taking in the changes. Sage green cabinets warmed up the kitchen and white countertops kept it bright. Danny had added pot lights around the work surfaces and the refinished wide pine floorboards gleamed. Paint on the walls made everything seem new again. But the old kitchen table, with its decades of dents and scratches was still there, and Linney was overcome with emotion. She was home.

"Clothes are in your dresser and Kirsten did the best she could to put your books and knickknacks into good places. Give her a call if you can't find something." Jake's words brought Linney back, and she nodded, noticing some small trinkets from London on the mantel, beside a new mason jar full of her stones. "Anna did some grocery shopping. Take a quick look in your new kitchen and see if there's something you need that she didn't buy. I can run into town before I go."

"Jake, you're amazing. All of you. I write for a living and I have no words to thank you." She turned around and he could see tears in her eyes. She ran her hand along the scarred kitchen table. "It feels so good to be here."

He took Linney's bag into her bedroom as she opened kitchen cupboards. "Looks like Anna did a great job," she called to him. "She even remembered popcorn!"

Jake came back into the kitchen. "I don't suppose you'll let me stay for a few nights?"

Linney put a hand on her hip and cocked her head. "Jake!"

"Okay, okay." He put his hands up in the air. "How about a cup of coffee and a sandwich for the road then?"

She smiled. "That, I can do."

Linney unpacked after Jake left and folded the quilt at the end of her bed. There was a gentle knock on her door mid-afternoon. Linney slowly made her way across the room and opened it to see Derek's face. She smiled wearily. She didn't need artifice with him; she could just be herself. "It's good to see you."

He hugged her gently, afraid she might break. "I thought I'd never see you again," he said, the emotion creeping into his voice made stronger because of their argument. He beat it back. "I'm so glad you're home. Tell me what you need."

"Let's sit. I'm just so tired." He took her hand and led her out to the porch swing where they'd sat so many times before. He put his arm around her and she leaned into him. "Where are the kids?" she asked after a while.

"It's a school day. They'll be off the bus in an hour."

"How are they old enough to be in school?" she asked, shaking her head in wonder.

"I know. It was hard to let Ivy get on that school bus for junior kindergarten the first time a couple of weeks ago. But what about Anna and Danny—they've got one going to university next year!"

"Impossible. Will you bring the kids over later?" Linney made a noise as she repositioned herself on the swing.

"Sore?" he asked, and she nodded. "Do you have painkillers?"

"In my purse on the counter. But—" Derek was already at the door. He returned a minute later with a bottle of prescription pills and a glass of water. "Thanks. I was hoping I was done with these, but all the travel has set me back a bit." She put two pills in her hand and swallowed them down with a sip of water. "Okay, more than a bit. But I'll be fine in a few days."

"What does fine look like for you right now?" he probed gently.

"All my bumps and bruises are gone. No brain damage." She tried to make a joke, but it fell flat as Derek flinched, reminded of the possibility. She started again, knowing there was no need for bravery with him. "Honestly? It's still a work in progress. My ribs are finally good—I can't believe how long they took to heal—and I have a limp that gets works when I'm tired. I won't be walking to town any time soon. And then there's this awful cane. The doctor said it would probably take two or three more weeks before I can get rid of it. Possibly even more, but I don't think so. They're sending records to the hospital here and I have an appointment with a Silver Lake specialist in two days who will monitor me."

Linney took another sip of water and rubbed her hip. "That's the easy part. Or maybe I should say the part with a known path forward. My eye, on the other hand? The vision limitations are taking some time to get used to." She rested her head on his shoulder and closed her eyes.

Derek said nothing, letting Linney take her time. "I still get dizzy sometimes," she said quietly. "And I keep bumping into things that I used to be able to see out of the corner of my eye. Door frames, tables, bookshelves—things like that.

"I was surprised that the crowds in the airport made me anxious," she continued, reluctantly, looking back up at him. "It's okay now while I have the cane, because people give me a wide berth, but I'm a worried about how it'll work when I look 'normal' again."

"How's your depth perception?" he asked, knowing that was important from the reading he'd done. Linney laughed. "Not so great then," he surmised.

She shook her head. "They say my brain will fully accommodate for it in time, but for now it's a work in progress. And that's important. I'll need that, and range of vision to get behind the wheel of a car again."

They sat together for a few more minutes and then Derek looked at his watch.

"Do you have somewhere to be?" Linney asked.

"School bus time. I'm sorry. I have to go," he said, standing up. "I'll come back when the kids are in bed." He didn't think she was up to them visiting just yet.

"That'd be nice," she said. "And Derek? Thank you."

Linney watched as Derek bounded down the steps and ran across the lawn, disappearing into his house, and wondered when she'd be able to do that again. She closed her eyes and rocked on the swing. It was so good to be home.

ANNA AND KIRSTEN video chatted with Derek that evening while he brushed Leo and Ivy's hair after their bath. "I'm going back over when the munchkins are asleep," he told them. "But here's what I can tell you based on what I saw this afternoon."

Derek suggested that for the first week at least, they go one at a time. Linney was far more tired than she was admitting to. She was only a few weeks post-surgery, and she'd had a long journey home.

"She's still taking strong pain pills, but I think that's because she's pushing herself more than she probably should," he started. "Also, she's having trouble with her eyesight, even though her eye looks perfectly normal." He switched subjects. "I can get her to medical appointments but Anna, maybe you can help with groceries for the next while? We don't know when she'll be able to drive. And Kirsten, Linney has some specialists to see at the hospital and I'm sure she'd appreciate your opinion on the doctors."

"Ouch! That hurts, Daddy!" Derek gave Ivy a kiss. The comb had come across tangles in his daughter's hair. He worked through them gently. "Sorry, sweetie. Go pick some stories, guys. Daddy will be there to read in a few minutes." They ran off and he turned his attention back to the grownups. "I'm back. Questions?"

"So many." Anna was trying to take in everything Derek had said. "But I'm not sure where to start. I'll come by tomorrow morning."

"I'll take the next day, after work," Kirsten chimed in. "Just call me, Derek, when you take Linney to the hospital. I'll come and help her manage the bureaucracy and run interference for her."

"Thanks, ladies," Derek said. "I'm going to text Jake later tonight and give him a status update. We'll get her through this."

"Come on in, Derek," Linney called out when she heard him knock on the door an hour later. "They're asleep?"

He nodded and held up the baby monitor. Linney was sitting on the couch, with her legs straight out in front of her and a bowl of popcorn on her lap. "Now tell me," he jokingly interrogated her grabbing a handful for himself. "This isn't dinner, is it?"

She grinned. "No. I actually made salad and an omelette. It was the first time I've made a meal in a full kitchen in a long time. Do you want a cup of tea?" She started to get up. "Or a beer?" she added as an afterthought.

"Stay there. I'll make us some tea. At least for this week, let us—me and Kirsten and Anna—take care of you. After that, you're on your own," he warned her, jokingly. Derek put on the kettle, dropping tea bags into oversized mugs.

Linney shifted on the couch, making room for Derek and they sipped their tea and polished off the popcorn, neither feeling the need for conversation. Finally, Linney looked over at him. "I have a long road ahead of me," she said quietly. "I realized today it's longer than I thought." She put up her hand to silence Derek as he started to speak. "I'm not too proud to admit I'm going to need help. I'm sure you've talked with the girls already." Derek nodded. "I'm going to owe you all a lot after this."

Linney slept better that night than she had in—well, she couldn't remember how long. The night was cool, but she opened the windows and lay in bed with heavy eyelids, listening to the comforting sounds of the waves on the shore and snuggling under the quilt that Gran made so many years ago.

29

Linney woke the next morning feeling rested. She was a bit nervous about the shower, but she saw that someone—Danny, she guessed—had installed a grab bar for her. She dressed and started reading the news on her iPad when she heard a car in her driveway. She made her way to the porch and broke into a huge smile when she saw Anna walking up holding what looked like two takeout cups of coffee and some kind of home-made treat.

"I can smell that from here," Linney shouted. "I love your baking."

They sat at the kitchen table and after Linney thanked Anna for stocking her cupboards, they made small talk as they dug into the strudel. Anna's daughters were both in high school now, so there were many stories to tell.

"They're totally boy crazy," Anna said.

"Do you remember our first dance?"

"It was Halloween, right?"

"Yep. You were a ballerina—as usual—and Kirsten dressed up as a clown."

"And you were—oh my gosh, you were Amelia Earhart! You

were an adventurer even back then." Anna's memories came rushing back. "I had my first kiss that night. Oh—and your crush kissed someone else." Linney nodded. It was so long ago. "Didn't Derek spend the rest of the night cheering you up?"

"He did. Even then, he was rescuing me."

"What's next for you?" Anna asked, after a few moments.

"I'm not sure," Linney said honestly. "The next month or two are just about getting better. I haven't thought beyond that." She put her fork down. "But I'm not going back to London. I know that for sure. My nieces and nephew are growing up too fast—and your kids too. I hardly know any of them. I think the explosion ..." Anna tried not to react to that word, but it was hard. "... the explosion taught me a bit about my own mortality. I suddenly feel the need to be close to family and friends."

Anna reached out across the table. "Well, we're glad you're back." Her voice lowered to a whisper. "Linney, we were so worried."

"Don't get all maudlin on me. I can't stand those pitying looks people give me and I'm tired of having to tell people I'm fine. Now," she said firmly, getting to her feet and reaching for her cane, "with all this travelling, I've been sitting too much. Will you walk around the property with me? It will be slow, but I'd still like it if you'd walk with me.

Linney took the porch stairs one at a time, with both feet on each step before tackling the next one like her grandmother had in her last years. It drove her crazy, but for once in her life, she was determined to follow the rules to the letter and her rehab team had told her that it would be up to her doctor at home. It was top of her list to ask about tomorrow. Until then, it was one step at a time. She didn't want to do anything that would make her recovery harder or longer.

They walked slowly around Linney's property. Up the side she shared with Derek, across the front by the road, down the other side where the creek ran and across the shoreline of the lake. It wouldn't be long before the trees were ablaze in colour. This was the first time Linney was walking on rough terrain and it was decidedly more difficult than the flat paths around the gardens she was used to or the long airport halls. It was humbling to be so tired when they stopped at the dock. She looked longingly out over the lake, wondering when she'd be able to get herself into her kayak again.

"Thanks for coming, Anna." Linney put on her game face, refusing to feel sorry for herself.

"You'll call me, or text if you need anything, right? I know you hate to lean on people, but now is the time. You can pay me back by rescuing me from my teenagers when you're feeling stronger."

Linney threw her head back and laughed heartily. "It's a deal," she agreed.

After Anna left, Linney went back to her online news and then puttered in the kitchen, making some soup and toast for lunch. She napped on the couch for a couple of hours and then did the exercises Ilse had drilled into her. Stretching her muscles felt good.

Linney poured herself a glass of water and took stock properly of the contents of her kitchen cabinets. She took out a bag of chocolate chips to make cookies. She beat together the butter and sugar and added eggs. Soon the other ingredients were added and she shaped small cookies and put the cookie sheet into the oven. The timer beeped ten minutes later. Linney's glasses fogged annoyingly when she opened the oven door and her stomach grumbled. Easing the cookies off the pan and placing them on the rack to cool, she grabbed one for herself and groaned with delight over the melted chocolate goodness. Linney found a tin to put the cooled treats in and waited. Soon, she heard the school bus, and saw two children wearing backpacks that looked bigger than them jump out and run next door. She picked up her cookie tin and her cane and slowly made her way across the lawn.

DEREK HAD a lunch box in his hand and a look of surprise on his face when he answered the door.

"Linney?"

"Are you going to let me in?" She lifted the tin slightly. "I made cookies."

Derek pulled the door open. "Of course. Come in. Just watch out for the kids." He heard the water turn off in the bathroom and the laughter of the children. "Leo, Ivy, come see your Auntie Linney." They came barrelling out to join them, and despite all his warnings, threw themselves at her.

"Oohh!" Linney wasn't prepared for that, and stumbled into Derek.

"Kids," he reprimanded sharply, as he helped steady Linney on her feet. "We have to be gentle with Auntie Linney for a bit, remember?"

"Are you okay, Auntie Linney?" asked Leo repentantly.

"I'm just fine, Leo," she replied brightly for the kids. But Derek could see through it and knew her confidence was shaken. "I brought you something. Maybe your dad will let you have it for your after-school snack." Linney sat down at the breakfast bar and gestured for them to join her. The kindergarteners scrambled up onto the high stools and she opened the tin.

"Cookies!" exclaimed Ivy, bouncing with excitement. "Daddy, can we?"

"Yes you *may*," he replied, emphasizing the grammar point and opening the fridge for some milk. "You'll spoil them, Linney. Home baking is pretty rare around here." He wiped out the lunch boxes and put reusable juice boxes in the dishwasher.

Linney listened as Leo and Ivy chattered away about their days. She nibbled on another cookie and Derek put a glass of milk in front of her with a wink. How many times had they had cookies and milk together after school, she wondered, remembering years gone by.

The kids slid off their stools to go and play.

"I'll let you get on with your evening," she said to Derek.

"Thank you for the cookies," said Ivy shyly.

"You're welcome, Ivy. We'll do it again soon, okay?" She started toward the front door and banged into the corner of a book shelf with her shoulder. "Ouch!"

Derek was at her side immediately. She shrugged him off and rubbed her shoulder. "I have to get used to this. I'll see you tomorrow, Derek."

LINNEY WAS MORE upset than she'd let on. As she made her way slowly across the lawn all she could think about was how she'd turned back into the awkward, klutzy kid she'd been. The capable and independent woman with a successful career had disappeared. She felt fragile and her body still didn't feel like her own. She was still frustrated as she climbed up the stairs to her porch. She wasn't paying enough attention and caught her foot on the lip of the top step and had to catch herself from falling. Her humiliation was complete when she closed the door behind her and smashed her shin on the coffee table. Linney collapsed on the couch and sobbed as the loss of everything— her career, her flat in London, her independence, her lover— overwhelmed her. She cried and cried until there were no more tears left and she fell asleep.

When she woke, it was dark, and she was hungry. Checking

her watch, Linney was surprised to discover it was almost midnight. She was stiff from sleeping on the couch for almost seven hours. Stretching, Linney picked up her cane and found leftover salad from the previous night in the fridge. She picked at it, leaning on the counter and then polished off two pieces of toast before peeling an orange. Hunger sated, but still sleepy, she lay down in bed and quickly fell back to sleep.

Linney was still feeling sorry for herself the next morning. Bruises were forming on her shoulder and shin, and her hip ached from the challenge of walking on uneven ground. She headed for the kitchen. Maybe coffee would shake this mood.

DEREK NOTICED the kitchen lights on next door as he waited at the end of the driveway with the kids. When the school bus pulled away, he decided to check in on Linney rather than go back home right away. He jumped up the few steps to the porch and was just about to knock on the door when he heard the sound of shattering china.

"Linney, are you alright?" He was alarmed and knocked loudly.

"Go away, Derek."

"Linney, what's going on? Let me in." Derek banged on the door again.

"Go away," she repeated, sounding upset.

"I heard something break. I'm worried about you."

"Go away, Derek. I'm serious."

Derek wasn't going anywhere. This was what he'd promised Jake. That he'd take care of her even when she pushed him away. The door wasn't locked, so he turned the handle and pushed it open. Linney stood in the kitchen with her cane and still in her pajamas, with tears sliding down her cheeks again. He came toward her to see what had happened. In the kitchen, he found the carafe on the counter, sitting in a pool of spilled coffee that was dripping onto the floor, a shattered mug by the opposite wall and what looked like a coffee explosion. "What happened?"

"I'm fine." Linney took off her glasses and swiped at the tears. She put them back on and wanted to scream when she saw the look of pity in his eyes.

Derek shook his head. "You're not fine. Not yet." He spoke sharply, to make the point and Linney felt her anger continue to rise. "You'll be fine again, I promise. But you need to learn to accept some help—at least for now."

"Derek."

"Linney, you were my lifeline after Olivia left. Let me help you now." She sighed with exasperation, but sat down. Derek knew a victory when he saw one. He grabbed a tea towel and started mopping up the mess. "What happened?" he asked again, gently now.

She sniffed. "I missed when I tried to pour the coffee. Depth perception. I keep forgetting." She hung her head.

"And the mug?" Derek gestured at the shards of china on the other side of the room.

Linney looked up at him sheepishly. "I got frustrated." They looked at each other, and burst out laughing.

LINNEY HELPED Derek clean up the mess, feeling lighter now. They talked for a while and then he headed into town to run an errand, returning early in the afternoon to take her to the hospital to meet with her new specialists.

Linney was nervous, but excited to meet her new team. She fiddled with the strap on her purse as Derek parked the car. He'd wanted to drop her at the door and then park the car, but she insisted she could walk the short distance. Slowly, they made their way in and Linney filled out a figurative tonne of paperwork while Derek texted Kirsten to let her know they'd arrived.

The orthopedic specialist was pleased with Linney's progress. What he saw in her charts convinced him that as long as she kept doing her physiotherapy, she'd be able to throw away the cane in no time. He thought she could be driving in four to six weeks, assuming her vision tests came back within an appropriate range. The most immediate thing was that he green-lit the return to walking up and down stairs normally. There was a knock on the door and Kirsten joined them, giving Linney a hug and the doctor a warm smile. The doctor picked up a list of physiotherapists from his desk and Kirsten reached out her hand and quickly scanned the list, nodding positively.

"There are some solid names here, Linney. Not just here, but in Bridgegrove too. I'll help you find someone who's a good fit, someone who will come to the house and push you just the right amount."

Linney smiled wryly, remembering her love-hate relationship with Ilse. She thanked the doctor for his time, and the two women left together and rejoined Derek. Kirsten helped them find the ophthalmologist in the maze of hospital corridors.

"It's silly for you both to be here waiting with me," said Linney, while they sat. "I can do this on my own, you know. I just need a ride when I'm done."

Kirsten nodded her head. "Derek, why don't you head home. I'll see Linney through her other appointments, and I can get her home. I was going to go over tonight anyway. This will give us a chance to catch up properly."

"Are you sure?"

"As long as Linney agrees."

Linney nodded vigorously. "You're doing so much for me already, Derek. I'll talk to you later tonight."

Kirsten stayed with Linney while the ophthalmologist

looked at her eye and then pored over her records, hoping to give Linney better news than she had received to date. Finally, he shook his head.

"I wish I had better news for you. Unfortunately, your doctor in Germany was right. The nerve damage is severe, and from what I can see, permanent." Linney nodded. She hadn't seen any change since she'd woken up that awful day in Germany, so this news wasn't unexpected. "But it's not all bad," the doctor continued. "Plenty of people live full, normal lives with monocular vision. Here's a list of therapists who can help with that. We just need to retrain your brain a bit." Kirsten scanned. She had less experience with the names on this list, but she still recognized several.

"What about driving?" Linney asked. This was the one thing that could cause a problem if she planned to stay in Silver Lake.

"Absolutely," he assured her. "As long as you have a normal field of vision, it won't be an issue. We can test in a month, but I see nothing in your charts that would suggest there will be any problems. And then you'll just need to retake your test."

Linney breathed a sigh of relief. This was good news.

The women walked to Linney's third and final appointment of the day. A psychiatrist. Linney bristled at this appointment. She'd always been able to deal with problems in her life and she didn't love the idea of accepting this kind of help. Kirsten was kind but firm. "You know, it's just as important to look after your mental health as your physical health, Linney."

"I know, I know. It's just..."

"Don't knock therapy, Linney. Give it a fair shake. It's helped me in the past, and you've been through something pretty traumatic." Linney raised her eyebrows at this revelation, but Kirsten ignored it and continued. "Dr. Aslan has a good reputation. I'm going to leave you and I'll be back in an hour and then we can figure out what to do next."

"Thanks. I seem to be saying that a lot these day. But I really will try to have an open mind about therapy. There was someone in Germany and TCN would have insisted on me seeing someone if I had come back from an assignment. Mac still sees someone. I just never expected I would need it."

Linney's appointment with Dr. Aslan was a pleasant surprise. She hadn't expected the therapist to be her age. She seemed friendly and had a faint accent that Linney couldn't place. Dr. Aslan took the time to explain her approach and together they set up a schedule of weekly appointments through the end of the year.

"I think I'll like her," Linney told Kirsten. "I wasn't expecting to."

"I told you. Dr. Aslan has been in Silver Lake for a couple of years now and she's built a great reputation. Now, I'm taking you out to dinner."

Linney didn't dissuade her. It had been a long afternoon, and she didn't feel like cooking. While they waited for their order to arrive, they talked with a number of townspeople who stopped by to welcome Linney home and offer their help if she needed anything. She smiled and thanked them, but was determined to be as self-sufficient as possible.

Over pizza and iced tea—she didn't want to drink while she was still on painkillers—Linney and Kirsten discussed the team who would be helping her. Kirsten talked about the various physiotherapists and agreed to call a couple in the morning to test how they'd work together. "Combined with the others, you'll have a crack team," Kirsten said. "You're in good hands, Linney."

30

Linney worked hard and pushed herself as fast as she could. Her physical therapist was impressed but in therapy, Dr. Aslan kept cautioning her to go slowly and take the time to figure out what she wanted to do next,. Linney was itching to make plans and had been thinking about getting an apartment in Toronto and doing some freelance writing, or maybe consulting. "Don't rush," Dr. Aslan kept telling her. "You have the luxury of time. Make sure your next move is right for you."

September turned into October, and Linney began to confidently walk without a cane, although she still limped when she was tired. To build back her muscles, Linney started making the two kilometre walk into town often. Suddenly she wasn't completely reliant on Anna, who was taking her to the grocery store every week. She was taking the time to cook properly, and rediscovering, after years, how much she loved being in the kitchen. Derek and the kids were often the beneficiaries of this rediscovered passion, but she also loved having Kirsten and Anna over for dinner.

She sometimes dropped into Vi's Café or the Doughnut

Hut, and old school friends would stop and say hello. And from time to time, she visited Anna at her dance studio, amazed at how she and her teachers kept the little preschoolers in line.

To keep the rumour mill at bay, Linney joined KnitWorks, at least until she figured out what her next move was, she told them. It was a tough decision—she had always thought that while the group's charitable activities were good, they also embodied all she disliked about small town life. And after the first week, she was sure she was right. They bombarded her with questions, many of which she didn't feel like answering. But she went back the next week and as she made progress knitting a scarf for the charity box, and listened to conversations about how to shore up some of the poorer families in town, she found herself being drawn into this circle and wanting to help as well.

So when Avril, who had been a year ahead of her in school, and who now had four school-aged boys, asked for some last-minute volunteers for their booth at the Fall Festival, Linney found herself with her hand up. "I don't know what came over me," she told Dr. Aslan.

"What do you think it means?" asked the doctor.

Linney thought for a minute, now used to the doctor's long pauses. "I guess I'm looking for some kind of community. I love Silver Lake, but I never expected to find that with KnitWorks."

Dr. Aslan nodded. "Sometimes home appears where you least expected it. I certainly never thought I'd find a small town in Canada as my home. But I love it here." It was rare for Dr. Aslan to share about her own life.

Linney sighed. "It's just strange when you consider how much I wanted to leave as a kid. Derek too. But he's found a home here with his kids."

"Could you be happy here?"

There was another silence while Linney pondered the question. She knew by now that Dr. Aslan wouldn't fill it, just as she hadn't as a journalist. "Maybe. I think so. I just don't know what I'd do here."

"There are your grandmother's books." Linney had made her way up the stairs beyond the blue door to the office and had talked with Dr. Aslan about Gran's drafts. "Or maybe you have a book you want to write about your experiences. You could go back to reporting. You could do something entirely different. Let's make that your homework for this week. To think about all the ways you could earn a living in Silver Lake." She closed her notebook. Their session was finished.

Linney nodded. "Thank you, Dr. Aslan."

"Same time next week?"

"I'll be here."

～

JUST BEFORE THE FALL FESTIVAL, Linney stopped in at Page Turners. It was quiet in the store, but then again, it never seemed busy. She struck up a conversation with the owners.

"Honestly, we're thinking of selling," the woman said to Linney. "We jumped into this without thinking. We've given it a good go, but it's just not a good fit for us."

Her husband nodded in agreement and he sounded frustrated when he added, "I just hope we can find a buyer quickly. We've spent more than six years trying to make this work."

"I'm sorry," Linney said kindly, putting the book she'd just purchased into her purse, but thoughts were suddenly turning over in her head, and when she got home, instead of reading, she started scribbling notes.

The day of the Fall Festival dawned crisp and bright—the perfect autumn day. The trees were at their peak, and Silver Lake was all dressed up in its finest. Anna and Danny's cottages were booked, and Kirsten was crossing her fingers that nothing bad would keep them busy at the hospital. It was one last weekend of high tourism before the cold of winter set in and Silver Lake families tightened their belts.

The festival grounds were crowded. Cottagers and visitors from other towns bought honey, cheese, and maple syrup, all produced by Silver Lake residents. They browsed at stalls that sold paintings, jewellery, and quilts. Linney did roaring business at the KnitWorks stall, selling mittens, gloves, and hats to raise money so the group could do even bigger things for the community. She was glad to finally be done with her cane. It would have been cumbersome with all the commotion. There were still people she hadn't seen in the weeks that she'd been home so there was lots of chatting and catching up. In the middle of the afternoon, Ivy and Leo came running up to her booth. Behind them was their father.

"Can you take a break?" Derek asked. They were spending most evenings together now. Either she would walk across the lawn to join him and the kids—they still liked it when she read bedtime stories, or better yet made up new ones—or he would come to her place, monitor in hand, after they were in bed. Sometimes they would play card games, or talk, or watch TV. Often Derek brought over his laptop or a book and Linney would have music playing quietly in the background while she wrote or read. They were just comfortable together.

Linney looked around the booth. There were several other KnitWorkers there. "Sure," she told Derek, and she took off her apron. "I'll be back soon," she called over her shoulder.

Ivy slipped her little hand into Linney's and Derek chased Leo as they headed down to the lake's edge. Derek opened a package of kettle corn he'd bought and they shared it as they watched the children play. Linney wandered down to the shore and picked up a flat stone. She flicked her wrist, expecting the stone to skip nicely on the flat lake surface, but it hit the water awkwardly and sank. She tried again. Same result.

"You've lost your touch," Derek joked, coming up behind her. He sent a stone skittering across the lake.

Linney tried again. Kerplunk. "I think it's my eye," she said and Derek suddenly felt guilty. "I can't get the angle right. Just one more thing to relearn." She was more matter-of-fact and less angry about it now. Therapy was helping, she realized.

~

RED, gold, and orange leaves were tumbling down in the wind when Derek saw Kirsten drop Linney at her house the following week. The two women hugged. But instead of going into her house, Linney started walking over to his. She had something in her hand and a huge grin on her face. He met her at the front door.

Linney waved the paper in front of him excitedly. "I got it! I borrowed Kirsten's car. I can drive again!"

"Why didn't you ask me? I would have taken you."

"A girl has to have a few secrets," she said slyly. "My field of vision tests came back last week and my ophthalmologist signed off." Linney hadn't banged into anything recently either and she knew her brain was finally adapting. "Kirsten and Anna have been letting me practise on their cars. But, if I didn't pass, I didn't want you to know it."

"Still," he said, "I'd have liked to have taken you."

"You can still help. How would you like to take me car shopping?"

~

LINNEY BOUGHT AN SUV. It was a bit bigger than she needed, but it was high off the ground, which made it easy to get into. An upgrade package gave her both front and back cameras that would alert her if she got too close to something. It was a small price to pay to help compensate for her vision.

But a new driver's license wasn't the only secret Linney was keeping from Derek. She'd had several more discussions with the owners of Page Turners and she thought she knew where they'd gone wrong. She was convinced she could make the bookstore a thriving part of the community again. What surprised her was how much she wanted to do it.

"Would it be weird if I talked with your parents?" she asked Kirsten as she sat on her friend's couch one evening. Tuesday dinner and drinks had become a regular occurrence for the two single women and this time it was upstairs from the bookstore. Kirsten poured wine into their glasses, chosen to accompany the charcuterie board she'd put together. "I think I can do this, but I'd love to have their input. They made Page Turners so special and I'm sure they'd have good advice."

"They'd be thrilled! But are you sure you want to take this on? I thought you'd probably be in Toronto by summertime and just come and visit us on weekends."

Linney took a long sip of wine. "I think I do. I have loads of ideas, and I'm comfortable here. Even when I was home last summer, it was hard to leave."

Kirsten put down her glass and gave Linney a hug. "Welcome home."

"Don't celebrate too soon—there's still a lot to sort out and it might fall apart. But I'm really excited. I want to bring in better stock, have a children's room, do author readings, and hold other events. I think with the right combination I can bring traffic from Bridgeport and maybe beyond. I have some great ideas about partnering with our old school and—"

"Stop!" Kirsten laughed. "You're making me dizzy with all these ideas."

"Sorry, I just get excited when I think about it." Linney

popped a cherry tomato into her mouth. "But I would like to talk to your folks. Maybe they'll temper my enthusiasm."

But that wasn't the case and with their encouragement, Linney was even more excited than ever. She crunched all the numbers with the help of the local accountant. It was a big decision—not just financially, but also in how it would tie her to Silver Lake—so she talked it over with Dr. Aslan as well, but she was convinced this was the right decision. She was almost ready to make an offer. All she needed now was a lawyer!

THE LAWYER next door had his own secret. A new stenographer in Bridgegrove had caught Derek's eye when he'd been in court recently. They'd spoken several times outside the courthouse and he learned Sharon was a single parent of two, like him. They shared a few stories, and he surprised himself one day by asking her to join him for a cup of coffee, and when that went well, for a dinner date.

Nervously, he pulled a blazer on over a button-down shirt and jeans. "Be good for Gabby, okay," he told the children. Danny had dropped his daughter off to babysit a few minutes earlier.

Conversation with Sharon was harder than Derek expected. It had been so easy at the courthouse and he thought they might have a lot in common. But tonight, he was having to work hard at it. Sharon spent most of their appetizers and main course complaining about her ex-husband. Derek thought her ex sounded like a real jerk, but it wasn't the conversation he was hoping to have with her. When their dessert arrived, he tried to change the subject. "So what do you do for fun in Bridgegrove?" he asked.

"Well, I haven't been able to do much since my ex left," Sharon started. And then she was off again complaining about child support and visitation. Derek found his mind wandering, and he was more than happy to pay the cheque and walk Sharon to her car, thanking her for a lovely evening. He made no promise to call. He was beginning to think he'd never get to a third date with a woman. As he drove home, his mind drifted to his next-door neighbour. Leo had extracted a promise from her to come for pancakes tomorrow. At least that would be easy.

EASY MIGHT HAVE BEEN AN OVERSTATEMENT. Derek watched Linney dodge the raindrops as she made her way over for the promised breakfast while he tried to supervise the chaos. Leo stood on a stool in front of the stove with a spatula in his hands, his nervous father by his side. Ivy was perched on a matching stool, enthusiastically stirring frozen orange juice concentrate and water with a wooden spoon. There was pancake batter on the counter next to empty egg shells and Ivy was dangerously close to splashing sticky orange juice out of the pitcher. Derek hovered over Leo, making sure he didn't burn the pancakes—or himself.

"Good morning everyone!" Linney called out as she let herself in. She surveyed the chaos. "Now, Ivy, I think that juice is done. How would you like to help me set the table?" She took the pitcher and wiped the outside before putting it in the fridge and then handing placemats to the five-year-old.

"Thank you," Derek said, not taking his eyes off the stove.

Linney ruffled Leo's hair and took knives and forks to the table.

After they finished their meal, and the dishwasher was loaded and counters wiped down, Derek sent the children off to watch television. He refilled coffee cups, and the adults sat down in the living room. The rain had picked up now—it looked like it was going to be an inside day. Linney absent-mindedly rubbed her hip. He wondered if the rain made it ache.

"Can I ask you something?" she began.

"Anything."

"I think I need a lawyer. Your practice includes real estate and commercial work, right?" Derek sat up with a worried look on his face. Was she going to sell the house and move to the city? "I want to buy Page Turners."

"Page Turners?" Derek was slow to catch up. "That's a big decision."

Linney nodded, and he caught the excitement in her eyes. "I've talked with Kirsten's parents and I've run all the numbers. I have so many ideas to bring it back to what it was—and even more. I really want to do this."

Derek ran his fingers through his hair, a little stunned at the news. "I didn't even know it was for sale."

"It's not really. Not yet. But I spoke with the owners. They know they made a mistake and are ready to wash their hands of it. They haven't officially put it on the market, but I'm sure if I make them a fair offer, we can do a quick private sale. I just need a lawyer. Are you interested?"

He was, and within a couple of weeks, the deal was done. Soon, Linney would have a huge bank loan and would own both the Page Turners business and the heritage house it was in —including Kirsten's apartment.

THE WEEK BEFORE CHRISTMAS, Linney signed the last of the legal documents, and shook hands with the previous owners of Page Turners. They were anxious to leave Silver Lake and put the chapter behind them but Linney was giddy with excitement. Page Turners was officially hers and she was brimming with ideas. Her hands shook as she opened the store's front door in the middle of the afternoon and stood there taking it all in.

Kirsten came downstairs in her nurse's scrubs with champagne flutes in one hand and bottles under her arm. "I thought I'd better get in the good books with the new owner so she doesn't make changes to my tenancy," she joked.

Linney whirled around. "I can't believe this is all mine!" She was like a kid in a candy store.

"I can't wait to see what you do with it."

"The first thing I'm going to do is close for a few weeks. I have so much I want to do in here. Then I'll have a grand reopening event!" Linney had already spoken with the aging editor of the *Silver Lake News*, who was planning to run a story on their local "celebrity" who had returned home and was about to make a big splash. Linney was counting on that story to help raise interest. She'd quietly set up social media channels for the store and couldn't wait to start building an audience and teasing about what was coming. Then there were the comfortable reading chairs she'd ordered last week, the painting she was planning, and of course an overhaul of the store's inventory system.

Kirsten popped open the bottles—champagne for Linney and an alcohol-free version for herself. "Here's to your new adventure!" They raised their glasses with a satisfying clink. "And I'll pitch in however you want."

Linney pointed at a roll of thick brown paper, scissors, and tape. "If you're serious, you can help me put this up in the window before your shift. I want the transformation to be a surprise."

Anna turned up just as they were finishing, with an armful of flowers. "I thought you were making improvements, not shutting the place down," she jested.

"Run while you can," Kirsten joked, "or she'll put you to work!" She headed upstairs for more champagne flutes.

Anna found a vase for the flowers in the old kitchen, where they'd all done homework together. She came back and put bouquet on the checkout counter. "I can't stay long today, but I'm at your service all weekend."

Derek arrived with a congratulatory hug, just as Kirsten returned and they all toasted Linney's new adventure.

Slowly the friends dispersed. Derek had to get home before the school bus dropped the kids off, Anna had after-school ballet to teach, and Kirsten headed to work. Then it was Linney alone in the store. She got to work, scrubbing all the wooden trim she wanted to keep, and then taping it so she could start painting in the morning. She covered bookshelves near the walls with drop cloths and moved mobile displays.

It was dark when Linney flicked on the store's ancient computer—another thing she needed to upgrade—and she started reviewing orders that had been placed before the old owners knew they were selling, and noted dates of their expected arrivals. The old bulky monitor flickered badly and Linney rubbed her eyes behind her glasses as she started making notes of titles she thought were missing. Hours passed without her knowing, and she jumped when her phone buzzed.

Do you know what time it is?

OMG. I lost track of time.

Don't work too hard on your first day!

I'm just so excited. But you're right. Locking up in 5 minutes.

Drive safe.

♥

Linney hardly left the bookstore for the next few days, only stopping when exhaustion set in. Anna and Kirsten worked with her through the weekend, and Derek even came one evening with the kids—and pizza—to check up on things.

Suddenly it was Christmas Eve and Linney reluctantly put away her paint roller. A long hot shower took care of most of her aching muscles, and she took the time to blow out her hair before dressing in black pants and a cheery soft red sweater. She zipped up her winter boots and buttoned her long coat before heading carefully through the deep snow to Derek's with a dish of apple and cranberry crumble. Her hip felt good these days, and she could almost forget about the explosion, but she was still nervous about falling on the ice.

Derek had made a simple supper and Leo gobbled up the crumble, but he and Ivy were just about vibrating with excitement. Santa Claus was coming soon!

"Church first," Derek said as they cleared the table. He didn't often take his kids to the little church in town, but Christmas and Easter were special. "Let's put our coats and boots on."

Linney helped get the children ready, and they went together in Derek's car.

Anna was already in the sanctuary with Danny and their girls when they arrived, and she watched them come down the aisle and find seats. Linney smoothed Ivy's hair when she took off her hat, and she straightened Leo's adorable waistcoat. Then she turned and laughed at something Derek said. They made the perfect picture of a family and Anna wondered, not for the first time, if something was happening between her friends. She waved at Kirsten up in the choir loft, who smiled back in recognition.

Linney loved church on Christmas Eve. The whole town seemed to be there and no matter their circumstances, everyone smiled, sang, and listened attentively to the minister.

She noticed several pairs of mittens and scarves that KnitWorks had donated and she was glad to know that they'd found the right homes. Kirsten assured her that the church made sure those families also had presents for the children.

By now, even without the *Silver Lake News* story, the whole town knew Linney had bought Page Turners, and everyone wanted to ask her about it. She kept an air of mystery around her answers and made sure younger folks knew about her social media channels. Ivy stayed close to her, still shy in a crowd.

Derek pulled into her driveway and she wished them all a good night. "You two be good for your dad and go to sleep soon," she told Ivy and Leo, who nodded vociferously. They knew Santa would only come if they were asleep.

Linney leaned across the front seat and gave Derek a quick kiss on the cheek. "I'll see you in the morning. Merry Christmas!" He waited until she had opened the door and waved before backing out of the driveway and turning into his own.

Derek's house was absolute chaos the next morning. Ivy and Leo had woken early and rushed into their father's room with the stockings Santa had left them. They jumped up on the bed and tore into them as Derek opened his bleary eyes. He'd been up late wrapping the last of the gifts under the tree and desperately needed a cup of coffee. But he sat up and with Leo on one side of him and Ivy on the other, he wondered how many more years he'd have with the magic of Santa.

"Daddy, look!" Leo was bouncing with excitement. Santa had brought superhero socks and Leo was putting them on already. On the other side of him, Ivy had found the orange at the toe of her stocking and poked his shoulder, asking him to peel it.

"I think maybe we should get up," Derek told them, rubbing a hand over the overnight growth on his chin. He looked at his watch. It was still far too early for Linney to be coming over with breakfast. "Let's snuggle in the living room and watch a movie until Auntie Linney comes. And then after breakfast, we can open presents under the tree."

It didn't take long for them to jump down from his king-sized bed, leaving a mess in their wake, to bicker over which movie to watch. Derek gathered the wrapping paper and put it into the garbage before joining the children. They sat cuddled together on the couch, under a big warm blanket. Derek kissed their heads and settled in. He had plenty of time to get dressed.

When Linney woke, she made a savory bread pudding, the same one Gran had served every Christmas that she could remember—and as it baked, she put on a carafe of coffee. After looking at the thermometer—it was going to be a cold day— she dressed in jeans and a chunky fair isle sweater for warmth. She swept her long hair into a low pony tail, brushed mascara onto her lashes and added lip gloss. When everything was ready, she packed an insulated bag that she slung over her shoulder before walking over and quietly sliding in the door.

Leo and Ivy were talking over each other so they didn't hear her come in. Linney watched the family vignette for a moment and realized she'd completely lost her heart to those two children and she was glad that she was putting down roots in Silver Lake so she could watch them grow up.

"Wake up, Daddy!" she heard Leo say. Derek startled and Linney realized he'd been sound asleep. "Okay, kids, the movie's almost finished," she heard him say in a sleepy voice. "And then we should get dressed before Auntie Linney gets here. We want to look nice for her." He yawned and muttered to himself, "And I'd better shave."

Linney put her hand over her mouth to stifle a laugh, but it wasn't enough and two little heads popped over the couch. "Merry Christmas, everyone!"

"Auntie Linney!" They ran to greet her.

"You heard your dad—run and get dressed, and then it's breakfast time!"

As Leo and Ivy clattered up the stairs to their bedrooms, Derek untangled himself from the blanket and got to his feet groggily.

"Well, look at you. I've finally caught you slacking!" Linney teased him. She reached up and touched his chin. "I don't often see you with stubble. It looks good!" In fact, Linney thought he looked really good, a thought she stuffed back inside as soon as she thought it.

"You think? Maybe I'll leave it."

"You've got time for a shower if you want. The kids and I will set the table."

When Derek came back in jeans and a button-down shirt with sleeves rolled up to his forearms, it was his turn to take in the scene. Linney looked lovely—more than lovely—and his kids hung off her every word. Something stirred inside him. It wouldn't be hard to imagine ... but no. He pushed the idea away. They were friends. Linney didn't see him any other way.

There were wonderful gifts under the tree. Linney, as the new book-seller in town, had wrapped books for everyone. Derek was touched when he opened a soft denim chambray shirt. Somehow she'd noticed that his was starting to fray around the cuffs. For her, he'd bought a simple silver necklace with a locket in the shape of a book, with the initial L on the front cover. He'd found an old photo of Linney's grandmother in his mother's things and had put it inside. Linney threw her arms around his neck when she opened it.

"It's perfect."

31

Boxing Day meant visiting at Danny and Anna's house. Linney went early to help Anna get ready. When she pulled up in her red SUV, Danny was using the snow-blower to clear the sidewalk.

"Merry Christmas!" she called out, and he waved to her. Linney made her way into the house where Emma and Gabby greeted her with hugs and sent her into the kitchen where Anna was pulling a second turkey out of the oven.

"I swear I cook more for Boxing Day than I do for Christmas," she said. She wiped her hands on her apron and hugged Linney. "I'm so glad you're here for it this year. It's been far too long."

The house soon filled with friends and family and Linney found herself the centre of attention as everyone wanted to know when the store was opening.

"Soon!" she promised. "That's the best I can do yet. As soon as I have a date, I'll let you know.

"Auntie Linney, will you need any help at Page Turners?" It was Emma asking. She was turning eighteen this year and was applying for universities.

Linney nodded. "I'll be putting up a help wanted sign soon. Let me know if you're interested." Emma and her sister had been babysitting for Derek for years and Linney knew she was a responsible young lady.

Linney's eyes drifted to the door as another family came in. She'd been hoping it was Derek. He wasn't here yet with Leo and Ivy, but she knew he'd taken the kids to see their grandmother at Graceful Care. Kirsten arrived before he did, making her way around the room with Christmas greetings for everyone. When Derek did arrive, he sent the kids downstairs to play under Gabby's supervision and joined the crowd in the living room.

"Hey, neighbour!" he joked with Linney.

"Hey, yourself!" she replied, her eyes sparkling behind her glasses.

As the afternoon sun started to set, the men drifted to the backyard, where Danny had a bonfire roaring. There was the usual grousing of happily married men about the challenges of marriage and fatherhood, and a lot of jesting about the current curling rankings. Derek listened, but his mind was elsewhere, and his eyes followed Linney as she carefully made her way down the driveway to her SUV when she headed home.

Danny and Anna collapsed into bed after everyone had gone home and they had cleaned up. Their Boxing Day party was always a lot of fun, but it was also a lot of work.

"I love you," Danny said, spooning into his wife.

"Speaking of love," Anna said, "am I imagining things or are there sparks between Derek and Linney? She was clearly waiting for him to get here today, and at church, they looked like a family."

"I don't think you're imagining it. Derek was having a hard time taking his eyes off her today."

Anna rolled over to face Danny. "I've always wondered what would have happened if neither of them had gone away. I hope this works out."

Danny kissed her. "Just don't go poking around. Let them come to it themselves."

"You're no fun!" she joked, but she rolled over again and he pulled her close. "I guess not everyone can be as happy as us. I love you."

"Go to sleep, my love."

❧

SEVERAL DAYS LATER, after giving Linney a hand at Pager Turners, Anna and Kirsten left her working on the inventory system.

"Want to grab a coffee?" Kirsten asked with a meaningful glance after the door closed behind them.

Anna agreed, and they walked up the street to the café. With cups of hot java in front of them, she asked Kirsten what she wanted to talk about.

"I don't think they know it yet, but I am sure there's something starting between Derek and Linney."

"What makes you think that?" Anna was holding her cards close to her chest.

"Haven't you seen the way they look at each other? The last couple of times at Page Turners, I've caught Linney looking at Derek dreamily. And he's been so protective of her since she's been back. Surely you've seen that. Maybe Linney is the reason he never puts his whole self into dating."

Anna laughed. "I totally agree with you. Danny made me promise not to get involved. It would be so great if they would get together. Did you see them on Christmas Eve?"

"It was hard not to from the choir loft. They looked so good together. And the kids adore her. I wonder if there's anything we can do to help them along."

"Danny says to leave it be. I'm tempted to agree, as much as I want to help too. They need to figure this out themselves."

32

I n the end, it took Linney three more weeks than she'd hoped to get Page Turners ready for reopening. But finally everything was done. The woodwork gleamed, the walls were freshly painted, new lighting warmed the place up, and several comfortable chairs had arrived for customers to curl up in.

Linney had sectioned off a corner and created a kids' area—a temporary one, she hoped, because she had plans to expand the store to the rest of the ground floor of the building she'd bought. Currently a portion was empty, having last housed a paper shop. She had placed a bright blue oversized chair off to one side where a parent and a child could cuddle up together and added a mural to the wall. Danny built her a platform, so the section sat up a little higher than the rest of the store, providing a step for children to sit on as well.

The old house's kitchen had been scrubbed clean, and Linney bought a new refrigerator to keep staff lunches and platters for signings cool. A new microwave and dishwasher were also installed, making heating lunches and dinners easier. She turned the old butler's pantry into her office. Outfitted with a new computer, Wi-Fi, and a good desk and chair, the private space pleased her. She wiped down the foldup chairs that Knit-Works used and oiled their stiff joints. The group was looking forward to using the new space for their next meeting.

The *Silver Lake News* article had come out well and Linney used it on her growing social media to garner more interest. The Bridgegrove radio station interviewed her, increasing interest beyond the town's borders. In both cases, Linney found it strange to be on the other side of the microphone answering questions instead of asking them. How life had changed for her!

More recently, Linney was focussing on the business end of things, updating the store's computer systems and placing orders with publishers for summer. Boxes seemed to arrive every day now, and the brown paper in the window had been updated with an opening date. Every time more money went out she gulped, but excitement outweighed fear. She hired Emma and two more part-time staff. If all went well, she'd be looking for more people for the summer.

The day before opening, she was so focussed that she didn't hear the back door open. Derek had taken to coming by for lunch several days a week, when he wasn't visiting his mother. If he didn't, he'd never see her. Linney left her house early, and often didn't return until nine or ten o'clock at night. Ivy and Leo missed her, and if he was honest, he did too. He'd gotten used to the evenings they spent together. It was a school holiday, so he had brought the kids along today.

"So, are you ready?" he asked, making her jump.

"I sure hope so," she answered. "And I guess whatever isn't done now will just have to wait." She stood up from her chair and stretched.

Derek held up a paper bag with the café's logo on it and stomped the snow off his feet. "We brought soup and sandwiches."

"We?" She rolled her shoulders, stiff from a morning at the computer. Suddenly she noticed the children and her face lit up. "Come here you two—I've missed you!" They were in her arms in seconds.

Derek pulled the table out from the wall so there was room for all of them. Linney brought spoons, and they sat down to eat. The kids chattered away about their friends and about school—Linney and Derek just smiled at each other. "That's great, Leo," Linney said when he told her about his perfect score on a spelling test. "Thanks for bringing lunch, everyone. I needed a break. Now, who wants a story?"

DEREK LEANED against the sales counter in the early afternoon light. Ivy was sitting on Linney's lap in the bright blue chair, snuggled into her soft curves as Linney read. Leo was lying on the ground moving his fingers along a line of text in the early reader book he'd chosen and waving his feet in the air.

Derek remembered Linney always saying she didn't want children—that it wouldn't have been fair, with her crazy career. But now, he wondered if her perspective had changed. She looked so tranquil there. The scene was serene, and if you didn't know better, you'd think the tableau was of mother and child. He shook his head. Back to reality, Derek thought to himself. Linney was off limits. A friend. His best friend. Nothing more. And yet, as he watched her chest rise and fall with her breath, and noticed the hollow at the base of her throat and his Christmas gift around her neck, he had to fight back feelings he knew could ruin everything. The back bell rang with one more delivery, and he went to sign for it, stuffing all of that back inside for another day.

WHEN STORY TIME was finished and Linney and Derek had bundled the kids up into their coats, Derek caught Linney off guard with a big hug. The hug lasted longer than usual and Linney was shocked to find her feeling something far stronger than friendship. For Derek? But she couldn't have those feelings for Derek. He was her friend. A very handsome man for sure, but her best friend. And the father of the two most adorable children she'd ever known. She had fallen in love with them, she knew. But their father? She shook her head as she headed back to unpack the boxes that had come. That was impossible.

OPENING DAY WAS A SMASH HIT, as everyone other than Linney had known it would be. The store was busy from the moment she peeled back the brown paper, and not just with curious townsfolk. Customers from Bridgegrove and even further afield made the drive, browsed, and made purchases. Emma was busy at the sales counter. To Linney's delight, Jake made the drive up with all three of his teenagers to support her as well. Books flew off the shelf and almost nobody left without a package under their arm.

There was a brief lull at dinner time, which gave Linney time to set up the KnitWorks chairs in the centre of the store. The Canadian author with a new thriller that she had been advertising was due shortly, to do a reading from his book and sign autographs. The big coffee percolator that Emma had filled with water fifteen minutes before started to gurgle on the counter, and Kirsten arrived with a platter of pastries Linney had ordered. Next time, she hoped to have a liquor licence and be able to serve wine as well. That was one of the many "little details" that hadn't gotten taken care of just yet.

People started streaming in just before the reading was to

begin. Gabby was baby-sitting Leo and Ivy for Derek, who was sitting in the front row. Anna and Danny were behind him, and Kirsten hung out in the back to usher in late arrivals as Linney welcomed her guests and introduced the author. After the reading, he answered questions, and together they sold several autographed books. He graciously signed another ten for her shelves and thanked Linney for the evening, wishing her much success.

When the front door bells jangled with the final customer leaving, Linney sighed with relief, kicked off her high-heeled shoes and rubbed her hip. She'd made it through day one. All that remained was to find out if people would come back. Derek sent Danny and Anna home and shooed Kirsten out the door. "I'll help her get everything cleaned up." He was awed by how she'd transformed the bookstore. Together they folded up the chairs and covered up the remaining pastries. He ran a broom over the refinished floors while she closed out the computer system. Linney locked the front door and turned off the store's front lights.

"You did it." Derek's voice was husky behind her in the dim light. "You're incredible, Linney."

Linney turned to face him. He found his hands on her hips. There was a moment of silence and then he reached down and his lips gently met hers. It was a slow, warm kiss, unfamiliar, but borne of years of friendship. Derek felt his pulse quicken when she kissed him back. She tasted so good. He kissed her again, more intentionally this time. Then suddenly he broke away, panic wild in his eyes.

"I'm so sorry ... I didn't mean ... I don't ... I have to go." He bolted out the back entrance and the wheels of his car slipped on the snow as he sped out of the parking lot.

Stupid, stupid, stupid. Derek's heart pounded in his chest and he shook his head. What had he done? Linney was his best friend. And he'd gone and kissed her. He could only hope their years of friendship would mean they could overcome this lapse. Good grief, what was he going to say to her tomorrow?

As it turned out, Derek said nothing. And neither did Linney. They both put it down to a momentary lapse. It wouldn't happen again.

PAGE TURNERS WAS DOING BOOMING business. Linney's first three months of sales were more than she'd budgeted, and summer was right around the corner. It would soon be warm enough to paint the store's deep porch. Linney had plans for that porch, including half a dozen Muskoka chairs that were due to arrive in a week. It had been too late to plant spring bulbs in front of the porch when she'd taken over the store, but she intended to put in summer annuals in a month's time and daffodil bulbs would be purchased to plant in the fall.

Linney left the bookstore in Emma's capable hands and pulled on a spring jacket. She walked up the street to surprise Derek for lunch and her hair blew in the warm breeze. When she opened the door to the law firm, she saw Janet was at lunch already.

"In the back. I'll be out in a moment." Derek's deep voice travelled beyond the door to his file room, sounding formal and lawyerly. Linney decided not to wait and headed back. She bashed into the door frame on her way into the file room, something that rarely happened anymore.

Hearing the noise, Derek rushed out from behind the tall file cabinets. He winced, watching her hold her shoulder. "Are you okay?"

"I'll be fine. Just my ego was bruised."

"Let me see." Derek placed his hand on her shoulder, rubbing it gently. She shivered under his touch. "Are you cold?" He rubbed her upper arms and Linney's breath caught.

"Derek," she whispered.

He smelled good. Linney took a step closer and then slid her arms around his neck. She stood on her tiptoes and lifted her chin. She could feel his heart as the small distance between them evaporated, and she kissed him hungrily. Fireworks went off in her head. Linney slid her hands down his back and realized his were tangled in her hair. Derek was kissing her back like he couldn't stop, and she didn't want him to. Derek. Derek! Derek? Linney's brain took over again, and she stopped mid-kiss. She stiffened in his arms and he opened his eyes, reacting to her body language. Something was wrong. He stepped back.

"Linney?"

"Derek, we can't ... I shouldn't have ... I ... I—" Linney was panicking and her face flushed as she fled.

Linney ran across the road and down to the pavilion at the park. She sat on the steps, taking deep breaths. She put her hands on her hot cheeks and willed the colour to leave her face What had she done? Twice now, they'd kissed, and it had been good. So good. How had she never thought of Derek like that before? They'd always had a lot in common and he had always been her champion. But now the sound of his voice gave her butterflies. It was almost criminal how handsome he looked dressed in his suit to go to court. Her hands itched to comb through his curls, and the feel of his breath on her neck, when they were close enough to kiss, was exciting.

His kisses. That could never, never happen again. They couldn't ruin this lifelong friendship. And yet, when he touched her—well she couldn't let that happen either. She pulled herself together and headed back to Page Turners. She could make a sandwich in the kitchen for lunch.

Linney threw herself into summer planning to ensure the bookstore was a success. She didn't stay away from Derek, but she made sure they were rarely alone together and that there were no hugs and no friendly kisses on the cheek. She was stiff around him, and he was as well. They spent evenings alone in their separate homes. She ached to tell Anna and Kirsten but she didn't want to put them in the middle. She didn't even want to talk to MJ about it. There was nothing to talk about, really. Two kisses. Two kisses that had to be ignored.

IT WAS AN UNSEASONABLY WARM JUNE, and with Ivy and Leo both at birthday parties, Derek had a rare Saturday afternoon to himself. He headed to the shore where Linney was skipping stones. It hadn't taken long for her brain to compensate for her monocular vision and she could rival him once more . "How do you feel about a quick spin in the kayaks?" Linney hadn't tried to get into one since her accident. "I'll give you a hand in and out if you like."

Linney hesitated. But her love of the lake won. "Let's do it."

They headed down to the dock and Derek put both boats in the water. As he watched, Linney sat on the dock with her life jacket on and slowly transferred her weight into her kayak. She looked triumphant to have done it without his help and he silently revelled in her happiness. Derek buckled his own life jacket and dropped into his kayak. They headed out over the water, leisurely paddling along the shore away from town.

Derek was the first to notice the rain. A single fat raindrop landed with a splat on the front of his kayak. It was followed by another. It had clouded over while they were out, but they'd been engrossed in conversation and neither of them had noticed how dark the sky off to their starboard had become.

"I think we'd better head back," he said, backpaddling to turn his kayak around. Linney followed suit and with swift strong paddles, they were soon skimming along the surface of the lake, but not fast enough to outrun the rain. Within minutes they were soaked.

"At least it's a warm rain," called Linney. Her hair was plastered to her head and her glasses were getting hard to see through. She squinted and focused on following the red kayak in front of her.

Derek looked back to make sure she was close. Linney's delicate cotton blouse was moulded to her body, and had been rendered see-through from the rain. As she pulled closer, he could see the lacy bra she wore underneath and the sight of it stirred feelings. "It's not the first time you've been wet in a boat with me," he yelled back, covering his rising desire. He didn't know she wore underwear like that.

Linney laughed, remembering the time they'd tipped over a canoe, and he saw the beginnings of laugh lines at the corner of her eyes. They were both older now.

Even through her spotted glasses, Linney could see how fit Derek was as she pulled closer to his kayak. His black T-shirt was stuck to his toned torso and water droplets dripped from the ends of his slightly greying curly hair. He shook his head, spraying water everywhere. He was a fine specimen of a man. Linney gulped. Why was she thinking of Derek like this? It was getting harder to push these feelings away.

The rain was still pelting down from the sky when they pulled their kayaks up to the dock. Derek jumped out and then reached down to give Linney a hand up. Getting out of the kayak would be harder than getting in. Taking care with her hip, Linney took his hand and managed to get back onto the dock, but lost her balance when she stood up as the dock swayed slightly under their combined weight. She stumbled into him and he put his hands on her waist to steady her. She grabbed his arms for balance and they stood pressed against each other for what felt like several minutes. Their eyes locked, asking unvoiced questions. After an eternity, Derek brought his head down to meet Linney's, and with mutual understanding, their lips met.

This was not like the kisses they'd shared before. This was a kiss filled with years of understanding each other, but now with a shared passion. It was a long, steamy, sensual kiss, between two equal partners with needs and wants. Linney heard a low guttural sound from Derek's throat as she wrapped her arms tightly around his broad back. His hands cupped her face, and he kissed her again, with even more intensity this time. The hairs of Linney's neck stood at attention and her legs turned to jelly. Derek thought he heard her moan softly but he couldn't believe it was real. Breathing heavily, they pulled apart to make sure they understood what was happening. Convinced that they were on the same page, Derek drew her in again and his lips crushed hers, making every nerve in her body tingle.

"Linney," he breathed raggedly, and the first crack of thunder broke the spell, making them jump.

"Run, Derek!" Linney held out her hand, and they ran together through the downpour to the relative safety of her porch. Linney reached out to open the door, but Derek spun her around. Another kiss sent her mind whirling like a child's top. Or maybe that was the sound of the wind, which was now thrashing through the trees.

Still with his arms around her, Derek pushed open the door, and they kissed their way into the house, as the sky flashed with lightning. Linney stood in front of him, dripping wet as he slammed the door behind them. He kissed her neck and her collar bone, making her shiver with delight. He cradled her face once more and kissed her again until they were both breathless. Their hands were busy exploring each other's bodies. Derek didn't know how much more of this he could take. "

Linney, are you sure?" he whispered hoarsely. He didn't want to do something rash, but at the same time, he was nearly vibrating with desire.

She took a step back, and he felt a moment of disappointment. But then she started unbuttoning her wet blouse as lightning lit up the room. Stepping out of her shorts Linney stood in front of him in her wet bra and matching lace panties, and she answered him in a husky voice. "I've never been so sure of anything in my life."

Derek didn't need to be told twice. As thunder shook the house, he pulled his T-shirt over his head, took a step towards Linney, and brought his mouth down passionately on hers. He picked her up and took her to the bedroom. Suddenly they were discovering each other in ways Linney had never dreamed of.

Afterwards, they lay in each other's arms as the storm continued to rage around them. His fingers traced the scar on her hip, illuminated by another crack of lightning. "Does it still hurt?" he asked, tenderly.

"Only when the weather changes. Like now." She laced her fingers through his. "Why have we never done this before?"

"I don't know," he whispered. "But I love you, Linney. I think I've always loved you."

"I love you too."

EPILOGUE

Turning Pages was extraordinarily busy that summer, but Linney and Derek spent every spare moment together. It was soon apparent that they couldn't keep their love under wraps. They thought they'd surprise everyone, but they were the ones surprised.

"I guess we were the last ones to know," Linney said, when Anna and Kirsten hugged her and told her they'd been waiting for this news for months. "I blame my poor eyesight for not seeing what was right in front of me!"

"Congratulations, man," said Danny. "It took you long enough."

The KnitWorks group had disbanded for the summer, but a steady stream of members came by the store to tell Linney how pleased they were for the two of them.

MJ squealed with delight when Linney called to tell her. "Finally. A man your own age. A good man. I want to meet him the next time I am in Canada. Enjoy, *mon amie.*"

Linney told Jake when he and the kids came up for a long weekend. "I'm happy for you," he said gruffly. "Derek's had a crush on you for years. And I expect you've had one too, even if neither of you knew it! Even Gran thought the two of you should be together."

Linney blushed and changed the subject. "How are things with you and Rachael?"

"Don't mind about us. She'll come around. She always does. Concentrate on your own happiness."

Derek wasn't surprised when Jake wandered over to his house before he left.

"So, you and Linney," Jake said. "You've been really good to her this year. I would have said thank you anyway. But now I need to add something." Derek raised his eyebrows. "Don't hurt her."

"You can count on me, Jake. The kids and I are totally in love with Linney. I'm not sure what she sees in me, but believe me Jake, this is the real thing. I just can't believe we never saw it before."

Derek and Linney took the kids for countless kayak rides that summer, and stone-skipping lessons for Leo were paying off. He could now occasionally get a stone to skip two or three times. Ivy was still satisfied with the "kerplunk" of throwing pebbles into the lake. She kept asking when Linney could sleep over.

WHEN IT WAS TIME, Derek talked to his mother first. It was fast, he knew, but it was right. He knew his mother wouldn't recognize him, but he felt he needed to tell her. She was sitting in her wheelchair and he gave her a quick kiss on the cheek. "Mum? It's Derek, your son. I hope you're doing well today." He knew not to expect an answer. It had been a long time since she'd spoken to him. Derek picked up one of her frail hands. "I've made a big decision. I'm going to ask Linney to marry me." He was startled to feel her squeeze his hand. "I know you and Mrs.

McDonnell always thought Linney and I should be together. It took us a long time to realize that for ourselves, but now we will be. I love her, Mum, and we'll be a good family together." They sat together quietly. "I need to get back to the office now. But I wanted you to know."

There was no sign that she'd heard him or understood the words. But as he turned to leave, he heard her voice in a low whisper. "Good."

Linney sat on the dock on a warm and sunny fall morning, listening to the loons call and sipping coffee from an insulated mug. She'd been home for a year now and the leaves were once again turning from green to brilliant reds and oranges, and pine needles were beginning to drop. Linney heard the school bus pick up the kids, and she knew Derek would come and join her shortly. She'd brought a second mug down to the lake for him.

Derek watched her as he walked down to the shore, his heart bursting. Some days he couldn't believe how lucky he was to have found love again—and that it was with his best friend made it all the more special. He picked up a smooth stone and expertly skipped it out over the almost mirror-like lake, thinking how much his life had changed in the last year.

"Well done, my love," Linney said, as he joined her on the dock. The boards squeaked as he walked out to the end where she sat. Linney held up his mug of coffee and Derek took it, lowering himself to join her.

"Good morning," he said, taking a sip. "You look like you're enjoying yourself this morning."

"Mmmmm."

"Linney, I want to talk to you about something."

Her eyes searched his face. Derek sounded serious. "First a kiss," she said and leaned over to press her lips to his. "I love you."

"I love you too. You're beautiful and you're fearless. You're smart and you're compassionate. I love us together and I love how you are with Leo and Ivy." Linney was blushing now, he noticed.

"I never expected to find love again after Olivia left me. What she did almost broke me. And then when you almost died—" Derek took a deep breath. "When you came home, I never expected to fall in love with you, Linney. But I'm head over heels, like a teenager. And I want to spend every day of the rest of my life with you."

Derek reached into his pocket and pulled out a ring box. Linney gasped. She put her hand to her throat and tears leapt to her eyes. "Derek?"

"I should probably do this over dinner in a fancy restaurant, but the lake is where you're most happy, and where we've built our lives. Linney, you would make me the happiest man in the world if you would be my wife."

"Yes, oh yes!" Linney threw her arms around Derek's neck and he almost dropped the box into the water. When she finally let go, he slid the ring onto her finger. It was a simple gold band with four small diamonds. "One for each of us," he said, his voice threatening to break with emotion.

"The kids?" she whispered.

"They gave me their permission. They want us to be a family."

Tears ran down her cheeks. "Me too. Me too."

THE END

A MESSAGE FROM THE AUTHOR

Dear reader,

I hope you enjoyed *Skipping Stones*, the first of my Silver Lake stories.

If Derek and Linney's story spoke to you, please could leave a review on GoodReads, the e-book retailer of your choice, or on your own social media. Reviews are so incredibly important to authors. They don't have to be long. Just a few words about how *Skipping Stones* made you feel can go a long way in helping people decide to hit the 'purchase' button.

I can't tell you how much I love hearing from readers. When I see a photo of one of my books "in the wild" or read your words, I am reminded that my stories matter to someone and that I made the right decision to start sharing them.

Until we meet again in Silver Lake!

Katherine

ABOUT THE AUTHOR

Katherine Ward was twelve years old when she won her first writing competition, but took a long detour in corporate communications before starting to tell stories of her own. Katherine lives in Ontario, Canada, where she raised her three children. When she's not at work on her next novel or belting out show tunes in the privacy of her own home, Katherine loves to garden, hike and travel.

Skipping Stones is her second novel.

You can find more about Katherine on  her website or on social media platforms including Facebook and Instagram.

9 781738 256525